PROLOGUE

When Will and his cousin, Jimmy, set off on a fishing trip one summer day in Smithers, British Columbia, they had no idea that following a little boy and girl through an opening in a cave would plunge them into an underground world.

For centuries there have been stories about legendary lost civilizations. The boys come face to face with an ancient Aztec civilization. Trapped in a world that is so different from theirs, they must find a way back to their worried families. The portal through which they entered this underground world will not open for the next twenty-one years. There are six similar caves, and the Aztecs agree to help them get to the next portal, in Peru. Will they make it to the portal in time? What unimaginable dangers await them on this action-packed journey?

*To My Husband, Jens
Who Always Encouraged My Dreams*

ACKNOWLEDGEMENTS

Healing Crystals the A – Z guide to 555 gemstones
by Michael Gienger

CHAPTER ONE

Summer, my favourite time of the year. Not because school was finally over, though, that was a bonus. No, it was time to go up north with my cousin, Will, my Uncle Steve, Aunt Jenny, my cousin, Katie and the best dog in the whole world, Buddy.

They live just outside of Smithers, British Columbia, and if you ask me, there is no place on earth as beautiful as this part of the province.

My Uncle Steve worked for the Canadian Forestry and he taught me how to fish, track and hunt. And this summer, he is going to teach me archery. I also know what berries we can eat and those that are poisonous, which mushrooms are edible and which ones are not. By the way, there are more poisonous mushrooms than edible ones, so it is better to be really sure before you eat anything in the forest. You can spend a whole day in the bathroom if you eat the wrong ones. I know this from experience. Anyhow, I loved being up here with my family. And Uncle Steve was the best wilderness guide you could ever meet.

My mom works for a law firm in Vancouver. That's where I live in a condo near Coal Harbour. It's nice there, and we live near Stanley Park. So Mom and I ride our bikes around the seawall, or we go for walks in the park. It's a beautiful nature reserve but nothing like the wide open spaces of the interior of British Columbia. Still, I'm grateful for where I live, and I love the times I spend with my mom. The ocean, the mountains, the trees. But give me miles and miles of forest, lakes, rivers and mountains, and I'm a happy camper.

My dad died in a car accident when I was two years old. Someone ran a stop sign and T-boned my dad as he was coming home from work. My mom still gets misty-eyed whenever I ask questions about him, so I try not to bring him up with her anymore. Uncle Steve, on the other hand, loves to talk about my dad all the time. You see, my dad and Uncle Steve were twin brothers. I think that is why my mom doesn't like coming up too often. They tell me Uncle Steve and my dad were identical twins. I guess looking at him is just too painful for her. I don't remember my dad at all, but when I look at Uncle Steve, it makes me feel good that I really know what he looked like when he was alive.

We came up to visit my Aunt Jenny and Uncle Steve for Christmas when I was about six years old. We really had a great time. We were out playing in the snow, throwing snowballs at each other when suddenly Uncle Steve came out of nowhere and pretended to be a snow monster, hooting and growling and making funny faces as he chased us around the yard. We laughed and screamed, but when I looked up to see my mom who had been sitting on the porch drinking coffee, she was nowhere to be found, except that her coffee mug was on the floor of the porch. When we finally got too cold, we came inside for hot chocolate. (Aunt Jenny makes the best because she uses only milk and always adds mini-marshmallows on top). When Mom came into the kitchen I could tell she had been crying. Her eyes were all red, and she kept blowing her nose. She said she was worried that she might be coming down with a cold, but I knew Mom had been crying. She cried lots of times when she didn't think I could hear.

Uncle Steve took her into the family room, and they talked quietly by the fireplace. I could tell he was doing most of the talking because she was just nodding and blowing her nose. I didn't know that my life was going to change forever because that is when Uncle Steve talked my mom into letting me come up north every summer. It was the best Christmas gift I could have ever received.

So here I am, Jimmy Wright, with my uncle and cousin sitting in the front of a pickup truck and me sitting in the back hugging Buddy. Like it has been for the past nine years. I had just turned fifteen in June, and my cousin Will turned sixteen in March. We are cousins, but he is more like a brother to me than a cousin. He has shared his dad, his mom, his sister and his dog with me and never once made me feel like I was an intruder into his world. Will was my best friend too.

As we hop out of the truck to our favourite fishing spot, Uncle Steve begins his usual safety dialogue.

"Okay, you two characters. Now you remember the rules:

Stay in this area, no hiking up river where I can't find you. Keep the walkie-talkie on at all times. You have your blow horn, Will?"

Will pulls it out of his backpack. "Yeah, Dad. Got it right here."

"Okay. I'll be up on the Cranberry Junction line, so I will still be in range of the walkie-talkie. You guys get your fishing gear out, and I'll be back in a couple of hours. Catch us some dinner; okay? And Buddy, you stay with these two and keep them safe; okay?" Buddy wags his tail and barks as if he knows exactly what his job is, and he is ready for action.

We grab our gear and head down to the riverbank. Uncle Steve honks as he drives away, and we are left on our own.

As we get our rods ready I look around us at the vastness of the mountains and trees, the smell of the air, the blue of the sky and the silence of nothing else but nature. Birds, tree branches moving, the river water lapping over rocks.

"Will, I know you see this every day, but man, I would never tire of it. When you live in a city, you really do appreciate the difference of our two worlds."

Will smiles. "Yeah, I have to admit it. I like going to the city to visit you and take in all the sights, but when I get back home, it just feels good to be back. The noise is gone, the traffic is forever behind you and the smells of the city are non-existent. I would never admit this to my parents, Jimmy, but I don't know if I want to leave here and go to university in Vancouver. I'm looking into a smaller university in Prince George or Kamloops. I just don't know if I could handle the big city life."

Jimmy didn't say anything. He was looking forward to have Will come to Vancouver and stay with him and his mom.

"Aw Will, that's still two years away. You got lots of time to think about plans, but I have to admit, it would be fun having you stay with Mom and me. I'd teach you to be a city slicker in no time, just like you have taught me to be a country bumpkin."

Will laughs. "Okay bumpkin, let's get these lines in the water."

With smiles on both boys faces, they cast their lines and began their afternoon of fun and rival banter.

Jimmy looks over at Will. "Hey, care to make this trip a little interesting?"

Will looks at him suspiciously. "What did you have in mind, Slick?"

"How about a bet? Whoever lands the first fish, the loser does his dishes for a week."

Will looks at Jimmy, smiles and shakes his head. "The devil went down to Georgia, but I believe I'll take that bet."

Jimmy laughs and turns towards Buddy. "You heard him Buddy. You'll be my witness." The wag of his tail was his only reply, and the game began.

It didn't take long before Jimmy started hooting and howling about the tug on his line. Will looked over in his direction and muttered, "Son of a biscuit. That guy is so lucky."

Jimmy's smile on his face went from ear to ear. "Now watch, cousin, this city slicker will show you how to land this monster." With a tight line and a few winds on the reel, Jimmy popped a good three pounder onto the riverbank.

"Read it and weep, cousin. That there puppy just got me out of dishes for a week!" Jimmy turned quickly when he thought he heard someone laughing in the bushes behind him. He spotted a young child, but as quickly as he caught sight of him, he disappeared deeper into the bushes.

"Hey, wait a minute," shouted Jimmy as he and Buddy ran into the bushes after the child. "Stop. Hey kid, you shouldn't be out here all alone. Wait a second, we can help you."

Will watched as Jimmy and Buddy disappeared into the bushes yelling at someone or something.

"Jimmy, Buddy, what are you two chasing?"

Running into the bushes after them he could hear Jimmy shouting back to him.

"Will, there is a little kid up here. I'm trying to track him and Buddy seems to be on the right scent of him."

Within seconds Buddy and Jimmy see the child stumble behind a tree.

"Got him. Come on, Buddy."

But just as Buddy and Jimmy came around the tree a young girl scooped the child into her arms and ran behind a large patch of bushes. When Jimmy and Buddy were about to follow Will jumped out at them.

"Where do you two morons think you're going? You could get

lost out here in no time if you don't take precautions."

"Will, there is a girl and a young boy who just ran into that hedge of bushes. Come on, I'll show you."

Buddy ran ahead and Jimmy and Will were right behind him. As they parted away some branches, both boys looked in total surprise at their encounter.

"Whoa, how long has that been there?" asked Jimmy to his cousin.

There in front of the boys was an entrance to a cave that would never have been seen had the boys not removed the thick branches.

Jimmy took a deep breath. "Come on, let's check this out."

"Wait here, Jimmy. I'll get our backpacks. We'll need flashlights."

As Jimmy and Buddy waited for Will to return, Jimmy could hear voices deep in the cave, as if someone was scolding someone.

Will was back in a flash, "Okay now, we stick together. And Buddy you stay behind us, I'm not having you run off on us."

Slowly the boys crept into the cave with Buddy bringing up the rear. They were maybe twenty steps into the cave when a thundering bang came from behind them. Turning quickly the boys realized the cave had a stone door, and they rushed back to it to see if they could move it.

Pushing and shoving with all their might Will said the words that Jimmy did not want to hear.

"Oh, my God, we're trapped"

Grabbing his backpack, Will searches for the walkie-talkie.

"Please let this work." He began pushing the call button hoping his dad would hear it, but all he got was static. He tried again.

"Dad, can you hear me? We're stuck in a cave." Only static could be heard coming back.

"Will, maybe there is another way out. That girl and little boy came this way, there must be another way out. We have to find them."

"Jimmy, I never saw anyone, but if you say there was someone here, I guess I have to believe you."

Picking up his backpack and handing Jimmy's to him he said, "Come on, Sherlock. Let's start investigating."

The boys slowly walked deeper into the cave, smelling the dampness of the moss and an odd smell, one that you would not expect in a cave.

"Jimmy, do you smell that?" Jimmy looked at his cousin and started to sniff the air.

"Yeah, smells like my mom's jasmine tea."

"There has to be someone close by. That is not a scent you would find in cave. Come on, let's keep going."

As the boys and Buddy came to a turn in the cave, they were met by two passages.

"Great Will, which one do we pick?"

Will holds his flashlight into the right passage and then holds the light into the left passage.

"They both look the same. Jimmy, you go down that passage about twenty feet and listen for any noise, and I'll do the same in this one."

Jimmy nods. "Okay, twenty feet and then listen."

Will nods. Both boys go quietly into each passage, Jimmy listens intently as Will gets settled into the other passage. Buddy starts to whine and both boys go, "Shhhh," in unison. Buddy lays down and watches closely at both passages.

Will listens and can only hear the drip of water far off in the distant. He goes slowly back to Jimmy.

"Anything, Jim?" Jimmy comes out of the cavern slowly,

"Will, I think I heard bells."

"Bells? Are you sure?" asked Will incredulously.

"I'm positive. It was bells. Do you think we should follow the sound?" he asked, looking at Will.

"What choice do we have, Jim. Follow the sound or stay here and die."

At the word "die," Jimmy's face paled. Will realizing his mistake said, "Oh Jimmy, I'm sorry. We're not going to die. Look, we have both been taught by the best forest ranger this side of the Rockies. We can certainly find our way out of here. And boy, aren't we going to have a story to tell!"

Jimmy smiled uneasily. "Yeah, after we get grounded for two years."

Will looked at Jimmy as he put on his backpack. "Only two? I'll take it." Jimmy laughs and adjusts his backpack as well.

"Okay Buddy, we're off to the Land of Oz."

Jimmy had no idea how real those words would become.

CHAPTER TWO

Steve could hear static on the walkie-talkie as he picked it up.

"Will, are you okay?" More static. "Will, can you hear me. Pick up. Over." More static. "That's strange. Why aren't you guys answering me?"

Steve threw his books into the truck and started heading for the boys. All the while on his drive he could feel his brother's presence in the truck.

"Mike I don't know why I don't hear back from them. That's why I'm going to check."

Steve was getting an uneasy feeling in his stomach. He only felt Mike's presence when something was wrong with Jimmy.

He thought back to a camping trip with the boys. Jimmy got up in the night to relieve himself and lost the trail back to the camp and began to follow the trail he was on. That trail led to the riverbank, which would be impossible to see on the moonless night.

Steve was fast asleep in his own tent. The boys insisted they wanted a two-man tent for themselves. But out of nowhere Steve felt like someone kicked him in the leg.

"What the hell!"

It took only a few seconds for Steve to know something was wrong. Grabbing his shoes and shoving them on as fast as he could, he started running towards the boy's tent. Popping his head in he called out, "Will. Jimmy. You guys okay?"

Will rustled in his sleeping bag and turned towards the voice.

"What? Dad, is that you?"

"Yeah, son, but where is Jimmy?"

"I dunno, must have gone to take a leak."

Steve headed for the outhouse down the trail.

"Jimmy! Jimmy where are you?" With no answer coming from any direction, Steve got to the outhouse, but it was empty. A strange chill came over Steve running down his back and tight down his legs.

"Oh, God. Mike, this can't be happening! JIMMY! JIMMY! Where are you?"

As Jimmy continued down the trail he began to hear the rushing river.

"This isn't right. We are not by the river."

He started feeling a warm presence beside him and a pull to turn around and go back the way he came. As he turned to go up the trail he heard Uncle Steve's voice.

"Jimmy, where are you?"

"I'm here, Uncle Steve," Jimmy shouted as loud as he could. Steve ran down the trail and scooped him up in his arms.

"Oh, man. Kid, you just about gave me a heart attack. You okay?" Jimmy lips started to quiver.

"I'm okay. Guess I took the wrong trail."

Steve hugged him and chuckled. "Next time kid, just pee in the bushes." Jimmy started to laugh.

"All the time?"

"No, just in the middle of the night, okay?"

"Okay, Uncle Steve." Steve got him settled back in his tent, and he was asleep in no time. Steve remembers he didn't sleep the rest of the night, pondering all of the "what ifs" and what he would have said to his sister-in-law, Carol, if anything had happened to Jimmy. And what about that kick that woke him. How did that happen? He began to think about his brother Mike and somehow he just knew that he had something to do with that kick.

"Next time, jerk, just shake me!" And he rolled over and closed his eyes.

As Steve drove up to the fishing spot he had left the boys, he jumped from the truck and started calling their names.

"Will. Jimmy. Where are you?"

Hearing nothing Steve ran to the riverbank. There on the grass was Will's fishing pole, and then he spotted Jimmy's laying up against a log. A fish was still attached to the hook.

"What could have made you guys leave a fish on the hook?" An uneasy feeling began to come over Steve.

"Okay, Mike. Okay. We'll find them."

Steve started surveying the area. Looking around he noticed the backpacks were missing.

"You took your backpacks? Where did you go?"

Looking at the bushes and noticing some broken branches Steve smiled.

"Okay guys, I've got your trail."

Moving along the forest and looking for broken twigs, trampled foliage and possible torn clothes, Steve continued on the boys' trail like a blood hound. Finally, coming up to the area the boys found the cave Steve stops abruptly.

"That's it? Where did you go from here?"

Searching every twig and bush in the area, backtracking but leading right back to the same spot.

"This makes no sense. You can't just disappear! Will. Jimmy. Can you hear me?" Reaching for the walkie-talkie Steve tries again.

"Will, it's Dad. Can you hear me? Pick up. Over."

Just the dreadful sound of static. Steve sits down putting his head in his hands. "Oh, Mike, what am I going to tell Jenny and Carol?"

But the only sound he could hear was the rustle of branches above him.

CHAPTER THREE

Following the sounds ahead Will and Jimmy crept slowly into the cavern. Will pulled Buddy's leash from his backpack and put it on him.

Whispering to his four legged friend he said, "Sorry Buddy, but I don't want you taking off without us. Now stay quiet, okay?" Buddy just whimpered quietly as if he understood every word Will just had said. "Good boy, now let's go."

Jimmy noticed markings on the cave wall.

"Will," he whispered, "look at these drawings. Who would have made these marks? Cavemen?"

Will started examining the carvings, putting his fingers into the markings as if he was reading braille.

"Jimmy, these carvings are old. Look at the dust and dirt that's accumulated in these holes. That takes years to happen in an airtight cave. You don't have a lot of wind in here blowing dirt around."

Jimmy looks around slowly shining his flashlight on the other walls of the cave.

"There's more over here. This one looks like a sun, and this one looks like some kind of bird." Will checks out the new findings.

"Jim, I've seen these markings before when we went to Mexico two years ago. There are a lot of these pictures in their

Mayan calendar."

"Mayan? As in Aztec people?" Jimmy looks incredulously at his cousin.

"Yeah, but that's crazy. Somebody's idea of a joke or something. Come on, let's keep going."

Will holding tight to Buddy's lead entered another turn in the cavern.

Both boys stopped in their tracks as they stood in front of two stone statues on either side of a large opening.

"Whoa, look at this!" Jimmy blows out quietly. Will put his light on the first statue.

"It looks like a big cat. Jaguar maybe?" Jimmy shines his light on the second statue,

"This is definitely a snake."

Will shines his light into the centre of the opening.

"Jimmy, this looks like an entrance into a really big room." Both boys move in slowly and as if by a motion detector the walls light up. Jimmy's eyes widen.

"Whoa, explain that to me, cousin!" Will goes over to the wall and looks down into small crevices carved into the side of the cavern. Each small crevice contained what appeared to be a glowing rock. Will touched one, and it was warm to the touch.

"Man, this is weird. These rocks look like they have a fire inside them. I wonder where they came from." Will looks at Jimmy and they both turn off their flashlights and slowly put them away. In the distant they can hear bells.

"That's the sound I heard before, Will. We have to be getting close to the two people I saw." Before Will could respond they heard a loud noise deep in the cave, like thunder rumbling in the distance. Both boys looked at each other. Taking a gulp of air Jimmy looks at Will.

"We have to go in there, don't we?"

Will trying to look brave said, "Yeah, Slick. I'm hoping it will lead us out of here. But I gotta tell ya, Jim, I'm getting a bad feeling about this."

Jim nods his head in agreement but follows his cousin and Buddy into the next cavern.

As they enter into a passage lit by the same rocks in the room before, both boys stop in their tracks to the vision in front of them.

Will whispers, "Oh my God. I don't think we are in Kansas anymore, Toto."

CHAPTER FOUR

Steve wasted no time notifying Search and Rescue. When the twelve men and women arrived, they stood in a circle with Steve in the middle.

"These are good kids. They would not have wandered away looking for adventure. They left a fish still on the line. That indicates to me that something got their attention, and they chose to follow it. They have our dog with them. He's a Labrador Retriever, and he's very protective of the boys. They also took their backpacks with them, and my guess is they wanted all their emergency equipment and supplies with them. I'll show you where I tracked them and where I lost their trail. Any questions?"

The leader of the team, Harvey Johnson stepped forward.

"Yeah Steve. How long have they been missing and what kind of clothes were they wearing?"

Steve took a deep breath. "They have been missing for about three hours. I left the boys here to fish, and when I could not reach them on the walkie-talkie, I headed right back here. So altogether, I have not seen the boys for about four hours. As for their dress, they were both wearing jeans and T-shirts. Will was wearing a dark green shirt and Jimmy was wearing a blue one. And both boys were in running shoes."

Each person nodded in response.

"Okay. if you follow me, I'll show you where I lost their trail."

The team followed Steve to the end of the trail and each member began to fan out to look for more clues. After an hour, they all met up at the original site.

The team leader looked around at his group.

"Anybody find anything?"

Most of them just shook their heads, but Fred Avery the team's top tracker said,

"I followed the trail from the riverbank right to this spot. Steve is right. It's like they just disappeared from this spot. There are some slightly broken twigs in this group of bushes over here, but there is nothing but rocks back there. No indication of a slide, no blood trail, so I think we can rule out grizzly bear, and no tracks leading anywhere. I'm as baffled as Steve is Harvey."

Harvey looked around at his team.

"Ladies and gentlemen, children just don't simply disappear. We have missed something. We have about two hours of good light left, and I suggest we use it wisely. Backtrack on your steps, search for anything out of the ordinary. There has to be a logical explanation to their disappearance." The team all nodded and headed off in different directions. As Fred was grabbing his gear, Harvey quietly spoke to him.

"Fred, check down by the river, it's running awfully fast for this time of the year. I hope no one fell in and the other jumped in to help." Fred nodded to Harvey then looked at Steve.

"Man, I don't envy Steve for one minute. Imagine having to tell your wife and sister-in-law that the kids are missing. What a nightmare for this guy!"

He headed off in the direction of the river and gave Steve a small wave, hoping beyond hope that he could find some answers for this poor guy.

After walking up and down the riverbed for about a half mile, Fred was convinced the boys did not come in this direction.

"Okay boys, I'm going back to square one." Fred headed back to the fishing spot. Slowly he looked at the twigs and branches and the ground for any footsteps he might have missed. It was easy to spot the running shoe marks, but he noticed that two sets went in the same direction, then one set came back just slightly off the beaten path.

"One of you two came back here for something. What?" Then a prickle of hair stood up on the back of his neck. "The backpacks! You came back for the backpacks. So what did you see that made you need them so badly?" Fred searched around the area, and that's when he noticed a few berries laying under a bush. He pushed aside a large group of trees and spotted the clue that he almost missed for a second time.

CHAPTER FIVE

As the boys ducked behind a stone statue they were in awe of their discovery. A crystal village. Large purple stones hung down like sparkling upside down trees. There was a yellow stone path meandering through the village. A large waterfall could be seen draining into a lake of shimmering glacier blue. The sound of thunder was definitely the waterfall. The small houses seemed to be made of a rainbow colour of crystals. Jade green, deep azure blues, purple, yellow, red and some that seemed to be made of clear stones, like agates. The kind of stones that Will and Jimmy always looked for whenever they were near a river or lake. The entire walls of this huge cave was lit up, like fire in crystal. The whole village was a breathtaking scene of colour and beauty.

Will whispered to Jimmy, "This looks like a Christmas card. Are we dreaming?"

Jimmy looking at Will with his eyes as large as saucers. "Will, there are people down there. What if they're not friendly?"

"Jimmy, this may be our only chance to get out of here. But you are right. We'll have to stay hidden and just watch and see if anyone shows us another way out."

The boys and Buddy sneaked down to an area of bushes and stone carvings and lay on their stomachs watching the villagers move in this strange and wonderful world. As Will was looking, he was mesmerized by a beautiful young girl standing in a doorway of what appeared to be her home. Suddenly a small boy about the age of three came running out the door, but in a split second the young girl scooped him up in her arms and started carrying him back with him kicking and screaming at her. She spoke in a language the boys did not understand, but it was obvious the little boy had been ordered to stay inside.

"Will, that's her. And the little kid, that's who I saw in the bushes," Jimmy whispered quietly.

Will looked at Jimmy. "Are you sure?"

Jimmy nodded to him. "Yeah, I'm positive. She had that same dress on, and the little guy had those blue shoes on. Only they looked more like elf shoes than human shoes now that I think of it. And her voice, that's the voice I heard in the tunnel of the cave. I think she must have been giving that little guy a bad time about having been spotted by me."

Will nodded. "That makes sense. I'll bet he wasn't supposed to come out at all. Jimmy, how mad will her family be if they find out we followed her?"

"Simple, we don't let them find us."

Both boys nod in unison.

"I hate to break this to you, cousin, but I have to take a leak. Care to direct me to the local gas station," Jimmy says with apprehension.

"Don't feel bad, Slick. I've had to go for the past hour." Looking around Will whispers to himself. "Where is a safe place to go?" Then he sees a small group of bushes behind three statues of birds.

"Jimmy, we can go behind those bushes, but we are going to have to stay low, or we'll be seen for sure." Jimmy nods,

"Okay, but what about Buddy. He's not very good at belly crawling, is he?" Will looks around.

"No, but I'll tie him up behind this bush and give him the command to stay. He should be okay for a few minutes." Will ties Buddy to the bush and whispers,

"Buddy, stay! Stay!" Buddy immediately sits. "Good boy." And Will gives him a pat on his head.

Jimmy and Will crouch down as low as possible and begin to sneak to the patch of bushes. When they reach the patch safely Will looks at Jimmy.

"You go first. I'll keep watch and then we can switch."

"Okay," says Jimmy as he moves in a little deeper into the foliage. Will watches closely as he hears his cousin's sigh of relief. He chuckles then starts to feel the pressure to go as well.

"Jimmy, hurry up. I'm going to burst my seams any minute." Jimmy comes out zipping his fly as he ducks down beside Will.

"All clear, Captain. Go water the trees." Will smiles at his cousin and quickly ducks into the bushes. He is just about finished when he hears Buddy bark and howl as a man grabs his lead and begins to drag him towards the village. Buddy is yanking on his lead and growling, but the man is relentless and continues to drag Buddy.

Will comes out of the trees, but Jimmy is nowhere in sight. Will scans the area and sees Jimmy crouched beside a blue house very near to where the girl and little boy live. The man dragged Buddy towards the girl as she stares in horror at the dog. Will is beside himself with terror and is just about to move towards Jimmy, when a very tall man with a necklace of jewelled rocks and headdress of feathers and beads comes towards Buddy. He emerges from the tallest crystal building in the village. Will thought he must be of some importance to these people. He points to the dog and then begins to yell at the girl in a very odd language. The girl obviously tries to explain, but she is silenced by this man when he yells louder at her. It becomes very obvious this man is the chief of these people.

The little boy comes out of the house and jumps with glee at the sight of Buddy. He runs to the dog and puts his arms around his neck. The chief yells at the boy, but he puts his face into Buddy's coat and continues to hang onto his neck. The chief then looks at the girl and says something softer to her. She nods and goes to pick up the little boy in her arms and returns him to the house. She comes back with her head bowed as if she is about to be sentenced to hard labour for life. The chief looks at the man holding Buddy's leash, says a few words. The man holding Buddy, nods his head and pulls out a huge knife from his sheath and raises it above Buddy's head. Jimmy and Will both scream out,

"NO, NO, NO!" and come running towards their dog from their hiding places. The chief, the girl and the man with the knife turn in shock to see these strangers running towards the dog. Jimmy got to Buddy first and pushes the man with the knife and grabs Buddy's lead. Will stops in front of the chief.

"Please, don't hurt my dog. He means no harm." The chief looks at the girl and begins shouting at her again. She begins to talk back, but again, he raises his hand, and she is quickly silenced. The chief looks at Jimmy who is just holding Buddy quietly by his side. He turns to Will. Will, as if by instinct knows this man holds the power, so he instantly bows his head in respect and holds out his hands, palms up to indicate no harm from him or Jimmy. The chief seems taken aback by this sudden change of respect. He looks at the girl and speaks to her quietly. She answers back with a pleading voice, but again, the hand goes up and she falls silent. The chief walks away. He turns to the man with the knife and says some words to him. The man sheaths the knife and walks behind the chief, leaving Will and Jimmy looking into the eyes of a very upset girl.

The girl turns to Will and Jimmy and looks at them with anger in her eyes. Will smiles feebly.

"Hello. We didn't mean to get you in trouble with your chief. We just didn't want anyone to hurt Buddy," he said, pointing towards his dog.

The girl looks puzzled and replies, "Buddy? His name is Buddy?"

Will and Jimmy both say in astonishment, "You speak English?"

The girl smiled slightly. "It has been many years since I have spoken these words. Yes, I speak English."

Will and Jimmy let out a cleansing breath of air. "Wow," said Will. "Can you help us get out of here? We have to get back home. Our parents are going to be worried sick."

The young girl said nothing at first then pointed to the entrance of her home.

"Please, come in and drink and eat with my little brother and me. We can talk later." The girl led the boys to her doorway and stopped to let them in first.

"No, after you," Jimmy said, trying to sound gallant an charming. Bowing a little and pointing the way with his hand. The girl smiled and entered first with Jimmy, Will and Buddy following behind.

Inside the little house was another shock of colour and design ingenuity. The floor was covered with soft mats of woven colourful cloths. The chairs were made of rock though they looked shiny and smooth, as if they had been tumbled by a rockhound. There were two beds in each corner of a small room next to the one they were standing in. The beds were covered with fur duvets like no animal fur that Will had ever seen before. The kitchen area had an amethyst sink that glittered, wet from the water. The water was being fed in by a hollow rock cut into the wall. Will looked closer and realized that this was being fed by an aqueduct system. Looking out the window he realized the whole village was being fed by this water system.

"Wow, this is ingenious!" Pulling his head back into the house Will noticed the girl, little boy and Jimmy starring at him.

"I beg your pardon. We have not even introduced ourselves. My name is Will, and this is my cousin Jimmy. You already know Buddy."

The girl smiled and replied slowly, "This is my brother Timtuk, and I am called Miria." Will smiled and extended his hand to the small boy,

"How do you do, Timtuk. It is so nice to meet you." Timtuk took the hand timidly as Will shook it gently. Looking at the girl he said, "And you as well, Miria. Thank you for inviting us into your home." She bowed graciously and extended her hand to the table and chairs.

"Please sit and I will get our food."

As the boys settled down in the chairs Jimmy was amazed by this table made of a polished stone. Timtuk walked over to Buddy and put his hand out as Will had just done with him. "Tayachou, mai appa Timtuk." Buddy held out his paw, and Timtuk laughed with glee at his wonderful breakthrough of friendship. Jimmy laughed and came and sat beside Timtuk and Buddy. "His name is Buddy," pointing to Buddy as he said the word again, "Buddy."

Timtuk looked at Jimmy and tried to repeat the name. "Bodee." Jimmy smiled. "Almost. Buddy," repeated Jimmy slowly.

Timtuk, looking very seriously at Jimmy said, "Baadee."

Jimmy smiled and nodded. "Yes, Buddy," he said pointing again to the dog. Then pointing to himself and looking at Miria for encouragement he repeated what Timtuk had said to Buddy. "Mai adda Jimmy."

Miria and Timtuk burst out laughing.

Jimmy turning a little red in the face said, "I said that wrong, didn't I?"

Miria smiled and said slowly, "Mai appa Jimmy."

Jimmy repeated the words. "Mai appa Jimmy." Then turning to Timtuk he repeated, "Mai appa Jimmy."

Timtuk slowly repeated Jimmy's name back to him, "Jimmee."

Jimmy smiled and nodded. "Yes, Timtuk. Jimmy and Buddy." Looking at Miria again he asked, "Just out of curiosity, what did I say?"

Miria smiled. "You said my nose is Jimmy."

Jimmy laughed and winked at Timtuk. "I'm grateful it was nothing worse."

Miria placed stunning crystal bowls on the table, each bowl a different colour of crystal. Timtuk took the blue crystal bowl, and everyone could see it was his favourite as he hugged it close to his chest.

Miria scolded him. "Timtuk, yetta more na." Timtuk quickly placed the bowl on the table in front of himself, looking at Miria for acknowledgement. She smiled at him and kissed his forehead. Timtuk seemed to glow from the affection. Will smiled at everyone watching this scene in front of him. Timtuk looked at Will and nodded his head at him.

"Oh," said Will with a chuckle. "Mai appa Will."

Timtuk tried forming the word. "Weo."

Will smiled and shook his head, this time saying his name slowly and making sure his emphasized the 'l's' on his teeth and lips.

Timtuk looked at Will and peeked into his mouth as if to examine his technique. "Wheelll," he said, holding his tongue out of his mouth and laughing.

Will laughed. "Not bad. Now say it fast. Will."

Timtuk smiled. "Will, Will."

Will laughed and nodded, "Yes Timtuk. Mai appa Will."

Timtuk crossed his arms and leaned on the table and smiled. Will realized how proud this little boy was communicating with these foreigners. *And that is what we are here*, thought Will, *foreigners in a strange world*. Will these people help us back to our world? Or will they kill us to keep their identity secret. Will shuddered at this thought and told himself to keep that awful feeling to himself. No sense in scaring Jimmy too.

Miria sensing Will's apprehension said, "Please Will. Have some food."

Will and Jimmy watched as Miria placed the food on the table. They both stopped and stared at each other in surprise.

CHAPTER SIX

Fred picked up the small basket half full with huckleberries. Looking at the basket's tight weave and colourful reeds he wondered in what country this could have come from. Definitely not native to our area. Baskets from our First Nations people tend to be brown and black with very distinct patterns from each band.

He noticed Steve approaching him.

"Find anything?" asked Steve.

"Yeah, look at this. What do you make of it?" Fred replied as he handed Steve the basket.

"Never seen any of our First Nation bands with a basket like this. It's just not their style. Where did you find it?"

Fred pointed towards the large clump of bushes, "Over there under those bushes. Darn near missed it, except I noticed some huckleberries on the ground under them."

Steve looked around. "Where is the nearest huckleberry bush?"

Fred pointed behind Steve. "I noticed some a little way back. Let's go over there and take a gander." Steve followed Fred to the small patch of huckleberries. On intense inspection Fred nodded to Steve. "Yup, they have been freshly picked." Steve and Fred searched the ground for any footprints.

"Definitely no sneaker tracks but Steve come over here. What do you make of this?" Steve came to Fred's side and looked down at a tiny footprint in the dirt.

"This is a small child's print. But aside from the size, there is no pattern on the sole of the shoe. Like it's a slipper or something."

Fred nodded. "I agree. But man, Steve, we're out in the boonies here. What is a child doing out here alone."

Steve sat down on a log and started to speculate in his mind what could have happened. After a few moments he decided to test his theory on Fred. "Fred, what if the boys spotted this little kid. They would go after him and try to help him if he was lost." Fred nodded in agreement.

"And one of them came back to the fishing spot for their backpacks I'm guessing. One set of prints came back and then went back into the woods."

"Let's go back to where we lost their trail."

Steve and Fred slowly started to methodically search the area.

"Steve, we're losing the light too fast. I can't see anything. We'll have to come back tomorrow before our prints start tracking over their prints."

Steve looked at Fred with a paleness that even Fred could see in the dim light.

"I know, man. You dread telling Jenny and your sister-in-law. I'll come with you if you think it will help."

Steve shook his head. "No, Fred. Jenny is just going to lose it, and I know she will be humiliated doing this around you. You're a good friend, but I have to do this myself."

Fred nodded in understanding and a little relieved that he didn't have to witness Jenny crying. He might start himself.

"Okay, then, buddy. What say we meet here at first light tomorrow?"

Steve nodded as he walked back to his truck. "I'll be here, Fred. And by the way, thanks a lot!"

"Just doing my job, buddy, but then I'd do it for a friend anytime. I'll go round up the rest of the troops and get them off this mountain before we lose anyone else.

Steve, I'll also contact the R.C.M.P. They will want to talk to us tomorrow and make a report if we don't find them within the twenty-four hours of disappearance."

Steve nodded his head slowly and walked back to his truck feeling the weight of the world on his shoulders. He started up his truck and waved to his friend as he headed home, praying silently to himself, *Please God, I need a miracle.*

Driving down the gravel road to his home, Steve got that funny feeling again, like he was not alone in the truck. "Mike, I need you to go be with Carol tonight. She is going to be devastated by my phone call. Help her to hold onto hope. Make sure she feels you, Mike. She is going to be so scared." In seconds Steve felt alone again. "And could you say a little prayer for me cause Jenny is going to want to kill me."

***

As Steve got out of the truck Jenny came out to greet him.

"Hey, you're late. I was starting to get worried." Looking around the truck, Jenny looked at Steve, "Where are the boys Steve?" Steve looked at Jenny with a look that no mother could deny it's meaning. Jenny's stomach dropped inside her and she started to feel hot tears in her eyes.

"Steve! Where are the boys?" she screamed. Steve grabbed her and hugged her to his chest.

"Honey, we don't know. We tracked them about a quarter mile from their fishing spot, and their footprints just disappeared."

She looked at Steve with tears streaming down her face and

asked incredulously,

"How could they just disappear? Both boys and the dog? Steve that's crazy. People just don't disappear!"

"Honey, I swear to you we looked everywhere. The team from Search and Rescue were out with me for hours. And Fred Avery was there. He's the best tracker this side of heaven, Jenny. I'm meeting up with him first thing tomorrow morning, and we'll find them, Jenny. I promise you, we'll find them." He said hugging Jenny closer to his chest.

Jenny pushed back. "Oh, Steve. We have to call Carol. God! Steve, she can't be alone when you tell her the news." Steve almost chuckled out loud when he realized he would have to be the bearer of bad news to Carol.

"You're going to make me do it, huh?"

Jenny looked up at him. "Seriously! You have to ask. But we have to call her friend, Sharon. Steve, she cannot be alone when she gets the news!" Steve nodded and hugged Jenny as she started wailing into his chest. Steve did what any good husband and father would do in these times. He cried too.

CHAPTER SEVEN

On examining the food Miria had laid out on the table, Jimmy looked at her in a puzzlement.

"Miria, where did you get this food?" For on the table was a basket full of blackberries, huckleberries and wild blueberries. Going to what appeared to be like an oven in the wall, Miria removed a platter that had obviously been in a steamer oven as steam permeated into the small kitchen. As she placed the platter on the table both boys were surprised to see sliced salmon as the main course.

"You have many questions for me. Let us eat first, and after I will try very hard to answer your questions." Both boys nodded and could not help but feel famished from smelling the wonderful smell of the salmon.

"Yes, Miria, you are right. Let's enjoy this delicious dinner you have made for us."

Everyone got settled in their chairs and the boys watched for Miria to make the first move. When she folded her hands and bowed her head, the boys did he same. Timtuk smiled at them and bowed his head too. Miria whispered a small prayer in her own language, but the boys could not really hear what she said. She finished with a "Elaso," as Timtuk repeated after her. Taking this as their cue both boys said in unison, "Elaso." Miria and Timtuk both smiled. Miria picking up the plater of salmon and handing it to Will said, "Let us eat." Will took the platter and smiled at her, and she blushed ever so slightly. She quickly handed the basket of berries to Jimmy.

"Please, take some."

Jimmy taking the basket replied, "Thank you Miria. This is very kind of you." Again Miria blushed and helped Timtuk fill his plate. Timtuk popped a large huckleberry into his mouth and smiled and said, "Mmmmm." Miria laughed at him and popped one in her mouth as well.

"These are my favourite, but the blueberries are very good too."

Will and Jimmy took bites of their salmon. "Oh, wow. This is cooked to perfection," said Will.

"Perfection?" Miria said the word slowly as if deciding on its meaning. Will smiled,

"Perfection means the best, and that is exactly how you have cooked it."

Miria smiled and again started blushing. "Oh I do not cook very well. I just steam food, and we eat it. My mother died before she could teach me all the wonderful dishes she made for us. I do the best I can for now."

Jimmy looked at Miria. "I'm sorry that you lost your mother. I know how it feels to lose a parent. My father died when I was very young. I wish I could say that I remember him, but I was about Timtuk's age when he died."

Miria held out her hand to Jimmy. "Is your mother still with you?"

"Yes," said Jimmy, "and boy is she going to be upset that Will and I are missing. Do you think you can help us out of here Miria?"

Miria rose slowly and took Timtuk into her arms. Reaching for a cloth she began to wipe his face and hands. Whispering some words in his ear he jumped down from her arms and ran into the bedroom. He returned with a long shirt, and it was quickly known that this was his night shirt. Miria undressed him quickly and put the shirt over his head. When he popped his head out of the shirt, Miria shouted, "Pooka!" and Timtuk laughed. It didn't take a genius to know that 'pooka' was peek-a-boo in her language. Taking Timtuk by his hand she began to lead him into the bedroom, but he quickly started to squabble and you got the meaning that he did not want to go to bed. Pointing to Will he spoke to Miria. Miria shook her head, but Timtuk started jumping up and down in protest.

Will asked, "What does he want?"

Miria looked at Will. "He would like you to put him to bed."

Will smiled. "I'd be honoured." He scooped Timtuk into his arms and hoisted him up on his shoulders. Walking like a grizzly bear and growling he popped Timtuk over his head and plopped him down on his bed. He knew it had to be his bed as it was much smaller than the other. He smiled at Timtuk and tucked him under the covers. Timtuk touched his hand, and Will could not help but tussle his head of hair and say, "Good night." At the sound of the words 'good night' Buddy entered the room. Timtuk's smile was from ear to ear.

"Okay, Buddy. You lay here and watch our new friend." Buddy turned around in a circle before settling down on the rug by Timtuk's bed.

Will smiled, "Okay, Timtuk?"

Timtuk smiled back and slowly said, "Okay." Rolling to his side he put his thumb in his mouth and closed his eyes. Will quietly walked towards the door never knowing Miria had been watching the whole scene.

He blushed slightly and shrugged his shoulders. "What can I say. Kids just like me."

Miria just smiled at him. "Would you like to go outside and sit by our pond. I will bring tea for us there." Will and Jimmy both nodded, but they both knew she wanted them to leave the house, so Timtuk would go to sleep.

"That would be lovely," Jimmy said in an English accent. "William, let's have tea on the terrace."

Will gave Jimmy a soft slap across the back of his head. "Smart ass." Jimmy and Will both laughed as they went outside to sit by the pond. Jimmy continued with the accent.

"Oh you brute! You are sounding more like your father each day."

Will looked seriously at Jimmy. "Want to guess what he must be going through right now."

Jimmy looked at his cousin and acknowledged this by saying, "And can you imagine what it's going to be like for him when he calls my mother?" Both boys just sat down on some carved stone chairs and said nothing.

CHAPTER EIGHT

"I can't breathe. I can't breathe!" Carol was crying in Sharon's arms still holding the phone. Sharon grabbed a paper bag and covered the front of her mouth and nose.

"Carol, breathe slowly into the bag. Just breathe slowly." Carol nodded her head and followed Sharon's direction. She took three cleansing breaths and then slipped to the floor and began to sob. Sharon could hear Steve on the phone and she quickly hit the Speaker Phone button, so she could hear him as well.

"Steve, it's Sharon. I think Carol is going to need a few minutes. Let me call you back." She clicked off the line before Steve could even reply. She knew exactly what had happened as Jenny had phoned her to tell her the horrible details. Now it was time to help her friend.

"Carol, Jimmy has been going up there for years. He's like a mountain man when he gets up there. He's not stupid or reckless. He knows how to survive out there. Steve has taught him that. You have to have faith in Steve and the Search and Rescue team that they will find the boys safe and sound."

Carol looked up at Sharon with tear-stained cheeks. "Sharon, I can't lose another one. I just can't."

Sharon held her friend in her arms. "You are not going to lose him Carol. You have to believe me. You are not going to lose him."

"Sharon, where can they be?" Carol asked trying to muffle a sob. Sharon smiled and held her friend close.

"Steve and this excellent tracker guy tracked the boys to the same spot. From there the tracks just disappear. So they are going back at first light to this spot, and tear the place apart until they have some answers. You know Steve won't rest until he finds the boys. He's got his son out there too. You have to believe in him, Carol. You know you do!"

Carol blew her nose and got up off the floor. "I guess I should call him back. You're right, Sharon. They're going through hell too."

She dialed the number and Steve picked it up on the first ring.

"Hello Carol."

Ah, call display, she thought. "Steve, I'm so sorry for the breakdown. It was just such a shock."

Steve replied in very soothing voice, "Carol, I'm so sorry I ever had to make this call, but you must believe me, I'll tear that mountain apart until I find the boys. I promise you. And about breakdowns, Jenny was given a sedative by our doctor. She just fell asleep about an hour ago, and I hope and pray she will sleep through the night." *Lucky her,* Carol thought.

"Steve, I'm going to make arrangements at work and fly up tomorrow night. I'll rent a car, so no one has to meet me. I can't just stay here and wait for your calls. I have to be there."

Steve knew she was right. "No problem, Carol. You and Jenny can support each other; you both could use it. I'm heading out tomorrow at first light. By the time you get here I hope I have positive news for us."

Carol bowed her head on the table. "Tell Jenny and Katie I love them. And Steve, I love you too. Please find them!"

Steve replied, "You know I will. Failure is not an option."

Carol hung up the phone, smiling a little. "Failure is not an option. How many times did I hear Mike say that to me?" She looked at Sharon and smiled. "Sometimes it's just darn spooky how alike those two are."

Sharon smiled at her friend. "You want me to stay with you tonight. I could go home and pack an overnight bag and be back in no time."

"You are a great friend. If I never tell you enough times that I love you, please forgive my silence because I cannot say it enough to you. I love and appreciate your kindness more than any words can say. Now you better get home to that wonderful husband of yours and make him realize how special you are to him. Besides, I'm going to be on this phone for hours making arrangements at work, airline and car reservations and the worst call I'll have to make is to my mother. Oh, God! Sharon, this might kill her. Her heart is not very strong."

Sharon came over and sat by Carol. "Don't tell her tonight. Wait until tomorrow night when you know more. Don't get her all upset when there is nothing for her to do but worry. Maybe Steve will find the boys tomorrow, and you can tell her all about it after it's all over."

Carol looked at Sharon. "I do like how you think. You're right. I'll leave her out of the loop until tomorrow. Please dear God let this be a happy ending."

Sharon gave her friend a final big hug. "Call me if you need anything. I'm only a phone call away, and I can be here in ten minutes if I file a flight plan. Twenty if I have to drive like you." Carol started to laugh as Sharon always teased her about her slow driving.

But after Mike's death, driving and its hazards became too real for her.

"You just make sure you get home safely, and I'll call you tomorrow night."

Sharon touched her friend's hand. "Okay. Carol, don't lose faith. They're out there. And Steve will find them."

Carol nodded that assured nod and slowly shut the door on her friend. She went to the couch, sat down slowly and started to cry again.

"Oh Mike. You gotta help Steve find our boys. You just have to."

Somewhere deep inside her head Carol could hear Mike's voice. "Failure is not an option!"

CHAPTER NINE

Miria came out of her house and seated herself on a chair near the boys. She looked at them and then gave a huge sigh. "You have questions?"

Jimmy looked at her with a smile. "Only about a hundred."

Miria smiled. "I will try very hard to answer them for you."

Will sat up straighter. "That will be great. First question, who taught you how to speak in our language?"

Miria smiled and spoke softly. "My father."

Jimmy moved forward in his chair towards Miria. "Your father? How did he learn it?"

Miria took a deep breath. "He is from your world." Both boys sat back in their chairs saying nothing at first, trying to slowly digest this information.

Will looked at Jimmy. "Didn't see that one coming. Okay then, how did he get here?"

Miria looked at both boys and smiled. "The same way you got here. He came through the portal of the sacred cave."

Jimmy slowly repeated, "Sacred cave. Portal of the sacred cave." Shaking his head in confusion he asked, "Miria, what happened to your father?"

Miria looked into the eyes of these two boys and realized they deserved to hear the complete story. But she was bound by law not to reveal her people's secrets, so she chose her words very carefully.

"Let me tell you what I am able to reveal to you. My father entered our sacred cave about twenty- one years ago. He like you was…" She tried to search for the word she was thinking of.

"Overwhelmed?" said Will.

Miria looked at Will "Does this mean what you feel?"

"Yes," said Will. "It is starting to get that way."

"Then yes," said Miria, "he was overwhelmed by our culture and our world. At first the elders thought to execute him and protect our secrets, but my mother saw kindness in him, and she stood up for him and pleaded for them to allow her to teach him our ways. If in two years he did not wish to stay in our world, she would help him leave. But only on the promise of his soul that he would never reveal the secret of our world."

Jimmy looked at Will with a stunned expression. "Miria, did your father leave this world."

She shook her head. "No, he fell in love with my mother and she with him. He stayed with her until he died. I was eight years old when he died. I am bound by our laws not to reveal how he died, but I can tell you that we were a happy family, and I miss them both very much."

Will spoke calmly hoping his voice would not sound shaky at this next question. "Miria, can we leave this world?"

"The portal that you came through is closed. It will not open again for many, many years. Tomorrow, the chief will decide your future. But please do not worry, for I will speak as my mother did for my father. I will guide you through our ways and help you. If you wish to leave our world, I will take you to another portal, but it will not open for another three years. Can you agree to what I speak? Do you understand?" Miria spoke these words slowly, so the boys would comprehend the meaning.

Will looked at her and his face was turning pale at the realization of her words. "Yes Miria I think I understand. Tomorrow, your chief will decide whether we live or die, and you are telling us that you will speak in our favour. But why would the chief even listen to you?"

Miria took another deep breath. "Because I am his daughter, by the marriage of my mother to him. He swore to honour me with love and respect the day they were married. I became his daughter by our laws. Timtuk is his son. I have raised him since his birth. My mother died two days after he was born." Tears started to well in her eyes, and Jimmy quickly took her hands into his hands.

"I'm so sorry Miria. You have lost both your parents?"

Miria let the tears fall. "I have Timtuk, and his father has been generous to me. Though I do fear him most of the time, he is a good leader, and I know he will listen to my plan."

Will looked at her. "Your plan. You have a plan? Don't hold back, let's hear it."

Miria smiled at Will. "I will ask of him what my mother asked for my father. I will teach you about our world. I hope by then you will realize the reasons why our world must remain a secret. If you still want to leave, I will travel with you to our next portal."

Will looked at her with shock. "But Miria, you said that won't be for three years. Are you saying we are stuck here for three years?"

Miria looked slowly into each boy's eyes seeing their fear and pain. "Yes, Will. This is what I am saying."

✷ ✷ ✷

The boys were curled up outside in some bedrolls given to them by Miria. Buddy came outside and snuggled between the two of them. Both of them listened to the quiet of the little village except for the sound of the waterfall in the distance. Jimmy, sitting up and leaning on his elbow whispered, "Will, do you think the chief will kill us?"

Will looked into his cousin's eyes and could read the fear on his face. "We have to put our lives in Miria's hands. I have faith that she will get the chief to listen. But Jimmy, we could be in this world for three years. I am having a real hard time wrapping my head around that little jewel. We will be eighteen and nineteen years old before we get out. And where will out be?"

Jimmy looked down at the ground. "And what about our families, Will? Will they give up on us?"

Will shook his head in total negation. "Not in this lifetime. Not ever! You know my dad, Jimmy. He'll move heaven and earth to find us. But where will we be? Should we stay here and hope he finds us, or do we follow Miria to who knows where? Man, I hope I can just fall asleep and forget this nightmare we're in. Get some sleep, Jimmy, we'll talk in the morning."

Jimmy nodded his head and rolled up in his blanket. He did not realize until just that moment how tired he really was. He was asleep in five minutes. While he slept he dreamed of his father and could hear him say over and over again, "I am with you son, and we will not fail. Failure is not an option." And he slept soundly for the rest of the night.

CHAPTER TEN

At first light Steve was out of his truck heading to the last spot where the boys just disappeared. To his surprise Fred Avery's truck was parked and empty.

Steve smiled knowing his friend was as determined to find the boys as he was.

Coming to the turn where they lost their trail he found Fred on his hands and knees crawling under the bushes. "Morning, Fred. You find something?"

"Morning, Steve. I think so, though it makes no sense."

Steve shook his head. "What about this whole scenario makes any sense? What did you find, Fred?"

Fred looked up from the bushes. "Come see for yourself, and tell me what you think." Steve crawled in under the bushes and slowly moved the branches away from his face to look at Fred as he pointed to the ground. Steve looked at the ground and saw another footprint. Much like the shoe from yesterday but this was adult size. Female size.

"Another print. The narrowness of the foot points to an adult female. There was someone else with the child? It's mother maybe?"

Fred nodded. "That's my theory too. Looks like they may have been hiding in these bushes but again, no prints to follow. It's like they all disappeared."

Steve held his head as if he was nursing a headache. "Not what I want to hear, Fred. Not what I want to hear."

Fred gave Steve an encouraging pat on his back. "Come on, buddy. I think we should go and visit my friend Chief Patterson at the First Nations reservation. He might be able to shed some light on this disappearance. It sure couldn't hurt to go ask."

"Yeah, I know the chief. He's a good man. But what will he know that we don't know?"

Fred smiled. "That's what we are going to find out. Now come on and follow me in my truck; okay?"

"Okay," said Steve as both men headed back to their trucks.

On arrival at the chief's home Steve was welcomed by the children, who came running up to him smiling and waving. "Hi kids. How are you all doing?"

Steve asked smiling at their little faces. "We're fine Ranger Steve. Did you come to see our fish?"

"No, I came to see Chief Patterson. Is he home?"

One little boy shouted, "Yeah, he's home. He's in his house. Do you want me to go and get him?"

Fred walked up to the group of kids. "No, that won't be necessary. We'll go visit him. This is just a social call." The children ran off laughing, and Fred and Steve walked towards the chief's home and knocked on the door.

A young native girl of about fifteen years answered the door. Looking at the men she spoke softly, "Do you wish to see our chief?"

Fred answered kindly, "Good Morning, Shira. It's nice to see you again. We would indeed like to speak to the chief on an urgent matter. Is he available?"

Shira smiled at Fred and blushed a little that he remembered her name. "Yes, Mr. Avery. He is sitting in the great room."

"Thank you, Shira." Both men took off their shoes as respect to the chief and his home and entered the great room. The chief was sitting on a large easy chair smoking a cigarette.

"Welcome my friends," he greeted them with a yellow-stained smile. "What has brought you two old friends here today?"

Steve cleared his throat as the smell of cigarette smoke was as thick as a fog.

"Well, Chief, I have lost my son, my nephew and our dog yesterday. Fred and his team searched everywhere for miles yesterday. We followed their tracks to a heavily bushed area and then simply lost their trail. We also found a child's footprint and a woman's print, but again, they just disappeared."

The chief looked into the faces of these two men, and he could feel their anguish and despair. He looked at his granddaughter, Shira, and spoke in his native tongue to her. She went out of the room and quickly came back carrying what appeared to be a very old book. It was covered in a soft moccasin-like leather and it had a large eagle painted on the front. The chief slowly opened the book and turned the pages to the middle of the book. The language on the page was as foreign to Steve and Fred as hieroglyphics. Yet the chief's finger moved across the page as if he was reading the local newspaper. He stopped his finger at a certain spot and slowly reread the passage. He looked up at Steve and Fred and shook his head.

"It is the time of the cave people. Your boys are with them. They will not be back."

He said it as calmly as if he was reading a grocery list. Steve's hair stood up on the back of his neck.

"Chief, what are the cave people? Where do they come from?"

The chief took a long puff on his cigarette and looked up at the ceiling. "Many years ago a chief's son from another village disappeared into a cave. His friend and brother were hunting with him when they discovered the cavern. The oldest son went into the cave to explore where it went. The other two boys waited outside the cave. Before the sun passed over the trees the cave shut its door, trapping the chief's son inside. He was never seen again."

Steve taking a hard swallow asked, "How long ago was this, Chief?"

The Chief looked into the book and read slowly, looking up at Steve he replied,

"About twenty-one years ago."

Steve looked at Fred. "I need some air. Thank you, Chief, for your time and information." Fred and Steve rose and the chief gave a chant to them in his native tongue.

As they left Shira was right behind them. "My grandfather wished your journey to end in happiness, Mr. Steve and Mr. Fred."

"Thank you, Shira," said Fred and left close behind Steve.

Steve was shaking his head from side to side. "This is crazy, Fred. Cave people!"

Fred looked at Steve with a complete understanding of this wild story. "Look Steve, I have heard of the missing chief's son, and I know what village he lived in. Let's go to that village and talk to the elders or maybe the brother and the friend that witnessed the disappearance. Maybe we can get a better light on this story."

Steve looked at him and said with a little anger in his voice, "Story! That's all this is, Fred, a story. A native folklore. What's next? Sasquatch?"

Calmly Fred looked at Steve. "What else do we have to go on? Steve, sometimes you have to come out of the box and see another world. I think this is our time to do exactly that. Are you ready?"

Steve shook his head in disbelief that he was even considering this fairy tale. "Okay, Fred. But I hope Jenny and Carol don't have me committed for this. Even you have to admit it's nuts."

Fred smiled. "Yeah, Steve, but I have seen things with the First Nations people that can make your hair stand on end. I trust the chief, and yes, it does sound nuts, but so did airplanes and rockets and telephones. But someone believed and I'm asking you to do the same. Have a little faith, brother!"

Steve walked to his truck. "Lead the way, Padre! You carry a Bible in your truck?"

Fred smirked at him and jumped into his truck and held his head out of the window. "Follow me you heathen!" Steve just chuckled and stayed close behind Fred on the highway to the next village.

CHAPTER ELEVEN

The boys woke up to the sound of Buddy barking and Timtuk laughing. Will rolled over to see Timtuk throwing a rolled up cloth and Buddy running and fetching and bringing it back to him. Will smiled at the playful scene and rolled over to look at Jimmy. "You okay," he asked.

"Yeah, I slept better than I thought I would. How about you?"

Will smiled. "Not bad. This is certainly a different way to sleep in the ol' outdoors."

Jimmy laughed. "Yeah, kind of missed those stars!" Before either one could respond Timtuk and Buddy ran over and jumped on Will and Jimmy.

"Oh, man. Buddy, you weigh a ton. Get off me!" shouted Jimmy but Buddy just gave him a morning hello lick on his face with Jimmy shouting his protests. Timtuk sitting on Will's stomach just laughed and laughed. Miria came out of her house to see what all the commotion was about. When she saw Buddy licking Jimmy's face and Jimmy howling at the dog, she started to laugh as well.

"Good morning, my friends. I have made the morning food for you if you would like to come in the house."

Will smiled at Miria. "Breakfast, Miria. You have made breakfast."

Miria smiled. "Yes, breakfast! I could not remember the word for the morning food."

Will and Jimmy crawled out of their blankets and began to fold them up neatly. Carrying them into the house, Miria showed them where to put them down.

Jimmy whispered to Will, "Ah, cousin. I have to make a nature call. Any ideas?"

Miria as if sensing his needs pointed to a small room in the back of the house. When Jimmy entered he was shocked to see a rock basin and a rock toilet full of water and a rock basin above it with a copper wire and stone chain. *Now if memory serves me right,* thought Jimmy, *I pull this chain when I am finished.* As if on cue, he pulled the chain and the water from the above basin flowed into the toilet forcing the water to disappear down a hole.

As Jimmy washed his hands in the basin he knew that Miria's father must have had something to do with this bathroom. On entering the kitchen and Will taking his turn in the bathroom Jimmy smiled and asked Miria,

"Did your father have anything to do with the bathroom?"

She smiled. "Yes, he … (then she thought slowly of the word she was looking for) modern? Modern?"

"Modernized the place," said Jimmy smiling.

"Yes, modernized. He was so happy to show our people this way. It changed our village. The smell went away."

Will laughed as he entered the kitchen. "Yeah, that would do it."

"Please, everyone sit and we will have….breakfast." Miria smiled as she remembered the word. They bowed their heads as Miria said a quiet prayer. "Elaso." "Elaso," everyone repeated. She smiled as she put the platters on the table. One had blackberries and more huckleberries. One had what appeared to be corn bread. Round and flat but warm to the touch. Finally, she brought out what looked like a baked omelette with mushrooms and small onions on it. She cut up slices and served each one of them a large piece and one for herself. When the boys took a bite of the omelette, they were amazed at the flavour. She poured water into mugs made of the most colourful stone. Each mug was a different colour. Even the water here was amazing. Cold and fresh, just like you get when you camp by a rushing river.

"Miria, you are an excellent cook and an even better hostess!" said Will smiling at her.

Miria crinkled up her nose, "What is hostess?"

"Someone who invites people into her home and takes good care of her guests. That would make you a hostess. Thank you for treating Jimmy and I so kindly."

Miria smiled. "I am happy to do this now. But yesterday I was angry at my chief for giving you to me. He said you were my fault, so I should have to suffer the punishment. You have not been a punishment. You have been very nice to Timtuk and me, and we are happy to have you in our home."

Jimmy smiled at her. "You are our friends. Timtuk and you, we are honoured to call you friends."

Miria looked at the boys. "Today, I will use this honour and hope my chief will honour my friendship to you as well."

At the mention of the chief, Jimmy lost his appetite.

***

There were about twenty men sitting in a horseshoe shape facing the chief. The chief spoke to the men and then looked up at everyone and repeated words that Jimmy and Will could not understand. Slowly Miria stood up and moved into the centre of the seated men. She spoke slowly but loudly, so everyone could hear. After a few moments of her speech everyone looked at Will and Jimmy.

Jimmy leaned over to his cousin. "Tell me your ears are not ringing."

Will chuckled into his chest and looked into Jimmy's eyes. "Man, I hope this lady can sell her plan. If not, you, Buddy and I may have to make a run for it. I've been watching these guys and that cavern over there (moving his head in the direction) seems like it's used a lot."

The chief started yelling in the direction of the boys. Will quickly took it as a hint to shut his mouth. Looking at Miria he nodded his head at her and smiled hoping she would grasp his meaning that he trusted her with their lives.

When Miria was finished talking she quietly came and sat by the boys. She did not look at them but looked straight ahead as if she had never met them.

Will's stomach was doing summersaults, and he was sure Jimmy's was doing the same. Finally, the chief rose, he looked around at his people and then at the men seated in front of him. He spoke to them in a gentler tone this time, and the men rose one by one. As each man stood up Will could hear Miria take a quick breath. He did not know if this was a good sign or a bad one. Finally, all but two men rose. The chief turned and spoke to Miria. At first she did not make a move, and then she put her head in her hands and began to weep.

Will looked at her and with shock in his face said, "Miria, what just happened?"

Miria looked at him through tear filled eyes. "I am to take you to the next portal. We will escort you to safety."

Jimmy looked at her in confusion. "But that's good; right? Why are you crying?"

Miria looked at Jimmy and Will and with a deep sigh said, "I must leave Timtuk with his father. He will not allow him to come with me. He has never been away from me!" She put her head in her hands and began to sob uncontrollably.

Will put her in his arms. "Oh, God. Miria, what have we done to you?" The court of men dispersed slowly and three young men came up to Miria and spoke gently to her. She nodded her head and touched their hands as if to thank them for their concern. One man in particular was very attentive and Will could read his face that he did not like Will touching Miria.

Miria stood up. "Come, Will and Jimmy. We have much to do." She nodded at the three men and started back to her house with Jimmy and Will close behind.

Back at the house Timtuk was playing 'fetch' with Buddy. Jimmy laughed at them. "Your arm will fall off before Buddy ever tires of this game. Come on, Timtuk, let's take Buddy for a walk." He made the gesture for Timtuk to take his hand, and Timtuk did it without hesitation. Jimmy looked at Will and gave a quick look at Miria and then back to Will. Will knew this was an indication to speak to Miria privately. He nodded at his cousin in agreement and watched Timtuk, Buddy and Jimmy walk down the small lane towards the lake.

"Miria, is there anything we can do to keep you and Timtuk together? Maybe the escorts could take us and leave you and Timtuk together."

She looked at Will without any expression at all. "No one knows your language but me. But the chief believes it is my fault that Timtuk came out of the cave. I did not know he had followed our party out, but now leaving him, this is the punishment. I must accept the decision, but I will never forgive myself."

Will held her hand, and she did not pull back but let his hand rest on hers. "Those three men who came to you today, are they part of the escort team?"

She shook her head. "No, they were a part of the party that Timtuk followed out. They too are sorry they did not notice him and were giving me their apologies. They did not want me punished, but the chief made it clear to everyone that Timtuk was my brother, and I should have taken better care of him." She started to smile and shake her head. "He really is good at hiding himself. It's a game he likes to play on me all the time."

Will rubbed her hand slowly. "How soon will we be leaving?"

With a huge sigh Miria took a breath. "It will take about three days to collect our supplies and plan our route. My father will decide who will go with us. I am sure that one of those three men who spoke to me will be joining us."

Will looked at Miria and hoped beyond hope she did not answer the next question in the way he did not want to hear.

"There was one man with the white stone necklace. Is he your boyfriend? He seemed very concerned for you."

Miria smiled. "Lian. His name is Lian. And no, he is not my boyfriend. But he would like me to change my mind. Maybe someday I will, but right now my heart does not feel right for him. Do you understand what I mean?"

Will smiled. "Yeah, you're just not into him. I get it!"

Miria laughed. "Oh Will, you talk so funny. You remind me of my father. He was always making me laugh."

Will gave her a quick hug. "Oh, Miria, I hope I can make you laugh for a very long time. But now I have just given you sadness because you must leave Timtuk behind. I don't know how to make this better for you."

Miria shrugged her shoulders. "You cannot make it better. I will have to suffer in silence like most women do in our village."

Will looked at her. "Your women suffer? How?"

"I cannot tell you anymore than this, Will. Maybe someday I can explain our ways and culture to you, but now we have work to do, and we must get started."

Will stood up and looked at Miria. "I am yours to command."

Miria smiled. "That would never be in my culture. But I am grateful for your friendship and understanding. Now let us get started."

CHAPTER TWELVE

Steve followed Fred to the village deep in the heart of the Kispiox Valley. When they parked their trucks, this time Fred was overrun with the small children of the village. He threw one on his shoulders and two others in each arm. He looked like a totem pole of human faces.

"Hey kids, where is Chief George? Is he in his house, or is he fishing?"

The children shouted in unison, "Fishing!" So Fred led the way to the nearby river. Steve and Fred looked around at the many faces standing by the river when the young boy on Fred's shoulder shouted,

"There he is, Mr. Fred," and pointed to a man standing alone with a fishing pole in his hand. Fred put the children down and started to walk over to the chief.

"Hello, Chief. How's the fishing."

The chief looked up and smiled. "Hello, Fred. A good day to fish. Always a good day to fish."

Fred pointed to Steve. "Chief, this is my good friend Steve Wright, and we have come to talk to you."

The chief looked at Fred. "Is there a problem that an old chief can help you with?"

Fred smiled. "I hope so, Chief. Though what we would like to talk about may bring back bad memories for you. For this, we are very sorry."

The chief looked at Fred.

"We have been brothers for many years. We can talk about many things. But let us go to my house, so this man's old bones can sit and rest." Fred smiled and helped the chief walk back to his house with Steve bringing up the rear.

As the chief got settled into his chair he called for his wife to bring some refreshments for their guests. Fred knew better than to protest against this, as the chief would be insulted by the refusal. So his wife slowly brought out coffee and some cakes and smiled at Fred as she handed him his mug of coffee.

"Thank you, Clara. This is most kind of you."

Clara put up her hand. "Fred, you are always welcome in our home. You are a good friend." Fred smiled as she slowly left the room.

Chief George watched his wife leave the room and then turned to Fred. "So what do we have to talk about?"

Fred looked into the old man's face and could read years and years of life in each wrinkle on the old man's face. "It's about your son, Chief. The one you lost many years ago. I was wondering if your other son would be available to talk about this day. Or maybe the friend that was with your sons on this tragic day." The chief took a huge slow breath before he spoke.

"The friend you speak of died many years ago. Some say he was too sad for the loss of his friend. Others say he just liked to take foolish chances. He was jumping off a rock cliff into the river. He never came up. The river never gave his body back to us. My son you wish to speak to is in his house. The dark green one just down the lane. He is married to a good woman, and they have three sons. When you speak to him, remember he was only twelve years at the time. He may not remember anymore." Fred nodded and stood to shake the chief's hand.

"I will speak with him with kindness and respect, Chief George. You have my word on this."

The chief shook Fred's hand too. "I know you will, my friend. Come back and visit us after we smoke the salmon. A big feast for everyone."

"I'll look forward to that, Chief. Thank you."

As Steve followed Fred he whispered to him, "He was only twelve years old. How much can he possibly remember?"

"Steve, do you remember where you were when the Challenger blew up? You were just a kid right? And how about 9/11? Do you remember where you were? Or how about the day your dad died? You were only about fourteen; right? But do you remember everything?"

Steve nodded. "Like it was yesterday."

Fred touched his friend's shoulder. "I'm betting this guy remembers everything about the day he lost his big brother. Let's go test my theory."

Fred knocked on the door of the green house and a beautiful native woman answered. "Hello, may I help you."

Fred smiled at her. "Yes, we're looking for Chief George's son. Is he home?"

"Yes, he is out in the back chopping some wood. Would you like me to call him?"

Steve piped out. "No, no, we'll go around and find him. Thank you." The woman closed the door as Fred and Steve went around to the back of the house. They found the chief's son chopping wood and stacking it neatly beside the house.

"Hello!" Fred called to him. The man stopped chopping and wiped his brow with his sleeve.

"Can I help you?" said the man looking a little suspicious at the two men. Fred held out his hand.

"My name is Fred and this is my friend Steve. And we were just speaking with your father, and he gave us permission to come and talk to you."

The man took Fred's hand and began to shake it. "My name is Reed. What would you like to talk about?"

Fred let out a huge sigh. "Well, Reed, would you mind if we sit. This may take a while?"

So each man sat on lawn chair by a fire that Reed was using to burn old twigs and branches.

Fred began, "Steve has lost his two boys and a dog. We tracked them until the footprints just disappeared into thin air. We may be in the exact area you lost your brother. Can you tell us what happened?"

Reed looked at Steve with a total understanding of his anguish. "I was just twelve years old when this happened. No one would believe David and I. They thought we were loco! But I remember it like it was yesterday. I still have nightmares about it. But I have three sons and if one went missing I would not stop until I found him. I cannot imagine your pain at the loss of two."

Steve nodded to him. "Thank you, Reed. I appreciate this so much."

"It was a sunny day in fall. You know the type of day, cool, fresh and the leaves on the trees were turning bright yellow and red. I was the kid brother and bugged Dean to let me tag along with David and him. He was going to show me how to track animals, recognize their prints and follow them as far as we could. It felt like what the elders have always told us, be one with nature, be the wind. After a few hours of tracking some deer tracks Dean thought he saw someone in the distance running into the bushes. We thought it would be so cool to track a human. So the chase was on. We had no idea how deep in the woods we were, but hey, it was a game. A game of skill and persistence. Dean had the tracks picked up in no time. The man was a genius tracker. But when they led us to the opening of a cave, the game took a dangerous turn. Dean told us to stay back, and he would go into the cave and investigate. We tried to talk him out of it. David was afraid there might be bears inside, but Dean assured us it was too early for bears to begin hibernation. He went inside the cave, and David and I stayed outside and waited for him to come back. But like in a bad dream the cave opening just vanished. There in front of us was just a huge rock where the opening had been. We screamed and tried to move it, but it was like it had been there for a thousand years. We ran back to our home and screamed for help. Many men came but they just did not believe our story. I cried for days and returned to that spot every day for a month. But he never came back, and I knew that he was gone for good. One of the elders, one of the oldest men in our tribe, simply said, 'It was the time of the cave people,' and that was that. Everyone thought he was crazy too, but I always wondered if he knew more. Unfortunately, he passed on before I could speak to him. My only hope of knowing the truth died with him. I don't know much more to tell you except if you lost the tracks check to see if they go near some rocks. They may have disappeared like my brother."

Steve looked at Reed and spoke slowly, "You lost your brother in the cave twenty-one years ago. Now twenty-one years later I have lost my boys too. Reed, would you take us to the spot where your brother disappeared. Do you think you can find it again?"

Reed nodded slowly. "I know exactly where it is. I go up there ever so often just hoping for a miracle. I'll take you there, but the light is going. How about first thing tomorrow morning? Say, eight o'clock."

Steve and Fred rose from their chairs. Fred spoke, "That would be great, Reed. Where would you like us to meet you?"

Reed smiled. "If you come here and pick me up then I can leave the truck for my wife to use. She'll be happy to have it all day."

Steve smiled. "Eight o'clock tomorrow, then. Thank you, Reed."

Reed looked into Steve's eyes as he shook his hand. "I don't know if I'll be any help to you, Steve, but I sure hope I can be. I'd like to solve this mystery as well."

As Steve and Fred went to their trucks, Fred turned to Steve with a look of apprehension. "Steve, I really don't know what to make of all this. But more to the point, what are you going to tell Jenny?"

Steve bowed his head before looking up at Fred. "I'm going to tell her the truth. We haven't found them yet, but I'll turn over every rock and stone until I find them. I believe Reed, Fred! Who could make up such a story like that and believe it for twenty-one years?"

Fred nodded at him. "I believe him too. I'll meet you here tomorrow morning. Good luck, buddy." He patted Steve on the back, and Steve felt like the weight of the world was still back there. He not only had to tell Jenny but Carol would be coming tonight. Two mothers to try to console. *Could it get any worse,* he thought as he jumped into his truck and headed home.

CHAPTER THIRTEEN

Miria was busy making bedrolls for the three of them. Food had been packed and stored in large containers with a stone top that seemed to air lock the container. There was a large container with odd writing on its sides, and when Jimmy tried to lift the lid to check out the contents, he found it to be locked though there was no sign of a lock or key hole anywhere. Jimmy looked at Miria.

"What's in here, Miria? And how does this box lock?"

Miria smiled at her friend. "What is in there are things we can trade with other villages as we travel. We have enough food for one week, but we should be at our first village in five days. As for how it locks, I do not know how to explain this in your language but the rock that this box is made of is heated, which makes the rock stick together tightly."

Jimmy looked at her and smiled broadly. "I know what you're talking about. It's Hematite. It's one of the most common minerals you will find on earth. It is made mostly of iron, and when you heat the rocks, they become magnetized. Holy cow! My science teacher would be so proud of me right now."

Miria laughed at Jimmy as Will came into the house with Timtuk on his shoulders.

"What's so funny?" he asked as he put Timtuk on the ground.

"Will, look at this. The box is made of Hematite. They have heated it."

Will cut in. "So it becomes magnetized. Clever!" Jimmy was a little miffed at his cousin for raining on his discovery.

Will looked at Miria. "Timtuk has been watching us very closely. Does he know about our journey?"

Miria shook her head. "I have not told him yet. I will tell him the day before we leave. I cannot bear to hear his cries for three days. I will comfort him the best I know how on the last day."

Will looked into her eyes and read the sadness, and he wondered if Timtuk saw it too. In the short time he had got to know Timtuk, he realized he was one smart little guy and was not easily fooled. He grabbed Buddy's rolled up rag and tossed it to Timtuk. Gesturing for Timtuk to take Buddy out for a play. Timtuk laughed as he called Buddy's name. Boy and dog happily ran out the door.

"He will miss you and Jimmy," Miria said sadly.

"No, I think he'll miss Buddy the most," said Will smiling. "I think Jimmy and I will come in third and fourth after Buddy and you."

Miria's eyes started to well with tears. "He will be sad, and there is nothing I can do to help him."

Jimmy started putting small plates and knives into a box. "Who will look after him when we are gone. Your chief doesn't give the impression that he'll be a good babysitter."

"There is an older tribal woman that usually cooks and cleans for the chief. She has agreed to take care of Timtuk. She is quite old, and I feel Timtuk will be a handful for her."

She smiled upon using the word "handful" as her father had said she was one, many times to her as a child. "I hope our chief will be a good father to his son. Timtuk will need a good man in his life, to help him grow and learn about our ways. I hope our chief will be patient with Timtuk. I hope Timtuk will not hate me for being away from him for so long."

Will looked at Miria and dreaded asking this question. "How long will it be before you see him again."

Miria sat down and rested her forehead on her hands. "Timtuk will be eight years the next time I see him." And she started to weep quietly into her hands.

Will kneeled down beside her and put his arms around her shoulders. "Oh, Miria, we are so sorry for bringing this on you. We feel like dirtbags in this sad story."

Miria looked up at Will. "Dirtbag. What is a dirtbag?"

Jimmy picked up the nearest garbage container. "It's what holds this," he said, pointing to the garbage.

Miria looked up and then chuckled. "You are not dirtbags, my friends. You are in need of help, and I am the only one who can help you with this journey. Me and three of my friends. The ones you met at the tribal council, the hunting party that was in your world. They have all said they want to help me. I think they feel bad about Timtuk too."

Will groaned quietly to himself for he certainly remembered the one young man that did not seem to like him in his female territory. Will whispered to himself, "Yup, this is going to be fun. Fun, fun, fun!"

Miria looked at her companions. "I'll fix us some food and then we must sleep early. Tomorrow we visit our tribal elders, who will help us with the map we will need to follow. Then we will do our final packing and leave early the next day."

And Jimmy thought, *And Timtuk will be told the whole story. I think no one will sleep tomorrow night.*

* * *

The next day started as the previous one. Timtuk jumped on top of Will and rolled onto Buddy. Each so happy to see each other. Jimmy rolled over and smiled, "You know, we have no sun, no sky and no stars and yet we know it's a new day. How is that possible, Will?"

Will just smiled and shrugged his shoulders. "Dunno. Must have something to do with our inner clock. Hello, Timtuk."

Timtuk looked at Will and repeated slowly. "Hello, Will. Hello, Jimmy. Hello, Buddy," and he laughed from his belly. Will picked him up and held him up over his body.

"Fly, little bandit, fly!" Timtuk laughed so loud that Miria came running out to see what was happening. She began to scold Timtuk, and he stopped laughing immediately and looked a little sad.

Will looked at Miria. "Aw Miria, he wasn't doing anything wrong."

Miria looked sternly at Will. "He should have more respect for you and Jimmy. He should not have woken you up."

Will looked at Miria with a stern face. "Miria, tell the boy we are not angry with him. We had to get up anyway, did we not? I do remember someone saying we had to get an early start. Oh yeah, that was you," he said, smiling and pointing directly at her.

Miria smiled in defeat and spoke to Timtuk. He smiled at Will and jumped into his arms screaming with glee.

Miria shook her head walking into the house. "I cannot win. They are all children!" As she came into the doorway she called back to the three amigos, "Our morning food is just about ready."

Jimmy smiled and yelled after Miria, "Breakfast, Miria. It's called breakfast."

Miria walked into her small kitchen and thought to herself, Yes, breakfast. I must remember, breakfast. She smiled as she put out the stone bowls and mugs. She slowly surveyed this little house she called home and hot tears started to well in her eyes. Timtuk came running in with Will chasing behind him. They both stopped

The Seven Sacred Caves

short when they noticed Miria's tears. She quickly wiped away her tears and turned her back to them.

"Please, sit down. I will get breakfast," she turned and smiled as she finally remembered the word. Will nodded politely and settled Timtuk in his chair. Jimmy came in yawning and stretching. "You know Miria, I sleep like a bear here."

Miria looked at him with a puzzled look. "A bear? What is a bear?"

Jimmy smiled as he sat down. "Big, furry animal. Big teeth, big claws and he sleeps for four months during the winter."

"Is he dangerous?" she asked slowly.

"Oh, yeah. You don't mess with a bear. Especially a mother bear. Get near her babies and you are toast!"

Again Miria looked at Jimmy. "What is toast?"

Jimmy smiled back at her. "Breakfast!"

Miria laughed. "I will remember not to mess with a bear. Now, everyone, let us begin." Miria said a quiet prayer and ended with "Elaso". All the boys echoed, "Elaso," and began to eat their breakfast.

***

When Jimmy, Will and Miria arrived at the elder's home Lian and his two friends were already there speaking with the man and looking over a chart. Lian looked up and smiled at Miria. He only glanced in the direction of Will and Jimmy then went back to the chart. The other two young men came over to Will and Jimmy.

One pointed to himself. "Mai appa Beya."

The other young man pointed to himself and smiled. "Mai appa Donat." It took everything for Jimmy not to laugh, as his name is pronounced donut.

"Mai appa Will," Will said as he pointed to himself.

Jimmy jumped into the introductions. "Mai appa Jimmy," and

hoped he said it right and didn't name his nose again.

Beya and Donat smiled at the boys and repeated their names slowly. Will held out his hand to shake theirs, but he was met with a startled look from each man. Miria stepped in and explained to Beya and Donat the meaning of this gesture. They slowly took Will and Jimmy's hands and the boys shook them gently but firmly. They exhaled together as if some weight had just been lifted from their shoulders. They smiled at Will and Jimmy and gestured for them to come to the table and look at the chart. As the boys neared the table Lian put his hand up to stop them. He spoke very sternly to Beya and Donat who looked shocked by their friend's attitude.

Miria stepped up to Lian and spoke to him quietly but very firmly. It was obvious she was not happy with Lian and was not afraid to let him know. When Lian did not seem ready to accept the boys, she shouted something to Lian and turned to the boys. "Come, we shall go to speak to my father. I do not wish for Lian to be with us on the journey."

As they were just about to leave the house, Lian called out and Miria slowly turned around. Lian spoke to her quietly and it did not take a genius to figure out she played the trump card. Miria looked at the boys and spoke in a very business-like tone. "Lian has asked for our forgiveness and would ask us to join him at the table. How do you feel about this?"

Will and Jimmy gave each other a questioning look. If anyone could read Will's mind it would say, *So long sucker, nice to have met you.* But Will wanted to show that he could be the adult here. "Tell Lian we accept his apology and we will try very hard to be helpful on this journey."

Miria spoke the words, and Lian came forward and put out his hand for Will to take. Will took the hand but was amazed by the over squeeze he was receiving from Lian. He did not think it was a mistake but rather a show of strength.

"Mai appa Will."

Lian smiled a funny smirk but Miria's face showed anger again. "Mai appa Lian."

Jimmy smiled at him. "Mai appa Jimmy."

Lian took his hand but did not squeeze it hard. He did seem to feel Jimmy would be of any threat to him.

The boys walked towards the table and were astonished at the complex map laid out in front of them. When Will looked closer at all the lines and what seemed like numbers, he looked at Miria.

"What line are we to follow?" Miria put her hand on the map and pointed to a red line meandering through the map.

"Miria why can't the route be more straight? It looks like we are going in the wrong direction, and then we head back down again."

Miria smiled at Will. "This is not a road, Will. This is a river, and we are going to take a boat down it. It will save us many days of walking."

Jimmy stepped up to look at the map. "A river? You have a river down here?"

Miria smiled and looked into the boy's eyes. "You are about to enter another world, my friends. You will see many strange things, some things that I will not be able to find the words to explain to you, but I will try my best. We will meet strange people, but you must trust us that they will do you no harm. This world is beautiful but dangerous. We must listen to our guides and trust that they will get us to the portal on time.

"On time? What do you mean, Miria?" Will asked in confusion.

"The portal we are heading to is many, many months away. If we do not get there on time, you will not be able to leave our world."

Jimmy piped in, "Miria, is this the only portal available to us?" Miria looked at Jimmy and could feel his apprehension.

"No, Jimmy. But it is the next one to open. The portal after that will open three years later."

Will looked at Miria and then to the rest of the group. "Am I to understand that each portal opens at different times?"

Miria spoke to the group and they nodded to Miria as if to say it was okay to tell them the truth.

"Will, Jimmy, each portal opens and closes for twenty-one years. There are seven sacred caves throughout our world. Each one opens in a pattern. The next portal will open in three years, and it will open here." She pointed to the map and both boys knew that they were in for a long journey.

Will looked at the group of men and then at Miria. "Will we make it?"

Miria smiled. "It is their quest to get us there. They will protect us and lead us, and they are very sure we will reach our goal."

Jimmy started to get flutters in his stomach. "Miria, what are they protecting us from?"

Miria looked down at her feet and then slowly started to speak. "There is much in our world I must teach you. Yes, there is danger, Jimmy. I will explain my world to you as we travel. But please know, there is little danger for many weeks. I will teach you everything about our world, but you must make a promise to us that once you leave our world, you must keep it a secret. Can you do this?"

Will could only imagine what he would tell his parents when he returned. But looking into Miria face he knew his answer held his life in a balance. "Miria, you have our solemn promise. We will never divulge the secret of your world. I swear to you on my soul."

Miria smiled at Will, for he could not know how true those words will become in his future.

CHAPTER FOURTEEN

Carol and Jenny looked at Steve with shock. Carol looked at Jenny.

"Is he on drugs?" Jenny smiled as her sister-in-law but could not blame her for not believing this ridiculous story Steve had just divulged.

"Steve, let me get this straight. You believe the boys have been swallowed up by a cave that swallowed up Chief George's son twenty-one years ago."

Steve looked at Jenny. "I know this sounds hare-brained, but when we talked to the chief's son, he was very convincing about what he saw and what happened to his brother."

Steve looked at Carol. "Carol, look at the facts that we do know. The footprints just disappear, all of them. There is no blood anywhere, so we know they were not attacked by a bear or cougar. One of them came back to the fishing spot and grabbed their backpacks, so we know they were going after something or someone. There were other prints, a child's footstep and a woman's footprint. Fred and I believe they were tracking them. The fact that everything just disappears made Fred come up with this scenario after we spoke to Reed, the chief's son. I know it sounds crazy, but sometimes you have to look at crazy with a serious attitude."

Tears started to well up in Carol's eyes. "Steve, what the hell am

I going to tell my mother? This story is just a little too far-fetched for her to understand any of it."

"Give us another day, Carol. I'm going to meet up with Fred and Reed tomorrow. I want to see if the boys disappeared in the same area as his brother. If they did, then we have to assume there is something to this story."

Jenny looked at Steve. "Or it's just a coincidence."

Steve shook his head. "Jenny, I don't believe in coincidence. Do you know how many miles of forest is out there? If they disappeared in the same spot, the odds are a million to one if not more. No, Jenny, it won't be a coincidence. But I can promise you two ladies, I will move heaven and earth to find them. I won't accept this scenario and then do nothing about it. I'll blast holes in every rock out there if I have to. I'm going to find the boys." Looking at Jenny he added, "And our dog too!"

Jenny ran into her husband's arms and began to cry. "I know you will, honey. I know you will."

Carol walked over to them and put her arms around both of them. "I believe you will too."

Steve held the two women in a group hug and said the first word before they all said the phrase together in unison. "Failure is not an option!"

※ ※ ※

As Carol lay in bed in the guest room, she could not sleep but only stared at the ceiling. She whispered, "Oh Mike I need your help. Our son is missing and I can't lose him too. God help me, Mike. I'm not strong enough for this. Please help Steve! Stay with him and find our boys. Please darling, help Steve find the boys." For the first time in this past two days a peace came over Carol. Like a warm blanket had just been put on her body, and she drifted off in a deep sleep. Far off in a distance she could hear Mike. "We'll find them, sweetheart. We'll find them." And she slept soundly until daybreak.

* * *

Steve was up at first light making coffee for his thermos and putting some of Jenny's muffins in a bag for later.

Carol quietly walked in on him. "Morning, Steve. Stealing all the good stuff, eh?"

Steve smiled. "Don't know how long we'll be out there. Don't want hunger to be the reason we have to come back."

Carol smiled. "In that case dear brother, let me make you some sandwiches from that delicious roast beef that we hardly touched last night."

Steve smiled and shook his head. "No Carol, you don't have to do that."

Carol smiled. "Yes, I do. Sorry for giving you so much static last night. I don't know why or how, but I dreamed about this last night and all I could hear was Mike's voice telling me it was going to be okay. Silly, huh?"

Steve just stared at Carol and spoke softly, "Not silly. I heard him too." He handed her a cup of coffee and sat down at the table with his cup.

"Carol, do you hear him very much?"

"Sometimes when I'm really upset or confused about something, he comes to me at night, In my dreams. I really believe this is how those who have left us can still communicate with us. Whether you believe it or not, is up to you."

Steve smiled. "Oh, I believe that, Carol. Mike woke me up when Jimmy took a wrong trail from our camp one night. The rat kicked me in the leg, but I got the message and everything turned out okay. That was a long time ago, and I swore I was never going to tell you. Didn't want you to worry."

Carol laughed. "For the record, Jimmy told me the whole story, but not about the kick in your leg. Sure it wasn't higher? Your butt would be more like the target he would have aimed for."

Steve laughed. "What can I say. The jerk missed. But I will be honest with you Carol, I feel his presence all the time. Especially when Jimmy is around here. I believe he protects him. I know that may sound crazy, but doesn't it just go with every other story we've heard lately?"

Carol nodded. "I feel him too. And no, it's not crazy. And if I can believe that then I guess I can believe a young native man and his story too. The world is a mystery, and we can't say we know all the answers, can we?"

"You, dear sister, have just said a mouth full. But I am going to try to solve one of them and find our boys." They both smiled at each other and drank their coffee in silence each deep in their own thoughts.

As Steve was just about to jump into his truck, an R.C.M.P. cruiser turned into his driveway. Steve waved at his high school buddy as he got out of the car.

"Constable Rick, how are you?" Steve held out his hand.

"I'm good, Steve. Heard about Will and Jimmy. I thought I would come and take your statement. Is this a good time?"

Steve shook his head. "I was just about to go and meet with Fred Avery from Search and Rescue. I can't really tell you much, Rick. We tracked the kids until their footprints just disappear. There is no blood, so we are ruling out animal attack. There is no evidence they fell into the river. We are just going to keep searching until we find some clues as to what happened."

Rick looked up from his recording book. "How's Jenny?"

Steve let out a huge sigh. "Holding on by a thread. And Carol too, my sister-in-law. She flew up yesterday. Rick, if you could put out a notice that the boys are missing, maybe some fisherman or hiker might have seen them. We would appreciate all the help we can get."

Rick smiled. "We'll do our best, Steve. Do you think I could talk to the mothers? Maybe they could give us a photo of the boys, anything to get their faces out there."

Steve nodded. "Yeah, Carol is in the kitchen, and I'm sure Jenny will be up by now too. And Rick, thank you. The more eyes out there, the better our chances are we find them. Right?"

Rick nodded. "Absolutely. You go meet Fred, and I'll go talk to the mothers. I'll keep you posted on our progress."

Steve shook Rick's hand while Rick looked into Steve's eyes feeling the anxiety and pain he was going through. He stepped in and gave his friend a huge hug.

"You hang in there, buddy. Kids just don't disappear without a clue. We'll find something."

Steve nodded and walked slowly to his truck as Rick knocked on the back door of his house.

***

Steve jumped from the truck and waved to Fred and Reed as they came around from Reed's house.

"Morning." Steve nodded at them.

Fred smiled. "Morning Steve. Ready to go?"

"Ready as I'll ever be. Come on, we can take my truck. You guys need any coffee or refreshments. I have a thermos of coffee, Jenny's muffins and Carol made us some sandwiches. But I think we should get more coffee and maybe some water at Belle's Diner."

"Good idea," said Reed, "Belle's berry tarts are really good too. If you think we will need more."

Fred looked at them both. "Man is this a search and rescue or a picnic?"

Steve laughed and then looked at Reed. "How much do you want to bet he'll be the first one to call lunch."

Reed laughed. "Yeah, and coffee break too."

Fred just chuckled as he got into the truck. "Come on, children, we have work to do." Steve and Reed hopped into their places as Steve started the engine and drove off for a day of hard work and hopeful answers.

***

Reed led the way into the forest and Steve and Fred were amazed to note that they were in the same vicinity where the boy's tracks were lost. Reed was quiet but sure he was in the right area. He had come back here many times looking for some clue to his brother's disappearance. Reed looked at Steve. "There is a lot of new growth, but I am sure this is where the cave was."

Steve's hair stood up on the back of his neck as he and Fred realized they were in the exact same spot that the boys had disappeared.

Steve looked at Fred. "Hundreds of miles of forest, rock and mountain and he brings us to the exact spot. That is not a coincidence. Not in a million years."

Fred let out a huge sigh and covered up his mouth in amazement. "No, Steve. This is no coincidence. The mystery starts here."

Steve started hacking bushes away from the mountain situated just behind them. "Reed, does this look familiar?"

Reed looked at the mountain side, "This is the right spot, guys. I'd bet my life on it."

Steve looked at Fred. "There is a mine about two hundred miles north of here. I want to go and talk to an explosive technician."

Fred's eyes bugged out. "Geez, Steve. You can't just go blow up a side of a mountain. This is First Nation land, and you have to get permission from the elders before you can do anything. Especially dynamite blasting! Crap, the paperwork will drown you."

Steve looked at Reed. "Do you think you can help me with this, Reed. We may find out what happened to your brother too."

Reed looked at Steve with sadness in his eyes. "I'll try my best for you, Steve, but I would not hold my breath. They didn't believe me twenty-one years ago. I don't know if they will believe me now."

Steve looked into Reed's eyes. "We believe you and that's two more people on your side than you had twenty-one years ago. I'll come to the council with you if I am allowed to attend and help state the case. But first, Fred, I want to talk to an explosive expert. I need to know how to do this right before I can even talk to the elders."

Fred just shook his head. "Yeah, let's not let fear and good judgement get in our way. Let's go talk to Dynamite Man."

Steve smiled and looked at Reed. "See, now he's talking my language."

Fred looked at Reed and shook his head. "We'll take you home first, Reed. No sense dragging you away from your family for the next day or so. Steve, let me make the arrangements at the mine, and we can get started tomorrow morning."

Steve nodded. "Sounds good to me, Fred. Will I need to bring anything with me?"

"An overnight bag wouldn't be a bad idea, notebook, and a real nice picnic lunch. Those sandwiches and muffins were excellent!"

Steve and Reed started laughing. "Man, we created a monster, an eating monster with a bottomless pit!"

Fred laughed as he began to pack up their backpacks. "Hey, I'm the single guy here. Home-made anything is a real treat for me."

Steve grabbed his pack and hoisted it on his back. "Then I won't disappoint you, Fred. Picnic lunch again tomorrow." Fred smiled as he began to walk back up the trail they had forged in the forest. Reed followed Fred but Steve held back a bit and looked at the rock face in front of him.

"I'm coming, boys. Don't give up." And he walked out of the forest behind his friends.

***

CHAPTER FIFTEEN

Timtuk cried all night. Miria tried to console him, but he was having none of it. Will had gone into the house to see if he could help her, but Timtuk was beyond reason. Will could not believe a little guy like that could scream and cry so much. Miria looked at Will to thank him for his help, but he could see she just wanted him to leave, so he did just that. It was hours before he finally settled down. When Will peeked into the window to see how Miria had created this miracle, he found Miria cradling him in her arms and rocking him slowly. Timtuk was sucking on his thumb, but every so often he took a deep breath and sobbed quietly. Will went back to his bedroll feeling like the worst person in the world for having to deal Timtuk this horrible hand that will change his life forever. He did not sleep this night as well.

In the morning Miria took Timtuk to his father's home. He went quietly and bravely. His head was held high as if he was a king, and this was how a king should act. He never even said goodbye to Will or Jimmy. Just walked away with Miria. Will and Jimmy were hurt but understood. After all, this was all their fault.

Jimmy looked at Will. "Do you think he'll get over this?"

Will was still watching Miria and Timtuk walking away. "He might, I won't."

Jimmy patted his cousin's shoulder. "Come on, cuz. We've got more work to do."

Slowly everything that Miria had put out was packed neatly into these very large rock boxes. When Miria returned, she was surprised to see that the boys had completed all the packing.

"Oh my, I did not expect you to do this. How very kind of you."

Jimmy smiled at her and crossed his arms. "Yeah, you can count on us, Miria, but one thing I don't understand. How are we going to move all the boxes? They weigh hundreds of pounds? Are we using animals to carry them?"

Miria started to laugh. "We could never use an animal for this work. It is much too heavy. We will use this." Miria walked over to the boxes and taking her hands she spread them out above the boxes. With a move like a magician would make before he said abracadabra, the boxes floated about two feet above the floor.

Jimmy and Will both looked at this in total shock. "Whoa! How did you do that?" they said in unison.

"There is much of my world you will learn. This is just the beginning."

Will walked up to Miria and took her hands. "Are you a magician?"

She smiled. "I do not know what this is, so I will say no, I am not. But some of my people have special gifts that we use when needed. Mine is what you just saw, and I am also a healer."

Jimmy looked at her. "What's a healer?"

She smiled at Jimmy. "If you are sick or hurt, I can make you well again."

Will looked at her. "Like a doctor or a medicine man?"

Again Miria laughed. "Clearly I am not a man. No, Will. The power to heal comes from within me. I do not need medicine or anything else. My mother was a healer, and I too have the power."

Jimmy looked at Will. "How cool is that?"

Will smiled at Jimmy and Miria. "I'm afraid I am a 'show me' type of guy. But, Miria, I sure can't explain how you lifted these boxes, and I'm still not certain how we are going to move them."

Miria gave one of the boxes a small push, and it simply floated in the direction of her push.

"Wow, it's like zero gravity!" Jimmy shouted with glee. And he gave another box a small push. "Too cool! Come on, Will. Try it."

Will walked over to the boxes and gave the third box a small push. Smiling he turned to Miria, "If you ever want to go into the moving business, I'd like to be your partner. We could make a fortune."

Miria laughed. "Will, you say words I do not understand, but you do make me laugh. What is a moving business?"

He pointed to the boxes. "This! Moving boxes and furniture for people when they move from one home to another."

She laughed again. "I think I am doing this already. But there is no fortune to be made."

Will laughed. "That's really too bad. You would make a fortune in our world."

Miria started to push the boxes outside. "Come, we have much to do." The boys followed her each pushing a box as well.

Miria and the boys pushed the boxes towards a cavern at the far end of the village where they were met by Lian, Beya and Donat. Everyone acknowledged each other with a nod. Beya and Donat took the boxes from each of them and began to tie them together.

Jimmy started to chuckle. "It looks like a floating freight train."

Lian quietly spoke to Miria as if he didn't want Will and Jimmy to overhear his conversation.

Will looked at Jimmy in defiance. "What a nimrod! Speaking quietly, so we can't hear. Like we understand his language. He could shout it to the highest rock, and we would still not understand him. Bright. Real bright!"

Lian looked in Will's direction, not knowing his language but feeling he was the butt of the joke since Jimmy was laughing but stopped abruptly when Lian looked at them. He spoke again to Miria, but she shook her head and touched his arm as if she was trying to calm him.

Jimmy looked at Will. "Oh, I can just see this turning into such a fun trip! Are we there yet, Will?"

"Shut up and help me," was all his cousin would say to him, though there was a laugh in his voice.

Beya and Donat were to lead the group. Will and Jimmy were to follow pulling the train of boxes. Miria and Lian would bring up the rear. Will wondered what the strategy for this formation was, but he was sure there definitely was one. He would ask Miria about it later. As for Buddy, he went wherever he wanted to be. Lian spoke crossly to Miria about this, but she showed him how well behaved he could be when all you had to do was call his name and pat your leg. Buddy wagged his tail and rubbed into Miria's dress, and she happily patted his head. But Buddy stayed close to Jimmy and Will and the train of boxes. It seemed he knew where the food supply box was, and he wasn't going to let it out of his sight. Lian called out to Beya and Donat and the journey began.

They followed a large trail as it descended deeper into the earth. They could feel wind and wondered where it was originating from. *More questions for Miria,* thought Will. After about an hour of walking they came to a large shelter carved out of the rock. There were benches carved from the mountain rock and Miria moved slowly to one of them and sat down.

Looking at Will and Jimmy, she patted the seat. "Come, we will rest while we wait."

Will looked confused as he sat beside her. "Wait? Wait for what?"

Miria smiled at him with twinkling eyes. "The boat, silly. I told you about the boat."

"Miria, there is no water for a boat to float on," Will said with confusion.

"Oh, but you are wrong, Will. The water is here. We will be on it shortly." Miria could not contain her laugh as Will and Jimmy looked at her as if she and the others were three light bulbs short on a chandelier. As Miria sat with the boys and Buddy, Lian, Beya and Donat pushed all the boxes into the shelter and for a few seconds it was very cramped. Then the shelter dropped through the rocks as if it was an elevator going down.

Jimmy yelled, "Whoa!" and Buddy started barking. Miria held him close and soothed his fears while smiling at Will as if to say, "*Surprise!*" They slowed to a stop and right in front of them was a beautiful river of the deepest azure blue. With the look of shock and total amazement, Will's mouth just dropped open.

"Miria, this is incredible! Where does the river go?"

"It goes in many directions, but we are heading to the village of Attaberra. It is where we will get new supplies before we head on our quest. It should take us about five days to get there. Are you ready to come on the boat?" Will and Jimmy both looked around for the boat and then realized the three men had disappeared as well with the supply train.

"Miria, where is everyone?" Jimmy asked.

"This is Beya's gift. He can make things disappear though they are right in front of you. Please step forward and follow me." Miria stepped to the edge of the river and jumped. Both Will and Jimmy tried to grab her, but she disappeared right in front of them.

"Now, it is your turn. Just jump as I just showed you," she said in a way a mother would tell her child to jump for the first time into a pool. Will and Jimmy looked at each other. Jimmy shrugged his shoulders.

"When in Rome!" and jumped. He disappeared. "Come on, Will. It's easy!" Jimmy shouted.

Will grabbed Buddy's leash and said to his companion, "Come on, Buddy. It's a leap of faith." And Will and Buddy disappeared onto the invisible boat.

Will and Jimmy could hardly believe their eyes. For here they were standing on a large wooden deck from a boat that looked like a pirate ship you see in all the movies. The huge difference was it sparkled and shimmered all around them as if they were in a cloud.

"It's Beya's gift. He can make things disappear. It is a very special gift, and it will help us to stay safe for the few days we will need to. Then we can go on as before,"

Miria said this as calmly as if we were just going to the grocery store, thought Will. "Miria, what is the danger?"

Miria looked down at her feet. "There are many different tribes in our world. Some are friends, others are violent and want our special gifts. They would keep us as slaves to achieve this. For this we must be very careful on our journey."

Will sat down beside Miria. "Jimmy and I know of your gift and now Beya's. What are Lian's and Donat's special gifts?"

Miria took a huge sigh. "I hope and pray that you will never see their gifts for they will be used if we are being attacked. I wish that this will not happen." Will nodded in understanding but was still not satisfied with her answer.

"Please, I would like to know their gifts."

She looked at Will and Jimmy. "Wind and fire," was her whispered reply.

"Wind. Yes, I want to ask you about that. When we went into the tunnel, I could feel the wind all around us. How can that be when we are underground?"

She smiled at Will's intelligence. "That was Donat. He was

clearing the tunnel of any bad smell that might hurt us."

Jimmy piped in. "You mean like a bad gas. Sulphur or even a natural gas can be harmful to us."

Miria nodded. "Yes, that is a concern for us. However, Donat was making sure none of our enemies put anything harmful in our caves. He can clean it in just a few breaths."

Will and Jimmy looked at each other before Will spoke, "Miria, these enemies could get that close to your village? Do you not have your people watching for them?"

Miria smiled. "Yes, of course. But Donat was making very sure we would be safe."

Jimmy chuckled softly. "Man, what I wouldn't give for a special gift."

Miria looked at both the boys and spoke quietly to them. "Your intelligence is your special gift, Will and Jimmy. Before this journey ends your gift will be well spent."

* * *

The hours drifting down the river was uneventful and beautiful. The hills were a bevy of colourful rocks and crystals. Jimmy was the rockhound of the family, and he was trying to impress Miria with his knowledge of the names of each colourful rock. Will thought that he could name them Huey, Duey, and Luey, and she would not know the difference. But Miria seemed genuinely interested in Jimmy's knowledge, and Jimmy seemed to revel in the attention she was giving him. Will also noticed Lian watching them as he steered the boat. He could read the jealous look, and he started to wonder if he was not feeling the same way, but he shook that thought away. He did not want to mess with Mr. Firebug in a duel for love.

Yet he did remember Miria said she did not have the heart for him. Maybe there is something to hold onto, the hope that Miria might have the heart for him someday.

Then Will just hugged Buddy and whispered in his ear. "For now Buddy, you're my only love, okay?" Buddy barked and wagged his tail, and Will laughed as he always believed Buddy could understand every word you spoke to him.

***

Jimmy looked at his watch. "Will, we've been on this boat for nine hours. Are we going to dock it or sail all night?"

Will nodded and looked at Miria. "What's the answer, Miria?"

"It is safer to sail all night. By putting us on the banks of the river, our enemies might get too close," Miria answered.

Jimmy looked confused,. "But Miria, we're invisible. How can they see us?"

She smiled. "Beya cannot use his gift for long periods of time. In fact we will soon be out of this mist, so we can let him rest."

Will looked at Miria with great concern. "Will we be safe?"

She smiled at him and patted his leg like a child being assured by his mother.

"Yes, very safe. Lian will see to it."

Will grumbled under his breath about her mommy pat and then having to lean on Lian for their safety. It was just forming into a perfect night of bliss.

Jimmy leaned into Will, so only he could hear. "You know, I could sure use that gas station, cousin."

Will laughed. "Yeah, me too. I guess we better ask Miria where the facilities are on this floating bucket."

Miria heard them and pointed to the stairs leading down into the ship. "Down the stairs you will find a room on your right side. My father called it the floating outhouse. Does this make sense to you?"

Both boys laughed out loud. "Yup, total sense," laughed Jimmy.

Then using his best English accent, he turned to Will. "Shall we remove ourselves old man and retreat to the floating water closet. Maybe we can ready ourselves for dinner as well. I'm a little parched. Are you not as well?"

Will just laughed. "Oh shut up and let's hit the head. You can be such a drip sometimes."

Jimmy laughed and looked at Miria. "Mother could never control his outbursts. But I find him endearing, don't you my dear?"

Miria laughed hysterically at Jimmy's funny accent. "I find him most endearing. And you dear Jimmy will always make me laugh just when I need it the most."

At these encouraging words Jimmy made a bowing gesture to his cousin and held the door open. "After you, dear boy. Age before beauty."

Will walked past Jimmy and muttered under his breath for only his ears. "Jerk." Jimmy smiled and bowed again to Miria before following Will down the stairs. She laughed again and was sure this trip was going to be anything but dull.

***

Miria put the food on plates she had packed from her house. She placed on each plate dried fish and two types of vegetables. One tasted like sweet potato and the other one tasted like celery but did not look anything like the vegetables from home. They tasted delicious or they were so hungry an old boot would have been great. Then she put out a bowl of berries that she had got from above their world. As she passed the bowl around she said,

"I am sorry to say that these are the last of my stock. I thought

I had packed more, but I think Timtuk must have got into them before we left." At the mention of her brother's name she became unusually quiet.

Will put his arm around her shoulder. "It's okay, Miria. I'm sure he is doing just fine with his father." Miria looked into Will's eyes and just smiled and lay her head on his shoulder. Lian walked away and took over the helm from Donat. They drifted quietly down the river totally unaware that some small berry stained hands were stealing some dried fish from the supply box below deck.

CHAPTER SIXTEEN

The drive back from the mine was unbearably quiet. Fred and Steve were both devastated by the answers the demolition expert had given them. No seemed to be the answer to all the questions they had to ask.

"No, you cannot just blow up a side of a mountain without geology tests. No, you cannot get the test without permission from the First Nation Council. No, they will not give permission without sound reason for the need. The need is insane and no one would believe you." This pretty much summed up the story of their trip.

After about an hour of total silence Steve looked at Fred. "What am I going to do, Fred? I can't just give up. Those are my boys in there."

Fred gave out a big sigh before he could speak. "Steve, maybe we could ask the council if we could do a geological dig only in the one spot and maybe give a timeline of six to eight weeks. If we can assure them we would do as little damage as possible and that we would see to it that we will put it back to the best of our ability, they may agree to it."

Steve looked at Fred as if he was crazy. "Fred, dig! How can you even suggest such a hare-brained idea? That's a granite mountain. I don't think shovels will do a whole lot of damage on that thing."

Fred nodded his head. "Yes, but we know there is a cave opening behind one of those rocks. All we have to do is find the exact rock, and then we can get to work on it."

"The exact rock! Please, sir, tell me how we find the exact rock?" Steve replied in a distressed voice.

Fred looked at him and smiled. "I didn't say it was a perfect solution! But at least the moment of opportunity hasn't been slammed shut just yet."

"How do we begin to look for the right rock?" Steve asked.

"We go look. We go look with a magnifying glass if we have to. We crawl on our hands and knees and look for any clues. We're good trackers. There has to be some small bit of something that will lead us to the answers we're seeking."

Steve smiled at his friend. "That's what I like about you, Fred. You're as crazy as I am! But you have my attention. Now it's up to you to come home with me and sell it to the two mothers waiting for our return."

Fred gave out a big laugh. "Does it come with a home-made dinner?"

Steve smiled coyly. "And apple pie too!"

Fred smiled. "I'd dig a hole to China for a home-made apple pie."

"You just might have to do just that, good buddy." Steve laughed as he turned onto the main highway and headed to his home.

✱ ✱ ✱

Jenny looked at the two men sitting at her kitchen table. "Is this our only option? Dig!"

Fred smiled at Jenny and Carol. "If we can get permission from the council, and that will take some time. However, Reed will present our proposal, and it helps that he will be with us for the dig."

Carol took a sip of her coffee and shook her head. "It all sounds like it will take weeks or even months. Steve, I don't think I have the strength for this. I'll go insane thinking of the boys and what they are going through right now."

Steve took her hands. "They are intelligent young men. I know in my heart they will keep each other safe. Carol, we have to believe that they will be okay. We have to have faith that we will find them as soon as we possibly can. But right now you have to decide what you are going to do. You can stay up here with us, or will you go back home and wait for our progress reports?"

Carol took a deep breath. "I can't go home right now. I'll go stark raving mad waiting for the phone calls. No, I have vacation time stacked up. Now is a good a time as any to use it up."

Fred smiled at Carol and was warmed by her bravery and her matter of fact charm. He looked at both women and marvelled at their stoic behaviour when in truth he thought they would be crying and screaming by now. He thought he would be if these were his boys.

Fred smiled gently at the women. "Would you ladies like to come and help us look for some clues? My mother always said that men couldn't find their socks in a sock drawer. Maybe female eyes would be an advantage for us."

Carol and Jenny both laughed and said in unison a resounding yes!

"Then it's settled," Steve piped in. "We start first thing tomorrow morning. If we find what we are looking for, it's off to meet with Reed and set up the proposal for the council. Fred, what do you think we should bring tomorrow?"

Fred eyes sparkled and with a devilish smile replied, "A picnic lunch with apple pie for dessert!"

Jenny blurted out loudly, "Men! It's always their stomach first.

Leave the gun but bring the cannoli."

Everyone laughed and it was just what was needed to cut the tension in the room.

***

Fred held the bushes back for Jenny and Carol as they rounded the last turn on the path. "This is where we lost their tracks, and also this is where Reed said he lost his brother."

Jenny looked at Steve. "I can see what you mean by a million to one shot. It would be like throwing two needles in a haystack and finding them both in the exact same spot."

Carol looked around at the topography. "I'm with you guys on this conclusion. This is not a coincidence."

Fred started to ease his way around the bushes and trees. "It's behind here where we found the woman's print, but after that the trail goes cold. This is where I hope a woman's touch might help."

Carol and Jenny both smiled at Fred before Carol spoke, "Hope that didn't hurt your male ego to say that."

Fred laughed. "I have three older sisters. My male ego was trampled on years ago, believe me."

Carol laughed and found herself liking his company. She had not felt that way for a very long time.

Jenny was on her hands and knees crawling against the rock face when she felt a shiver go up her spine. "Oh my!" she said.

Steve moved over to her side. "What is it, honey?"

She looked at him and stated rubbing her arms. "I'm not sure, Steve. It was like a feeling of a small electric shock right when I touched the bottom of this rock."

Steve started feeling along the bottom of the rock but felt nothing. Shaking his head to Fred he said, "I don't feel a thing."

Carol came over and started moving her hand over the same area and jumped back. "Ow, that hurt!"

Fred quickly came to her side. "What did you feel?"

Carol looked into his eyes and could read the concern he had for her at this moment. "Just like Jenny said, an electric shock."

Fred and Steve looked at each other and got right on their hands and knees and swept the area with their hands. The both shook their heads at each other and in unison said, "Nothing."

The women looked at each other before Jenny spoke, "Could we as women be picking up a current that only a female body can feel?"

Fred shook his head. "Jenny, normally I'd say that wasn't possible but right now I'd believe anything. Steve, I think bringing these ladies with us was the smartest move we've made all week."

Steve nodded in agreement. "Yeah, there is definitely something here that only they can feel. How do you want to address this?"

Fred took a piece of chalk from his pocket. "Carol, would you take this chalk and mark on the rock when you first feel the current and Jenny, would you take this piece and mark where you last felt it. Maybe we can judge the distance between the two marks."

Jenny went to the right of the huge rock and Carol crawled over to the left of it. Carol made a mark when she could feel the current begin and Jenny marked her spot where she believed it started on the right side.

"Okay," said Fred, "that's about seven feet apart. Big enough for an opening, eh, Steve?"

Steve nodded. "Yeah, but hidden well enough so that you wouldn't see it until you were right on top of it."

Jenny looked at Steve. "Now what?"

Steve looked at his wife and wished he had the answers she so desperately needed to hear. "Now, my love, I have to do some calculations. Why don't you guys go set up the picnic lunch down by the river, and I'll join you in about twenty minutes."

Jenny smiled at her husband. "There's that stomach of yours. Always growling for food."

Steve laughed. "I think better on a full stomach, didn't you know?"

With a cheeky smile Jen whispered back at him. "That's not all you do better on a full stomach."

Steve gave his wife a playful pat on her bottom. "Careful, young lady. We are not alone you know."

Jenny chuckled as she and Carol followed Fred back to the truck for the lunch cooler. Steve started taking sight calculations hoping to figure out how big this rock was and how deep they would have to dig to get it moved. Then the hair began to prickle at the back of his neck.

"Okay, Mike. I feel you. Now help me. What am I missing?" Steve shut his eyes and let his mind drift as if he was floating on a cloud. He could hear Mike's voice far away as if he was in a tunnel.

"Mark! What mark?" Steve started to crawl around the rock and slowly feel the stone under his fingers as if he was reading braille.

"Mike, what mark?" He continued feeling and looking at each dent and curl of the rocks. "A mark. You want me to find a mark? But where is it?" At the moment the hair on the back of his neck stood straight up. Steve looked closely into a crack, "Holy Mary Mother of God!"

CHAPTER SEVENTEEN

Will and Jimmy lay on top of their bed rolls looking up where the sky should have been, but instead it was the ceiling of the cavern. It sparkled from the crystalized rock formation made over a million years ago.

Jimmy spoke quietly, "Look Will, if you use your imagination this could be a sky full of stars."

Will didn't smile but looked seriously at his cousin. "Jimmy, will it be three years before we ever see the sky again? How do these people survive without the sun? Don't we need the sun for some vitamin?"

Jimmy looked at Will. "Yeah, vitamin D but you can get that from some plants too."

Will raised himself up on his elbow. "Okay. So how do you grow plants without the sun?"

"Good questions, cuz, more for Miria to answer for us tomorrow. Right now I'll just marvel at this cavern we're in, enjoy the slow ride as we meander down an underground river to a place we have never heard of and wonder what new adventure this next day will bring to us."

As Jimmy spoke the words Will could tell he was nodding off to sleep. Will smiled at his cousin that he could sleep so easily, anywhere and on anything at all. Hard or soft Jimmy could sleep on it. Will always envied his cousin for this trait. Will just lay beside Jimmy listening to his deep breathing and shut his eyes hoping to drift off as well. It didn't take too long before his breathing became deeper, and he too drifted off to sleep. Buddy lay his head on Will's leg and closed his eyes too.

They awoke to Buddy's barking and knew from the way he was barking that something was wrong.

"What is it Buddy? What do you hear?" Will said to his dog as he patted his head. Buddy began to growl and went to look over the side of the boat. He growled as he searched for positive proof of danger.

Lian stepped down from the helm and spoke to Miria as she too was checking what Buddy was growling at. Miria came to Will and Jimmy. "Lian thinks Buddy heard the sound of the rocks as they crack in the heat. It would be alarming to hear for the first time. Come on, Buddy. You are safe." She rubbed his chest and gave him a nuzzle into her chest. Will was starting to feel envious of Buddy at this moment. But Buddy was not to be settled. He sprang to the edge of the deck and barked down at the water.

Will and Jimmy both joined him. "What is it Buddy?" Looking at the water both Jimmy and Will jumped back.

"Whoa, what the heck is that?" screamed Jimmy. Miria looked over the edge and screamed. Instantly a snake the size of a mac truck sprang from the water and lashed down at Will and Buddy. With the fangs as big as cow horns it lashed again at Will, but he ducked behind a barrel. Buddy was barking and took a bite out of his back, but it moved so quickly that Buddy was thrown half way up the deck. Jimmy yelled from behind the ropes on the deck, and that's when Lian sprang into action. His hand circled above his head and instantly a fire ball appeared in his palm. He threw it at the serpent, and it landed on its chest. It bounced off without any damage to the snake. Donat came running to Lian and nodded to him. Lian quickly made another fire ball appear in his palm. As he threw it Donat blew on it, and Lian looked like a flame thrower. The impact of this fire ball made the snake flinch and make this hissing sound of pain. It quickly slithered off the boat and into the river. In a flash Lian sprang for the edge and threw a fireball at the huge snake-like serpent popping its head up from the water. In an instant he threw another one at the beast, and it disappeared beneath the water. Waiting for it to reappear Lian stood on guard with another fireball sizzling in his hand. After what seemed like eternity Lian moved his hand and the fire disappeared. Will looked at Lian and nodded to him in understanding of his special gift. Lian's face was without emotion. He just walked back to the helm like nothing had just happened.

Will and Jimmy looked at Miria. "Some gift he's got! That thing out there, do you think it will be back?" asked Jimmy.

Miria tried to speak bravely. "I do not think it will return. Lian did hit it. But you can believe me that he will listen to Buddy next time. Buddy too has a special gift, and we will not ignore it again."

Will crouched down to Buddy. "Ya hear that, Buddy. You have a special gift, but I've known that since you were a puppy." He gave his dog a big cuddle and Buddy basked in the love hug. Miria and Jimmy laughed and joined in on the dog pats. Will and Jimmy looked at each other and blew out a huge sigh of relief. Then everyone went back to their bedrolls and tried to settle in for the rest of the night. Thankfully, all was quiet and sleep did come to everyone.

✻ ✻ ✻

Will awoke to a large wet tongue licking his face. "Oh, Buddy. Yuck!"

Miria started laughing as Buddy jumped on Will and Jimmy to welcome them into a new day. Jimmy looked at Will. "He just loves that we're sleeping on the floor. So easy for him to get to us!"

Miria walked over and pulled Buddy off Jimmy. "It's my fault. I told him to wake you. I have breakfast ready for you."

At the sound of Miria saying the word breakfast, Will smiled. "You remembered the word."

Miria smiled. "Yes, and next will be lunch and then dinner. Is this right?"

Will laughed. "Right as rain." Then realizing his metaphor mistake he added, "I mean right as water."

Miria laughed. "I know what rain is, Will. I have been outside before. Remember?"

"Oh, yeah. My mistake, Miria. You are worldly."

Then her look changed to confusion. "What is worldly?"

Will smiled at her. "You are, Miria. You have seen many wonderful things in your world and some from mine. That would make you worldly."

Miria smiled and blushed at this compliment. "You are very kind, Will. It is not very often someone says nice things to me."

Will made a mental note to himself to say something nice to Miria every day. Scoring points as his mother used to say to him when he complimented her. He remembered when his mother came out of the bedroom dressed for a night out with his dad. She looked beautiful in a red dress that sparkled in the evening lights.

"Wow, Mom! You look fabulous!"

"William Wright, what are you going to do with those hundred points I just gave you?"

Will remembered answering, "Could I cash it in on your famous chocolate fudge cake?"

She laughed. "Done!"

He remembered his dad entering the living room and gave a loud wolf whistle.

"Sorry, but only one chocolate cake per family," she said and gave Will a peck on the cheek.

Will remembered his dad whispered something in his mom's ear, and she laughed and said,

"Done." But he never knew what his mom had promised him. He knows now, and he blushed at the thought.

"Will, are you feeling well? You are red in the face." Miria looked at him with concern.

"Oh, no, I'm fine, Miria. Just thinking about my parents."

Miria sat down beside Will and handed him a plate of dried fruit, some flat corn bread and a piece of smoked fish. It looked delicious.

"Thank you, Miria. This is really good." Will smiled at her.

Miria smiled back. "You are welcome, Will."

Will thought, *Score one point for Will.* Beya came and sat down with Jimmy, Will and Miria.

He spoke to Miria and Miria looked at Will and Jimmy. "Beya would like to know if you would like to learn how to drive the boat and learn how to use the sails when we get into big water?"

Both boys said in unison, "Big water?"

Miria smiled. "Yes, we will be coming to it by the time we have lunch in our tummy."

Will and Jimmy both laughed. "Stomach, Miria." Will corrected her, and he could see she was hurt by their laughter. Will tried to backtrack as fast as he could. "No, Miria, you are correct about the word tummy, but it is used on children. Adults use the word stomach."

Miria stood up quickly. "Maybe I should find an adult first." And she walked away.

Will thought, *So much for the extra point you moron!*

Jimmy looked at Will. "Did we just make her mad?"

Will looked at Jimmy. "Yes, Einstein, we made her mad." Will got up leaving Beya and Jimmy wondering what he was going to do. Will took a deep breath and headed in Miria's direction. He could tell she was crying, and he felt even worse than before.

"Miria, I am so sorry if I offended you."

Miria looked at him with anger. "More difficult words for me! Do you like to make me feel stupid?"

Shocked, Will answered, "Oh, Miria. No! If I ever make you feel this way, you may slap me across the head. It would serve me right."

Miria looked at him in stunned amazement. "I could never hit you, Will. It is forbidden in our culture."

Will smiled. "How do they feel if you kick me in the shin?"

"What is a shin?" Miria whispered.

Will pointed to his lower leg.

"No, that would be forbidden."

"Then tell me, Miria, what could you do to me if I ever hurt your feelings again?"

Without hesitation she said, "Burn your food."

Will started to laugh and Miria did too. "Aw, come on, Miria. That would really be nasty!" They both laughed again before Will spoke again.

"Miria, do you remember when Jimmy called his nose Jimmy?" She nodded and he continued, "You laughed at him. Did you mean to hurt him?"

In shock she looked at Will, "No never!"

"Exactly, Miria, and Jimmy and I did not mean to hurt you either. It just sounded funny when you used the word. And by the way the word 'Offend' means to hurt your feelings. Did I offend you? Another way to say it is, did I hurt your feelings?"

Miria looked up at Will. "Then why did you not just say that?

"Why do you use difficult words?"

Will smiled. "Because I'm stupid!"

Miria laughed and put her head on Will's shoulder. "No, Will, you are not stupid."

Will put his arm around her. "Tell you what, Miria? If I ever hurt your feelings again, you have my permission to call me stupid or fat head or jackass. Stop me when you get to one you like."

Miria laughed and hugged Will back, and for the first time in his life Will felt a feeling in the pit of his stomach that he had never felt before. And it felt good. But what Will didn't see was Lian's knuckles go white holding the wheel of the ship. And the feeling in Lian's stomach did not feel good at all.

* * *

The rest of the morning was pretty quiet compared to the excitement from the night before. Beya was teaching Jimmy how to steer the boat and hoist the sails and bring them down again and properly stow the sails and ropes. Jimmy was enjoying the school of sailor and Will laughed at him when he got tied up in some tie-down ropes.

Jimmy looked at his cousin. "Think you could do better? Get over here and try!"

Will sauntered over to Beya and Jimmy. "I sure couldn't do any worse." And he began to pull on the lines hoisting the sail up and then pulling the jig line in to bring the sails down again. It went off perfectly, and Will just smiled coyly at Jimmy.

"Oh, man, that's just beginners luck," Jimmy said with anguish.

"Is it, or maybe I've done this before," said Will with a cocky smile.

Jimmy looked at Will in confusion., "When? When have you ever learned to sail?"

Will laughed. "You don't know everything about me, cuz. I

learned in Mexico when we went down for spring break last year."

Jimmy just growled under his breath and Will could have sworn he called him a smartass. Will just laughed and repeated the pattern again with total success.

Jimmy snarled. "All right. Now you're just being a show off!"

Will laughed. "Watch and learn, cousin. Watch and learn." And Jimmy did just that. He was not going to let his cousin outshine his capabilities. Within an hour Jimmy had the technique down pat, and he felt pretty proud of himself. Will had to admit he was a natural. He would not tell Jimmy that it took him three days to learn what he just picked up in a few hours. No sense in making him gloat all over the boat, he thought.

When Beya and the boys were just rolling up the last of the lines, Miria called out to them, "Lunch is ready." The young men sauntered over to Miria with a swashbuckler attitude in their step, feeling very proud of their morning accomplishments. Miria would have to be blind to miss their cockiness. "You have been very busy this morning, and it makes me happy to see you both get along so well with Beya."

Jimmy chimed in with a smiling face. "Yeah, Beya's a great teacher! Neither of us can speak each other's language, but he taught us by example, and he was easy to follow. Please thank him for us, Miria. Tell him we appreciate his patience even though Will can be slow and pig-headed at times."

The last part Jimmy said with laughter, and Will wacked him across the back of his head with his T-shirt that he had removed earlier. Miria repeated the words to Beya, and he laughed as he understood the antics the two cousins just played out in front of him. Beya spoke to Miria, and she laughed as she repeated the words to the boys.

"Beya says you are both fine students, and he would be proud to sail with you anywhere." Both Jimmy and Will smile and nodded at him.

Will looked at Miria. "How do you say 'thank you' in your language?"

Miria smiled and said, "Mena."

Will nodded and then turned to Beya, "Mena Beya."

Beya smiled back. "Mena Will."

Everyone sat down around a small table that Miria had set up for lunch. On the stone plates was a corn bread, some vegetables that taste like beans and squash, and a paste that she spread on the corn bread. It tasted like egg salad, and Will wondered what it was made from.

"Miria, what is this?"

She smiled. "Do you not like it?"

"Oh, no, it's very good. It tastes like eggs. Is it made from that?"

Miria smiled. "Just one egg from a large bird you will see in Attaberra. It does not fly. You will see why later."

Jimmy and Will both looked at each other. "Ostrich?" they said in unison.

"Nah, can't be," said Will.

Jimmy looked at him. "Please don't tell me it's a pterodactyl. I really want them to be extinct."

Will smiled. "Yeah, me too!"

Will looked at Miria. "When will we be at Attaberra?"

Miria brushed her mouth of some crumbs. "We will be there in two sleeps. We will be on the big water for two days, and then we will arrive."

Jimmy looked at Miria. "This big water. Does it have any more of those big snakes like the one we met last night?"

"It is not likely we will meet one in the big water. They stay mostly in the river, but we must be on our guard for other animals that live in the big water."

Will stopped eating. "Such as?"

Miria smiled. "Hopefully we will not meet anything that will cause us a fright. Don't forget Lian and Donat make a good team; do you not agree?"

Jimmy laughed. "Yeah, our own weapon of mass destruction!"

Will laughed but Miria looked confused. "I do not know these words."

Jimmy laughed. "That's okay, Miria. They are our very own private army. I feel safer having them around. You can tell them I said so."

Miria laughed and repeated the words to the men. They laughed and nodded in agreement. Lian said something back, and Miria's mood quickly turned angry. She voiced her anger to Lian, who merely got up and walked back to the helm.

"What did he say, Miria?" Will asked quietly.

"It does not matter," she quickly replied.

"Yes, it does. What did he say?"

She looked at Will with sadness. "He thinks you and Jimmy are not worth the trouble we are having to go through. It would have been better if the serpent had killed you."

Will took a deep breath. "Wow, he really hates us, doesn't he?"

Miria touched his hands. "I am so sorry, Will. Lian can be so…"

Will piped in, "Conceited, jealous, pig-headed! Stop me when you find one you like."

Miria started to laugh. "I think you describe him very well. Though I do not know what conceited means, but I am sure it fits his face."

Will squeezed her hands. "I guess I will have to try to win his friendship or die trying," he muttered under his breath. These words could not have been more true as Will would soon find out.

***

"Look, the big water!" Miria shouted as she pointed towards the bow of the ship.

Will and Jimmy both ran to the bow to take a look.

Jimmy's eyes popped. "Whoa, Will, that looks like an ocean. An underground ocean!" Will could not believe his eyes either. For the cavern opened up to a height surpassing his guess as to how high. It seemed like a sky was above them, but on careful observation he realized the ocean water was reflecting onto the roof of the cave giving it a sky colour atmosphere.

"This is incredible! Miria, this is unbelievable and fabulous all at the same time," Will said loudly as the boat passed over large waves as they pushed away from the river's mouth.

Miria laughed. "It is beautiful, isn't it?"

Jimmy laughed and shouted, "As if we were dreaming. We're not, are we?"

Will laughed. "Fraid not, cuz. This is as real as you and me."

Jimmy whooped and hollered as they passed through the waves and settled slowly on the ocean.

Beya shouted to Miria and she turned to the boys. "He wants to know if you would like to help with the sails?"

In unison they shouted, "Oh yeah!" and ran towards Beya to hoist the sails.

Jimmy started to speak in a strange way to Miria. "Avast yee, matey. We're going to sail the seven seas and then add one more – an underground sea full of mystery and danger. But alas, we're pirates and the ocean is our home. Born in our blood. We fear nothing. Aha!"

Miria laughed at Jimmy and the strange way he spoke. She found him amusing and was feeling happy knowing these two strange and wonderful young men. No matter what Lian thought of them. They were worth the trouble, and in time she hoped Lian would feel this as well.

The ships sails went up and then the wind came up. Will looked at Donat and realized how his gift was not only amazing but truly wonderful as well. He walked over to Miria.

"Please tell Donat that I find him amazing. His gift is truly a blessing."

Miria nodded and related the words to Donat. He smiled and blushed a little. He held up his hand as if to wave in salute to his new admirer, and Will waved back. Slowly a friendship was beginning to form, and Miria smiled at the prospect of these two young men becoming just that.

***

Miria went below deck to take care of the lunch dishes and to make a decision about the evening meal. When she looked in the supply box she stopped suddenly noticing the container of corn bread was open, and she was sure that she had closed it. She also noticed the fruit container was not in the same spot she always left it. She started to look around to see if there were anything else out of place. Then she noticed a fur blanket behind a large container box. She quickly moved the box and gasped in surprise, for there sleeping in the blanket was Timtuk, sucking his thumb and twirling his hair as he always did when he slept so soundly. Miria slumped down and began to cry quietly for her emotions went in every direction. She was elated to see him again but feared his father would think that this was all her idea of stowing him away.

When her head was spinning with emotion Lian came down

the stairs and stopped suddenly seeing her tears. She looked at Lian and began to whisper her discovery and her fears. He looked at Miria and shook his head and assured her that he would make the chief believe that Timtuk did this without help from anyone. He looked down at the sleeping child, smiled and called him a little scoundrel. Miria was relieved that Lian was not angry and thanked him for his kindness. Lian touched her arms and gave his promise that he would protect Timtuk with the same oath he gave to protect her. Miria looked at Lian and gave him a huge hug. Lian was taken aback by this show of emotion but hugged her back and laughed. At the sound of the laughter Timtuk awoke and peeked out of his hiding spot.

Miria spoke to him very sternly and he looked down at the floor as if he was about to cry. She quickly swept him into her arms and hugged him with all the love she could show him. Timtuk was confused with Miria's duel outburst. Mad or happy, he was not sure. But he hugged her back and started to cry in her arms, and she told him she loved him and missed him with all her heart. But that he should not have done this as his father was going to be very cross with him and her as well. Timtuk looked at Miria, "Then let's not go back. Let's live far away from him. He scares me!" Miria tried to reassure her brother that the chief loved him very much.

Timtuk shook his head and repeated, "He scares me. He scares me." And began to cry again. Miria rocked him back and forth in her arms, and he slowly fell back to sleep. She wondered how he had managed to stay hidden from everyone for so many days. He was a scoundrel! And she wondered if the chief would be coming after him. The thought of this gave her shivers up her spine. But for now she had her sweet little brother in her arms, and she was basking in her happiness. She would deal with the chief when the time presented itself. For now she was with her baby brother, and no one would take this happy feeling away from her.

It was as it should be, she told herself. And she rocked her brother and hummed a lullaby to him as he slept. Lian watched the scene with awe. He knew that Timtuk should be with Miria and the chief was wrong to separate them. He swore silently to himself that they would never be separated again. He swore an oath to himself that Miria would never be that unhappy again.

CHAPTER EIGHTEEN

When Fred held his flashlight into the small crevice even he felt the hairs on the back of his neck. Steve looked at him, "Well, what do you think?"

Fred shook his head. "Looks like those signs you see in Mexico. Aztec or Mayan."

Jenny and Carol crawled in for a closer look, shining the light into the crevice. Both women drew back suddenly.

"Ow, that hurts!" Carol said softly.

Jenny nodded. "Why do we feel it and not the guys?"

Carol smiled. "Oh, you know, we just have that magnetic personality thing going on."

Jenny snickered. "Yeah, but is it supposed to hurt like that?"

Carol took a deep breath. "Don't you feel we get more questions than answers out here?"

Steve sat next to them. "Not really, Carol. First, we are ninety-nine percent sure this is where the boys disappeared. Second, we know that there is some force field for lack of a better description, that only women seem to feel. Third, we have some ancient markings that we will have to take a photo of and send to a professional who studies this stuff."

Fred nodded and took out his phone and took a photo of the

marking. He took several for good measure.

Carol walked over to Fred. "May I see what you took." Fred handed her his phone, and she slowly scanned the photos. "I think I know someone who can help us. He's a client of my firm, and he studies Aztec and Mayan history. You might say he's a leader in this field."

Steve looked at her hopefully. "Do you think he would mind looking at this, and maybe we could even go and talk to him."

Carol smiled. "Sending the photos would be the easy part, but seeing him would be a little difficult. He's a little eccentric. Doesn't like people very much. He never comes to the office. One of the partners or myself go and see him whenever we have legal issues to discuss."

Fred touched her arm. "But he's comfortable with you? So maybe you will be our ace in the hole to reach this guy."

Carol shrugged her shoulders. "I could try, but let me send the photos first and see how he reacts to them."

Everyone nodded in agreement. "Okay, so I guess there is nothing more to do except eat that wonderful lunch that you lovely ladies prepared this morning," said Fred with a loud gusto voice.

Jenny shook her head. "Come on, you guys. Let's deal with those growling stomachs of yours. And I am sure Carol and I can use a little something too."

Carol laughed. "I hate to admit it, but all this fresh air does give me a ravenous appetite."

Fred laughed. "Good. I hate women who only eat raw vegetables and yogurt! Bring on the good stuff, Jenny!"

Everyone laughed and headed back to the riverbank to set up their picnic.

✷ ✷ ✷

The following morning Carol came out of the guest room carrying her phone. "Morning. Hey, I just got a text from my office. It seems Professor Marlin has been trying to reach me. Must have something to do with the photos I sent last night."

Steve looked at Carol. "Professor Marlin? Is that his name? I didn't know he was a professor. What's he a professor of?"

Carol laughed. "Slow down, Speedy Gonzales. It's the client I was telling you about. I didn't mention his name until I was sure he would help us. Besides, he not exactly a professor like in a university though I'm sure he could be. He has more letters behind his name that a can of alphabet soup. We call him professor as a courtesy to his status. He likes it!"

Jenny smiled at Carol and handed her a cup of coffee. "Thanks Jenny," she said as she took a sip and sat down with them at the table.

Jenny passed her a platter of muffins. "What did your professor want?"

Taking a blueberry muffin and putting it on a small plate Carol looked at Jenny. "Apparently he wants to talk to me on the phone. Said he doesn't trust text messages. You know, that eccentric thing I told you about. He might have a few conspiracy theories he's dealing with."

Steve started to chuckle. "Are you sure he's right in the head or better yet right for us?"

Carol smiled but got a little serious look on her face. "Steve, I'm not kidding you. This guy is a genius in his field. I find him fascinating."

"Okay, sis. If he's as good as you say, we're on board with you."

Carol breathed a huge sigh of relief. "Great. Now I just hope he answers his phone." Carol started dialing the number her office left her, and she got an answer on the first ring.

An excited little voice piped in, "Carol is that you?"

"Yes, Professor. Did you get the photos I sent to you?"

With an excited and squeaky voice he said, "Yes, dear. That is what I must speak to you about. Where did you discover this mark?"

"Professor, I'm up north with my brother and sister-in-law. I'm afraid we are in trouble up here. Our boys have disappeared, and we discovered that mark."

Before she could say another word the professor cut in. "Disappeared! Oh, my dear. They have found the key. They found the key!"

Carol started to have a panic in her voice. "Professor, what key? What are you talking about?"

"Oh, my dear," he squeaked again with excitement. "The key to the womb of the earth. I must come see you immediately. How do I get there?"

Carol sat down hard on the chair. "Professor, you'd come here? You would get on a plane? Are you sure?"

"Yes, yes my dear. Oh this is so exciting. How soon can I get to you?"

Carol spoke in a business-like voice. "I'll make all the arrangements for you to be on an afternoon flight. Can you be packed and ready?"

The professor laughed. "I'm packed now! This is so exciting, Carol."

"Okay, Professor. I'll make all the arrangements and have a car come and pick you up and take you to the airport. I'll call you as soon as I have everything confirmed."

"Oh, Carol, I feel as giddy as a school boy."

Carol smiled a little. "I'll talk to you soon, Professor." She hung up the phone looking a little confused.

Steve was the first to speak. "Did we hear you right? He's coming here?"

Carol nodded slowly. "Apparently, this is exciting. He said the boys have found the key. The key to the womb of the earth, his words exactly." Steve and Jenny looked at each other in shock and confusion then Jenny turned to Carol. "Make the arrangements for him. Steve we can set him up in our travel trailer. It has all the comforts of home, Carol. Heat, water, shower and toilet."

Carol hugged her sister-in-law. "Jenny, that's a great idea. He'll be happy on his own but near us just the same. I love you."

Jenny was taken aback by the huge hug Carol was giving her. "I love you too, Carol," Jenny said with a quivering voice.

Carol held her back in her arms. "That's the first time we have ever said that, isn't it?" Jenny nodded slowly with a quivering lip and tears forming in her eyes. Carol started to softly cry. "About time huh?"

Jenny nodded. "Way about time!" And they held each other for a few more minutes of hugging and crying. Steve had to walk out of the room wiping his eyes as he did. He didn't want the girls to see what a big suck he really could be.

✱ ✱ ✱

"Professor! Professor Marlin! Over here." Carol was shouting and waving her hands to the little white haired man walking through the doors of the airport. Jenny and Steve were taken aback by this tiny little man not much bigger than their daughter Katie. Professor Marlin walked up to Carol and seemed all out of breath from the walk.

"Carol dear. So very nice to see you. My, what excitement we are having today."

Carol kind of smiled at the irony of that statement. "Professor, this is my family. Steve, Jenny and my niece Katie."

"Very nice to meet you all. Now, where did they take my satchels? I need them desperately for our work."

Steve smiled. "Luggage pick up is over here, Professor. I'll take you over."

Professor Marlin smiled at Steve. "Thank you, young man. Then will you take me to see the key?"

"We'll have to wait until tomorrow morning, Professor. By the time we get you to our home, it will be nightfall. Not a good time to be wandering in the woods."

The professor looked a little disappointed. "Yes, of course. No sense in all of us getting lost now, is there?"

Steve smiled and whispered under his breath, "Glad Jenny didn't hear you say that."

✱ ✱ ✱

"He's not quite what I expected," Jenny said to Carol.

"What were you thinking?"

Jenny laughed. "I don't really know, but I sure wasn't expecting Einstein."

Carol laughed and took Katie's hand. "Well, I can tell you he's really fascinating. Katie I hope you really get to like the professor too. He's a real nice man."

Katie looked at her mother. "He's little, isn't he?"

Jenny smiled. "But very smart, so don't let size matter; okay?"

Katie nodded to her mom. "Okay, Mommy."

"At least not at your age," muttered Carol under her breath. Jenny burst out laughing, and Katie wondered what her mother and Auntie Carol were laughing about. She was just about to ask when her father and the professor walked up to them, luggage in Steve's hand.

"Okay, everyone, let's get this show on the road," Steve piped out.

"Show? We're going to see a show?" the professor looked at Carol with confusion.

"No, Professor. Just a way of saying it's time to go and get in the car."

"Oh, then why did he not just say so?" asked the professor.

"Because my brother-in-law is poetic!"

"Really? It didn't sound like poetry to me," the professor said looking down at the ground as if he expected it to answer. Carol just chuckled and guided him to the car.

Carol muttered under her breath, "This is going to be so fun." She slid into the back of the car with Katie in the middle and the professor on the other side of Katie.

✳ ✳ ✳

Steve carried the luggage into the trailer with the professor following close behind.

"Oh my!" said the professor. "This will be fine. Yes, just fine."

Steve nodded to the professor. "I'm so glad to hear you say that, sir. Let me show you where the light switches are," he said, pointing to the walls. "The bathroom is in here," he said, opening the door at the back. You have water, so you can shower whenever you would like. Jenny does most of the cooking, so meals will be served in the house if that's okay with you?"

"Oh, my boy, that would be wonderful. Cannot tell you the last time I had a home-cooked meal. Where can I set up my office?" he said as he looked around the unit.

Steve pointed to the table at the front of the trailer. "You can set up right here, Professor, and your bed is in the back just past the bathroom. Closet and drawers are in there too."

The professor had a funny little coy look as he turned to Steve. "It's like first class camping, isn't it?"

Steve laughed. "You are so right, Professor. It's the only way I can get my wife to come camping with me. But please don't tell her I said that; okay."

"Okay, but what did you say?" the professor asked with a blank face.

Steve realized how tired he must be from all this travelling and all. "Professor, why don't you come with me and join me for a light refreshment before Jenny and Carol call us for dinner."

"A refreshment! How nice. What would that be?" asked the professor.

Steve smiled. "For me it will be a beer. How about you?"

"Oh my! I haven't had one of those in years. Yes, I would very much like a beer."

Steve smiled. "Then follow me, Professor. I have a beer with your name on it."

"You do! Oh I must see that. How did it know my name?" the professor asked quizzically.

Steve chuckled under his breath. "Oh God, this is going to be fun!" and he led the professor to the house.

***

Dinner went by quietly. The professor seemed interested in the meat that Jenny had cooked. He chewed it slowly and smiled at every bite he swallowed.

"It's venison, isn't it, my dear?"

Jenny smiled at the professor. "Yes, it is. Do you like it?"

He held up his hands. "My dear, it is delicious. I have not had this since I was a very young boy. My father used to hunt in the

Kootenay region. I lived just outside of Cranbrook when I was a boy. This meal is a memory I had long forgotten. Thank you, my dear. What an absolute pleasure this has been for me."

Carol laughed. "Well, it's not over, Professor. Jenny makes the best lemon meringue pie you have ever tasted. Would you like a piece?"

The shocked look on his face was as if Christmas had just been announced to a small child. "Pie! We have pie?" he looked at Katie, "Pinch me, dear child, for I know I must be sleeping. Is this a dream?"

Katie jumping at the chance pinched the professor on his arm. "Ouch! Oh, you sweet little child. I'm not dreaming. Yes, please, dear lady. May I have some pie?"

Everyone at the table started to laugh as Jenny presented her wonderful dessert to the table. And no one was disappointed. It was the best lemon meringue pie.

* * *

Fred pulled his truck into Steve's driveway, and he was surprised to see Steve wandering about the yard this early in the morning. Fred parked and jumped out of his truck.

"Morning, early bird. Didn't think I'd find you out and about so early."

Steve taking a sip from his coffee mug smiled at his friend. "Got a lot on my mind. Trying to put it all in perspective."

Fred frowned at his friend. "What's going on?"

Steve pointed to the travel trailer. "Our new guest. He is a workout."

Fred started to laugh. "You mean Carol was not exaggerating on the eccentric personality."

Steve smiled. "No, she wasn't exaggerating on that. But it's what he said to me last night when I was walking him back to the trailer that's bothering me."

Fred frowned. "Like what?"

Steve smiled and shook his head. "Oh, no. You have to meet this guy and get the full meal deal. Come on, I heard him moving around about an hour ago. I'm sure he is ready for house guests."

Fred followed Steve to the trailer and waited as Steve knocked loudly on the door. The door opened quickly, and Professor Marlin stuck his shaggy white head out.

"Good morning, good morning. Do come in. I have so much I want to show you."

Steve and Fred stepped in, and Steve was stunned to see how the professor had transformed his trailer. Books lay open on the couch, papers were taped to the walls, maps were taped to the curtains, and the floor was a medley of papers and books strewn everywhere. Steve trying not to show his shock.

"You've been busy, Professor!"

With a wide smile and clapping his hands he said, "Yes, indeed, young man. I wanted to share all this with you."

Steve nodded and mumbled about Jenny seeing this mess but only Fred heard his words. He started to chuckle before Steve shook himself away from that thought.

"Oh, Professor Marlin, this is Fred Avery. He has been with us from the beginning of this hunt for our children. He's an excellent tracker and one of my best friends."

The professor looked up at Fred. "Delighted to meet you, old boy. Please sit down and we can begin."

Fred chuckled at two things. First, he noticed Steve was referred to as a young man, but he was an old boy. Second, where the hell was he supposed to sit? There wasn't enough space for a mouse to find an empty spot.

Steve opened a closet and grabbed two folding chairs handing one to Fred. Fred nodded a thank you and tried to set it up around the mess on the floor.

"There you go. Now we can begin," said Professor Marlin as if he was about to start a grade three reading class.

Again, Fred started to chuckle under his breath, but Steve gave him a knock on his arm and whispered, "Hang on, buddy. There is more fun to come."

Professor Marlin looked up from his book and patted the page for Fred and Steve to look at.

"There, this is where we will begin. It's about the time the Aztec natives really started to shine. The word Aztlán means 'the land of the north,' the land from where the Aztecs came. They became known as Aztecs, and they eventually migrated from Aztlán to the Valley of Mexico. In some books it was viewed as a place of paradise for all inhabitants. However, the Aztec people were subject to the Azteca Chicomoztoca, who were known as the tyrannical elite. The physical identification of Aztlán has been described as an island, an island within a lake. However, no one knows where it is or where it could have originated from. Some scholars believe Atlantis and Aztlán are the same place. But this has been disputed and all indications point to two definitely different places on earth. One mystery, though, is how far north did the Aztec people go. Some indications and searches extend as far as Utah. However, what you have found indicates even farther north.

"Now, I know you must be asking yourself how does a small mark on a rock indicate a great find. But it does, my boys. It does. You see, they didn't travel above ground. They travelled below it. Many of the Aztec people started to question their faith and beliefs and decided to leave their city to escape the tyranny of human sacrifice. They fled Aztlán to Tenochtitlan, and this is very important to Aztec history. It began on May 24, 1064, which was the first Aztec solar year.

"They were hunted, but what you must understand is these people were genius in science, engineering, farming and building. They simply found the mouth of the seven sacred caves, closed the door behind them and expanded under the earth. But they have ways to open each cave door in a particular time frame, take from above the earth what they need and go back to their underworld. All indications of my studies is that each cave door opens every twenty-one years. But they open every three years in a different part of the world. You my dear boys have found one of those doors. Now, when can we go and see it?"

Fred started to shake his head trying to catch up to the quick history lesson the professor just shared with them.

"Professor, you think we have found you one of the doors to the sacred caves?"

"Exactly, dear boy. And if it is confirmed by me, I can add it to my map." He pointed to a map taped on the curtain.

"Your map?" Steve said as he edged his way towards the map.

"Yes, dear boy, my map. You see, I know of three other doors around the world. If I confirm your find, I will know of four sacred doors." Fred and Steve looked carefully at his map, one mark indicated a place in Utah, one near Mexico City and one in South America around Lake Titicaca.

"Professor, do you know when one of these other doors will open?" Steve said holding his breath in anticipation.

"I believe I do, dear boy, but it will not be for another three years," the professor said in a matter of fact tone.

Fred let out a giant burst of air. "Three years? The boys could be stuck under there for three years?"

The professor looked insulted by this statement. "Not stuck, old boy! A learning experience. They will see worlds you can never believe, see architecture beyond your realm of thinking and witness worlds beyond our dreams. Stuck! My boy, I would give my right arm to be where they are right now. They are experiencing the very best of a lost civilization and will forever be changed by this journey. I envy these boys. When they return to you, they will come back as a Marco Polo. No one will believe their stories, but my dear boys, I will and I will record their every word."

CHAPTER NINETEEN

Miria came up the stairs carrying a sleeping Timtuk in her arms.

Jimmy noticed her first. "Holy Christmas, it's Timtuk!"

Will quickly turned and looked into Miria's eyes. Just the sight of her happiness melted his legs to rubber. He walked towards her with his hands spread and shaking his head. "How?"

Miria spoke quietly, "He has hidden himself all this time. I now know the disappearing food took place on board not back at my house. I told you he is very good at hiding. It was always his favourite game with me.

I had no idea he followed us, his father will be furious with me. I doubt he will believe Timtuk did this all on his own."

Will and Jimmy both looked at her seriously before Will spoke. "Will he come after us?"

Miria looked sadly into Will's eyes. "He will probably send men."

Jimmy looked at her. "Will they hurt you, Miria?"

Looking at Jimmy and then at Timtuk in her arms. "I don't know, Jimmy, but Lian wants us to keep going and try to stay two days ahead of anyone who might be chasing after us."

Will smiled. "Sounds like a good plan to me. When are we supposed to be at that city you said we're heading for?"

Miria smiled. "Attaberra. We should see it soon. It is right around that point of land over there." She pointed to their left and Jimmy and Will followed her direction. Beya called out and turned the boat to port side. There far off in the distance was a small city shining above the shore.

Will took a deep swallow. "Oh, my God, Miria. It looks like the city is made of gold!"

She smiled. "It's beautiful, isn't it?"

Jimmy looked at her in shock. "Beautiful! Do you know what this city would be worth on the stock exchange?"

Miria started to chuckle. "Jimmy, I do not understand anything you just said."

Will looked at her seriously. "Miria, is gold precious to your people?"

Looking a little confused. "It is an easy stone to mold and create with. It is in abundance in many of our villages. What do you mean precious?"

Will took a deep breath. "What do your people use to trade with? How do you buy things from each other?"

Miria smiled. "We trade with what we have. The berries and fish we got from your world will get us other types of food and materials that these villages have in abundance."

Jimmy asked, "Then the gold rock that you have at this city is not traded?"

Miria looked at him in confusion. "Some things they make from the rock is traded. Men trade for some jewellery for their women if they wish to do so. But no, it is a pretty rock, but not a precious rock to trade. You find it everywhere. However, the magic men like to use it in their work."

Will shook his head. "What's a magic man?"

Miria smiled. "I'm sorry, that is what my father always told me their name was. It must have another name, but I do not remember it."

Will looked at her. "Would scientist be the word?"

Miria thought about that for a second and repeated the word slowly. "Scientist. Yes, I believe I heard my father say this. Will, is this rock precious to your world?"

Will and Jimmy nodded at her before Jimmy spoke,

"Kind of makes our world go around. Miria, it is what we use to back our money."

Putting Timtuk down softly on a blanket and some fur she turned to the boys. "What is money?"

Will smiled at her. "Something I envy you for not having and not ever needing. Miria, is there nothing precious to your people?"

She looked shocked by the question. "Life is precious to us. Family and friends. Food, of course. But sadly it was not always this way with my people."

Jimmy started to try to remember some of his history lessons on the Aztec people. And he feared where this might be going. Miria looked at them and sat on a bench.

"Our people escaped from the bad people above, hundreds and hundreds of years ago. My people escaped to the sacred caves for they didn't want any more killings for the God of Rain and Sun. You asked what is precious to my people, life. To the people they ran away from, blood."

Will's eyes widened in shock. "BLOOD! They cherished blood!"

Miria nodded sadly. "They killed children for the rain god. They killed thousands of people and painted their temples with their blood. My people ran away. They could only see death if they stayed. So they were led by a priest who also did not believe in their faith anymore, and he took my people away from the God of Rain and Sun. He took them to the sacred caves where the gods could not find us."

Will looked at Miria with admiration. "And your people have been here ever since? How many years, Miria?"

Miria smiled with a little bit of pride in her voice. "My father told me a thousand years."

Both boys let out a huge blast of air. "Wow, that's incredible!" Jimmy said with a huge smile.

Miria smiled too. "It is, isn't it?"

Will smiled too. "I have so many questions for you, Miria. Like how do you grow food without sunlight? How do your people stay healthy without the sun? Where do you get fresh water from? And how did that rotten cave door just shut behind us?"

Miria just started to laugh. "All good questions, Will, but I will have to answer them later. Beya is calling you to join him with the sails. I will answer your questions tonight after dinner."

Will and Jimmy stood up and began to walk to Beya and Donat. "Okay, Miria. We'll talk later." Will smiled at her. She smiled too and then turned her attention to her little brother, who was just waking from his nap.

* * *

With everyone sated after dinner it was a quiet time for everyone except Buddy and Timtuk. Timtuk was playing fetch with Buddy, his favourite game. And everyone watched and laughed too. Even Lian, who seemed a bit mellower since Timtuk was discovered.

Will smiled at Miria. "Are you ready for my questions now?"

Miria smiled. "I will try to answer them the best way I can."

Will nodded. "Great. How do you grow food without the sun?"

Miria laughed. "You don't need the sun, just light. We get that from the stones you must have noticed in the cave. The harder you bang them, the longer they glow. You can see how we light up the caves as we travel. We get these stones from our village, not far from here, but we trade with them. Which will come into your next question you asked. Where do we get fresh water? We make it."

Will's eyes popped open. "You make it! How?"

Miria smiled. "Our magic men, they can make water from a blue stone that is abundant in many of our sacred caves. We have rivers as well, but they must be cleaned before you can drink it."

Jimmy looked at her in a puzzled look. "Pollution down here?"

Miria looked back in the same way. "What is pollution?"

Jimmy smiled sadly. "When man makes your water or air dirty by complete stupidity."

Miria looked down and chuckled. "Our rivers are polluted because of your people. They put things on your soil, and it seeps into the earth and makes our rivers dirty. You should never drink from the river."

Will thought about that for a few minutes and then asked, "Miria, the lake and small river where you live, I thought you could drink from this."

She smiled. "You could, it was all made from the stones."

Both Will and Jimmy looked at her incredulously. Finally Will spoke, "All that water flowed from the blue stones?"

She nodded. "Yes, made by our magic men." Jimmy and Will just looked at her in amazement.

"What were your other questions?"

Jimmy smiled. "How do you stay healthy without the sun?"

Miria smiled again. "We've been doing it for a thousand years, however, our food is rich with the veenims you need to stay healthy. And the magic men make veenims from plants and fish oil for us all to take."

Jimmy looked at Will. "Veenims?"

Will smiled. "Must be another name for vitamins."

"And at least once a year we go to the cave of holes for real sunshine. My father called it a holiday in the sun. He loved it."

Will sat up straight. "Miria, there is a place where sunlight can get through?"

She wrinkled up her nose, "Not exactly. It's called…" She looked up to the sails as if she was trying to find the correct word. "Flection. Yes, father called it that."

Will looked at Miria. "Could the word have been reflection?"

"Does that word have a good meaning?" she asked slowly.

"Yes, and it would explain a few things, but I sure would like to see this cave,." said Jimmy.

"Oh, we will go there, but it is very far away. But we will go there someday on our journey."

Both boys smiled and in unison said, "Excellent!" Miria liked to see the boys smile like this. It made her feel special to them.

"Now, have I answered all the questions?"

Will shook his head. "Not quite, the cave door. How did it just shut?"

Miria spoke slowly and quietly. "This is a very big secret to my people. But you have sworn an oath on secrecy, do you remember?" Both boys nodded their heads, and Will could feel the hair on the back of his neck rise. Miria took a deep breath and said, "Each portal is only open for three days. When you two entered the cave our time was up. That is why I ran like the wind to catch Timtuk. I knew it was going to shut, and if I did not get him, he would have been lost in your world."

Will and Jimmy looked at each other and seemed to know what the other was thinking. Will nodded to Jimmy and then looked at Miria.

"How far away is the next portal?"

Miria looked at Will and then at Jimmy. "How old are you now?"

she asked.

Will looked at Jimmy. "Fifteen and sixteen years," Will said with a choked voice as he was fearing this next answer.

Miria spoke softly, "You will be eighteen and nineteen when we reach the portal."

Both boys sat there in stunned silence. Miria noticed their faces had paled, and she worried they might get sick to their stomach.

"Will, Jimmy, I thought you understood it would be a long journey. Will, I told you how old Timtuk would be when I saw him again. Did you not understand?" Will had understood the three years until the portal opened. He did not understand it would take three years to get to the portal.

"Do you mean we will be travelling for three years?"

"Yes, are you understanding this journey now?"

Jimmy whispered slowly, "What if we don't make it?"

Miria looked at the deck and spoke softly, "Then we go back to the elders. If they agree, we will take you to the next portal, which will open three years later."

Will took a hard swallow. "And if they don't agree?"

Miria refused to look at them. "Then you will have to join my people and wait for twenty-one years for the portal you entered to open again."

Jimmy and Will both jumped up, looked at her in shock and each boy walked to different parts of the ships rail, lost in their own thoughts.

***

Jimmy was the first to speak as they lay in their bedrolls. Neither had spoken a word after their talk with Miria.

"Will, did you know it would take this long to travel?"

Will rolled over and looked at his cousin. "Jimmy, I had no idea we'd be travelling for three years, but I'm going to level with you. It's an exciting thought. Jim. We're going to see places we could never have dreamed of, meet people who have survived a thousand years down here. We are going to be explorers in a whole new world. Don't you find that incredible?"

"Yeah, but Will, who will we be able to tell? They've survived because it has been a secret. Can you imagine what our people would do to try to find them? Can you imagine what they'd do with that golden city we're going to see tomorrow? Let's face it, Will, we won't even be able to tell our parents about this place. We can't. Their very survival depends on it. And I for one will not jeopardize this life of theirs. I find them incredible."

Will looked at his cousin and smiled. "I think we'll feel like Marco Polo when we're done."

Jimmy looked at his cousin. "Yeah, and they killed him because they wouldn't believe his stories."

Will looked at Jimmy. "Point taken, cuz. We keep our mouths shut."

Jimmy chuckled quietly. "Will, what if we don't make it on time. The worst case scenario is twenty-one years from now. Our families will think we're dead?"

Will looked at his cousin and tried to sound as positive as he possibly could.

"Our fathers have a motto, Jim. Do you know what it is?"

Will and Jimmy both smiled and said in unison, "Failure is not an option!" And they both fell asleep with smiles on their faces.

CHAPTER TWENTY

Fred and Steve walked out of the trailer as the professor began to gather up his papers to bring with him to the site.

Fred gave a huge sigh and looked at Steve. "Is that what he told you last night? Three years?"

Steve nodded his head. "I couldn't bring myself to tell Jenny and Carol. God! Fred, this will devastate them!"

"So what are you going to do?" Fred asked.

Steve put his arms in the air as in an 'I surrender' mode.

"Let's take the professor to the site. Maybe it won't be what he's looking for. Maybe this will be just a bad dream. Maybe I'll grow fairy wings and fly to Care Bear land."

Fred smiled and patted his back. "You'll need to pack lots of cookies. The Keebler Elves don't live there."

Steve laughed. "Good to know. I'll write it down."

Jenny came out of the house. "There you are. Where have you been?"

Steve walked to his wife and gave her a hug. "Just getting my morning history lesson from the professor."

Jenny looked directly at Steve's face. "Anything I should have to worry about?"

Steve smiled then looked at Fred with the God help me look.

Fred chimed in. "Mostly he was introducing me to his world of knowledge. He is a fascinating man. Carol was right about that."

Carol walked out of the house. "I heard my name. What are you talking about?"

Fred smiled at Carol and felt a little jolt in his stomach when he saw her. "Your professor friend. He is exactly as you described him."

Carol laughed. "He is something, isn't he?"

Fred laughed. "And then some!"

At that moment the professor came out of the trailer carrying a large satchel stuffed with papers and books. "I am ready now. Can we go see the rock?" asked the professor with excitement in his voice.

Carol smiled and walked to the professor. "Good morning, Professor Marlin. Would you be comfortable just going with Steve and Fred? I would like to stay here with Jenny and Katie, if that is okay with you?"

The professor put up one hand. "No, my dear. That would be quite fine. I mean I will be with two wonderful trackers, so I know I won't get lost up here. I won't, will I?"

Fred took the satchel from the professor. "Not a chance, Professor. We won't let you out of our sight." Turning to Carol he added, "You don't want to come?"

She smiled at him and caught the sound of disappointment in his voice. "No, Jenny is going to teach Katie and I how to make her world famous chocolate fudge cake."

Steve groaned under his breath. "Man, I'm going to have to kick up my jogging time. You two are going to make me fat!"

Jenny laughed. "No chance. I'll put you on celery and water if you start showing a pot belly. Fred, you're invited for dinner tonight. You will stay, won't you?"

Fred smiled at Jenny. "And miss the chocolate fudge cake?

Not a chance." Steve gave Jenny and Carol hugs goodbye and the three men hopped into the truck and drove off.

The professor was the first to start the conversation. "How far away do we have to travel?"

Steve groaned quietly, afraid he was going to start the "Are we there yet?" routine. "It should take us about an hour to travel by truck and then about a twenty-minute hike to the rock."

The Professor started to jump a little in his seat. "Oh, I'm so excited. I feel like a young explorer again!"

Fred turned to look at him. "Professor, if this rock turns out to be what you are looking for, is there any way we can open the portal?"

The professor started to laugh and then in a shrieking high voice he said, "Oh, no, old boy. If we could do that I would have done it years ago in Utah. There is no way to open it. It's locked."

Steve piped in, "What about dynamite?"

The professor starting laughing in hysterics. "Oh, you silly boys. You could blow that whole mountain to Alaska, you will never open the portal."

Steve and Fred looked at each other in total confusion. Then Fred turned to the professor again. "Sir, have you ever tried?"

The professor's face changed from laughter to serious in a split second. "Of course I have. I was a young crazy fool at the beginning of this research. I thought I could get in by digging and blasting. All we managed to do was make a huge mess with a whole lot of nothing to show for it. That's when I really started to dig into the Aztec history books and discovered something earth-shattering."

Fred and Steve looked at each other before Steve spoke. "Earth-shattering? What was earth-shattering?"

"Our ignorance, dear boy! Our ignorance. We believe that we are the most scientific people of all time. We have all the answers.

The truth is, dear boy, we are light years behind these people. Do you know that these people were more advanced than the Roman Empire ever was? They are the most brilliant people we have ever had on this earth, and we almost destroyed them. For what? Land, gold, superiority? We, my boy, are the ignorant fools. We can only guess at their achievements, but I would stake my life to the claim that these people are so advanced. We're one step over the dinosaurs compared to them."

The professor sat back and crossed his arms, shutting off all further conversation. Fred and Steve just looked at each other with total shock and fear. Any feelings of hope to get to the boys was just flushed down the drain. The rest of the drive was quiet as each man was lost in their own thoughts.

※ ※ ※

They reached the site in good time. The professor practically pushed them along. He was so excited.

Steve pointed in the direction of the crevice. "Over here, Professor. Is this what you are looking for?"

The professor grabbed his book of notes and crawled to the spot that Steve had indicated. Opening his notebook to a certain page, he took Steve's flashlight and shone it into the crevice. After what seemed like an hour but was only a few minutes, the professor sat on his bottom and began to write in his notebook.

Steve sat down beside him. "Professor, is it what you are looking for?"

The professor looked at Steve, and he had tears in his eyes. "Oh, my dear boy, it is exactly what I have been seeking. Look here in my book. This symbol is the jaguar, and this is the serpent. Together it marks the entrance to the womb of the earth. You have found a key. Now we know that twenty-one years from now this key will be used to open the portal. I only hope I will live to see the day."

Fred came to sit with them. "Professor, you said this is your fourth key. Do you know when any of the others will open?"

"From all indications of my research, the next portal will open in the mountains near Lake Titicaca."

Steve jumped up. "You mean in South America. The boys will have to travel to South America to get back home?"

The professor looked at Steve and Fred with a matter of fact look on his face. "Yes, I thought I explained that to you last night. Were you not listening?" Steve covered his face with his hand and groaned silently.

The professor looked at Steve with a confused expression. "Why are you so unhappy, dear boy? Your boys are on the adventure of a lifetime. If they were to climb Mount Everest or join the Cousteau Research Team, would you be so upset? I envy your boys. They are with the most brilliant society that has built an underworld, and I can only imagine what their eyes will feast on each day of their journey."

Steve tried to look a little less remorseful. "Professor, I understand your excitement for this discovery. I really do, but my son is sixteen years old. My nephew is fifteen years. I kind of thought I had a few more years with them before I sent them out into the big bad world. Instead through my fault, I lost them to another world. Their mothers are going to be devastated that they won't see them for three years, and that is just us assuming they will make it to that portal in time. Professor, how the hell do you think they are travelling?

By bus or underground subway?"

The professor just shook his head. "My boy if I knew that

answer, I wouldn't be sitting here with you now, would I?"

Steve covered his face again in anguish and Fred looked at the professor and quietly spoke. "Professor, how does the portal work? How does it just appear and then disappear?"

The professor sat up happily. "Glad you asked this. I have a theory." He tore a piece of paper from his notebook and rolled it into a tight cylinder with a pointed end. "Do you see this cylinder shape? Now watch what I do with it." Taking Steve's coffee mug, he took off the lid and slowly slid the cylinder of paper into the coffee. "You see how the cylinder disperses the coffee and makes a tunnel to the bottom without letting any coffee in. I believe they have a way to melt rock in this same matter. However, they can't do it for very long, a few days maybe. But it gives them enough time to come out of their world, take what they need from our world, go back and then remove the cylinder."

Steve and Fred just sat there with their mouths open. Finally Steve spoke, "Melt rock! How?"

The professor laughed again at Steve. "My dear boy if I knew that I'd have joined their society years ago. I told you they are so advanced from us. We can't imagine everything they have achieved."

Fred stood up and shook his head. "Professor, this is just a theory. What proof do you have to come to this conclusion?"

The professor hung his head and began to shake it. "Thirty years of research, old boy. Come back to the trailer, and I will show you documentation that will turn your hair white. It did to me."

Steve stood. "Okay, Professor. Do you need anything more from this site?"

"Just a few more photos and the correct bearing as to where we are on a map, so I can mark it on mine."

Fred helped the professor with the photos, and Steve wrote

down the coordinates for the professor's map. Then the three men slowly headed back to the truck.

"Would you like me to explain to the women the boy's discovery and how proud they should be of them?"

Steve and Fred both chimed "No!" in unison. When Steve saw the shocked look on his face, he explained. "Professor, mothers are not easily excited about their teenage boys going on a three-year excursion. Please, sir, let me tell them in my way."

The professor faintly smiled. "Yes, of course, dear boy. But be sure to tell them what a wonderful opportunity this is for them."

Steve muttered under his breath, "Yes, I'm sure they will be thrilled."

He looked over at Fred. "And don't even think of abandoning me, buddy. I'm going to need all the support I can get."

Fred chuckled under his breath. "It better be a really great chocolate fudge cake!"

***

"Ladies, that meal was nothing short of fabulous. And Katie and Carol, you get A+ for your chocolate fudge cake. Jenny you should have a cooking show!"

Fred praised.

Steve smiled and joined in. "Yes, my girls could put Martha Stewart to shame. Honey, that was excellent."

Jenny smiled at all the compliments. "Thank you, gentlemen. My crew thanks you, and you can thank us by doing the dishes."

Fred snorted. "I knew there would be a catch! But Jenny, Carol and Katie it would be my pleasure. After all, a home-made dinner is worth a million dollars to me. Doing dishes is a piece of cake – if you pardon the pun."

Everyone laughed as Carol stood to clear the table. "Hey, I said I'd do the dishes. That includes clearing. You lovely ladies just go sit in the parlour and just look pretty."

Jenny and Carol both let out a loud laugh. "Man Jenny, all this sweet talk. Are they up to something?" Carol said jokingly.

Jenny turned to look at Steve and then quietly whispered to Carol. "Something is wrong. Steve seems too quiet, and the professor hardly spoke a word during dinner. Is that like him?"

Carol snorted under her breath. "I think he's hammered!"

Jenny started to laugh. "Oh, I don' think one beer could do that, do you?"

Carol's eyes popped out. "I told you he was eccentric. He's probably trying to dispute the theory of relativity in his head."

Jenny laughed. "Come on, let's go and enjoy some peace and quiet while the guys do the dishes. I've got the newest rag magazines to share."

Carol laughed. "Oh, I don't even have to go to the beauty salon. It's the only time I get to read up on Brad and Angelina."

Jenny grabbed the magazines from the shelf. "Here, take your pick."

"Oh this one. What are Kate and William up to?" Carol said as both women settled into their chairs.

✳ ✳ ✳

As the final dishes were dried and put away Fred looked at Steve. "What's your plan, old man?"

Steve smiled. "Oh no, you don't. I'm the young lad. You're the old boy."

Fred chuckled. "How can a four-year difference make me so old?"

Steve smiled and smirked. "Guess I just know how to live right and look young. You old bachelors don't age well. It's in all the magazines. Ask Jenny if you can read them someday."

Fred looked at his friend with a squinted eye. "The next time we go hunting, be afraid. Be very afraid."

Steve let out a loud laugh. "You couldn't hit the side of a barn let alone Bambi or me."

Fred laughed. "Hey, I don't have to take this crap. I have drunken friends who insult me better."

Steve slapped him softly across the back. "Yeah, but do they give you chocolate cake?"

Fred just laughed. "Okay, you got me there. God, I'm so easy to buy."

Steve smiled and started to whisper, "Fred, we have to tell them. Should we go talk to the professor first or not?"

Fred shook his head. He had had enough of the history lesson. Tomorrow would be soon enough to continue. "Let's go talk to the girls, but Steve, be gentle, and if you need any help I'll be right outside going for a walk."

"You leave me and I swear I'll break one of your legs," Steve said in a high whisper.

"Okay, okay. It was worth a try." Fred chuckled.

"Yeah right, nice try coward!" Steve laughed. Both men entered the living room. One look at the women and they both felt sick to their stomachs.

※ ※ ※

"Three years!" both women shouted in unison.

"Steve, you have to be kidding," Jenny shrieked.

"I'm not honey. The professor explained it very well. They will have three years to get to South America and hope they will be there before the next portal opens."

Carol jumped up. "And what if they don't make it?"

Fred held her hand. "Then they will have three years to get to the other cave and portal."

Jenny shrieked again, "And where will that be?" Steve tried to hold her hand, but Jenny seemed too mad at the world to want any comforting.

"We don't know, love. The professor just knows the portal by Lake Titicaca is next. After that, it's a guess."

Carol let the tears fall. "This is a nightmare. How do we know if the boys are okay? How do we know if they haven't been…"

Jenny screamed, "Don't say it! I couldn't bear to hear that!"

Fred chimed in. "Ladies, the professor totally believes the boys are safe and are on the adventure of a lifetime. You really must listen to him, and you might feel a little better about their safety, but the three-year period is real. There is nothing we can do to change that outcome."

Jenny buried her face in her hands and started to cry. Steve put his arms around her, and this time she did not pull away. Carol buried her face in her arms as she sat on the floor by the coffee table.

Fred came to her side and took her in his arms. "Not again. I can't do this again," she sobbed.

Fred helped her to her feet. "Come on. Let's get some fresh air." As if in a trance Carol followed Fred out the door. He grabbed her sweater from the coat rack as they headed out. He put it around her shoulders. They walked towards a patch of trees where Steve had built a picnic table and fire pit. Fred sat Carol at the table and began to light a fire in the pit. When it was in full burn he guided Carol to the carved chairs Steve had made from old logs.

Carol looked at Fred and quietly said it again, "I can't do it. I can't do it again."

Fred looked into her eyes, "Yes you can! You have no choice! This is your son. Are you just going to give up on him?"

It was as if he had slapped her across her face. "No! Of course not!" she shouted.

"There, that's the fighter I expected to see. Nice to have you back," Fred said firmly.

Carol looked at him. "Fred, have you ever loved someone so much and then just lost them in a heartbeat?"

Fred was quiet for a moment. "Once, about fifteen years ago. My wife. She died of cancer. We lived in Kamloops. We were married for about four years. I loved her with all my heart, and when she died, I thought I died too. It's why I moved up here, away from the memories, away from the pain. What a joke. You don't run away from any of it. You just have to get through it. One day at a time. Yeah, Carol, I know what you have gone through. But this is different. Jimmy is not dead. He'll be back. You have to believe that. And if you will let me, I'll help you through this. I'll stand by your side. Hold you up if you need it. I won't leave you. What do you say?"

Carol looked at him in a daze. "What are you saying, Fred?"

"I'm saying, for the first time in fifteen years I feel like I'm alive again. I want to be a part of your world. Can I come in?"

Carol started to cry and fell into his arms and sobbed uncontrollably. "That's right, sweetie. Get it all out. Tomorrow we'll make a plan with Steve and Jenny." He just held her and rocked her until her sobs just became a soft sniffle.

Carol looked at him through tear stained eyes. "I'm so sorry about your wife. I didn't know. Do Steve and Jenny?"

Fred shook his head. "No one knows. I just kept that part of my life a secret."

Carol sat up but still stayed in his arms. "I haven't been held by a man for thirteen years. I thought I died too. But I had Jimmy, and that's the only reason I held on. If I had not had him, I don't know how my life would have turned out."

Fred smiled at her. "You are not alone this time. Just say the words."

Carol looked into his eyes. "Fred, I want you in my life." He came down on her lips and kissed her with the passion of an end of the movie kiss. When he gently let her fall back in his arms, she smiled.

"Didn't know wilderness men could kiss so well."

With a chuckle in his voice he said, "That ain't all we can do well."

***

Steve held Jenny in their bed. He brought her in here, so Katie would not hear how upset her mother was. "Steve, this is a nightmare. How can we live through this?"

"Jenny, what we have to get over is the age of the boys. They are capable young men, and I know they will do everything right to get back home. I've taught them how to survive, how to hunt, fish and track. Will is an excellent marksman with the bow, and Jimmy is intelligent and can assess any situation with bells on accuracy. If it was Katie down there, I'd be suicidal, but it's not. It's our young men down there, and when we get them back, I know we will never look at them as children again."

Jenny lay her head on his chest. "What is it the professor is going to explain to us?"

"His theories. Some seem a little far-fetched, but I do believe him. The man has been studying this for over thirty years. I think we should keep an open mind when we listen to him. Can you do that?"

Jenny looked up at him. "You mean put my hysterical motherhood on hold?"

Steve laughed. "Yeah, can you do that?" She pinched his arm. "Ow, that hurt!"

"Sorry, must be that hysterical part of me again."

He held her close. "Jenny, we're going to get through this. We are going to get our boys back. I won't accept anything less."

Jenny laughed. "Failure is not an option! Yes, I believe in our boys. I believe they will come back. And Steve, we will be in South America when they do."

CHAPTER TWENTY-ONE

When the boys woke up the next morning they found the ship anchored in a bay just beyond the city. Will and Jimmy could hardly believe their eyes. For there in front of them was a city made entirely of gold.

Jimmy spoke quietly, "Oh God, pinch me, Will. Are we dreaming?"

Will looked at his cousin with a shocked look. "Jimmy, I don't think I could ever dream of anything like this."

The buildings were pointed, looking like upside down ice cream cones. That is except the one in the middle. It was double the height from every other building, and it resembled a large church. There was only one large door in the front, but at the back of the building it rounded out to a large circular annex reminding Jimmy of the capital building in Washington only it was shorter. There were many small windows on each floor and Jimmy wondered what kind of markings would be on each building. He could hardly wait to explore. Miria came to greet them followed by Timtuk and Buddy.

"Good Morning. Are you amazed by the city?"

Will looked at Miria. "Amazed? Miria we're blown away. This is incredible!"

Jimmy looked at her as Lian came towards them. "Why are we anchored out here? Can't we dock closer?"

Lian whispered to Miria and Will chuckled again. "Einstein still hasn't figured out we don't understand the language."

Jimmy smiled, "He said something about boats and water."

Will looked at his cousin in amazement. "You're starting to learn their language?"

Jimmy smiled. "Look, cousin, if we're going to be down here for three years, don't you think we ought to learn it?"

"Who has been teaching you, Miria?"

"Some words, but mostly from Beya. I would point at something, he'd say the word, and I would repeat it. You know, I feel like a two-year old again, but how else can I learn it."

Will looked at his cousin. "I'm impressed, man. I'm a little ashamed that I didn't think of it first."

"Well, sometimes I just like to impress you," Jimmy smiled.

Miria came back to the boys. "I hope you will not be mad at us, but we cannot go into the city until we properly bath ourselves and burn our clothes."

"Burn our clothes! What are we to wear, then?" Will asked incredulously.

Miria smiled. "New clothes will be brought to us. No one may enter this city without being all bathed and clean. It is the way to keep sickness from the city."

Both boys nodded and then looked at Buddy. "What about Buddy, Miria. Will he have to have a bath too?"

Miria laughed. "Yes, I'm afraid this is also needed. Will he be unhappy to do this?"

Will started to laugh. "Well, it's not his favourite pastime, but he will handle it."

Jimmy laughed. "Where does all this bathing occur?"

"Below the deck. Lian and Donat set it up early this morning when the people from Attaberra brought all the needed supplies."

Jimmy shook his head. "They were here? And we slept through it all?"

Miria smiled. "They did not come on the ship. Lian and Donat rowed out to them."

Jimmy laughed. "Good. I was beginning to think I go into a coma when I sleep here."

Miria smiled. "I think we should bath Buddy first then you two can be after him."

Will smiled. "Lead the way, my lady. We shall bathe the filthy canine immediately."

Miria looked at Will with a scrunched up nose. "Canine?"

Will smiled. "Another name for a dog."

Miria laughed and repeated slowly, "Canine. I think I like it better than dog. Dog does not sound special enough. Canine is a nicer word."

Jimmy chuckled. "I'll alert Webster's Dictionary. Remove the word dog. Not grand enough for such a wonderful beast."

They all laughed as they headed below deck.

Lian and Donat had set up screens at the back of the ship. Above their heads was a large blue water rock just like the ones they had seen in Miria's village.

There was a round bar that Will concluded must be soap and a bucket of pink solution that he was not sure what it was exactly. Over in another corner was a large barrel made from stone filled with warm soapy water.

"Is this for Buddy?" Will asked.

"Yes, I used it this morning for Timtuk and then got it ready for Buddy. Will you need help with him?"

Jimmy laughed. "Only an army of fifty to hold him. But we'll put him on his leash, and he should be okay."

Will lifted Buddy up and plunked him into the water. He was receptive at first until the bottle of soap came out then he tried to jump out.

Will hugged him. "Whoa Buddy, you're not going anywhere!" Buddy started to whimper, but no one was feeling sorry enough to free him from the bath. After three great lather jobs he was ready for the rinse.

Miria held out the pink solution to Will. "You must wash him with this. It will kill all bad things on his body."

Will smiled. "You mean germs. It will kill all the germs."

Miria repeated the word. "Germs. Sounds better than bad things."

Jimmy and Will both laughed as Buddy tried to shake off the solution, but Will and Jimmy quickly massaged it in and lifted him out of the barrel. Will quickly put two large towel-like blankets on him and said, "Okay, shake!" While holding the towels in place Buddy shook like a dog on a mission. Then Will and Jimmy started rubbing him down and drying him off.

"There, all clean and ready for inspection!" Will smiled.

Lian came down just at that moment and spoke to Miria. She turned to the boys,

"I will take Buddy to the upper deck and tie him up, so he will get dry in the warm breeze that Donat will provide for him. It is time for you two to bathe. Beya will come and show you how to do this."

Jimmy started to laugh. "I feel like a kid again. Don't touch the faucets or you might get burned!"

Miria looked at Jimmy with a confused face. "You talk so funny, Jimmy. But Beya will show you how to make the water rocks work and please rinse off with the pink water to kill all the…germs."

Jimmy bowed gallantly and went into his pirate talk again. "Aye me lady, we shall scrub our bodies so clean they we shall squeak when we walk!"

Miria started laughing again and took Buddy by the leash to the upper deck. Beya came down quickly carrying a box that Will and Jimmy had never seen before. He opened it and showed them the clothes they were to put on after the shower. He indicated with his hands that their old clothes were to be put in the box after the new clothes were removed.

Jimmy took the box. "Mena Beya." Beya gave a small bow in response. He moved over to the blue rock on the stand behind the screen. With a smaller rock that he took from a nearby table, he held it up for them to see it. He went over to the blue rock and tapped it lightly three times. As if by magic, water started to flow out of it. Both boys looked at it in shock and Beya started to laugh. He then tapped the stone again two times, and it stopped flowing. Jimmy looked at Beya, "Amazing!"

Beya repeated the word slowly, "Amazing."

Jimmy scooped up some water in his hand and pointed. "Water. Water."

Beya repeated the word. "Water. Sala," he repeated back slowly and pointed.

"Sala." Jimmy repeated the word, "Sala. Water is Sala."

Beya and Jimmy smiled at each other knowing slowly they were making connections with each of their worlds.

Will interrupted the word lesson. "Okay, then. I'll go first Jimmy, if you don't mind?"

Jimmy smiled. "Age before beauty, cousin. Age before beauty!"

Will looked at his cousin and smiled. "Yeah bite me, beauty queen." And he started to remove his clothes. It will feel good to get out of these things. We've been in them for longer than a good dance."

Jimmy laughed. "My mother would have a fit if she knew I have worn the same shirt and pants for a week. We won't even talk about the underwear."

As Will stripped down he looked at his clothes "Goodbye Calvin Klein. I'll miss you." And he rolled them up and put them on the floor. Entering the screened in shower he took the small rock and tapped the blue stone three times. Magically, the water came out and to Wills' surprise it wasn't cold. Not hot but definitely not cold. Tepid would be a good description, he thought. As he lathered himself with the bar of soap he began to sing, "Splish, splash, I was taking a bath."

Jimmy cut into the song. "Spare us your vocals, cuz. Stick to Row, Row, Row Your Boat."

Will laughed. "Man, there's always a critic around when you don't need him."

He was totally enjoying the shower when Beya called out to him. Will took this as a sign to hurry up. He grabbed the pink solution and using the sponge that was in the bucket, he rinsed his body down. It tingled a bit and Will wondered what this stuff was made of. He grabbed the large soft towel hanging by the shower and totally dried off before coming around from the screen.

Wrapped in the towel he did a complete turn in front of Beya with a nodding head. "There Beya. Do I look clean enough?" Beya seemed to know what Will said and nodded his approval. Then Jimmy stripped down and folded his clothes neatly on the floor.

Will started to laugh. "Jim, they are going to burn them. What's with the neatness?"

Jimmy laughed. "I don't know. Mom coming through, I guess." Will fell silent at this. He was missing his family too.

Jimmy stepped into the shower and tapped the stone. "Oh

man, this is so cool! I feel like Merlin."

Will chuckled at his cousin as he turned to Beya. "Well, my good man, how are we going to dress me today?"

Beya took out the shirt and pants for Will and to his surprise there was a soft linen-like pair of underwear. "Oh, thank heaven. I thought I was going commando for three years."

He slipped on the clothes and was surprised at how soft they were, and they smelled of lavender. He looked down at the pale yellow shirt which had beautiful stitching on it resembling some flora bush. The pants were black and needed no belt. They just fit snug against his waist. He laughed when he thought of his dad. *Old man stretch pants, who knew!*

Jimmy came out all washed and dried and took a quick look at his cousin. "Hey nice look. Are we going to an Abba concert?"

Will looked at him with a smirk. "Shut up and get dressed!"

Jimmy started to chuckle as Beya handed him his new clothes. "No, dear boy, I'll take mine in a size sixteen, and I prefer a starch collar rather than no collar." Beya stood there holding the clothes wondering what Jimmy just said.

Will took the clothes from Beya and threw them at Jimmy. "Quit being a smart ass and just get dressed."

Jimmy put on his hurt look routine. "Cousin, you hurt me to the core of my being. Calling me names and everything. I'm so saddened by you, my mentor!"

Will just burst out laughing. "I swear, Jimmy, you are comic relief, if nothing else."

Jimmy just smiled at his cousin as if he had won a bet then looking at his clothes said, "Oh underwear! Wasn't expecting that."

He got dressed quickly and admired his soft blue shirt with the embroidered stitching of leaves down the front. The black pants were the same as Will's and Jimmy chuckled at the waist.

He looked at Will, "Yeah, I know. Old man pants."

Jimmy laughed, "Could be worse."

Beya handed them four pieces of soft cloth. Will took them and looked at Beya in puzzlement. Beya took one of the cloth pieces from Will and lay it on the floor. He motioned for him to put his foot on the middle of the cloth. Will did so, then Beya pulled the front up and then flapped the sides over the front flap. He brought out a leather tie and tied it several times around his ankle. Will smiled, "Voila, instant shoe. And real comfy too!"

Jimmy proceeded to put his shoes together. When finished he strutted around like a dancer. "I like these. Mena Beya!"

Beya smiled as he collected their old clothes and shoes in a box for destruction.

Will just smiled his approval at his cousin's new look. "Come on, let's go see Buddy."

Everything on the upper deck was being prepared for removal to the waiting skiffs. The stone boxes were floating along the rail and Will and Jimmy still marvelled at this ingenuity.

Miria came up to the boys and nodded in approval of their new look. "You both look very beautiful."

Jimmy batted his eyes, and Will gave his arm a soft punch. "I think you mean handsome, Miria. Beautiful is for girls and ladies. And may I say, you look beautiful in your new clothes."

Miria blushed at the compliment. "Thank you, Will. We are almost ready to leave the ship. Will you take Buddy, so he is not afraid of the new smaller boat?" Will nodded and untied Buddy and held him close to his body. Buddy whimpered but Will just kept patting his chest to comfort him.

Finally Lian started to shout from the helm and Beya and Donat came towards Jimmy and Will.

Miria turned to them. "It is time to leave. Can you climb down the stairs to the small boat?"

Jimmy looked over the side and was amazed to see the floating boxes were stacked neatly at the back and the front of the skiff.

"No problems, Miria. Will, I'll go first then I'll help you with Buddy."

Will nodded and grabbed a tighter hold of Buddy as he could feel his anticipation. As Jimmy got to the skiff he turned to Will. "Okay, let's lower him down." Will was just about to lead his dog to the edge when Miria touched his arm.

"No, Will, let me do this." With a flat hand over Buddy he levitated from the deck and she slowly placed him over the side and floated him slowly down to the skiff. Will stood there with his mouth open and could not believe what he was seeing.

"Miria, you are amazing!"

She blushed again at his compliment. "It is one of my gifts. Would you like me to lift you?"

Will smiled. "No, really I'm fine. See I'm fine," he said as he headed down the ladder to the skiff.

Miria laughed at his uneasiness. Then she turned to Timtuk looking so handsome in his red shirt and white pants. "Come little brother. It is your turn." She waved her flat hand over his head and slowly levitated him over the side of the skiff. Will reached up to take him, and Timtuk belly laughed at the ride. Will hugged him as he settled him beside Jimmy and Buddy. Miria was next and came down the ladder like a sailor on a mission.

"You've done that before!"

Miria laughed. "A few times."

They all got settled into the skiff, and Beya and Donat came and sat beside them. "What about Lian? Is he not coming?" Will hoped.

Miria smiled. "He will be along after everything is removed

from the ship. It should not be too long."

Will looked at Jimmy and whispered, "Oh goodie. He's still coming with us."

Jimmy started to chuckle knowing how Will felt about this guy. And vice-versa. "You know darn well that we need him. His gift is paramount to our protection." Then going into his English accent he added, "Try to get along with the boy, my dear son. We have such an awfully long journey ahead of us, and I do hate to see my two little ones quarrel."

Will started to laugh. "Yup, comic relief. That's what you are! Oh, Jimmy, if I had to get stuck anywhere, I'm glad I'm stuck with you."

Jimmy was taken aback by the compliment. "Whoa, where did that come from?"

Will looked seriously at Jimmy. "I mean it! If I never told you before, I'm saying it now. You're my best friend as well as my favourite cousin."

Jimmy laughed. "I'm your only cousin!"

Will laughed. "And that makes you my favourite!"

Jimmy looked at Will and said in a very serious tone, "I'm glad I'm stuck with you too, Will. You're more like a brother to me than a cousin. And since Katie came into our lives, you fell off the favourite cousin wagon. She stole it from you, cuz. What can I say? I'm a sucker for cute little babies!"

Will laughed. "Just couldn't give me a complete compliment, could you? Had to use the Katie card, did you?"

Jimmy laughed but playfully bumped his cousin arm with his body. Miria watched this playful banter and smiled. She could feel the love these two young men had for each other, and she knew this would be important for their long journey.

As the skiff drew closer to the city it became brighter and

brighter. Though it looked like the entire city was made of gold, on a closer look, they could see wood incorporated into each building. The dock was a timber walkway with gold bollards stretching on both sides of it. A rope was laced through each bollard preventing someone from falling into the water. The walkway was made for a king. With so much gold sparkling as they walked, it was hard to keep your mouth closed and look completely shell shocked by the vista.

Will whispered to Miria, "Where exactly are we going?"

"To my mother's home before she met my father. I have an aunt who lives there, and she will welcome us into her home for the night."

Jimmy looked at her. "Is there room for all of us?"

Miria laughed. "I think we will all squeeze in."

Will wondered what that meant, but it did not take long before he had the answer. For there in front of him stood a home like a small palace. It's golden columns glistened, and the cone roof rose thirty feet high.

"Is your aunt some kind of queen or something?" asked Jimmy.

Miria just smiled but did not answer, and Will wondered why. On entering the columned walkway to the huge carved golden door, Jimmy started to feel like this was the Land of Oz. Without any attempt to knock on the door, it opened as if it was a shopping mall door. Will looked around for the electronic eye but could not see anything. As they entered the great hall, white linen lace fell from the ceiling and swooped over golden rings hanging on the walls. A beautiful round table was in the centre of the hallway covered with a white table cloth and a vase of fragrant pink flowers. The vase of course was gold. There were paintings on the wall of water scenes, forests, and a cave of lighted stones similar to the first cave Will and Jimmy entered.

A small lady dressed in a white linen dress escorted the group into a room full of flowers and a waterfall fountain. It smelled like a garden of roses and cool from the water feature. Out of nowhere, a voice came from behind them. Miria turned and ran to hug this lovely lady. Obviously the aunt, thought Will. When they were through with the crying and hugging, her aunt turned her attention to Timtuk. She screeched with delight though Timtuk cowered behind Jimmy. Miria laughed as she went to pick him up. She held him close as she introduced him to his aunt. The aunt kissed his forehead and held his little hands in hers.

Miria turned to Jimmy and Will and introduced them to her aunt. At least that is what it looked like to them. She could have said look what I brought for us to eat for supper, and the boys would never know the difference. Will and Jimmy made a small bow to the lady and hoped it seemed sincere to her that they were pleased to make her acquaintance. She smiled at the boys and gestured for them to come with her into another room.

They all followed and were stunned at the size of the dining room table. It had enough chairs for twenty people, and the legs of the table and the chairs were carved in gold. But that was not what really set them back. For on the table was enough food to feed a small army. The aunt gestured for everyone to sit, and it was at that very moment that Will realized they had not had breakfast. With all the excitement of the Golden City, food went right out of their minds. Now here in front of them was a smorgasbord of the most delicious aromas he had ever encountered. They all sat down, the aunt at the head of the table, Miria and Timtuk to her left, Jimmy and Will to her right. Beya and Donat sat at the same side of the table as Will and Jimmy.

Will wondered who was going to sit with Miria and Timtuk. His answer came quickly when Lian entered the dining hall. The aunt stood and gave a hearty hug to welcome him. Will realized the aunt and Lian were good friends. Lian sat down beside Miria and smiled at the aunt as if he was a permanent addition to this family affair. Will growled under his breath.

Jimmy leaned over. "Careful, we need him."

Will looked at Jimmy with that, 'I know but I still hate him' look.

Buddy curled up under the table by Will, and Miria's aunt did not seem to mind. Will smiled as his mother would never let Buddy into the dining room. Taboo in her home rules.

They all followed their aunt's lead as they bowed their head in prayer. When she finished everyone said, "Elaso," including Will and Jimmy. The aunt seemed very pleased with this and smiled approvingly at the boys. Everyone started passing the golden plates of food around the table and each person helped themselves to the delicious lunch.

Timtuk kept the mood light as he made different sounds every time he took a bite of some new food. But when he bit into what looked like a sausage, his nose squinted up and he dropped it out of his mouth like it was a piece of raw liver. Miria began to scold him, but Jimmy and Will could only laugh because they had tasted the sausage, and they didn't like it either. The aunt just made a little fuss about Timtuk, wiped his mouth and gave him a bowl of fruit, which put a beaming smile on his face.

Will thought, *Ya got her kid. Wrap her up and take her home. She's all yours.*

After lunch everyone was escorted to their rooms. Jimmy whispered, "Does she have room for us? She could put up half this city in here. Will, what does this woman do?"

Will looked at Jimmy. "I don't know, but it has to be something important. I'll ask Miria as soon as I get her alone."

Jimmy snickered. "Yeah, good luck with that. Lian's hooks

seem to go far around here."

Will growled under his breath again.

Will and Jimmy were led to the left side of the spiral staircase. Miria, Timtuk and her aunt went up to the right. Will gave a sigh of relief when Lian was led to the left side as well. When they were shown their room both boys exclaimed "Holy Moly!"

Their room was made for a king. They had adjoining bedrooms, but they shared a common room with two large couches and two oversized easy chairs. Pillows were on the floor as well, and Jimmy jumped into them like it was a foam pit at a gymnastic studio. The rooms were painted white with gold encrusting the moldings. Soft white linen hung from the windows, and the view outside was to a courtyard with fountains and flowers. Each bedroom had a large bed with a mattress covered in a goose down blanket. There were white and blue pillows accenting the blue throw spread at the end of each bed.

Jimmy looked at Will. "Oh man, I'm going to sleep like a baby. How about you?"

Will smiled. "It feels like a year since we've been in a bed. I can't believe it's only been a week."

Jimmy put on his old man voice. "Yup, old man. These bones ain't what they used to be. My lumbago has been bothering me lately. Must be rain coming."

Will looked at his cousin, put his hand over his mouth and started to laugh. "Do you ever quit?"

Jimmy held up his hand and pretended to have a cigar in it. "I've got a million of them, cuz. Wait for the dinner show."

Just as Will was about to throw a pillow at Jimmy, there was a knock on the door. Will went to answer and was pleased to see Miria standing outside their room.

"Come in, come in," he said.

"I just came to see if you were happy with your room and if you need anything."

Jimmy shouted out, "Happy? It's the Ritz, Four Seasons and The Astor all rolled up in one big present. Miria, what does your aunt do? She must be someone very important to this city to live in such affluence."

Miria sat down on the couch and gestured for the boys to join her. Buddy came and lay at her feet. She smiled at him.

"My grandmother, my mother, my aunt and myself are all healers."

Will looked at her. "You mean like healing the sick?"

She nodded her head. "And more than that. If you have a bad cut on your body, I can heal it immediately. No scar, no pain. If you are very sick inside your body, it may take a few days, but I can heal you."

Will looked at her. "This is your special gift, isn't it?"

She nodded. "As well as making heavy things float, but many people can do this."

Jimmy looked at her. "Really? Can you teach us?"

"It took me five years to master the gift. I don't think you could learn it in our short time together, but I will show you how we do it. It will be up to you to master the gift."

Jimmy jumped in the air. "All right! Now we're talking?"

Miria scrunched up her nose and looked at Will. "Yes, we are talking. What does he mean?"

Will chuckled again. "He means he's excited about trying this new technique of yours. I mean gift of yours. Sorry about the big word, Miria."

Miria looked at him. "Technique. What does this mean?"

"Your ability to show us how you do something. It becomes your technique for us to follow."

"It sounds like a word the magic men would use."

Will nodded. "Very much so."

"If you are not too tired, would you like to come with me and walk the city streets?" asked Miria

Both boys jumped up and said, "Yes!" in unison. "Can Buddy come, or will he be a problem?" Will asked.

"No, bring Buddy. He will have many new smells to sniff and people to pat him," said Miria.

All four of them walked out of the house and into a whole new world. Together the journey continues and their lives will be forever changed.

CHAPTER TWENTY-TWO

Carol came out of the bedroom and joined Jenny in the kitchen.

"Morning, Carol. Coffee?"

Carol settled down on a kitchen chair. "Love one. How are you this morning?" Jenny putting a mug of coffee in front of Carol, sat down on a chair across the table from her.

"I had a restless night. But I think that's standard for any mother worried about her son. How about you?"

Carol said after taking a sip from the mug, "I don't think I slept a wink all night. Jenny, I'm going through every emotion in the book."

Jenny sat up and leaned on the table. "You and Fred were by the fire pit for a long time last night. Care to share with me?"

Carol blushed and Jenny stared to laugh. "I knew something was brewing between you two. Steve thought I was nuts, but you can't fool a woman's intuition. Come on, spill the beans."

Carol covered her face with her hands. "Oh Jenny, this is the last thing I thought would happen to me. I come up to find my son and find a new love instead. Can this get any more bizarre?"

Jenny came flying out of her chair and hugged Carol with the might of a bear.

"Oh honey, love doesn't have a road map or calendar. It shows up wherever and whenever you least expect it. I'm so happy for you. Now tell me, did he kiss you?"

Carol blushed and smiled. "He kisses real nice. And just being held in his arms, everything just seemed so right."

Jenny got up and refilled her coffee mug. "Is he coming back this morning?"

Carol smiled. "Yes, he said he wants to be with us when we talk to the professor. He really likes him. Finds him fascinating to talk to."

Jenny chuckled. "I find him a little absent-minded. Do you know he left his socks in the bathroom? Why would he take his socks off in the house? And why did he not notice when he walked outside to the trailer? You got to admit, Carol, he's a few bottles short of a six-pack."

Carol laughed. "You should see his apartment. You can't find a place to sit. Everything is covered in papers and books. Plates with old food are left everywhere. I think he has someone to do his laundry, but he has a pile of clothes four feet high in the hall closet. At least it's been there every time I've been to the apartment. We tried to talk him into a housekeeper, but he just about had a fit at the thought. Don't mess up his file system! But we have people bring him meals three times a week. There's always plenty of food to last him over the weekend. So we know the old guy is kept fed and clean, has a roof over his head and he is happy with his research. What more can you ask for?"

Jenny smiled and shrugged her shoulders. "If he's happy, I'm happy! Would you like some breakfast? Steve and Katie left early to go check on the fire line in the valley. They should be back within an hour. Would you like me to make some pancakes, French toast or is it a fruit and yogurt morning?"

Carol perked up. "Oh fruit and yogurt would be just perfect. But don't tell Fred. I think that man eats a lumberjack breakfast every day. I can't eat like that first thing in the morning."

Jenny laughed. "It's the mountain air. Brings out the appetite in all of us. Even you, kiddo. And any other appetite you might have." Carol blushed again and drank up her coffee. "I'm so embarrassed." Jenny laughed and hugged her sister-in-law once again.

* * *

Fred arrived about an hour after Carol's breakfast and morning rituals: shower, hair, make-up. When he saw her come out to greet him, he couldn't help but whistle and give her a big hug. Carol felt wonderful in his arms.

Jenny came out and stopped dead in her tracks as she stumbled upon this scene. "All right you two, get a room!"

Fred laughed as he set Carol back on her feet, "Can we use yours?"

Carol gave him a playful punch in the arm. "Behave yourself! Jenny, my apologies for this big bear with no manners."

Fred just smiled. "Bears have no manners. We just steal picnic baskets and beautiful ladies' hearts." Carol blushed and he put his arms around her and walked her towards the trailer. He looked at Jenny and then around the yard for Steve's truck. "Steve not here?"

Jenny shook her head. "He should be back any minute." Just as she said this, Steve pulled into the driveway. As he got out of the truck Jenny searched for Katie.

He smiled at her in reassurance. "Met the Patterson family at the gas station. They asked if Katie could come for a playdate. I thought it would be good to keep her life as normal as possible. That okay with you, Mom?"

Jenny smiled, "A-OK Dad! Good call. When do they want us to pick her up?"

Steve smiled. "Gerry said he would drive her home after dinner. She was thrilled!"

Jenny was happy that Katie was oblivious to any of this nightmare. As far as she was concerned, the boys were on a camping trip. And Jenny was determined to keep this up for a little while longer. After that, she didn't know how to explain this to her. She and Steve had not thought that one through yet.

Steve stopped in his tracks when he noticed Fred's arm around Carol. He looked at Jenny with a confused look, and she smiled at him.

"Don't look so surprised. I told you I had a feeling something was up. And you told me it was just wishful thinking. Well, my wish came true."

She gloated as she smiled. Steve walked over to Fred and put his hand out for a shake. "Guess that pep talk last night got to you. You know, old bachelors and stuff."

Fred laughed as he grabbed his hand. "Yeah, that was it." Both men laughed and gave each other the one arm hug and pat on the back.

Carol laughed too. "What about me? Do I get a hug too?" Steve reached for her and gave her a big hug taking her feet right off the ground.

Carol screamed, "Oh, my God. I wasn't expecting that!"

Steve looked at her and then at Fred. "You two will be good for each other, but I'm not sure how the demographics are going to work for you."

Carol laughed. "Slow down, Steve. This just happened last night. We're not talking marriage or anything right now. Give us time to figure it out; okay?"

Everyone smiled at each other, and then the professor opened the trailer door.

"Oh, good morning everyone. Come in, come in. I have so much to show you."

The four of them followed the professor into the trailer. When Jenny stepped in she gasped at the tornado of destruction in front of her.

Steve hugged her close and whispered, "It's okay, honey. It's just papers and books. When he leaves, it will all go with him." She sighed and nodded her head in agreement, but the shock still stayed on her face.

Carol chuckled and whispered to her, "At least there is not four feet of laundry by the front door."

Jenny whispered back, "Are you sure? Have you looked in the closet?"

Carol snickered. "Not me. Haven't had my shots lately."

Jenny chuckled under her breath.

"Now ladies, if you would take your seats, we shall begin." Carol and Jenny looked at Steve with the 'where' look. He opened the closet and took out the two folding chairs from the night before. Steve set them up over the professor's books he had piled on the floor and the mothers gingerly sat down. Fred and Steve just leaned against the walls.

The professor looked up from his papers. "There now. Shall we begin?"

"Begin what, Professor?" Carol asked.

"Why the proof I have that your boys are safe and will return to you in three years' time. Are you ready?"

Jenny and Carol looked at each other, took a deep breath and said in unison, "Absolutely!"

"Good," said the professor. "Now let's begin."

"It was nearly thirty years ago that I was a part of an expedition in Utah. We were in the Uinta Mountain region looking for any proof that the Aztec Indians had truly come this far north from Mexico. We were there for about eight months with absolutely no proof of their existence. Then one cold morning I was looking among some berry patches when lo and behold I found what we had sought for so many months. Can you guess as to what it is I found?"

Carol and Jenny looked at each other and nodded before Carol looked at the professor. "The same mark that we found here?"

With a wink and a smile the professor jumped up. "Exactly! But I didn't understand it's true meaning until years later, but I took these photos of it."

He handed each one of them a photo of the jaguar and snake exactly like the one they found on the rock where the boys disappeared.

Fred examined the photo then handed it back to the professor. "So Professor, when did you discover the meaning of the symbols?"

The professor started scrambling about for more papers.

"Look here, these are the photos I took in Peru. Twenty-four years ago I was with another expedition looking for more proof that the Aztec people came south as well as north. Things were not going very well, but I was determined to stay long after our expedition group left. I got to know the local people. They welcomed me into their lives, and I became very fond of these lovely people. When I showed them the symbols I found in Utah, one very old man told me I had found the womb to the earth. A link to the sacred caves.

"About three years later I heard of two young people terrified of the cave they found near the lake. The young man was about to enter it until his sister convinced him to get their father. As they were just about to leave they said a beautiful young woman emerged from the cave and smiled at the children. She took some plants that the children had not noticed were bundled nearby. As she took the plants, she stopped and walked over to the children and gave them each a shiny stone. When she re-entered the cave, they said it just melted shut, like a candle melting in a fire. Of course they ran back to their family to tell them what happened. But of course no one would believe them.

"When I heard of the story, I jumped into my jeep and drove the fifty miles to this village. I desperately wanted to speak to these children. At first, the father did not want me to talk to them. He felt like I was encouraging their fantasy.

But he finally relented, and I asked the children to show me where they saw the cave opening and the lady. It did not take us long to reach the site, but the girl would not go near it, and I asked her why? Apparently, she got a huge shock the last time they were there, and she was frightened."

Carol sat up and leaned towards the professor. "Professor, Jenny and I were getting shocks near the mark of the cave. But only us, not Steve or Fred. What does that mean?"

The professor stood up and rustled more papers. "Apparently, there is an electrical jolt that can only be felt by the females of our species. Males do not experience this discomfort. I believe it has something to do with the chromosomes. Men have the XY chromosome and women only the XX chromosome. Leading the circuit, so to speak, to attach itself to this lone chromosome. However, with each passing day the circuit gets less powerful. I doubt you and Miss Jenny would feel anything now, it's been over a week since it closed.

"The children I spoke with could not give me the exact day of the cave closure, but I do know it was in August, eighteen years ago. Leading my research to conclude it will open again in three years' time."

Steve straightened up. "Professor, what proof have you that it will open in three years?"

The professor looked at Steve as if he was insulted by the question.

"The pattern, my good man. The pattern. I was searching in an old church just outside Mexico City, and I happened upon this extraordinary book. The Padre was kind enough to allow me to have it. Inside -- here it is, I found this chart. You see, the jaguar and the serpent and around them the paths of the seven sacred caves. Around that it divides into three segments around each path. This represents three years. Around this is the final circle broken into twenty-one years. My research points only to this conclusion. There are seven sacred caves, each opening in a three-year pattern, in a circle of twenty-one years. I now know that your cave will open twenty-one years from now. The portal in Peru is due next since that is the next twenty-one-year cycle. I do not know the pattern of the portal in Mexico nor the one in Utah. But I know the portal in Peru is next because I was there."

Jenny cleared her throat. "Professor, you say you have proof that our boys are safe. Please tell us how."

"Ah, yes." The professor looked through his pile of photos.

"The stones the children received. They are known as Philo Stones, given to people travelling from village to village over a thousand years ago. It was a sign of peace and goodwill. No danger from the carrier. Those stones the children received are like the ones in a museum in Mexico City. There is nothing like them found anymore, and yet a lady gave two of them to the children. I believe she wanted the children and their people to understand they mean no harm or ill will."

Fred looked at the photos and then at the professor. "And you believe the boys are with these people right now."

The professor nodded. "Absolutely, old boy, and as safe with them as I am with you."

Steve moved forward and stood behind Jenny. "Professor, you were in Utah thirty years ago. Did you miss the opening of that portal?"

The Seven Sacred Caves

The professor gave a huge sigh. "Alas dear boy, I did. I did not understand the pattern until years later. I missed the timeline. And I also do not know the whereabouts of the last three caves, so calculating would only be speculative. But I can guarantee you that the next portal will be in Peru, by Lake Titicaca in three years' time. If the boys make it, they will emerge from this portal."

Jenny and Carol both shivered at the thought that the boys would not make it in time.

Jenny looked at Steve. "How far away is Peru from here?"

Steve and Fred both looked at each other and shrugged before Steve spoke. "About eight thousand miles give or take."

Carol put her face in her hands. "How can they do this? They are only kids!"

The professor took Carol's hands from her face and smiled. "These kids are with good people. Trust your instincts, Carol. They will make it. Have faith in your boys."

She looked into the eyes of this soft-spoken gentle man and her fear melted away.

"Okay, Professor, if you say they are safe, I believe you."

And then the professor did something totally out of character. He hugged Carol.

CHAPTER TWENTY-THREE

The first thing Will noticed was the ceiling of the cave, which had to be three hundred feet high. But it was the colour of the sky and the feeling that you were outside was so overwhelming. Clouds were interspersed throughout the cave.

"Miria, did someone paint the ceilings of the cave?"

Miria laughed. "Many people did this. About two hundred years ago they decided to bring the sky back to us with the proper paint and lights from the stones. I think it is very nice, don't you?"

Jimmy piped in. "It's amazing. It reminds me of Vegas at the Caesar's Palace."

Miria looked at Jimmy. "You have been to a palace?"

Jimmy laughed. "Not the kind that you are thinking of. More like a large building for people to come, stay overnight and take a holiday."

Miria nodded. "Sounds very nice."

Jimmy smiled and nodded. Then he stopped in front of a vendor where small trees were growing out of large rocks.

"Whoa, Will. Take a look at this."

Will holding Buddy on the leash walked over to the vendor. He took one look at Buddy and began to back away in fear. Miria held her hand up and spoke to the man, explaining Buddy was totally harmless and asked him to come and touch him if he would like. The man shook his head at first, but Miria's gentle voice guided him slowly towards Buddy. Buddy took his cue and began to wag his tail. The man slowly touched Buddy's head, and Buddy sat and enjoyed the attention. The man laughed and crouched down to Buddy's face. Without a moment to spare Buddy gave this man a great big lick. The man fell back on his butt and began to laugh as Buddy came forward, wagging his tail and going in for another face lick. But Will held him back and Jimmy helped the man up onto his feet.

The man told Miria that he would like to give the boys a gift and handed them a small bonsai tree growing out of a rock.

Will smiled at the man as he handed it to him and said, "Mena, mena!"

The man looked pleased at Will and nodding his head said, "Pasha."

Miria smiled. "That means you are welcome."

Will looked at the bonsai tree. "Man, this is so cool. A tree growing out of a rock."

They continued on down through the marketplace. Jimmy stopped to look at some carvings from the most colourful crystal stones. Some were small and would fit in your hand, others were about three to five feet tall. One was carved like a fir tree that sparkled from the light of the cave.

"Hey Will, instant Christmas Tree."

Will admired the work and shook his head. "I'd love to buy this for Mom but two things come to mind. One, we can't drag that thing for three years and two, we have no currency. Come to think of it, Miria, what do you do to buy these things?"

"Remember, we trade. We have the light stones. They are only found in my village, so they are valuable to trade. I think that I would like to get one of these carvings for my aunt as a gift. Which one should I get her?"

Both boys pointed to the fir tree they had just been admiring. Will said, "The Christmas Tree, but can you afford it?"

Miria turned to talk to the man selling the carvings. His eyes lit up when she produced three stones from her satchel. She gave him the stones and exchanged more words. She smiled and began to walk away. Jimmy and Will both looked confused.

"I have asked him to take it to my aunt's house for us. It is very heavy."

"Three stones and free delivery. Good deal Miria, said Will."

She laughed at these words. Suddenly they heard what sounded like firecrackers just down the street. When they walked towards the sound, they were astonished by the sight before them. The sound was coming from a firecracker, but it did not explode into lights but rather in scenes. For above them was a waterfall coming out of a large cave. You could almost believe it was real. Then it melted and bang another scene appeared. This was deep inside a cave grotto with deep blue water and stylolites decorating the grotto. It was breathtaking. Then it melted and bang, another scene. This was of a city that looked like it was covered in snow.

Will looked at Miria and asked, "You get snow down here?"

She smiled and shook her head. "It is a fine rock that is mined far from here."

Jimmy looked at her. "It's sand Will. This village is covered in sand."

Miria nodded. "Yes, sand. That's the word. The village is empty; no one can live there now. It is in the dead area."

Will and Jimmy both looked at her before Jimmy spoke. "The dead area. What's that?"

Miria began to walk slowly down the street. "Your people

destroyed this area. Many years ago, long before my mother was born. There were large bangs that shook this part of our world very badly. It destroyed that city as the sand fell and blew all over it. The people were all killed and many men and women got very sick when they entered this city to help. Even the healer could not save anyone. They were badly burned or their insides were too sick to cure. We call it the dead city, and we are forbidden to enter into the area. To do so would still make you very sick."

Jimmy and Will were silent for a moment when Jimmy snapped his fingers. "Nevada. The nuclear testing in the fifties or early sixties. God, Will, they destroyed a whole colony of people. And for what? So they could test their precious toys. What a waste!"

Jimmy started to walk away, angry at the stupidity and devastation.

Will came over to Miria and put his arm around her. "Miria, I'm so sorry. Our people are far from perfect and the destruction of this village was accidental. Stupid but accidental. Remember, we don't know you exist. But I can assure you, there will be no more testing like that. They realized that it is too dangerous for our environment. Our people got sick too."

Miria hugged Will. "This is good, Will. I am happy to know that it will never happen again."

Will smiled at her and started to walk down the street towards Jimmy.

"Come on, Jimmy is pretty hot under the collar. Let's go cool him off."

Miria laughed. "What does this mean, Will?"

"Jimmy's mad, and we need to make him happy again."

"Oh, I know just how to do this. Come, we can have some fun."

She pulled his hands and grabbed Jimmy's hand as she approached him.

"Come, I want us to have some fun. Follow me."

She led them to a small opening in the cave and they had to duck their heads to enter. Miria spoke to the man inside the cave and handed him a small light stone from her satchel. She turned to the boys. "Come, I think you will like this."

They followed her deeper into the cave and came to an edge that looked about fifty feet deep. Will and Jimmy looked down the edge before Will spoke,

"Ah Miria, what are we doing here?"

Without saying a word, she dropped her satchel on the ground and threw herself over the ledge. Will and Jimmy both screamed her name and looked over the edge. There was Miria bouncing and floating in thin air.

She was laughing and cried out, "Come on, jump. It is safe. I promise you."

Jimmy and Will stood there with their mouths open and then looked at each other.

Without hesitation they both shouted, "Geronimo," and jumped over the ledge. They bounced, they screamed in delight, going upside down, making somersaults.

"It has to be like sky diving but with no parachutes," shouted Jimmy.

Buddy lay at the edge and peered over at the sight. He whimpered and whined, but Will kept yelling at him to relax, and he finally settled down. Will whooped and hollered in delight and Miria laughed at their gymnastic skills.

After about twenty minutes Miria shouted, "Watch me and I will show you how to get out of here."

She pushed herself slowly to the edge of the rock and jumped with all her might and landed on the edge where they started.

"Now you do it. Push off hard from the wall and aim for the edge."

Jimmy nodded and went first. He held on to the side and took a huge spring to the edge. Unfortunately, he missed by about ten feet.

Miria laughed. "Try again. You'll get it."

Jimmy took up the challenge as Will just smiled, and bounced upside down in front of him. Jimmy curled his lip in anger and growled a bit, and then he took a huge push upward. This time he was successful and he cheered as he looked at Will. "Your turn."

Will turned himself upright and went to the side of the cave. With a deep breath he took a huge push off the side and landed directly in front of Miria and Jimmy.

"Piece of cake," he gloated to Jimmy.

"Lucky. That's all!" Jimmy protested.

Will looked at Miria. "That was awesome! How does it work?"

She shrugged her shoulders. "The magic men found it. It has no value but is fun. Did you have fun?"

Both boys yelled in unison. "Absolutely! That was unbelievable."

"Good. Now I believe we must return to my aunt's home for dinner. Are you ready?"

Both boys nodded and smiled and followed Miria from the small cave.

✳ ✳ ✳

When they returned to Miria's aunt home Lian was waiting for them at the front gate. Will sarcastically said, "Ah oh, I think Daddy is mad at us. Stayed out past our curfew."

Miria looked at Will with a confused face but answered Lian with a smile and a salutation. Lian, however, was angry and started to speak to Miria in a very nasty tone. Miria was taken aback by this greeting, and you could see her back stiffen with anger. She laced into Lian with everything she had within her. Will and Jimmy could tell by the tone and face this was a knock-out drag out fight.

Will started to chuckle under his breath. "Atta girl, Miria. Don't take any crap from the army."

Jimmy turned to him and said, "Shhh." But Will only looked at him with that, 'What did I do?' look.

Lian finally shut his mouth and stormed away. Miria looked down at the ground, took a deep breath and then turned to face the boys. "Come, dinner is prepared."

The boys just looked at each other but knew better than to discuss what just happened. Let her cool off was their quiet response. Miria just looked straight ahead and headed for her bedroom.

"Please clean up before we enter the dining room. Clean clothes have been put on your beds. I'll meet you back here in thirty minutes."

She did not wait for them to respond, and Will was sure he could see tears welling in her eyes as she ran up the stairs.

"That creep. He's always ragging on her. What's his problem anyway?"

Jimmy looked at his cousin. "Oh, I dunno. Maybe he's a tiny bit jealous of us He-Men stealing his girl. If he could, he'd pee on her for ownership."

Will looked at Jimmy. "She says we need him. For what?"

Jimmy looked at Will. "Oh, I dunno. That big snake scared the poop out of me. I was really glad Lian was on our side at that moment."

Will rubbed his forehead. "Okay, point taken. We need the jerk and his fire throwing skills, but where is it written that he has to get Miria so mad. You know darn well it was about us. He can't stand us!"

Jimmy smiled. "Then we will just have to earn his love and respect," he said, fluttering his eyes at Will.

Will muttered, "Three years won't be long enough to earn that. Besides, who needs it?"

"Come on, we have to get cleaned up. Don't want Miria mad at us, do we?"

Will gave a quiet grunt but followed his cousin up to their room.

***

Miria was waiting at the bottom of the stairs as Jimmy and Will descended to her. She was dressed in a sky blue dress with gold lace embroidered at the collar and down the sleeves. Her hair was off her shoulders and a sheer scarf was wrapped over it and then over her shoulder. She looked stunning. Will was just about to compliment her when Lian came down the stairs and started speaking before anyone else. Miria blushed but turned her back to him and greeted Will and Jimmy.

"You both look very nice. Shall we go for dinner?"

Will held up his arm for her. She looked at him confused. He smiled and took her hand and slipped it around his arm. She smiled at him and together they walked into the dining room, arm in arm. Jimmy looked at Lian and gallantly held out his arm. Lian just pushed past him.

"Why, sir, you wound me." Jimmy chuckled as he followed Lian.

Miria's aunt was standing by the tree Miria had bought that morning. She ran over and gave her niece a huge hug, and they could tell by the way she was speaking that she loved it.

Miria looked at the boys. "She said she will cherish this since it was from all of us. And she thanks you for your good taste in gifts. It's perfect."

Will and Jimmy both looked at her and in unison said, "Pasha."

The aunt seemed even more pleased with their response. She took their hands and motioned for them to sit in the chairs on each side of her. Will could see Lian's back stiffen. Will just smiled smugly and enjoyed the attention.

All at once Timtuk came flying in with Buddy running at his heels. He jumped into Miria's arms with a scream of glee. She gave him a big hug and kiss and settled him down on a chair beside Will and she sat down beside him. Beya and Donat came in with smiles and salutations and Miria's aunt motioned them to the two chairs, one by Miria the other by Jimmy. Lian was motioned to the chair by Donat on Jimmy's side of the table.

Will smiled smugly and knew that auntie was aware of the little outburst in her courtyard. Lian was being put in his place very subtly. He liked her aunt more now than ever.

❋ ❋ ❋

After dinner Lian, Donat and Beya went to check on the supplies they would need on the next leg of their expedition. Jimmy and Timtuk went upstairs to play with Buddy, and Will and Miria strolled outside on the terrace.

Will said, "Do you want to talk about it?"

She looked out at the gardens and shook her head. Then she sighed and looked straight at him. "Lian is trying to make me feel bad about showing you and Jimmy our world. But that is not what is bothering him. He believes you have feelings for me. The feelings he wants me to have for him. I do not have them for him, he is so…"

Will jumped in, "Conceited, pig-headed, stubborn, a dick. Please choose one you like or all of the above."

Miria started to laugh. "Oh Will, you and Jimmy make me laugh so much. I don't think I have laughed so much since…"

She fell silent.

Will looked at her, "Since your father was alive?"

She nodded. "He was so much fun, Will. I miss him so much. I miss both my parents. They would have liked you."

Will smiled at her. "Miria, Lian is not wrong. I do have feelings for you. I was kind of wondering how do you feel about me?"

She looked into his eyes. "I feel warm and happy when I am with you. I cannot wait for morning, so I may see you again. I think my heart stops a beat sometimes when I see you. Do you have the same feelings?"

Will slowly pulled her into his arms and kissed her softly on the lips. He gently released her, so she could look into his eyes.

"Like you were reading my mind."

She smiled and wrapped her arms around his neck and kissed him with a soft passion, and Will's head started to spin like he was back in the jumping cave. And his arms held her tight.

CHAPTER TWENTY-FOUR

They followed each other out of the trailer, Carol was the first to speak.

"I feel sick. What are we to do for the next three years? Are we to pretend this isn't happening? How do we explain this to our family and friends? Somebody please help me."

Fred grabbed Carol and put her into his arms. "We'll figure it out, Carol. Together. All four of us."

He continued to hug her and tears began to fall down her face.

Jenny turned to Steve. "Honey, what do we tell Katie? I won't tell her Will's missing and let her think he's dead. But if all her friends know he is missing, they are going to convince her he's gone forever."

Steve pulled Jenny into his arms. "Jen, we have to think of a logical story to tell her to convince her he's not gone forever. And we must ask her to keep it a secret from her friends. What choice do we have?"

Jenny shook her head. "She's eight years old, Steve. Eight-year-old kids are not noted for keeping secrets for very long. I don't know if this could work."

Fred looked at Jenny and Steve. "We have to make it work. Katie is a smart kid. We have to make sure she understands the seriousness of this situation."

Carol blurted out, "Situation? Is that what this is? A situation." Jenny shook her head. "No, it's a damn calamity. And I can't believe we have to wait three years before we can fix it. And then how do we explain their miraculous reappearance? And from Peru of all places. Steve, Carol, we are going to have to protect our boys from this situation! If the press ever hears of this story, their lives will become a nightmare. They will never leave them alone. And the people they are with, what about them? According to the professor they've been hidden for a thousand years. They don't want to have their lives changed by us, I'm pretty sure."

Everyone fell silent and just looked at each other. Jenny finally broke the silence.

"Coffee, we need coffee. Then we can sit and try to make up a good story for Katie and for Carol's mom."

Carol groaned. "Oh my lord, my mother. This will be a challenge. I never got away with anything as a kid. She always knew when I was stretching the truth." Everyone looked at Carol. "Okay, also known as lying. The point is, she knows I'm a terrible liar, and she'll see right through me."

Fred looked straight into her eyes. "Then we tell her the truth. She'll protect her grandson, knowing how important this will be to his wellbeing when he returns home."

Steve and Jenny looked at each other before Steve spoke. "Fred's right. I think we should tell Katie the truth and let her know it's imperative to keep it a secret, for Will and Jimmy's safety. I trust her Jenny, don't you?"

Jenny nodded her head. "But it's such a lot of information to put on her plate. Can she handle it?"

Steve held her hand. "Then we give it to her in small doses. The main thing for her to understand is that Will and Jimmy are alive and will come back to us. Isn't that the most important thing for her to know?"

Jenny and Carol both nodded and said, "Absolutely!"

"Then that's what we'll do. Now how about that coffee, Jenny. I could sure use a strong cup. Maybe with a shot of whiskey to make it a Good Attitude coffee," Steve laughed.

"It must be five o'clock somewhere," added Fred, laughing.

* * *

Fred held Carol's hand as they walked along the stream at the back of Steve and Jenny's property. Neither spoke. They just listened to the birds and the wind rustle the trees.

Finally Carol spoke quietly. "I forget how beautiful it is up here. Always knew why Mike liked to come back to visit. I was always grateful that he chose Vancouver and me over the wilderness."

Fred felt a thud in his stomach but chose to change the subject.

"How did you and Mike meet?"

Carol smiled. "At university. He was studying engineering, and I was studying law. The big dummy knocked over all my books at the library. He said it was an accident, but I think it was just him trying to break the ice and meet me. But he would never admit to that or deny it for that matter. Anyway, one thing led to another, and we got engaged. We graduated, and I was offered an excellent position at my law firm. Mike and I agonized over what to do. I knew he wanted to come back here and work as a civil and structural engineer for the government. But that job takes you everywhere, so we decided to make Vancouver our home base. That way I could have my job, and he could have his job wherever it took him. And believe me, he was all over the province."

Fred just smiled. "And when did Jimmy come along?"

"About three years later. Believe me, he was a surprise package.

But I got into the mother thing pretty quick. My firm was excellent with my maternity leave. And when I returned, they allowed me to work three days a week for the first two years. That's when I got Jimmy into a fantastic daycare, and I could go back to full time work. Everything was going great. Mike was home supervising a job in Richmond, I was working with a great new client and Jimmy was thriving in preschool. All was wonderful until the constable came to our door. My life crashed. My mother, bless her heart, stayed with me for three months while I tried to get my life in order. And slowly, very slowly I did. Steve and Jenny have taken Jimmy every summer since he was six years. He loves it up here, and I know Mike would have totally approved. And now another crash. But this one is different, Fred."

Fred looked at her waiting for her to finish her thoughts.

"This one is different. Jimmy is not dead, just a little lost according to the professor. And in this nightmare, I found you."

He stepped closer to her and kissed her with the same passion as their first kiss. He held her close but looked into her face. "You will never be alone again. That's my promise to you. But Carol, we do have to talk about where you want this relationship to go."

Carol frowned before she spoke. "I'm not sure what you mean."

Fred walked to a downed tree and sat down on the trunk, patted the spot beside him and Carol sat down.

"Carol, I can't survive in the city. My life and work is here. The city is okay to visit, but I can't wait to get back to this life. I hate the traffic, the noise, the smells and worst of all, the bright lights. No stars at night. I think I'd go mad without star gazing. Honey, I want you with me. I really do. But can you be happy up here with me?"

Carol crawled into his arms and sat on his lap.

"I have to take the professor home. I'll have to talk to my boss and his partners. But honestly, I settle most cases. If I have a computer and the internet I can do eighty percent of it from a home office. I know I'll have to go down at least one week per month, but I think we can live with that can't we?"

Fred looked into her face. "You've been thinking about this, haven't you?"

Carol laughed. "Didn't sleep a wink last night thinking about it. But I wanted to hear what you wanted before I opened my mouth."

Fred grinned. "Oh, and it's such a pretty mouth." And he gave her another long sensuous kiss.

"Should we tell Steve and Jenny or just let them stay in the dark a little while longer?" she chuckled.

"Let them wait. They have enough to deal with, Katie and all. How about I take you and the professor to dinner, so they can have some alone time with Katie?"

Carol looked at him incredulously. "You know Fred for someone who doesn't have children, you sure are thoughtful."

He chuckled. "Yeah, a regular Santa Claus. Now what about dinner?"

"I'd love it, but the professor will have no part of it. So, I'll make him something to eat in his trailer, and we can go out after that; okay?"

He nodded. "Sounds good to me. And I know just where I'll take you."

"Where," she asked.

"Nope, gonna surprise you!"

"Okay. What should I wear?"

He smiled devilishly. "Oh honey, with that question I might just take you to my house and have you leave your clothes at the door."

She gave a huge laughing breath. "Down boy, I like the romance first. So I take it, casual dress would be appropriate?"

He laughed. "Casual dress is all that is appropriate up here!"

She laughed. "I have so much to learn. City girl trying to become country girl. But I don't care how long I live up here, I'll always wear my make-up, do my hair and watch my weight. Deal?"

He laughed. "Deal! But that doesn't include yogurt, does it?"

Carol laughed hysterically. "And raw vegetables too. You will learn to eat a bit healthier; okay?"

Fred started to grumble. "Maybe I should think this over." He started to laugh as she hit him in the arm.

He grabbed her and hugged and kissed her with as much tenderness as an old wilderness man could muster.

***

Gerry Patterson drove into the driveway and stopped in front of the house. Katie hopped from the car and ran up to the front steps. Steve stepped out and gave his daughter a warm hug and waved at Gerry.

"Thanks, buddy. Do you want to come in for coffee?"

Gerry shook his head. "Rain check; okay? Got to get back to the family, bathing the twins is a two-man job."

Steve laughed. "Thanks for having Katie over. We'll have you and Gail over soon for a game of cards and munchies; okay?"

Gerry laughed. "Oh, we'd love a night out. Let us know, so I can bribe at least a few babysitters in our neighbourhood."

Steve laughed "You got it, buddy. I'll have Jenny call Gail."

Gerry drove off and waved as he honked goodbye.

Steve turned to Katie. "Did you have fun, sweetheart?"

Katie beamed. "Oh yeah, and those babies are so cute, Daddy. Do you think we could have a baby, Daddy?"

Steve stopped in his tracks. "Ah. Yeah, fine with me but we need to talk to your mother." He picked up Katie and threw her over his shoulders with her screaming in glee.

***

After her shower Jenny rubbed Katie's head with a soft towel. She smiled at her daughter and gave her a hug.

"Oh, you smell so nice. I like the smell of a clean on you, Katie."

Katie laughed and then became a little quiet. "Mommy, Hannah said something to me today that really scared me."

Jenny took a big gulp. "What did she say?"

Katie looked at her with tears forming at the sides of her eyes. "She said Will is lost and probably dead. Oh Mommy, that's not true, is it?"

Jenny held Katie in her arms and rocked her back and forth on the bathroom floor.

Jenny took a big breath and said, "No, Katie. That's not true. And Mommy and Daddy are going to talk with you about what has happened; okay. Now look at me."

Katie turned her tear-stained face up to her mother.

"Katie, what we are going to tell you is real grown-up stuff. It will be a little hard to understand, but I'm begging you, sweetheart, try to understand. But I give you my cross my heart promise, Will and Jimmy are not dead. Okay?"

She sniffed and then nodded her head. "Okay, Mommy, but are they lost?"

Jenny looked up to the ceiling. "Let's get your nightgown on and then go talk to Daddy."

Katie looked at her mother. "Are you mad at me, Mommy?"

Jenny hugged Katie again. "No, sweetie, never. Let's just go get dressed for bed and have a family talk; okay?"

Katie smiled. "Okay, Mommy."

***

Steve sat Katie on his lap with Jenny sitting right beside them rubbing her knee.

"Okay, Doodlebug. Mommy and I have some real important stuff to talk to you about. It's about Will and Jimmy."

Katie chimed in. "They're not dead, but are they lost?"

Steve shook his head slowly. "Not really. We know where they are, but we can't get to them. The boys are on a big adventure, and they had to go by themselves. We have to be patient and wait for them to return. Now Doodlebug, no one is to know about this adventure. Everyone will think they are lost and possibly dead, but we know better. They won't be home for a long time, but when the adventure is over, we will be waiting for them. People will say they are lost and possibly dead, but that's okay with us. We know better. Your brother and cousin will come home one day. The professor told us this, and we believe him."

Katie started to giggle. "The professor is funny. I like him."

Jenny smiled. "So do we, honey. Now if Hannah says Will is lost what will you say to her?"

Katie looked at her mother and gave a small sigh. "I'll say nothing. I will just look sad. Then she won't talk about it anymore."

Steve looked at Katie. "How old are you? That is a very wise answer, sweetheart."

Jenny laughed a little. "Katie, I'm so proud of you. That's a perfect solution. Your dad and I didn't even think of that."

Katie rocked back and forth on her dad's knee. "Can I have hot chocolate before bed?"

Her mom smiled at her. "Sure, why not. I think we can all have some."

Katie jumped off her dad's knee and skipped into the kitchen behind her mother. Steve watched them leave the room and thought, *When do we break the three years to her? But for now, all was good.*

"He said what?" Jenny said a little louder than normal. Jenny stormed back to Steve. "You told her we can have a baby?"

All right, he thought, *maybe not so good.*

✱ ✱ ✱

Carol sat across the table from Fred in a cozy log cabin restaurant. He smiled at her and took a sip of his wine.

"Have I told you how stunning you look tonight?"

She chuckled as she took a sip of her wine. "Only about three times. But don't stop, I'll take all I can get."

The waitress came over and placed their plates in front of them. Fred had ordered the dinner as a surprise to Carol. "Be careful, the plates are hot," warned the waitress.

Carol took a deep smell. "Oh wow, this smells delicious."

Fred smiled. "Wait until you taste it."

Carol took a forkful of the stew like meal and began to savour the taste.

"Oh, my lord. Is this ever good!" she said with a huge smile on her face.

"I'm so glad you like it. It's one of their specialty dishes," Fred boasted proudly.

Carol stopped after another taste. "What is it? I can't quite put my finger on the taste."

Fred just smiled and took another mouthful himself.

Carol's face paled. "Oh God! It's not testicle of yak or something like that, is it?"

Fred almost choked on his food as he started to laugh.

"No, Carol, it's mountain goat."

She froze in her seat with her fork in mid-air. "Goat? This is mountain goat?"

Fred started to look concerned. "Carol, are you okay? It's not freaking you out or anything, is it?"

Then she started to laugh. "No, not at all. I've just never tried this before. I can still say it's delicious. It really is good, Fred."

Fred sighed. "Oh, good. I didn't want to make you sick or anything. Glad I was the first one to introduce you to this game. It's my favourite of all the venison meats."

Carol just smiled and enjoyed eating her goat stew. She wondered how her vegetarian friends would react if they knew what she was doing at this moment. But with a flourish of her wine glass she didn't care either.

The rest of the meal was spent just enjoying each other's company. The wine, the music, the food and the conversation. It was all perfect in Carol's mind. Then Fred cleared his throat and she knew right away this was his "tell" for nervousness.

"What's wrong, Fred?"

He seemed surprised that she could tell he was nervous.

"Carol, would it be too presumptuous of me to ask you back to my house tonight?"

She smiled down at the table and then looked him in the eyes.

"Fred, I would really like to say yes, but I feel responsible for the professor. And he kind of has me on a pedestal as a working single mom and all. I just don't feel right about him thinking me as a loose woman. Do you understand?"

Fred started to chuckle. "Never thought of myself as a cradle robbing sinner."

"Oh Fred, I am sorry. Let me take the professor home, get my business affairs in order, and then I'll return to you. Then we take this relationship to the next level; okay?"

Fred looked at her with an unreadable face. "So how long are we talking? Two weeks or a month?"

She started to laugh. "In a rush, are we?"

Then he laughed. "No, I just want to know how long I've got to get my house cleaned."

She squealed in laughter. "How bad is it?"

He grinned. "Let's just say I need the time."

She laughed. "Okay, Martha, shall we say at least two weeks but no more than three. Can you have the new duvet covers and curtains hung by then?"

He looked at her with a stunned face. "Curtains? We need curtains?"

When he saw Carol's stunned face he started to barrel laugh.

"Oh I wish you could see your face," he said.

Carol started to laugh, "You jerk! You really had me going there."

Fred picked up his wine glass and motioned for her to take her glass.

"Let's toast. To our new life, starting in three weeks."

She smiled and tapped her glass to his glass. They sipped slowly, both lost in their own thoughts. But each happy in them.

CHAPTER TWENTY-FIVE

Will lay on his bed starring up at the ceiling. A smile was on his face from ear to ear, and he wondered and hoped that this feeling would last forever. After the kiss on the balcony, he walked Miria back to her room. She kissed him softly on the lips and gently touched his face before saying good night and entering her room.

Will was sure he floated back his room. Jimmy was there and seeing Will's glazed look he didn't need any explanation as to why. He sat down beside him.

"Will, be careful. You're treading on Lian's hopes, and we need Lian, remember?"

Will just looked at his cousin and shrugged his shoulders. "I won't stop our feelings for each other just because Lian has high hopes. She's not interested in him Jimmy. She told me so. Far as I'm concerned, he can go spit."

And then he plopped himself on his bed and began to stare at the ceiling with that love sick, goofy smile.

***

Miria tucked Timtuk into his bed and Buddy lay on the floor beside him. She smiled at Buddy and gave him a pat on his head. She whispered to him, "You're good to him Buddy. I'm so glad you are here to protect him as well."

Buddy wagged his tail and then put his head down on the rug. She smiled as she went into her bedroom. She undressed and hung her dress on the clothes rail by her bed. It was then she noticed the note sitting on her side table. She opened it and began to read, tears began to well in her eyes and she crumpled up the note in her hands. She slipped slowly to the floor and began to sob quietly in her hands.

"How could he? How could he?" was all she mumbled as she cried herself to sleep right there on the floor.

✱ ✱ ✱

The next morning found Will and Jimmy waiting for everyone to join them at the dining room table. Will looked at the door anticipating Miria's entrance but was only disappointed by the sight of Lian, Beya and Donat. Beya and Donat were both friendly and nodded and greeted the boys. Lian just looked bored by their presence and said nothing.

Will thought, *What an arrogant creep,"* but he kept his thoughts to himself.

Miria's aunt entered the room with Timtuk by her side. She gestured for everyone to take their seats and Will and Jimmy both wondered where Miria was. When the aunt started passing the platters of fruit and breads around Jimmy looked at her and said, "Miria?"

The aunt understood his question and pointed to her head. As if she had a headache. Jimmy seemed satisfied with this answer and started to take fruit from the platter. Will on the other hand was not satisfied. Her aunt is a healer. If Miria had a headache, could she not fix her immediately.

For that matter, could Miria not fix herself. He quietly excused himself from the table and headed to Miria's room. Lian watched him with the eyes of a cougar waiting to pounce his prey. Jimmy caught the tension and pushed the platter of bread into his hands. The look he gave Jimmy sent chills up his spine.

Jimmy thought, *Oh man, this is going to be one long trip!*

***

Will tapped on Miria's bedroom door and waited patiently. Then he banged a little louder before she answered with an angry face.

"What do you want?" she said with such coldness Will took a step back.

"Whoa, Miria. What's wrong?"

Again, with the same coolness. "Nothing is wrong. I simply do not feel like eating this morning. Is there something wrong with that?"

Will felt like he had been slapped in the face. "No, nothing wrong with that at all. Miria, are you angry about last night? Did I go too fast for you? Are you confused about our feelings?"

She gave him a cold stare. "There are no feelings! Last night will never happen again, Will. I will remain your friend, but that is all we can be. Do you understand?"

Again, Will felt like he was being slapped and kicked without a blow being thrown. He looked at Miria and stared back at her and with the same coldness in her voice he answered her. "Fine! We'll be friends. Understood!" He turned on his heels and stormed back to the dining hall.

Miria closed her door and slipped down to the floor and began to cry hysterically.

When Will came back into the dining hall Jimmy could tell all was not well with his cousin. As Will sat down, he gave Miria's aunt a pleasant smile and asked Jimmy to pass the platters to him. He filled up his plate like a hungry man getting ready for war. He looked at Lian and had a suspicious feeling he had something to do with Miria's foul mood. Taking a corn muffin and stuffing it in his mouth, he gave Lian a look of pure hatred. Lian only grinned slightly at the side of his mouth. He knew he had won this battle that Will had started. And yet in Will's mind, he was thinking, *This means war buster. And I will win her, just you watch me.*

* * *

Supplies were packed, and boxes were sealed and tied together. Beya and Donat had them tied together like a toy train. Miria finally joined the group and Jimmy welcomed her with a huge smile and hug. "You okay? Your aunt said you had a headache."

She smiled at Jimmy. "I'm good, thank you. Are we just about ready to go?"

She turned to Donat and Beya and began a long conversation. Jimmy knew she was going over what had been packed and where they were on the train of boxes. She slowly put her hands over the boxes and they began to float about two feet from the ground. Will watched her and was always amazed by this strange power she possessed. Jimmy tried to push down on the last box but it felt like an opposing magnet being pushed down. Just wouldn't let it stick to the ground and bounced back with little force at all.

Jimmy smiled at Miria. "Amazing! You are just amazing, Miria."

She smiled at him but did not respond to his compliment.

Lian began to shout out orders and Donat and Beya jumped to their stations. Miria's aunt came to see them off with Timtuk in her arms. Miria took Timtuk from her arms and put him softly on top of a box. Her aunt gave Miria a huge hug and kissed her forehead. She handed Miria a small satchel and helped her put it on. She went over to Timtuk and have him a final kiss on the cheek. He squirmed but returned her kindness with a big bear hug.

The aunt was overjoyed by the affection. As she turned to walk away, Will noticed her wiping tears from her eyes. She smiled at the boys and said something to them. Miria translated. "She wishes you safe passage back to your world."

Both boys responded. "Mena."

She smiled and waved her last goodbye before turning and entering her house.

Miria turned to the boys. "We are going to walk for a few hours then we will take another way to get to our next village."

Jimmy looked at Miria. "What is the name of the next village, Miria?"

She looked at them without expression. "Napo. It is a village deep into the centre of our mountains."

Will looked at her. "How long before we get there?"

She looked up at the train of boxes avoiding Will's face.

"Three days. It will take three days." And she walked away.

Jimmy came up beside Will. "Did I miss something? She seems as cold and distant as she could possibly be. Did you do that?"

Will turned and looked at Jimmy with a little anger in his eyes. "No, meatball. I did not do this. But I'd bet the farm that creep Lian did. He's been gloating around here all morning. I'd like to put my fist in his face."

Jimmy started to chuckle. "So this is what two roosters in a hen house look like. Look, Will, maybe this is for the good. What will you do if you two become madly in love? She has to stay in her world, and you have to go back to yours. Tell me how this ends happily?"

Will looked down at the ground and then at Jimmy.

"How did you get so smart? You been watching a lot of Dr. Phil or something?"

Jimmy just smiled at his cousin and put his hand on his shoulder. "Come on, let's get Buddy set for our walk; okay?"

Will nodded sadly but followed his cousin to Buddy and Timtuk.

Lian gave an order and Beya and Donat pulled on the lines. The boxes moved with total ease, and the next step of their journey began. Timtuk laughed as he enjoyed the ride on his train box. Miria walked beside him followed by Buddy. Jimmy and Will took up the rear and walked quietly down the path.

Jimmy looked at Will. "Cheer up, cuz. Maybe there are some other hot chicks in Napo. Then we could all be happy."

Will just snorted at his cousin and shook his head.

"Like I said before, Jimmy, I'm glad I have you with me. I need comic relief. Know what I mean?"

Jimmy smiled. "I got a million of them, cuz. I got a million of them!"

And the boys smiled as they descended down into a cavern on the outskirts of Attaberra.

* * *

It was a quiet two hours. No one talked. Will and Jimmy just took in the scenery of the caverns, some crystallized, some like crusted rocks with a green moss growing on them. It looked like a green valley if it hadn't been for the low ceiling of rock all around them.

They came over a wall of sand and gravel when Lian yelled out an order. Everyone stopped while Beya and Donat started to untie the attached lines.

Jimmy looked at Miria. "What's happening? Are we setting

up camp?"

Miria smiled. "No, we are getting ready for the next ride. You will enjoy this, I promise."

They watched Beya, Donat and Lian pull the boxes over to a platform at the edge of the cavern. Everything was tied to hooks attached to the platform. The process took less than fifteen minutes. Donat took a large piece of cloth from one of the boxes and attached it to the front hooks of the platform.

Miria called for Jimmy and Will to sit on the middle boxes already attached to the platform. Jimmy did so without hesitation, but Will just stood still. It took Miria a few minutes before she noticed Will not making any attempts to move.

Coldly she spoke to him. "Is there a problem, Will?"

Will just looked at her with a cold stare. "Many! But right now I would just like to know what is happening. What is this contraption?"

Miria started to feel badly about this attitude she has been giving Will. It was horrible seeing him so miserable.

As politely as she could muster, she replied, "This is our ride for the next day. If you go and sit by Jimmy, I know you will enjoy it. This is Timtuk's first time too. I can hardly wait to see his face."

Will started to soften his cold stare. "Okay, Miria. I'll do what you ask, but in the future, please keep Jimmy and me informed. We feel like hitch-hikers. We're here but not part of the group."

"Do you mean you would like to help with the jobs needed to be done?"

Will nodded. "Exactly. We'd like to feel like we belong to this group."

Miria smiled. "We can arrange this. But now, it's only Donat who can help us now. Please sit with Jimmy."

Will nodded and hopped up on the box next to Jimmy. He sat cross-legged and looked at his cousin. "Well, another adventure for us, cuz. I hope you are keeping a diary."

Will chuckled. Jimmy looked at him. "Who could we let read it? Remember our oath?"

Will smiled. "We could read it. I have a feeling we are going to forget so much of this if we don't start writing it down. I'll ask Miria if it's possible to get some pen and paper when we camp tonight. I don't want to forget one thing about this journey."

As if on cue, Lian shouted and everyone settled to their positions. Miria took her hands and passed them over the platform, like magic it lifted as lightly as a dandelion clock blown in the wind. And speaking of wind, Donat spread the cloth in front of him and blew a tremendous gust into the cloth. The cloth spread out in front of the platform and Jimmy realized it was a sail. Will was smiling at the ease of the platform as it started to move through the cave.

Lian was at the back, holding a large wooden handle. Will surmised that it had to be the steering helm of the train. Timtuk was laughing with glee as he sat on Miria's lap. Miria laughed too. *She looks so beautiful when she laughs*, thought Will.

The ride was everything Miria promised. It was fun, fast and exhilarating. Will wondered how long Donat could keep up the wind routine, but he didn't look a bit tired by the process.

Jimmy kept saying "amazing" and "awesome."

And Will had to admit it was exactly that. They rode for about four hours, but it just seemed like an hour. When they did finally come to a stop, they were by an underground river.

Lian called out orders, but this time Will jumped down and began to help Beya and Donat untie the boxes. He looked at Donat and held out his hand for a friendly shake. Donat understood and grabbed Will's hand.

Both men smiled as Will said, "Mena Donat. Mena."

Donat answered back with, "Pasha Will. Pasha."

Each man smiled at each other as they guided the floating boxes to the side of the riverbed. Will started to feel at ease again around Beya and Donat. But Lian, well there are not enough years in this century to build a friendship. Tolerance would be all he could muster on this trip.

CHAPTER TWENTY-SIX

Steve knocked quietly on the trailer door and waited for the professor to let him in. The professor called out, "Come in" and Steve entered.

The professor looked up from his papers. "Come in, dear boy. I'm just packing up my books and such for my trip home this afternoon."

He noticed Steve was carrying one of his books. "Oh, good. You are returning my book. My boy, you are a scholar for a librarian."

Steve smiled and handed the book to the professor. Steve hesitated a second and then sat down on a chair by the table.

"Professor, there is something I need to clarify with you. I read your book about the Aztec people. I must admit, Professor, they were really an amazing group of people. Their architecture and farming techniques were beyond modern day practices. Their scientific knowledge and medical reference are incredible. However, they were also the most barbaric group of people. Professor, according to this book they worshipped blood. Human sacrifice was done on a regular basis for the sun and rain gods. How can you tell me that my boys are safe when clearly these people do not honour life?"

The professor looked at Steve with a dazed look. At first, Steve wondered if he even heard anything he just said.

The professor put his papers down and folded his hands in his lap.

"Well, my boy, I have a theory about that. You see, you must ask the question, why would some of the people want to run away? It's clear as crystal. To remove themselves from the senseless killing. According to the history of the book I gave you, they slaughtered twenty thousand people just to fill their vats with blood. Twenty thousand men, women and children. Can you imagine such senseless brutality? So if you are angry with this practice, what do you do? You can't run and hide in another territory. They would hunt you down and slaughter you as an example. No, you go underground. Use your scientific knowledge to seal the entrance. They took their people, those who chose to leave, away from the sun and rain gods, where the people had no sun or rain. Therefore no remorse. Just build a new life, a safe life, a happy life. And yet, when they do emerge every three years, it is not to kill anyone from our world, but rather take what they can from the land and use it in their underworld. The basket of berries you found, obviously they were picking them for their supplies. The children in Peru saw the lady take some bundled plants into the cave. Obviously for their farming needs. I believe these people to be peaceful. All evidence in my research points to this conclusion. So my dear boy, rest assured your boys are safe and are really on a wonderful adventure. I would wager my life on it."

Steve gave a huge sigh of relief. "Thank you, Professor. I didn't want the mothers to know of my concerns. Thank you for putting my mind at ease."

The Professor replied in his high, squeaky and excited voice. "Oh don't thank me. I should thank you for this wonderful adventure I have had up here in the woods. It brings me back to my childhood memories when my parents first settled here from England. What a glorious time I had as a child. Someday, maybe I'll go back there and spend my final years. Wouldn't that be a full circle for me?"

Steve smiled at him. "Professor, that sounds like a marvellous plan to me. I hope your dreams come true. Now, about your trip home, I'll come and get your things right after lunch. It will take us an hour to drive to the airport, and your flight is at four thirty getting you into Vancouver before dinner. How does that sound for you?"

The professor clapped his hands together reminding Steve of his childlike ways. "Oh, my boy, that sounds wonderful. Maybe that sweet Carol will allow me to take her for dinner at the airport. They do have eating establishments, do they not?"

Steve nodded. "They do, indeed, Professor. I'm sure Carol and you will find a great place to dine."

The professor just laughed and skipped around putting papers into his suitcase and his books into his satchel.

Steve started to open the door but turned to call back to the professor. "Lunch will be in about two hours. If you finish packing before that, I'd be happy to drive you back to the cave for one last look."

The professor turned and with a scream of glee. "Oh yes, dear boy. I'll be ready in five minutes. Thank you so much for this."

Steve nodded and shut the door. Sometimes he thought, he's like an absent-minded professor and then he seems like the most intelligent man he has ever met. He walked back to the house shaking his head at the paradox.

* * *

"Where did Steve and the professor go, Jenny?" Carol asked as she entered the kitchen.

"Back to the cave site. You know, one last time before he heads home. Do you want some coffee?"

Carol shook her head. "No, thanks. I've had enough for the day. Can we talk privately?"

Jenny turned and looked at Carol with a serious face. "Sure, Katie is in her room playing with her dolls. She won't come until I drag her out for lunch. Come on, let's go sit in the living room. It's a little quieter in there."

As the ladies settled themselves on the two easy chairs, Jenny noticed Carol looked a little nervous.

"Carol, is something wrong?"

Carol shook her head. "On the contrary, Jen. Everything just seems so unusually right."

Jenny started to smile. "I hear some love talk coming on. Come on, what did you and Fred talk about last night?"

Carol smiled., "Everything! Jen, I haven't felt so at ease with a man since Mike. He just has a way of making me feel all warm and squishy. I feel like a teenager again."

Jenny laughed. "God, let's not go back that far. Did you make any plans?"

Carol started to nod and then began to fidget with her fingers. "He wants me to move in with him." She looked up at Jenny. "I said I would. Oh Jen, am I going too fast?"

"No, not at all. I told you before. Love does not get measured by a road map or a calendar. If it feels right, go with your heart. And speaking as your sister-in-law, it's about bloody time!"

Carol put her head on the back cushion of the chair and closed her eyes.

"Oh Jenny, I have to go an explain all of this to my mother. She probably will want to have me committed. I'm sure there is insanity on our family tree. She'll use that as an excuse."

Jenny chuckled and tucked her legs underneath her.

"Come on, Carol. You're a lawyer, for Pete sake. You can start with an opening statement and then nail her with your summation. If there was anyone I'd like in my corner, it would be you. I know you can handle your mother. She's a lovely lady and your happiness is front and centre on her mind. Believe me, mothers only want happiness for their kids. No matter how old we get."

Carol smiled. "Okay, so you think she'll handle the Fred situation but what about Jimmy?"

Jenny took a deep breath and covered her eyes for a second. "Carol, we believe it. Take the professor to her, have him explain it the way he explained it to us. She'll either believe you or have you committed. If this happens, I promise to visit once a month, and if you're really good I'll bring cake."

Carol started to laugh. "Thank you so much! But maybe the professor's visit is the right ticket to this crazy play. With any luck he'll sweep her off her feet, run away with her and my problems will be solved."

Jenny laughed hysterically. "Yup, and Care Bear land will have two more new residents. I like it!"

Carol laughed until tears fell from her eyes. "Can life get any crazier?"

Jenny shot her a shocked look. "Lord, don't ask that. I don't think I want to know."

With a nod in the direction of the kitchen. "Come on. I have chicken salad sandwiches in the fridge and a veggie platter too. Let's get the table set for lunch; okay?"

Carol jumped up. "I'm yours to command, my lady."

Jenny smiled and remembered Jimmy always saying that when he was here. She got an odd feeling in the pit of her stomach. She hoped it was just nerves and not motherly instincts.

"Please Lord," she silently prayed, "let our boys be safe."

***

Carol and the professor were walking to the luggage carousel at YVR. Carol noticed the childlike way the professor was walking. He had eyes everywhere but in front of him, looking at the carvings and paintings that hung along the walkway and stopping at different little shops to see what they were selling.

"Carol, come here. They sell smoked salmon here. Oh, I do think I should make a small purchase. Do you mind?"

Carol smiled. "Not at all, Professor. Do you have enough money?"

The professor shook his head. "No, but I can use this card, can I not?"

Carol approached him. "Yes, of course, Professor. It's a charge card. Do you remember your PIN number?"

The professor looked at her in confusion. "My what number?"

"Your PIN number, Professor. It's your passcode for the card. Do you remember it?"

He looked at the card as if it was the first time he had ever seen it before.

"Carol dear, I don' think I have a code. What do I do?"

Carol patted him on the back. "It's okay, Professor. We can use mine. It will be my gift to you; okay?"

Now he became agitated. "No, I wish to purchase this myself. Carol, how do I retrieve my code."

Carol scratched her head. "Well, Professor, what four numbers would mean something to you. Your birthday, your mother's birthday, your street address as a child. What four numbers would you code in that has meaning to you?"

He thought for a moment then replied without any emotion in his voice, "9-6-76."

Carol smiled. "That's good, Professor. How are those numbers significant to you?"

Without looking at her he said in a matter of fact voice, "The day my parents were killed. I'll never forget that horrible day." And he walked into the store to purchase the salmon.

Carol just stood outside the store stunned.

He walked out the store with his purchase in a bag and smiled at her as if nothing was amiss.

"My dear, do you think we can find an eating establishment in this place. I would like to take you to dinner, if I may."

Carol smiled at him and started walking towards the luggage carousel.

"That would be lovely, Professor. Let's go get our luggage then we will have a porter take them for us until after we eat."

"Where will he take them, dear girl?"

She chuckled. "Oh not far, just into a room until we need them. What kind of food would you like to try, Professor?"

He looked at her with confusion, "Type of food. Edible would be preferred!"

Carol started to laugh. "No, I mean Thai, Chinese, Mexican or maybe a little French cuisine."

He started to chuckle. "Oh, my dear, you choose. As long as it isn't rare or raw, I'll eat it."

She smiled. "I think we should try this Chinese Restaurant just around the corner. The food is excellent, and I am sure you will like the different flavours I'm about to introduce to you."

The professor followed Carol like a little duck follows his mother. In no time they had their luggage stored with a porter, and they were seated by the window of the restaurant. The professor was thrilled like a child as he watched the planes taxi away and then eventually take off. The waiter came to the table, but the professor was too enthralled with the airport traffic to notice him. Carol quietly ordered the dinner and a beer for the professor and jasmine tea for herself. She enjoyed watching the professor as his head bobbed up and down trying to look over one plane as another would taxi in. It was as if he was seeing a busy airport for the first time in his life.

"Professor, you have been to an airport before; right?"

He looked at her as if she was insane. "Of course I have, but never like this. No one has ever let me see this. Oh it is so exciting. Just think, Carol, each one of those planes is about to fly off this earth and land far away from here. Maybe tropical, maybe cold as the arctic or rainy as London in the wintertime. Isn't it fun to guess where they might be headed? It's all so thrilling!"

Carol laughed as she thought how wonderful and simple his life was and how he appreciated everything.

Finally their food arrived. "Oh, what is this?"

Carol pointed to the flat patties on the plate. "This is like a rice taco shell. You spread some of this sauce on it, put a green onion on and then some crispy duck skin. Roll it up and then eat it like a taco."

"A rice taco!" His eyes flew open wide and his expression was pure bliss.

"Oh my dear, that is extraordinary! How have I never experienced something so wonderful?"

Carol laughed as she ate her patty with the crispy duck skin. "Have some more, Professor. There is plenty."

The professor ate with flourish and the sound effects coming from his mouth were of complete exhilaration. The second dish came, a plate of iceberg lettuce followed with a bowl of ground meat.

Carol picked up a piece of lettuce and scooped a tablespoon of meat into its centre. "Now, Professor, this is what they do with the rest of the duck. This is called a lettuce wrap and it's simply delicious."

She handed him the lettuce leaf and told him to roll it like a taco again. He did as was told and took a big bite. This time his eyes remained closed but the sound effects of mmmmm could be heard across the room.

"Professor, I'm so glad you're enjoying this food, but I think the rest of the guests here would prefer a little less exuberance."

His eyes flew open. "Oh, my dear. Where are my manners? But I don't think I have had anything as extraordinary as these two dishes. Carol, you have expanded my horizons, and I thought that was impossible for me."

Carol rested her chin on her hands. "I'm so glad you liked it. I didn't order anything else. Thought this would be plenty for the two of us, but if you would like anything else, I can order more."

He rolled another lettuce wrap and took a huge bite.

"Oh, sweet heaven! This is food for the gods."

She wanted to ask him about his parent's death, but he was having such a good time, she refused to kill the mood. Watching him enjoy every last morsel was fun and humbling. Something as simple as an airport restaurant and gourmet Chinese food can bring one down to reality.

Life's true happiness can be just the simple things that matter. Or is it the way to a man's stomach. She would have to think about that later.

***

The phone was ringing as Carol opened the door to her condo. She grabbed it just in time. "Hello, I'm here," she huffed out.

"Hi, sweetheart. You sound winded. Did you just get home?"

She smiled at the endearment. "Yeah, barely got my luggage in the door to answer the phone."

Fred felt bad for the rush he had just put her through. "Sorry, honey. I can call back later. When you get your breath back."

Carol plunked herself down on the couch. "No, not at all. It's good to hear your voice."

Fred smiled. "Trip home okay?"

"Absolutely perfect. And the professor treated me to a Chinese food dinner. Fred, he was priceless. He had never had it before. Man, I think that man was raised on the moon. But he loved every bite and believe me he ate everything!"

"That's great, Carol. I'm sure he appreciated the culinary experience."

Carol laughed. "It wasn't just the food. He had never watched planes at an airport before. We had an outside window at the restaurant and he was like a five-year-old. It was hilarious."

Fred laughed. "Hey, I'm jealous. You didn't tell me you were going to watch planes. I like planes."

Carol laughed. "Okay, the next time you fly into YVR we'll eat at a restaurant by a window, and you can watch too."

Fred laughed. "Oh goodie! Cause that will be next week. I'm coming on Tuesday."

Carol sat straight up. "What? You're coming here?"

"Yeah, strictly business, though. I am going to a seminar at the Fairmont. So do I get a dinner by the window or not?"

Carol was silent for a moment. "Or we could have dinner here. Would you like that?"

Fred smiled and softened his tone. "I would love to see where you live. But I'll be staying at the Fairmont and the seminar starts at 6:30 am. So I'd kind of prefer it if you could join me there. I could spend more time with you. Then just quietly go to the seminar and not disturb you."

Carol had a confused look on her face. "Fred, are you asking me to spend the night with you?"

Fred chuckled nervously. "Yeah, but I don't think I said it right. Can I have a do-over?"

Carol laughed softly. "Go ahead. Do your best."

Fred cleared his throat. "Honey, I volunteered to come down for this seminar just to be close to you. I couldn't stand the thought that I might not see you for three weeks. I hear this hotel is top notch, and I thought it would be nice for us to see each other on neutral ground. This way, you don't have to go nuts getting your place fixed up. And don't deny it, you'd do something."

He could hear Carol laughing quietly.

"So I hoped I could wine and dine you in a five-star hotel. I won't even watch the planes! I just want to be with you. What do you say?"

Carol was quiet for a moment. "Fred, that was a very articulate do-over, and I really do appreciate your effort, but you had me at the dinner by the window."

Fred let out a howl. "Oh man, I thought I blew this with you. Carol, I can't wait to see you."

Carol laughed. "Me too, darling. This is such a wonderful surprise."

Fred's stomach took a dip and a flip. This was the first time she had ever called him an endearment. It sounded so good.

"I'll let you go, so you can unpack and all. But I'll call you tomorrow; okay?"

Carol's face just beamed. "That would be great. Talk to you tomorrow."

Fred whispered back. "Sweet dreams, love." And slowly hung up the phone.

CHAPTER TWENTY-SEVEN

The bedrolls were all laid out along a sandy area near the river. Will noticed that Miria had set her bedroll and Timtuk's in a small cavern about twenty feet from them. He wondered if she was trying to get away from him or if it had to do with Timtuk. Keeping him inside the cavern, so she could protect him from getting out. Timtuk would definitely go near the river, and that would spell disaster. So he felt a little better with this scenario in his head than the first thought. Jimmy walked over and sat down beside him.

"Apparently, we have to shower before we eat. These people are really into hygiene. Beya and Donat are setting up the water rocks behind a bunch of rocks over there."

He pointed to a group of rocks to the left of the camp. "Apparently, they are like our mothers. 'Wash your hands before dinner' but here it's wash everything. And oh yeah, clean clothes too."

Will squinted up his face in confusion. "This is taking hygiene to a whole new level, isn't it?"

Jimmy smiled. "Either that or they really like to see our bodies."

Will smirked. "Yeah, that's it."

Jimmy smiled and then got that mischievous face on. "Yeah, but Will, I miss our bathtub. My bubbles, my bath toys and most of all my rubber ducky. Showers are so clinical. Do you think Lian will get us a bathtub?"

Will just kept on walking. "Shut up, you moron!" And Jimmy just laughed as they walked over to Beya and Donat.

* * *

Jimmy and Will were showered and into their new clothes. Donat took their old clothes from them. Jimmy pointed to the pile.

"My good man. No starch in the collars, it makes my neck chafe." Donat looked at Jimmy with a total confused look before Will stepped in.

"Mena Donat. Jimmy is just being a dork."

Donat looked at Will. "Dork?" he said slowly.

Will smiled and nodded. "Yes, Jimmy. Dork."

Donat began to laugh. He understood their teasing of each other. He was just about to walk away when he stopped in his tracks.

He yelled for Lian and Beya. The both came running and Donat pointed to the rock. Jimmy and Will came closer to see what the fuss was all about. On inspection, they noticed a small carved out symbol on the rock. A sun with a serpent encircling it. Miria came running over with Timtuk in her arms. She looked at the symbol and paled.

Will looked at her. "Miria, what does this mean?"

She looked at Will and Jimmy. "It's a symbol from a very bad people. We may be in danger."

She walked away before Jimmy or Will could ask another question. Will noticed Lian and Beya looking at the map.

Donat was opening one of the boxes and looked like he was taking out weapons that Will had never seen before. Except two crossbows. Will knew exactly what to do with them. He picked one up and held it up to check the scope.

Donat watched in amazement as Will took an arrow and set it properly in the bow. Miria came over and Donat started to speak to her.

"He wants to know if you can handle this weapon?" Will looked at Donat and nodded his head. Donat handed him a sheath of arrows. Will took the hint, these were now his to use.

Jimmy walked over. "Will, did you already get lessons? I thought that is what we were going to do this summer."

Will smiled. "Guess what cousin? You're going to do exactly that. Come on, I'm going to give you a quick lesson."

Jimmy let out a slow whistle and followed Will. Will rolled up a blanket and placed it on top of a rock about thirty feet away. He came back beside Jimmy.

"Now watch me. I slowly scope the blanket, lift it ever so little to allow for draft, hold it tight and pull the trigger." Will shot and hit the blanket dead centre.

"Whoa, good shot," Jimmy cried.

"Now it's your turn," said Will. "Take the arrow and slide back the bow and place the arrow in this slot." Jimmy followed his instructions.

"Now, take aim. Use your scope to choose your target, lift it slightly, hold tight, and fire." Jimmy did but hit the rock below the blanket.

He turned and smiled. "I meant to do that."

Miria started to giggle.

Will looked at Miria. "Don't encourage him! Come on, Robin Hood. That wasn't bad for your first shot. Try again, but hold up the bow just a little higher before you shoot."

Jimmy followed the instructions perfectly and then shot. This time it hit the blanket. Jimmy let out a howl of delight. Will had to admit, Jimmy was a prodigy at most things. He started to feel envious of his cousin.

"Good job. Now keep your voice down. We don't know what's in these rocks. I got a feeling this is serious. Miria what is happening? What bad people are you talking about?"

Miria looked over at Timtuk, but he and Buddy were playing, so she felt safe leaving him for a few minutes. She sat down on a flat rock and asked the boys to sit as well.

When they did she began. "Many, many years ago some of our people wanted to go back to the religion that our great parents left behind. They wanted to sacrifice people again. Many of our people were angry and sent them away. They were to go to the bottom of our world and stay there. No one would trade with them or even see them again. Slowly they started to die, so I guess they did what they had to, to survive. The began to fight other villages, steal from them and take prisoners as slaves. Our people began to hide our special people. Put them as far away from these people as we could. You see, they want the special powers we have. And they will keep looking for us until they take us as slaves."

Jimmy started to think and then asked, "Miria, your village. It's the farthest away from these people, isn't it?"

She nodded. "Then why would your chief risk your lives to help us? Could he not have given us some good warriors and left Lian, Donat and Beya alone?"

Miria smiled at Jimmy. "They asked to come. And my father was afraid to let you stay. I think he feared what happened to my mother would happen to me."

Will spoke quietly, "You mean, fall in love with one of us."

Miria nodded her head.

"But, he sent Lian to make sure this didn't happen, didn't he?" Will sneered.

Tears started to well in her eyes. "He sent me a letter saying if this happened I was never allowed to come back to my village or see Timtuk again. But he did not know that Timtuk came with us. The message was clear. I would have no home or Timtuk if I let this happen."

Will looked down at the ground and let out a huge sigh. "So that's what happened. He threatened you."

Miria looked at Will. "I am so sorry, Will. But this is my village, my family. Without them I'd be lost. You have to go back to your world, and I must stay in mine. I can't lose you and then my home too. Do you understand?"

Will nodded his head. "I totally understand, Miria, but I wish you had been honest with me from the beginning. That scene at your bedroom door almost killed me inside."

Tears fell down her cheeks. "Me as well, Will. I cried for an hour."

Will put out his hand and she took it. "We'll always be friends; okay. No matter what," Will whispered.

She nodded. "Friends forever, Will."

They both smiled at each other and walked back to Lian and Beya who were still looking at the map. It was evident they were arguing about a new route. Miria tried to intervene but Lian shouted and she backed right off. Will wanted to put his fist in his face for that. He knew that would be senseless, but it sure would make him feel so much better!

Will looked at Miria. "What are they arguing about?"

Miria looked at Jimmy and Will and shook her head.

"They cannot agree on the safest route. Lian wants us to go through that path, which will lead us way off our map and will take many weeks to be able to connect with the route the elders planned for us. Beya thinks we should stay on this route and just be careful. He says he can use his gift to protect us. He can keep us covered for a few days, but it would take many days to get his strength back. It could be dangerous for him."

Will and Jimmy looked at each other before Jimmy spoke.

"So let me get this straight. We go off route and it will take us a week or so to get back on route. But we'll be safer. Now Beya thinks we should stick to the original route, which may have these bad people waiting for us, and he thinks he can keep us invisible for a few days. Then what? We'd have to fight them; right?"

Miria and Will both nodded. Jimmy took a deep breath.

"I vote for Lian's route. Safety first, I always say."

Will snorted. "When do you ever say that?"

Jimmy sat down beside Miria. "Look Miria, your chief knows exactly what route we are taking. You said it yourself. He will send men after Timtuk. Why not do as Lian suggests. Let's go off the map for a while. We can totally lose these guys and Timtuk would be safe with us. What do you say?"

Miria looked at Jimmy with a stunned look and then a smile came across her face. "Yes, Jimmy. I like this plan. I like Lian's plan too."

Will shook his head. "Why not? What possible harm could come of this?"

But he had to admit, Jimmy's plan was well thought out. Why didn't he think of it first?

The three of them went to Lian and Beya as Miria stated the case. Lian sat back and looked at Jimmy and Will. For the first time that arrogant jerk smiled at them. He nodded his head, and Beya rolled up the map. Obviously the vote was in and Lian won. Will grumbled in his head, *that's the only thing you're going to win if I can help it.*

***

Everyone was snuggled in their bedrolls. Buddy stayed beside Timtuk, as if to protect him from any harm. Will smiled at Jimmy. "That dog is turning into a little traitor. When's the last time he slept with us?"

Jimmy scratched his face. "Come to think of it, not since we've met Timtuk. He stays at his side every night. Even on the boat. You're right, Will. No Scooby treats for him."

Will chuckled. "It must be the paternal instinct in him. That's my story, and I'm sticking to it."

Jimmy chuckled and rolled over in his blanket and fell asleep immediately. Will just stared at the rock formation of this huge cave and listened to the river flow. He was asleep in minutes.

✷ ✷ ✷

The next morning was a bustle of breakfast for everyone and then packing up the boxes. Beya and Donat took a few things from each box and put them into small satchels for each one of them to carry. Lian came and took the third one and put it over his shoulder as well. When Will came forward with the cross-bow it was made clear to him that he was to carry this with him. They gave Jimmy the other one to carry. It was at that moment the boys realized this might be a dangerous trip after all.

Timtuk seemed oblivious to any danger and sat up on one box making noises that only a three-year-old could make. Miria smiled at him and tussled his hair with affection. Buddy sat down by the box and started whimpering for some affection. And of course Miria was there for him too with a pat on his head and a chest rub. Life was good according to Buddy.

Everything was set, all the boxes were tied and Miria did her magic and the boxes levitated from the ground. Lian called out and led the group into a far-off tunnel, away from the route that had previously been planned. Miria and Timtuk followed Lian, Jimmy and Will followed them, and Beya and Donat were at the back. Lian pulled on the lines and the boxes moved with the ease of a feather floating in the air. Jimmy and Will still marvelled at this.

As they entered the tunnel Will and Jimmy immediately felt colder. The river was far off in the distance, but the cold did not seem to come from the water. It felt more like it came from the wall of the tunnel.

Jimmy looked at his cousin. "Should have brought a coat. Man this is cold. Where is this cold coming from, Miria?"

She looked back at him. "It comes from the rocks. These rocks are known to keep cold for many months. Like the water stones and the fire rocks, these rocks are taken and traded with from village to village. It is how we keep our food fresh. But they do not take from this area as the river is too close to take the rock safely. So it is just a cold area. We will be back in the warm air in a few minutes."

Jimmy's teeth started to chatter. "Man, a polar bear would be happy down here."

Will looked at Jimmy. "Should we stop and get you something warmer to put on? Jim, your lips are blue. Are you okay?"

Before Jimmy could answer, he blacked out. Will screamed out his name and Miria went into action. Beya and Donat picked him off the ground and placed him on top of one of the larger boxes. Miria rubbed her hands together and held them flat above Jimmy's body. She closed her eyes as if in a prayer and guided her hands back and forth over Jimmy's body. After a few minutes Jimmy's lips started to turn pink again, and his skin didn't look so pale and sweaty. Miria took her hands away, and slowly Jimmy started to move and mumble some words.

"What happened? Why am I on this box?"

Will stepped beside him. "You passed out, Jimmy. The cold really seemed to have bothered you."

Miria felt his forehead. "You will be good in a few minutes. But I want you just to lay on this box, Jimmy until we get to a warmer space."

Donat handed her a blanket from one of the boxes, and she wrapped him in it.

"But why am I the only one affected by the cold? Even Timtuk seems okay."

Miria answered, "Some of us are affected differently than others. The tunnel is very cold, and some bodies cannot get used to such a quick drop of..." she tried to find the word.

Will cut in, "Temperature. His body couldn't adjust to the quick drop in temperature."

"Yes, temperature. So I put a healing of warmth on you, and your body adjusted to the heat I gave you. Now rest Jimmy, and we will be out of here in a few minutes."

Jimmy rolled up in the blanket and lay on the box as Lian called out for them to get going. Everyone took their places, and they continued down the tunnel.

It didn't take long before they felt warmth wafting up the bottom of the tunnel. Will looked at Jimmy and found him fast asleep.

Will quietly whispered to Miria, "Is this normal? I mean he just got up and now he's fast asleep again."

Miria smiled and whispered back, "After a healing your body will go to sleep to finish what I started. Our bodies are wonderful vessels. We just need a little push, and we can heal ourselves. And right now Jimmy is still healing. He should have his strength back within an hour. I assure you, Will, he is well." Will gave a huge sigh of relief and continued to look at his cousin.

As they came out of the tunnel Will's mouth dropped to the

ground. The whole cave was covered in white crystals. Everything glistened like diamonds. Will thought, *Come on, Jimmy. Wake up. You just have to see this place.* And no sooner said than Jimmy began to rustle.

"Will, where are we?"

Will touched his cousin's shoulder. "I don't know, but maybe you can take a look and tell me what kind of crystals these are."

Jimmy sat up and slowly looked around. "Wow, this is crystal white amethyst. The whole cave is this? Wow."

But before he could admire anymore of this fabulous view, Buddy started to bark. Will quickly went to his side. "What's wrong, boy?"

Buddy was looking at some large crystals and began to growl and bark. Lian quickly looked around but did not see anything, and then a lizard the size of a house came out of a large crack. Lian turned but the lizard's tongue slapped him up against the rocks. Lian fell like a rag doll. Donat blew as hard as he could, but it only stopped the lizard for a second. He was about to attack Miria and Timtuk when suddenly an arrow struck him in his neck. The lizard howled but was not stopped. Will was reloading the cross-bow when another arrow was fired at the beast. It hit him in the eye and the beast screamed in agony. Will turned to see Jimmy starting to reload his bow. When Will was just about ready to shoot again, a fire ball came out of nowhere. Will looked over his shoulder and saw Lian holding tightly to a rock. Will could tell he was seriously hurt. Donat ran up to him and together they became a blow torch of fire. The lizard screamed a horrible cry and fell back into the crack. Lian and Donat continued to burn him and then all was quiet except for Timtuk crying.

Lian fell against Donat and Beya flew to his other side. Miria gave Timtuk to Will and ran towards Lian. She gave him a quick look and gave directions to Beya and Donat. They supported Lian on both sides and slowly walked him to the boxes. Lian lay on a box face down, and Miria started moving her hands up his spine. When he screamed at her touch, she immediately stopped touching him and began to rub her hands together. She held her hands flat over the sore spot, and taking a deep breath of air she flecked her hands stiff. Will could have sworn he saw a ball of heat come from her hands. But on a second look, he saw nothing.

In about five minutes Lian's breathing was returning to normal as was his colour. The lizard had definitely knocked the wind out of him, but Will wondered if his back was broken as well. Lian slowly stood up as Miria talked to him. She asked Donat to help him to a rock that Beya had put blankets and cushions on for him. Lian slowly sat down. He looked at Will and Jimmy, and for the second time since they met him, he smiled at them.

Looking at Will and Jimmy he said, "Mena Will. Mena Jimmy."

Both boys looked at him and said, "Pasha Lian."

He spoke to Miria quietly, and she smiled at him and touched his shoulder.

She looked at the boys. "You are warriors. You did not tell us before."

Will started to laugh. "Not warriors, hunters. We hunt for deer, elk and moose when the leaves turn colour back home. We never kill for fun; we kill for the meat. Here it was necessary to kill for survival, Lian's and yours."

Miria smiled at both boys. "We are grateful for you both and your hunter skills."

Will and Jimmy smiled at each other. "Score one for Uncle Steve," said Jimmy. When they looked over at Lian, he was fast asleep.

After a few hours of rest Lian started to walk around slowly unassisted. He wanted to move on, but Donat and Beya insisted they rest for the day and get an early start in the morning. They knew Lian was seriously hurt as he agreed with them very quickly, which went against his character of stubbornness.

So they began to set up camp all the while Buddy played with Timtuk. Beya talked to Miria and she relayed the message to Will.

"Beya says he's grateful for Buddy. His hearing is a gift."

Will nodded and smiled at Buddy and Timtuk.

"As long as he doesn't bark or growl, I feel pretty safe."

Miria relayed the message to Beya, and he nodded in agreement. Slowly but surely this group was coming together as a unit.

***

Dinner was over, and Timtuk was asleep in his bedroll, Buddy by his side. Lian was asleep as well as Beya and Donat kept watch over the camp. Will looked at Miria. "Tell Beya and Donat that Jimmy and I will share the watch with them tonight so that they can get some sleep too."

Miria relayed the message and both men nodded and said, "Mena."

Will looked at them and said, "Pasha." Then looked at Miria.

"How about telling them we can do three hour shifts."

Again she relayed the message and both men nodded in agreement.

"Good. Jimmy we're up in three hours. We better get some sleep before then."

Jimmy looked at Will. "Hey, what's with this volunteer garbage. Don't you know I need my beauty sleep? Take Buddy. He hears better than me anyways."

Will started to chuckle. "Look, Sleeping Beauty, we're going to help if we are ever going to fit into this group. You can spare a few hours of your beauty sleep for the good of the group."

Jimmy scrunched up his nose. "Man, when you put it that way, you make me sound so shallow. Miria, am I getting wrinkles on my forehead? Or rings under my eyes? What do you think?"

Miria just laughed at him. "Jimmy, you are so funny. Thank you for this. I haven't laughed so much in years."

Will remembered she said something similar to this on the balcony back at her aunt's house.

"Miria, do you mind if we ask about your father and what happened to him?"

Miria looked at both boys sadly. She took a deep breath and nodded.

"I will tell you about my father. He came from the same portal that you and Jimmy walked through. So I believe he must have lived near your village. His name was Dean George. He told me his father was a chief in his village. When he came through the portal, our village was unhappy that he was there. But we are against human sacrifice, so they had to accept him and teach him the ways of our people. My mother was one of the people who was asked to teach our ways. Over time, they fell in love. My father said he fell in love with her the first time they met. My mother said it took her a little longer, but she always laughed when she said it. Anyways, they asked the chief of our village if they could be together in a blessed union."

Jimmy piped up, "We call that marriage."

Miria smiled. "Yes, my father used that word. But in our culture a blessed union must be agreed to by all our villagers. And many were not sure if my father was the right man for my mother. So my father took two years to prove himself to every one of our people. He learned our language, helped our elders, help build new homes or fix the ones we had. He introduced the toilet that was in my house and how to take the smelly stuff away from our village to a huge hole with rocks in it."

Will laughed. "A modern day sewage plant."

"Yes, and later we used the dry dust from the rocks in some of our gardens. It helped everything grow so much bigger. Anyways, over time the village accepted my father as one of them and allowed my mother and him to join in a blessed union. I came within the first year of their union. We were so happy until our chief died, and his son joined our village. His mother had died when he was a baby and he was raised by his aunt in Napo. The new chief, who you know as Timtuk's father did not like my father. He felt he did not deserve my mother. But the union was blessed and the villagers loved my father, so the new chief did not have any rights to change this union. When I was eight years the chief sent a group of villagers to take our light stones to Napo for trade. My father was told he had to go, but my mother would not let him go alone, so we packed up and went with him. The chief was angry about this, but a chief cannot keep a union couple apart if they do not wish it. So we headed for Napo. I was so excited as I had never left our village and of course the boat ride and going to Attaberra as well. I felt like it was the best adventure of my life. It was in Attaberra that I met my aunt, and we stayed with her for a week, which was a mistake, but we did not know it at the time. You see the rest of the people travelling with us went on ahead after two days. But my mother was so happy to see her sister that my father agreed to stay a few days longer. We lost our guards but the way to Napo was not thought to be dangerous, so we went on ahead just the three of us. I loved it. We camped by a river, sang songs that my father taught me and swam in a pool made by the river over some crystal stones. It was all so magical. We could not have been happier."

She looked at the boys. "What is the word in your language when you are taken by surprise by bad people?"

Will looked at her. "An ambush?"

"Yes," she nodded, "That is what my father yelled. 'It's an ambush.'

He found a small cave and put my mother and me in it, and warned us not to come out until he came for us. There was screaming and yelling and all the while my mother held me tightly, so my screams could not be heard. After what seemed like a very long time, all was quiet. We waited for my father, but he did not come. My mother told me to stay in the cave, and she went out to look for my father. She found him. He was not alive.

"I came out when I heard my mother crying while holding him in her arms. If he had just a little life left in him, my mother could have saved him. But he had been stabbed many times, as if to make sure he would never wake up again. We wrapped him up in blankets and just as my mother was wondering how we would get him back to Attaberra, I discovered my first gift. I made him float, and we took him back with ease. We put him in my mother's family's tomb, and we stayed with my aunt for many months. When we finally went back to our village the chief stayed by my mother's side until she finally agreed to a blessed union with him. I was twelve years when they were joined and Timtuk was born two years later. My mother died a few days later. She was the healer of the village and my skills were just being learned. I could not stop her bleeding, and she died in my arms."

Tears were flowing down her cheeks, and she closed her eyes as if to erase the pain of the memory.

"I did not have all my healing powers. Today I could have saved her." She put her face in her hands and started to cry.

Will got up and put his arm around her. "I'm so sorry, Miria, but it's not your fault. You can't blame yourself."

"I know," she said. "My aunt came to stay with me for many months after Timtuk's birth. She continued my healing lessons, and she is the reason I have the power of the gift at such a young age. Our chief promised my aunt he would take good care of me and

Timtuk, so my aunt went back to Attaberra. She wanted Timtuk and me to go back to Attaberra with her, but our village needed a healer, so I had to stay. The chief promised my aunt that he would take good care of me and Timtuk, but I have raised him. The chief did not know how to love a baby. I believe the chief did not know how to truly love anything. When my mother died, he was nowhere to be found. Some people say he was so sad he had to go away and be sad by himself, but I don't really know. He never showed any sadness when he was with me or speak of my mother. He just ignored Timtuk, as if he was to blame for her death. There are so many things that I don't understand, and I guess I never will."

Will and Jimmy remained quiet for a few moments. "Thank you for sharing this story with us, Miria," said Jimmy softly. "We know now how painful this memory is for you. For that, we apologize."

She smiled at the boys through the tears brimming in her eyes. "I think I will go to bed now."

She got up and headed towards Timtuk but stopped and turned around and looked straight at the boys.

"Ambush. How did they know we were coming? I always wondered about that."

She then turned and crawled in beside Timtuk.

Will and Jimmy just looked at each other. "Are you thinking what I'm thinking?" asked Jimmy.

Will looked at his cousin. "What are you thinking?"

"Will, it sounds to me like a set up. It's like the detective shows on television. Who had motive? Who could carry out the plan? Who benefits from the plan? Can you guess my answers to all of the above?"

Will looked at Jimmy and blew out a huge breath. "The chief, who seemed to have the hots for Miria's mother."

Jimmy sat up and spoke a little softer. "And the chief didn't want her to go with Dean, but because of their laws he couldn't stop her."

Will spoke quietly too. "And where were they going? To Napo, the chief's old stomping ground. Do you think he had friends to help him?"

Jimmy sighed. "Why wouldn't he? He grew up there. Probably a juvenile delinquent from way back."

They were silent for a moment before Will spoke. "I'm liking going off the map more and more. How about you?"

"Will, you and me both," said Jimmy with a wink in his eye.

"Now let's get some shut eye before our turn on the watch," said Will with a slight note of apprehension.

Jimmy smiled. "Don't worry, cuz, I've got your back and you've got mine. Just like always." Will curled up in his bedroll as Jimmy curled up in his.

"See you in two, cousin," said Will as he slipped off to sleep.

Jimmy just lay there beside him, thinking and not liking what he thought about at all.

Multiple stab wounds. Someone really wanted to make sure Dean George stayed dead. Yes, sir. No chance for a healer to do her job. This whole story smells a little fishy.

And Jimmy wasn't too fond of fish.

CHAPTER TWENTY-EIGHT

Jenny came into the house carrying two grocery bags when the telephone rang. Putting the bags on the table she rushed for the phone. "Hello."

"Hi Jenny, it's Carol."

"Hey, sis. How's things going down there?" Jenny said as she tried to take off her sweater.

"Oh Jenny, I have so much to tell you that I don't know where to start."

Jenny plunked herself down on an easy chair. "From the beginning, please. It makes more sense that way."

Carol started to laugh. "Okay, here goes. Fred came down yesterday. We met up at the Fairmont and had a fabulous dinner. I stayed with him all night, and he asked me to marry him this morning. Yeah, that about covers it."

Jenny sat on the chair totally speechless. "Holy crap. Carol what did you say?"

Carol started to laugh hysterically. "I said yes. Jenny, am I nuts or what?"

Jenny started to laugh. "Certifiable. But I couldn't be happier for you. Wait until I tell Steve. He's going to flip."

"Jenny, I have to ask you for some advice. Fred would like to get married sometime soon. But I kind of would like Jimmy to be there. Am I asking too much for him to wait three years?"

Jenny smiled. "Do you remember that calendar I told you about. If he loves you, the wait should not matter. As long as you two are together, everyone should be happy. Besides, I think Peru, The Andes would be a perfect backdrop for a wedding. What do you think?"

Carol laughed. "I think Jimmy would be shell shocked by it all."

Jenny spoke quietly. "Not when he sees how happy you are. You know Jimmy only wants the best for you. I know secretly he has always wanted you to find a new partner. And no he didn't mean a business partner."

Carol laughed., "Darn, you just stole my line. You think he wants me to find someone, Jenny?"

"Absolutely, Carol. Last year I overheard him say to Will that he wished you had a boyfriend, so we could all be together like one big family. Does that convince you he'll be happy about this?"

Carol let out a huge sigh. "Oh, Jenny, thank you. You always know just what to say to make me feel better."

Jenny laughed. "Hey, it's my job. Dr. Phil in drag, that's me. Now, when is the big move up here?"

Carol spoke nervously, "Next week. My firm is on board with me working through the internet. I sublet my condo to a really good friend that just got back from Europe. Fred is making sure he's all hooked up to the internet. I can't believe he wasn't already. Man, talk about the dark ages."

Jenny laughed. "Don't be too hard on him. Steve just learned how to use his phone. He didn't know you could video tape on it."

Carol really started to laugh out loud. "Wow, those wilderness men. How are we going to drag them into the twenty-first century?"

"We put a steak in front of their faces, they'll follow us anywhere."

"Jenny, how do you know all this?"

Jenny laughed. "Been married for twenty years. Kinda picked up a few pointers."

Carol started to choke with laughter. "You should write a book for us novice women just starting out on this quest."

"Nah, you figure it out as you go along. It's so much more fun that way," Jenny chuckled.

"You see, you even knew to answer that properly. I'm telling you Jenny, you're a maharishi on marriage."

"Come to me, grasshopper. I will share with you all my knowledge. Should take about twenty minutes and a cup of coffee." Jenny laughed.

Carol started to sound a little more serious. "I'm scared, Jenny. This is moving so fast."

Jenny put on a serious tone as well. "Carol, we're all scared in the beginning. It's the learning curve. Where do we fit in each other's life? But honestly, Carol, you have to try. Come on in. The water is fine."

Carol let out a giant sigh. "I always feel so much better after I talk to you. I can't wait to have you so close to me. For the first time in my life I'm going to have a sister, up close and personal. I am so looking forward to this as well as my life with Fred."

Jenny smiled as she spoke, "Me too, Carol. It will be so nice having you up here with Fred and the family. I feel like we're adding a new chapter to our Book of Family. Get here soon; okay?"

"I'm packing as we speak. See you in seven sleeps."

Jenny laughed. "Seven sleeps. Can't wait. Take care, sweetie."

"You too, Jenny." And Carol hung up.

Steve drove up to the Forestry Office and was surprised to see Fred's truck in the driveway. As he entered the inner office Fred was leaning against a counter with a mug of coffee in his hand and a smile that stretched from ear to ear.

"Why do you look like you swallowed the Tweety Bird?" asked Steve.

"Oh I didn't swallow a birdie, but I found a certain sister-in-law who agreed to marry me."

Steve stopped in his tracks. "You and Carol? So soon? Man that must have been some night in Vancouver!"

Fred put up his hands in defence. "Please, young man, I never kiss and tell. However, I will tell you she makes me so happy. I didn't think I'd ever feel this way again."

Steve looked at him in confusion. "Again? You've been married before?"

Fred nodded and spoke quietly. "Fifteen years ago. Lost her to cancer."

Steve sat down hard on his chair. "Fred, I never knew. You never mentioned it once in all the years I've known you."

Fred looked at the floor then slowly looked at Steve. "A part of my past that was just too painful to talk about. Thought love would only come to me once, and I lost it just as quickly as I got it. Then I met Carol. Man, I just want to run through a daisy field with her. She makes me so happy. Are you okay with this, Bro?"

Steve jumped up and hugged his friend. "Welcome to the family, Fred. Promise me you'll keep her happy. She needs happy, Fred. Just as I suspect you do too. I wish you my absolute best, buddy. I really do."

Fred grinned his crazy grin. "Thanks Bro."

Steve picked up the phone then looked at Fred. "Do you think Jenny knows?"

Fred started to laugh. "I don't know. Do women keep this news a secret for very long?"

Steve hung up the phone. "You're right. She knows. Come on home with me. I know she will want to congratulate you in person."

Fred gave a sly grin. "Well that all depends."

Steve looked at him in confusion. "On what?"

"Are we having chocolate fudge cake or banana cream pie?"

Steve started to laugh. "I don't know, Buddy. Let's go and find out."

The men grabbed their bags and headed back to their trucks.

"You know if Jenny we're available, I'd have a tough time choosing between those ladies," said Fred.

"I'll sleep better tonight knowing she's not," Steve said as he hit Fred on the back of his head. Both men drove away with silly smiles on their faces.

✼ ✼ ✼

The phone rang and Steve picked it up on the first ring. "Hello."

"Hi Steve, this is Harvey Johnson from Search and Rescue."

Steve sat up straighter. "Hi Harvey. What can I do for you?"

Harvey cleared his throat. "I was wondering if I might come and see you in your office. I have something I'd like for you to see."

Steve rubbed his chin. "Sure, Harvey. I'll be here all morning if that suits your time schedule."

"Yeah, Steve. That's great. I'll be there within the hour. See you soon."

Steve hung up and wondered what it was he wanted to share with him. Steve got that funny feeling in the pit of his stomach, and he hated that feeling. It never meant anything good. He picked up the phone and called Fred.

"Hello," said Fred.

"Hi, Fred. Are you busy in the next hour? Harvey Johnson from Search and Rescue wants to see me about something. I've got a lousy feeling. Fred could you be here too. I think I might need a little moral support."

"Sure, Steve. I can be there in twenty minutes. Did he say what he wanted to see you about?"

"No, just that he had something for me to see," said Steve quietly.

Fred nodded. "I'm on my way." Fred turned his truck back onto the highway heading for Steve's office.

Harvey entered the office with his usual loud jovial voice. "Hello, Steve. Oh Fred, didn't think I'd see you too. Nice surprise."

Fred took his hand. "Nice to see you too, Harvey. Just happened to be in the area. Steve thought I might be interested too."

Harvey nodded and sat down on a chair next to Steve's desk and removed his hat.

Steve looked at Harvey. "Can I get you a coffee, Harvey?"

Harvey smiled. "Oh yes, please. Black, no sugar. My wife always says I'm sweet enough." He smiled and winked at Fred.

As Steve handed him his mug of coffee he said, "What's this about, Harvey?"

Harvey took a sip of his coffee. "Well, Steve, we were doing a follow-up in the area your boys disappeared and one of my men found this caught up in a tree branch. Darn near missed it but the sun just shone on it for a second, catching the shine of the gold." Harvey pulled a necklace from his pocket. "Did this belong to one of your boys?"

Steve looked at the necklace. "This is a Tsimshian native art piece. I know Will didn't own a piece, but I don't know about Jimmy. I would have to ask his mother. She'll be here tonight. She's moving up here. As a matter of fact, Fred and her are engaged."

Harvey jumped up and slapped Fred on the back. "Why you old

hound dog. I thought you were a confirmed old bachelor."

Fred laughed. "Not anymore."

Harvey smiled at him. "Fred, I'm happy for you. I really am. Hope to meet the little lady soon. Tracey and I would love to have you for dinner. Get to know each other."

Fred laughed. "Gee, I had to get engaged to finally get invited to dinner?"

Harvey choked on laughter, "Oh God, no. Didn't mean it that way. But you know how wives are. They want to meet all the new ladies settling in up here."

Fred smiled. "Okay, you're off the hook for now. But I'm sure we can arrange dinner in a few weeks or so. Let her get adjusted to the wilderness life. City girl, you know."

Harvey laughed. "You may have your work cut out for you. We're pretty dull compared to the city."

Steve cut in. "She'll have plenty of support from us too. By the way, Harvey, could I keep the necklace and ask Carol if she recognizes it?"

Harvey smiled at Steve. "Absolutely, Steve. This is an expensive piece. Solid gold and all. Sure would like to get it back to the rightful owner."

"Thanks, Harvey. Appreciate your time for the delivery and all."

Harvey grabbed his hat. "No problem, Steve. Thanks for the coffee, and Fred, congratulations again." He shook each man's hand as he exited the office.

Fred looked at Steve. "Do you think this belongs to Jimmy?"

Steve shook his head. "No way. He wears a necklace that belonged to his dad. He never takes it off. But there is an engraving on the back. It looks like initials."

Steve took out his magnifying glass from his desk.

Fred chuckled. "You keep a magnifying glass in your desk?"

"Yeah, so I can read real small things like this. I'm a regular boy scout." He held the glass up to the back of the necklace.

"It looks like the initials, DLG. Here, Fred, you take a look."

"I agree with you, Steve. DLG. Who could that be?"

Steve grabbed the phone. "I have a hunch."

He waited for an answer on the line. "Hello. Is this Reed?" There was a slight pause, "Reed, it's Steve Wright. I was wondering if your brother had a middle name. Ah-ha. And did he by any chance own a gold necklace? I see. Can I get back to you on that? Thanks."

And Steve hung up. Steve grabbed his face in his hands and rubbed his forehead and cheeks.

"Dean Lyle George. And yes, he owned a gold necklace. It was his sixteenth birthday gift from his parents."

Fred shook his head. "Could it have been in that tree for twenty-one years?"

"No way," said Steve. "With a twenty-one-year growth that necklace should be twenty feet up the tree. They found it on a low branch. That means it was recently lost."

Fred blew out a long breath. "Did Dean George come out and return to the cave?"

"Or did the lady have the necklace on and lost it in the tree. And if she did, who gave her the necklace?" Steve asked slowly.

Fred spoke slowly. "He either gave it to her, or it was taken from him. Steve, he didn't come out. That leads me to conclude he might be dead or a prisoner."

Steve put his head in his hands. "The professor said they are peaceful people. He swore his life on that fact. So I think prisoner is out of the question. But Dean didn't come out. If you were away for twenty-one years, wouldn't you want to contact your family?"

Fred nodded. "In one way or another. I don't know how long the cave stays open. The professor's theory was three days, but he wasn't sure. But if Dean had at least one day, he would want to contact his family, don't you think?"

Steve nodded and held up the necklace. "Maybe this was his way to contact them."

Fred sat back in his chair. "He's been gone for twenty-one years. Why didn't he try to get to another cave? He could have been back in three years, just like the professor said. Why didn't he?"

Steve sat up in his chair. "What would make a young man leave his family?"

Fred smiled and nodded. "Only one thing I can think of."

They both said it in unison, "The love of a woman."

Steve rubbed the necklace in his hands. "You know this is all speculation. But I think Chief George deserves to see this, don't you?"

Fred nodded. "Absolutely, but what are you going to tell him. Your son was swallowed up by a cave, probably fell in love with a girl and left you this necklace as proof he is alive and well."

Steve mumbled. "Sounds horrible when you say it that way."

"Steve, it sounds horrible no matter how you say it. This is just a theory. What kind of wounds are we going to reopen for the chief? Is it worth it?"

Steve took a deep sigh. "It could be closure for him. For Reed as well."

Fred rubbed his neck. "Let's ask the girls. Maybe they can give us another way to look at this."

Steve shook his head. "If they conclude that he may be dead, we sir, are screwed. Those mothers will be beside themselves as we wait out the three years. And if they think there is a possibility they could die, you live with them. I'm going camping for three years."

Fred nodded. "Okay, good point! We think about this for a night, and we'll get back tomorrow. In the meantime, I have a lovely lady to pick up at the airport, and I sure don't want to be late."

Steve smiled. "Give her a hug from me, and we'll see you tomorrow for dinner. You did know the girls already planned this?"

Fred laughed. "No, but I'm sure I'll hear about it tonight. Take care, bro." Fred started for the door.

Steve called out to him just before he walked out. "Do you think he's alive, Fred?"

Fred turned and smiled. "I'd leave my world if Carol wanted me to. I'm just so glad she never asked me."

And he shut the door.

CHAPTER TWENTY-NINE

The next morning though a little tired, the boys seemed a little happier about their new route. Will asked Miria what the next village's name was and how long would it take to get there. Miria stopped and looked at him.

"On the map the next village is Kaitoona. It means "the small village." She honestly did not know how long it would take to get there.

"None of us have travelled here before. But Lian believes we should be there by tomorrow."

Jimmy looked at Miria. "How far have you travelled, Miria?"

"I have travelled only as far as Napo. Our chief took my mother and me there about a year after they were blessed. I'm sorry you will not be able to see it. It is a beautiful village."

"Well, I'll bet Kaitoona will be beautiful too. And we can all have an adventure discovering its charms."

"Yes, we shall all learn together. Come Timtuk, it's time to leave." Timtuk came running with Buddy right on his heels.

Jimmy looked at Miria. "You spoke English to him and he understood."

Miria stopped in her tracks. "Did I? And he understood? Timtuk do you understand me?"

Timtuk smiled at her then nodded his head.

"What colour is your shirt?"

Timtuk answered in his language. Miria's jaw dropped, so Will and Jimmy could only guess he answered correctly.

"Did he say blue in your language?" asked Will.

Miria nodded. "I can't believe he is picking up this language so fast."

Jimmy picked up Timtuk and tossed him over his head. "Cause he's so smart. Aren't you, Timtuk?"

Timtuk laughed. "Yes!"

Jimmy almost dropped him. "Wow, he is smart."

Will spoke quietly to Miria. "How old are children when they start showing their special gift?"

Miria looked at Will in confusion. "Each child is different. Some don't show their gift until about twelve years and some can show as young as two. It depends on the child."

Will nodded. "It might be possible Timtuk's gift is understanding different languages. Can you imagine how wonderful that would be to possess? No matter where he goes, he can understand anyone. Man, I'd like that."

Just as he was about to test Timtuk's gift, Lian called out for everyone to take their places. Lian started pulling on the lines, Miria and Timtuk were second with Buddy right behind Miria. Will and Jimmy were behind them and Beya and Donat took up the rear. The next journey was to begin, with everyone going into unknown certainty.

* * *

It was hours before Lian found what appeared to be a flat spot for all their boxes. Will and Jimmy were surprised to see the green moss growing on just about every rock on the ground. It looked like mountains of grass everywhere and for a fleeting moment, Will missed home. Everyone was setting up the camp for a mid-day lunch when they heard a strange noise coming from a cave tunnel on the other side of the mountain of rocks. At first it sounded like thunder, in the far-off distance. But then it got louder and Lian screamed out some orders.

Miria screamed, "Will, Jimmy it's water. We must climb for safety."

Jimmy grabbed Timtuk and threw him on his back, piggyback style. "Come on, Timtuk," he yelled. "Hold on tight."

As if in the all-knowing Timtuk squeezed Jimmy tighter as they climbed the rock wall. Jimmy climbed to a ledge and put Timtuk safely beside him.

He shouted at Will, "Look out!" The water burst out of the tunnel like a raging river. It was flooding the cave in a flash. Miria and Will were sitting on a rock formation that resembled a large oak tree. But the water was cascading up to them.

Will shouted to Miria, "We have to go higher. Follow me."

Will grabbed her hand and she stepped slowly upward onto another rock branch. This time the water did not climb any higher, but it rushed past them with the force of a speeding truck.

"We have to wait it out!" yelled Will to Jimmy.

Jimmy looked around. "Where's the rest of the group?" Will looked around but could not see Beya, Lian or Donat. He gestured to Jimmy with a shrug. Jimmy kept looking but could not see anyone.

"Oh man, I hope they're okay. Just then Jimmy's stomach dropped. "Buddy! Where's Buddy?"

Will went white. "Buddy! Buddy where are you?" they heard nothing but raging water hitting the sides of the cave.

Timtuk started to cry, "Buddy! Buddy!"

Jimmy held Timtuk in his arm. "It's okay, Timtuk. I'll bet he's safe with Donat or Lian. Or maybe Beya has him. We just have to wait for the water to go away; okay?"

Timtuk stopped crying. "Okay."

Jimmy looked at him in amazement and shook his head. "You are one amazing kid, Timtuk." Timtuk nodded and laughed.

It seemed like hours before the water slowly rushed out another tunnel. Jimmy and Timtuk slowly descended from the ledge and Will and Miria climbed down from the rock tree. They started to walk around a corner of the cave where Donat, Buddy, Lian and Beya were climbing down from a tunnel way up the cave wall.

Will looked at the height of the tunnel. "How did Buddy get up there?" Miria asked the men, and they all laughed.

"He swam," she said. "In fact he helped Beya get up there. Beya can't swim."

Beya crouched down by Buddy and rubbed his chest and put his head next to Buddy.

He said some words to Buddy and Will looked at Miria.

"He said he owes Buddy his life. And he will be forever in his ..." she stopped trying to find the word.

Will responded, "Debt. Forever in his debt."

Miria smiled. "They are grateful for you and Jimmy as well for keeping Timtuk and me safe."

Jimmy smiled. "Our pleasure my lady. We are here to serve you."

Everyone started to laugh.

Then Will looked around. "The boxes? Did we lose them?"

Miria asked Lian the question. He shook his head and gestured for them to follow him. Around the corner the boxes were shoved into a crevice. The weight of them kept them anchored.

"Wow, that was good thinking, Lian," said Will to him.

Miria translated and Lian smiled. Will began to look around at the drenched cave.

"Miria, which tunnel do we take? And I vote we don't follow the river; okay?" Miria spoke to Lian and Beya. Beya brought the very wet map out of his shirt and slowly unfolded it on one of the boxes. Lian and Beya looked around the cave, trying to get their bearings. Finally Lian pointed to a tunnel at the far end of the cave. Thankfully, it was not the tunnel that the river had drained into. Everyone started to stand in their line formation. Miria did her magic and the boxes lifted. Lian started to pull the lines.

Timtuk called for Buddy and he barked and joined in the line just behind Timtuk.

Miria grabbed some things from a box before coming into line. She gave Lian a dried piece of meat then gave everyone a large piece as well. When Will and Jimmy took a bite they both looked at each other.

"Jerky! Holy cow, it's jerky," said Jimmy happily.

Miria smiled. "Do you like it?"

Will laughed. "It's one of our favourite snacks. My dad makes beef jerky, deer jerky, moose jerky and salmon jerky too."

Miria looked at Will. "Are these animals you speak of?"

Will nodded. "Yes. Is this not made from an animal?"

She shook her head. "A vegetable."

Both boys looked at her in shock. "Really, a vegetable? It's delicious."

Miria started to laugh and said, "We do not eat much meat here. Mostly fish, if any. I have had a yak dish, but I did not like it very much. I prefer our vegetables."

Will and Jimmy both smiled and took another bite.

Will spoke, "Delicious Miria. I would eat nothing but vegetables if they all tasted like this."

"Please teach that to Timtuk. He can be so fussy with his food." Timtuk took a piece of the jerky and chewed with gusto. Miria started to laugh, "That is the first time he has ever eaten that. Do you like it, Timtuk?" He nodded happily.

"Atta boy, Timtuk," said Will.

"See Miria, he'll eat it if we eat it, right, Timtuk?"

Timtuk stopped chewing and looked at Will with a sly smile. "No," he said and began to laugh. So did everyone else.

✱ ✱ ✱

About an hour down the cave the air turned very warm and humid. Behind them, Donat started blowing a cool breeze at them, and it was a welcome relief. As they entered the large cavern, it was full of growing mushrooms. Mushrooms of all sizes, some as large as cars, others bite size. Everyone was in awe of the sight. Then Buddy started a low grumble in his throat. Everyone was on high alert. Buddy's alarm was not to be ignored. Then he went to a large mushroom and started to wag his tail and gave one small bark.

Will went up to him. "What is it, boy? What do you see?"

Then a shock came over Will as he fell back off his heels. For there in front of him was a tiny little elf creature no bigger than four inches high with tiny luminous wings. At first she ducked behind the mushroom but peeked out when Buddy began to whimper and wag his tail.

Will stammered, "Ah, guys. We have a visitor."

Jimmy, Miria and Timtuk slowly walked up to the mushroom. Miria gasped at the sight and Jimmy just smiled. Timtuk held out his hand to try to touch the little lady. She ducked back behind the mushroom, but Timtuk started to speak to her in a dialect that no one knew what he was saying. No one, except the elf. She started to speak to Timtuk, and he spoke back. Lian, Donat and Beya were standing there with their mouths open. Miria whispered to them of the discovery of Timtuk's gift.

Lian just shook his head and smiled. He then whispered to Miria, and she chuckled. Will looked at her. She smiled and said, "He said he is so grateful the little scoundrel sneaked onto this trip."

Will nodded and smiled at Lian in agreement. Timtuk continued to talk to the elf. She was feeling better about the group and floated gracefully on top of a mushroom. Her wings as fast as a humming birds and just as quiet.

Will looked at Timtuk. "What's she saying, Timtuk?" Timtuk looked at Miria and translated.

Miria translated first to Lian and then to Will and Jimmy.

"She is from Kaitoona. She is picking these vegetables for the feast tonight."

Jimmy looked at Timtuk. "Ask her what the feast is about?"

Timtuk relayed the question and she happily answered back. Timtuk looked at Jimmy. "To celebrate the new baby prince."

Jimmy smiled at Timtuk. "Good job, Timtuk. You're talking to me."

Timtuk smiled at Will and Jimmy. "You are friends. I like you."

Will picked him up and hugged him. "We like you too, Timtuk."

The little elf started to speak again, and Timtuk spun his head to hear her. He listened and then smiled and spoke back to her.

He looked at everyone. "If we help her pick these vegetables, she will take us to the feast."

Miria laughed. "So we're invited for dinner if we pick these. We can do that."

Will, Jimmy and Timtuk started picking the small mushrooms. The little elf came up and shook her head. She pointed to the large ones.

Will looked at her. "Really, you want those ones? Thought they would be too tough to eat." Timtuk relayed the message and she giggled like a small bird. Then she spoke again to Timtuk.

"She says they can feed the whole village if we take three of them."

"Okay, let's get to it," said Jimmy with an army sergeant command.

At first, Jimmy thought he could just push on it really hard, but that proved fruitless as he fell on his butt.

"Whoa, I think we're going to need a saw. These are like small trees."

"Miria, do we have any tools for this job. Sharp sword or something," asked Will.

Timtuk started talking fast to Miria.

Miria translated to everyone. "Do not bring out any weapons. They will frighten her and all her people."

Lian brought out a large saw from one of the boxes. Lian and Donat held the handles and started cutting the mushroom. In a few moments the mushroom fell. The little elf clapped her hands and seemed to dance in the air. Will and Jimmy put their hands out for the saw. Donat smiled and gave it to them. Will and Jimmy started cutting another large mushroom, and after a lot of sweat and perseverance, it finally fell. The little elf clapped and spun in the air. Lian held his hand up indicating another mushroom. The little elf nodded and Lian and Beya began the cutting. After about five minutes the mushroom still had not fallen. Will and Jimmy offered to take over, Lian and Beya happily gave them their positions. Will and Jimmy worked like lumberjacks and with a final cut the mushroom finally fell over.

The little elf flew among them clapping and laughing. Jimmy looked at Will. "Now I know what Peter Pan felt like around Tinker Bell. I'm getting dizzy." The little elf talked to Timtuk again, and he came back to Miria.

"She says if we bring the vegetables, she will lead the way to Kaitoona."

Miria went to the mushrooms and levitated them to the boxes. She placed them on the boxes at the back then took Timtuk and placed him on his box. The elf flew slowly around Miria as if she was in awe of her gift. She touched her hand and Miria said it was like a butterfly touching her.

Jimmy looked at Miria. "You know butterflies? How?"

"My father used to give me butterfly kisses. Then he drew some for me, so I understood what they looked like. I saw some when I was out of the cave. They were orange, yellow and black. They were beautiful. She reminds me of them."

Jimmy laughed. "Yes, I can see the resemblance but butterflies don't talk and look like little people or invite us to feasts. When are we leaving? I'm starving." Everyone laughed and took their positions and the little elf fluttered in front of them into a sparkling blue tunnel.

The tunnel was alive with an iridescent colour of blue, purple, gold and green. Will looked at Jimmy. "Well, Mr. Rockhound, tell me about this rock."

Jimmy smiled and touched the walls that were close. "It's called Peacock Ore because the colours resemble a peacock's feather. The official name is Bornite, though, that's not as fun or colourful as the Peacock Ore name. But it is the chief ore of copper, which is important to the electrical business and also in creating brass. But here it's just a rainbow of beautiful colours. I can't believe this whole cave is made out of it."

Miria looked around and smiled at the little houses built into every small crevice of the cave. Moss lined roofs and rock facing. Each with a different colour of stone on each house. The doors seemed to be made of bark and the windows were open with colourful stones for shutters. She was just about to speak when Timtuk broke in, "Fleera wants us to come to the middle of the village."

Miria looked at Timtuk. "Who's Fleera?"

Timtuk looked at Miria and laughed. "Our wing friend."

"Fleera, what a pretty name. Tell her we will follow," said Miria.

Timtuk spoke to Fleera, and she buzzed around Miria's head like a hummingbird. Then she fluttered in front of Lian. She slowed her wings and looked at him with a cautious look. Lian turned to Timtuk and spoke to him. Timtuk nodded and then spoke to Fleera. Fleera nodded and pointed in another direction. Lian lead the team in that direction with Fleera flittering about in front of him.

Will asked Timtuk. "What did Lian ask?"

Timtuk looked at Will. "He wanted to know where we could safely put our boxes, so no one will be hurt. She leading us to a new place."

Fleera led them to a cleared spot on the far wall of the cave. Lian ordered everyone to store their gear before they went to the feast.

"I wish we had time to clean up. I think we all look a little drowned from this morning," Miria said to Jimmy.

Jimmy laughed. "We may look a little wrinkled, but you, my lady, are always stunning. Wet, dry or a little in between, you look wonderful."

Miria blushed at such a beautiful compliment. "Sir, you make me blush. But I thank you," she said as Jimmy tried to shake out his pants a bit.

"No problem, but now I'm a little self-conscious about my looks. Will, do we look bad?"

Will took his hand to his forehead as if staying off a headache.

"Jimmy, we're in a cave full of fairies. Do you think they give a rat's butt as to how we look? We could be naked, and I don' think they would care. Now let's focus on the task at hand. We have to take these gigantic mushrooms to the village, and hopefully Fleera will introduce us to the big wigs. Can you stay focused now, Mr. Dior?"

Jimmy went into his usual routine of accents. "Sir, you wound me. You make me feel so shallow. Hey, a funny! Shallow, water, us wet. Ha-ha!"

"Shut up you idiot," said Will. But when Jimmy turned Will was chuckling under his breath. *What would we do without him,* he thought. *He makes everyone laugh just when you need it the most. He's a comedic gift to all of us.*

As they entered what seemed like the centre of the village at least fifty small elves came out of their homes and fluttered in a group in front of the team. One of the elves was older looking with white hair and a little portly. He had on a beautiful gold chain around his fur coat. He spoke and Timtuk listened intently.

He then turned to the team. "This man is the chief of the village. He thanks you for the mushrooms and invites us to the feast. A feast to honour the birth of a new baby prince. The king and queen will join us after the feast to introduce us to the new heir."

Miria, Jimmy and Will stood there with their mouths open.

Will looked at Miria. "I swear, he speaks better than me. How is this possible? He used "heir" and "introduce" in perfect order. Where did he learn those words? Have you been teaching him, Jimmy?"

"Not me, cuz. This is all Timtuk," said Jimmy in just as much awe as Will.

Miria smiled. "It's the gift. The power within him is unfolding. He will learn faster each day. He might know thirty or forty languages by the time he is twelve years. Maybe more, I really don't know."

Timtuk spoke loudly to the team. "They wish us to sit by the stream. Everyone will be safe if we are there. However, they worry about Buddy. I told him he is the best guard dog and will not cause any harm to anyone. Of course I did not tell them he will eat them if they harm us." He started to giggle mischievously. Jimmy and

Will snorted out their laughter.

Miria was not amused. "Timtuk, tell them Buddy will do them no harm, and they have nothing to fear. Tell them now, Timtuk!"

Timtuk knew that voice and, it was never good to hear. "Okay." He pouted and Miria gave a sigh of relief.

Jimmy and Will still muffled their laughter and Miria gave them a warning look. They both came to attention and pretended absolutely nothing just happened.

She shook her head. "Children. I'm surrounded by children."

Jimmy looked at Will. "Please tell me she's talking about those elves."

Will smiled coyly. "Yeah, that's exactly what she meant. Come on, let's go and behave ourselves. No fun in it, but Mom will really be ticked off if we don't."

Miria gritted he teeth. "I heard that!"

Jimmy and Will muffled their laughter again as they found a nice place to sit down by the stream.

The whole village of elves were swarming around the air, each with a different sound as if they were softly whistling. Then a larger elf came out of his house and went to the top of the highest building and stood on its peak. Clapping his hands and holding them up in the air as if he were about to conduct an orchestra. The elves fell into a horseshoe formation around this elf. And to the surprise of the team they started to whistle in a chorus of beautiful music. It was soft like a flute and yet sometimes it sounded like a lute, all coming from each elf. It was mesmerizing.

Will leaned over to Jimmy. "I could sleep to this sound."

Jimmy nodded in agreement. "It's beautiful!"

When the song was done, each elf joined hands and circled the centre of the village. The chief put his hands up and slowly brought them down. As he did this, each elf slowly drifted down to a bench or rock within the village centre. The chief elf spoke and doors from a building opened and elves carrying dishes and bowls flew out. They flew to each seated elf and distributed the dishware and cutlery as well. Then with a clap of the chief's hand, elves flew out of the building carrying steaming bowls of food for everyone.

A very small group of male elves brought larger dishes to the team. Will, Jimmy and Miria gestured their thanks while Lian, Beya and Donat made small bows to our hosts. Timtuk thanked them in their language and the male elves smiled and clapped in surprise. One of them spoke to Timtuk, and Timtuk laughed so hard he fell down on the ground.

Will looked at Timtuk. "What did they say to you, Timtuk?"

Timtuk looked at Will. "They thought Buddy was your real hairy child."

And Timtuk started to belly laugh again.

Will looked at Jimmy and Jimmy nodded. "Well he does have your eyes."

Will just covered his mouth and shook his head. Miria covered her mouth as she tried to stifle her laughter.

Will looked at all of them. "I could do worse. He's handsome and brave. What more could a father hope for."

And he started to laugh too.

Finally the food elves brought the steaming bowls to the team. The did not scoop it to them but rather left the bowls on a stone table and hurried away.

Jimmy looked at Miria. "They seem afraid. Do we frighten them?"

Miria smiled. "We are giants in their world. Would you not be nervous too?"

Jimmy laughed. "Point taken."

Miria took a bowl and started to scoop tiny amounts on each of the seven plates. When all the food was dished out she gave each person a plate. The team looked at the small amount of food and then looked at her. At first she scolded Lian, Donat and Beya, and they quickly looked down on their plate and began to eat.

She turned to Will, Jimmy and Timtuk and said, "Don't be rude by the amount they have given us. This amount of food would feed twenty of them for a week. I will make you more before we rest for the night."

They nodded their understanding and slowly began to eat the food. It was delicious. A spicy stew that had a hint of chillies in it, which made it hot and slightly spiced. A tomato dish with onions and cilantro, and a slice of squash the size of a walnut. Will wondered where they got their food from, but before he could ask Timtuk answered him.

"They grow their food in an energy cave. They grow potatoes, squash, tomatoes, peanuts, sweet potatoes, corn and limes."

Will looked at Timtuk. "How did you know I was just thinking that?"

Timtuk looked at Will with an innocent face. "I don't know."

And he continued to nibble on his food.

Jimmy looked at Will. "What's up?"

Will shook his head. "I'm not sure. But I think the little mugwomp is reading our minds now."

Jimmy started to laugh. "Now there's a scary thought. Let me try."

Without saying a word to Timtuk, Jimmy asked him to pass a spoon to him. Without missing a beat of his chewing, Timtuk handed Jimmy a spoon.

Jimmy looked at Will. "Okay, I'm spooked."

Will whispered, "This could be to our advantage if nobody else knows of it. We can learn what Lian is thinking or anyone else for that matter."

Jimmy looked at Will. "Our own little spy. But how do we keep him from spilling the beans?"

Will chuckled. "He loves berries. We hoard the dried ones and use them as a reward to him. He's three, food talks."

Jimmy snorted back his laughter. "I like it. I'll keep Miria entertained while you go make the deal with the midget mind reader."

Will nodded and moved closer to Timtuk. He didn't speak but looked right ahead and thought, *Timtuk, Jimmy and I would like to play a game with you. Are you interested?*

Timtuk nodded.

Will thought again, *Good. Now here's how it works. We don't want you to tell anyone that you can hear our thoughts, just Jimmy and I will know. Nod if you understand?*

He nodded. *Good. Now, when I ask you, I would like you to listen to Lian's thoughts and tell me what he is thinking, but the game must be kept a secret. Lian must not know that you can hear him. Nod if you understand.* Timtuk nodded.

Good. Now, each night before going to sleep, I'll give you ten dried berries as a prize. Is that a deal? Nod if it is?

Timtuk nodded.

Timtuk, I think you are one super kid. And I'm so proud to be your friend. Timtuk looked at Will and smiled his toothy smile and nodded. Will tussled his hair and pulled him in for a hug. Timtuk laughed and held on to Will as well.

From the village centre there came a sound of horns blowing a signal of authority.

The king and queen were entering the village. The queen was holding a tiny little wrap of cloth in her arms. This had to be the baby prince.

Will whispered to Jimmy, "He's no bigger than a peanut shell."

Miria turned to them. "Shhh. We must bow to them."

Will and Jimmy took their cue and gave a gallant bow as the

royal family passed by. The queen looked at the giants and held her baby closer to her chest.

"Ah man, they're afraid of us," whispered Jimmy.

Timtuk whispered to Will, "She's afraid you might steal the baby like the last giants."

Will looked at Timtuk. "Some people stole their baby? Who? When?"

Timtuk looked at the queen for a few moments.

"Some bad people came a long time ago and took their baby girl. She thinks you are going to take this baby."

Will went to Miria. "Miria, can we give the queen a small gift from us. Maybe a light stone for the new prince?"

Miria looked at Will in amazement. "What a thoughtful idea, Will. Why did I not think of it? Timtuk, will you come with me and speak for all of us."

Timtuk smiled and held Miria's hand as she entered the small village centre. She bowed to the royal family and asked Timtuk to repeat her words. He smiled and nodded.

"Your Highnesses, as a token of our appreciation to be included in this festive time, we would like to show our thanks and bestow on your baby son this gift."

She took out the blue stone and tapped it two times. It glowed in the light of the child.

"May your son grow in this light of friendship."

The king and queen both nodded at Miria and smiled. The queen handed the baby to the king and fluttered over to Miria. She curtsied in front of Miria and held out her hand. Miria took it in her pinkie finger, and the small touch was a huge gesture of appreciation and friendship. Miria was just about to take a final bow and leave when a chorus of screams could be heard behind them.

When Will and Jimmy turned their heads to the noise they saw bugs the size of cars barrelling into the small village. Will noticed they were coming from a large crack at the side of the cave. He shouted to Lian and Donat but they were already taking action. Lian started to throw fire bombs at the bugs storming down on the village. Elves were flying everywhere but some bugs had long tongues and sucked them in like a vacuum cleaner.

Jimmy screamed at Will and threw him his bow and arrows. Will loaded as fast as he could and took aim at the large grasshopper swooping down by the royal family. He shot and the bug fell to the ground, mortally wounded. Lian and Donat started working together as a flame thrower. The bugs started to scream a shrill cry and fall down in flames. Jimmy shot a huge bug coming towards them, Miria screamed and grabbed Timtuk just as the bug fell dead to the ground. Lian and Donat started to send the fiery stream into the swarm and they all retreated back to the crack in the cave. But Lian and Donat continued to throw the flames into the crack hoping to kill as many as possible in their retreat.

When all seemed quiet, Lian and Donat returned to the village. Will and Jimmy began to pick up elves that had been hit by the swarm. Some elves were still stunned but flitted their wings to show a sign of life. Others were not so lucky.

Miria picked up the chief of the village. He didn't move, but she waved her hand over his body several times and slowly he moved his wings and then his body. He looked up at Miria and smiled. She heard rustling behind her and she quickly placed the chief down on some soft moss and turned to see the problem. The queen was under a table. She was not moving. Miria gently picked her up in her hands and cradled her in one palm letting her other hand cup over the queen. She closed her eyes and Will saw a light come from her hands. She held the light over the queen for a few moments then looked at the queen. She still did not move.

Miria spread one hand flat over the queen and Will then noticed a green light coming from her hands. Seconds later, the queen began to flutter her wings. Miria gave a sigh of relief as the queen slowly regained consciousness. The queen sat up in Miria's hand and held her head, then she slowly began to stand up. Miria held out her pinkie finger to help the queen. She took it and began to flutter her wings. Slowly, she levitated herself over Miria's hand. She blew her a kiss and fluttered down to the king, who was waiting by Miria's feet.

Timtuk listened to the king and nodded to him. "The king is forever in our debt, for saving his wife, the chief and the village. He wishes for us to stay here for as long as we wish to stay. We are honorary citizens."

Miria bowed to them. "Timtuk, tell them we are honoured but we are on a long journey, and we must leave in the morning. If there is anything we can do to help them before we leave, we are at their service."

Timtuk relayed the message and the elves fluttered around their heads and blew kisses or bowed to them. Will and Jimmy smiled knowing now the queen did not fear them. He wanted to ask Timtuk to find out about the kidnapping of their daughter, but there did not seem to be anytime to get a quiet moment with the royal family. So he had to let it go and hoped they would find eternal happiness with their new son.

***

As everyone was settled around the stream, Miria tucked Timtuk into his bedroll and gave him a kiss on his forehead. Timtuk whispered to her and she nodded.

She walked over to Will.

"He wants you to tuck him in too. Do you mind?"

Will looked at her in astonishment. "Of course not. My pleasure."

And he headed for Timtuk with his pocket full of berries. As he approached Timtuk, he put his finger on his lips. Timtuk smiled and took the berries Will slipped into his hand.

Timtuk put one in his mouth. "The king said the bad men took the baby far away. They chased after them but they just disappeared. It was about the same time I was born, the king said."

Will smiled at Timtuk. "You were listening to my thoughts. Who else were you listening to?"

Timtuk smiled. "Lian's. He is so surprised at you and Jimmy. You're not as worthless as he thought you were."

Will started to chuckle but tried to keep his thoughts in check.

"What's a jerk?" asked Timtuk.

And Will started to muffle his laughter.

"So much for keeping my thoughts to myself. Between you and me, Lian is a jerk. But I am starting to like him a bit; okay?"

Timtuk smiled. "Okay."

Will kissed Timtuk on his forehead. "Good night, you little bandit."

Timtuk chuckled and rolled over in his blanket. Buddy lay down beside him and wagged his tail at Will.

"Good night to you too, my faithful son," he said as he gave Buddy a big rub on his chest.

When Will returned to the rest of the group Miria handed him a bowl with a sweet potato and a corn muffin. He thanked her and sat down by Jimmy.

Jimmy quietly whispered, "Well, what did our little secret agent tell you?"

Will chuckled quietly. "Lian doesn't think we're as worthless as he originally thought."

Jimmy went into his Dana Carvey churchgoer voice. "Well now, isn't that special?"

Will tried to stifle his laughter.

"Yeah, and the little princess was stolen three years ago. When they chased after the kidnappers, they simply disappeared. Sound familiar?"

Jimmy looked at him in confusion.

"Someone else has the same gift as Beya? I wonder if they know," pointing to the rest of the group."

Will looked at Jimmy.

"You think Beya could have been a part of that group?"

Jimmy shook his head. "No way. Not in a hundred years. He's a good guy."

Will nodded. "I thought so to, but I just wanted to hear you say it. I'm going to talk to Miria about it. Maybe she knows more people with the gift."

Will sat down by Miria who seemed lost in her thoughts. "Hi, can I interrupt your peace?"

She smiled. "Of course you may. What do you want to talk about?"

Will whispered to her. "The gifts you all possess. By the way, fantastic job today. I am so glad we have a healer with us. You were absolutely wonderful today."

Miria blushed. "I did my job. And I too am glad of our gifts. It would have been a tragic day today had we not been here."

Will nodded. "Miria does anyone else hold those same gifts as you all do?"

Miria looked at him. "Well, you know my aunt is a healer as well. But no, I do not know of anyone with the same gifts of Lian, Donat and Beya. Why do you ask?"

"Just wondering. Could their relatives have the same power?"

"Lian's father can move things by just looking at it. Donat's father can grow anything he's given to grow. A seed or a plant, he can make it thrive and grow in our world. That's why we take berry bushes, plants and trees whenever we go to the outside world. And Beya's father was killed a long time ago when he was on a trade mission to another village."

Will looked at her in a serious way. "Another killing? I thought you said your people are peaceful and against killing people."

Miria looked hurt. "We are! But I told you there is a group of bad people out there. We may come across them ourselves, but I pray every night that this will not happen."

Will whispered again, "Miria, you told me once that if they did ambush us, your team would probably be enslaved by them. They want your powers?"

Miria nodded. "Yes, we are sought after by them. Why do you ask this?"

Will gave Miria a quick kiss on the forehead.

"I'll get back to you on that later." And he jumped up to go speak to Jimmy.

CHAPTER THIRTY

Fred watched with sheer anticipation as the passengers descended from the plane. When he saw Carol at the top of the stairs his heart took an extra beat and he felt light-headed. It was a great feeling that someone could cause such a feeling in a big burly guy like him. As she entered the passenger gate she ran into his waiting arms.

"Oh, I've missed you!" he said picking her up off the ground.

"You took the words right out of my mouth."

He smiled. "No, I'd rather take this from your mouth." And he gave her an earth-shattering kiss.

"Whoa boy, that's the kind of hello kiss I'd like from you every night." He gave her a quick peck on her cheek.

"It's a deal. Now let's get your bags."

* * *

As they drove up to his log cabin Carol was getting a little nervous. She had never seen it before and she wondered what kind of startling surprise she was in for, him being a bachelor for so long. When he opened the door and let her step in front of him, her mouth dropped to the ground. The rooms sparkled. The gingham curtains had been freshly laundered and pressed. There was not a speck of dust anywhere. The floor shone from a new wax job and the kitchen table was set for two with a red checkered table cloth, wine glasses and a bud vase with a red rose. She turned and looked at Fred. "It's beautiful! And so clean. Did you do this?"

He smiled at her. "I would like to take all the credit, but I had a team of seven come in and do their magic. The Magnificent Seven, I call them. And they even did the grocery shopping for me. They think I'm an idiot, I'm sure of it. But I am grateful for all their hard work."

Carol smiled. "Me too."

She walked around the house. She loved the river rock fireplace, the big leather couch. *So masculine*, she thought. She stopped and looked at a photo on the wall. "Are these your parents?" He nodded. She smiled and continued her stroll through the house.

She opened a door just down the hall.

"Oh, a powder room. Didn't see that coming."

She avoided going down the hall but went into the kitchen instead. She loved the big stove with six burners.

"Do you have gas out here?"

He shook his head. "Propane." She nodded in approval.

She opened another door, the laundry room. "Have you ever used these machines? They look brand new."

He laughed, "They are. They were delivered three days ago. My old ones were just not going to impress you at all."

Carol slowly turned to face him.

"Fred, is that what you're doing? Trying to impress me?" He nodded his head slowly.

She walked up to him and put her arms around his neck. "You could live in a bear cave, and I would be happy. As long as you're by my side, I'm happy."

He kissed her softly and hugged her to his chest. "Oh man, I could have saved a fortune if I'd known that!"

She laughed at him and softly punched his arm. "But I appreciate the gesture, Fred, I really do." She slowly walked into the living room and turned to him.

"Are you as nervous as I am?"

He smiled at her, walked over to her and swept her up in his arms. She screamed with glee. "Let me relieve you of your nervousness my love." And he carried her down the hall.

✻ ✻ ✻

The next morning was picture perfect, blue sky, sunny with just a wisp of a cool breeze. Fred drove to Steve's office and parked his truck in the driveway. Steve stepped out with a cup of coffee in his hand. "Morning, love bird. How's it going?"

Fred actually blushed while grinning at Steve. "Could use a cup of that," he said as he pointed to the coffee cup.

Steve smiled. "Oh, did you have a rough night? Couldn't sleep? Poor baby!"

Fred started to snort his laughter.

"Shut up and let me have some coffee. And no, I slept like a baby, thank you. But that's all I'm saying, if you get my drift."

Steve smiled and followed Fred into the office.

"You're just no fun for details."

Fred looked at him with a scowl. "Come on, she may be family, but she's also a lady. I don't kiss and tell."

Steve smiled. "Good to hear. I wasn't prying, just giving you a bad time, old man. Now what do you think we should do about the necklace?"

Fred looked at Steve and took a long swig of his coffee. "I think we should talk to Reed. He should be able to tell us how we should handle this scenario, and if we should involve the chief. Let's face it, Steve, he's the only one who really knows what happened to Dean. We can discuss it with him."

Steve nodded. "That's exactly the same conclusion I came to. I'll call him and ask if we can see him this morning."

Steve picked up the phone and started dialing. Fred took his coffee to the veranda outside and enjoyed the vista of the mountains, trees and blue sky. It didn't matter how many times you looked at it, it never grew tiresome. *You appreciate every second you have up here,* he thought. He whispered to himself, "Please God, let Carol love it as much as I do."

Steve opened the door.

"He says we can come right over. He's not committed to anything until about two this afternoon."

Fred finished his coffee and Steve took the mugs into the office.

Fred asked, "Are we taking one truck, or do you have to be somewhere else this morning?"

Steve stopped for a second to ponder the question. "Let's just take one truck. I don't have to be out in that area until the end of the week. I have to go to the valley this afternoon, and that's in the opposite direction. Let's go together. I'll drive, that way you can catch up on your beauty sleep. Man you look old!"

Fred started to chuckle. "The only gray hairs I get is from your driving skills."

Steve laughed. "I guess that hair dye is just not working for you, eh?"

Fred jumped into the truck.

"Abuse, that all I take from you. Verbal abuse."

Steve laughed and backed out of the driveway.

✱✱✱

Reed was in the back of his house splitting firewood. His pile was sizeable and Steve was impressed.

"Wow Reed! You expecting a huge snowstorm this winter?"

Reed smiled. "No, I'm cutting this for the elders. That's what I have to do this afternoon. Deliver all these cords of wood. It keeps me busy for the band."

Fred and Steve nodded and smiled their approval.

Reed looked at Steve.

"So, what was with all those questions about Dean yesterday?"

Steve pulled the necklace out of his shirt pocket.

"Do you recognize this?" he asked.

Reed gently took the necklace in his hand and turned it over. He nodded.

"This is Dean's. No doubt about it. Where did you find it?"

Fred quietly said, "Search and Rescue went back for another look and found this tangled in a tree branch."

Reed shook his head. "Dean couldn't have dropped it. The tree growth would have put it up ten to twenty feet."

Steve nodded. "That was our conclusion too. So we think someone wore it out of the cave. We have two possible scenarios, and we wanted your feedback on them."

Reed sat down on his log chair and motioned for Fred and Steve to do the same. Reed took a deep breath. "Okay, let me hear them."

Steve looked at Fred, but he nodded to Steve to give the conclusions.

"Okay," said Steve, "the first scenario is that Dean is well and living with these people, and he left his necklace as proof to you and your family that he is alive and well."

Reed nodded. "Okay, and the next conclusion?"

Steve took a slow deep breath. "We know a woman came out of the cave with the child. We believe she might have been wearing it and lost it running back to the cave."

Reed looked at Steve and Fred without expression. "How do you think she got the necklace?"

Fred cut in. "It's pure speculation, Reed, but Dean could have given it to her."

Reed was quiet for a moment.

"You mean you think she was a girlfriend or wife to him?"

Steve nodded. "That's a possibility."

Reed was quiet again.

"If he was alive and well he would never have left the necklace. It was a badge of honour to him. My father gave it to him, and I know he would never leave it out there for anyone to find. If he wanted to leave a message for us he would have built a rock formation like this."

He pointed towards his house. There were six large stones in the formation. Three were on the bottom standing on their edge, two were balanced on top of the three and finally a lone rock was sitting at the top.

Reed looked at them.

"Whenever we went hunting or fishing or were just fooling around, if we got lost we were to build this "hocuta." It was a guide to follow, so we could find one another. It is also a family tradition to place it near our homes to keep our family safe from the spirits. Dean would have built this if he was alive and well and wanted us to know it. The necklace leads me to believe he is dead, and the woman who lost it, must have been someone special to him."

No one spoke for quite a while. Steve cleared his throat. We did have a theory like that too, Reed, but we were hoping we were wrong."

Reed just twirled the necklace in his hands.

Fred whispered to him, "What should we tell your father, Reed? Or should we say nothing?"

Reed bowed his head and kept rubbing the necklace between his thumbs.

"I believe Dean has already come to my father. Many years ago, my father dreamed of him riding to him on a white stallion. He said he looked happy and waved to my father as he disappeared into a white cloud. My father accepted that Dean was gone then. It was me who needed closure. There are still too many unanswered questions, but I know beyond any doubt now that Dean is dead. I just wish I knew what happened to him."

Steve sat closer to Reed and whispered, "I'll have the answers you need in three years. My boys will be back then, and I am sure they will have all the answers you need to put peace back into your life."

Reed looked up at Steve. "You believe your boys will be back in three years? How?"

Fred patted him on his back. "A very wise old man convinced us. We'll have your answers, Reed. Trust us."

Reed nodded his head and held up the necklace. "Thank you for this. I feel like a part of Dean is back with me."

Steve shook his hand. "You're welcome, Reed. If you ever want to talk about this or anything else, you know where to find me."

Reed smiled and gave Steve a huge hug. He turned to Fred and gave him one too and then slowly walked towards his house, looking at the necklace the whole time.

✳ ✳ ✳

Carol and Jenny looked at the men as they ate their dinner. Jenny broke the silence, "You two seem unusually quiet tonight. Is anything wrong?"

Steve and Fred both looked up from their plates. "Absolutely nothing," Fred said with a little more conviction than he intended.

Steve touched Jenny's hand. "Dinner is excellent by the way."

"Thanks, and Carol made the dessert. It looks fantastic." Jenny said with a smile to her sister-in-law.

Carol smiled. "Thanks, Jenny. It's my grandmother's recipe. It's an English trifle with a little more sherry in it that what the recipe calls for. I think it's an improvement. Katie, I made you a special one. No sherry but lots of raspberry jam."

Katie grinned from ear to ear. "Thank you, Auntie Carol. Raspberry jam is my favourite."

Carol smiled at her. "That's what I hear. Hope you like it."

Katie's eyes became as big as saucers. "Oh, I will! I will!"

Fred chuckled at Katie. He just thought she was the cutest thing he had ever seen.

"Steve and I will do the dishes," he said happily.

Steve rolled up his nose. "We will? Is it someone's birthday or something?"

Jenny started to laugh. "Aw, my knight in shiny armour. No, dear. I think Fred is just being very considerate. Take a page from his book; okay?"

Steve laughed. "Okay. Okay. I know when I'm being made to feel like a heel. Why don't you ladies go into the living room, and I'll put on the kettle for tea. We can have dessert in there. Katie honey, how about you have your dessert in the kitchen with me and Uncle Fred?"

"Oh boy!" she shouted and jumped down from her chair. "Can I sit at the counter?"

Steve laughed. "Wouldn't want it any other way," he said as he watched Katie scoot into the kitchen. Fred picked her up and settled her on the counter stool.

"Don't wiggle too much, Katie. Don't want you falling and hurting yourself."

She grinned at her Uncle Fred and giggled. Then she asked the million-dollar question. "Are you going to marry Aunt Carol?"

Without skipping a beat Fred replied, "Yup!"

Katie smiled at him. "Good. How about babies? Daddy said we can have one but my mommy said we can't."

Fred started to laugh into his chest. "Well Katie, to tell you the truth, we haven't talked about it yet. But when we do, you will be the first person I'll tell; okay?"

Katie gave one of her smiles that showed the dimples around her mouth.

"Okay, Uncle Fred."

Fred thought, *If we do have children, I want a little girl just like Katie.*

Steve walked into the kitchen with all the plates and cutlery. Fred took the single bowl of trifle from the refrigerator and handed it to Katie. He quickly got a spoon for her and handed it to her slowly.

"You sure you can eat all this. Maybe I should help you," and he took out a spoon as well.

"NO!" she laughed, "You have the big bowl in the fridge."

Fred's eyes popped out and his mouth dropped as he ran to the fridge and pointed. "That big bowl is all for me?"

Katie almost choked with laughter. "No, you gotta share with the parents."

Fred tried to look really disappointed. "Darn, I was really excited there for a minute. You sure I gotta share, Katie?"

Katie nodded her head with a spoon in her mouth.

"Boy, tough rules. But if you say so, I'll do it." Fred smiled.

Katie just giggled. "You're funny, Uncle Fred."

Steve piped in. "Yeah, Uncle Fred. Now grab the rest of the dishes from the table since you volunteered us for KP duty."

Fred winked at Katie and went back into the dining room.

Carol and Jenny sat comfortably on the two recliners in the

living room. "Is it just me, or do the guys seem a little quiet to you?" asked Jenny.

Carol nodded. "Come to think of it, Fred did seem like he had a lot on his mind. I was afraid to talk to him about it. Thought it might be because of me. Second thoughts and all."

Jenny snorted a laugh. "Sweetie, he has no second thoughts about you. He was so excited that you were coming. By the way, how did the 'Magnificent Seven' do with the cleaning?"

Carol laughed. "Oh Jenny, it was spotless. And do you know he ordered me a new washer and dryer? Said the old ones came over on the Mayflower."

Jenny laughed quietly. "He wanted everything to be perfect, was it?"

Carol's eyes glistened over. "Oh Jenny, it was all perfect. I can't tell you how happy I am right now. I feel as guilty as hell about it, though."

Jenny sat up straight. "Why for heaven's sake?"

Carol started to fidget with her fingers. "Because of Jimmy. What is he going through right now? Is he happy, or is he in trouble? And here I am back home -- no in my new home, feeling like a giggling school girl. I think that deserves some guilt, don't you?"

Jenny held Carol's hand. "I was reading this book last week. It was about two young native boys coming of age. They had to leave their family and meet three challenges the elders gave them to accomplish, and they could not come back until it was done. They were to kill a buffalo with only a knife and return the hide to them. They had to climb a mountain and obtain a feather from the nest of a golden eagle. And their final test, a claw from a grizzly bear. They had to survive in the wilderness with only a knife and their brains for as long as it took them to accomplish the other tasks. The boys were thirteen years old, and guess what? They did it! Because it was important to them and their families. Now take that story and ask yourself, would our boys rise to a challenge? My answer is absolutely yes. Steve taught them survival skills. He was always so proud of them and how fast they learned. He believes they can do it and so do I. And I will wait for them patiently and with pride because I know our boys will make it. I don't see it any other way."

Carol looked at Jenny and left her seat to hug her. "Oh, I am so glad I'm up here with you. I need a shot of optimism ever so often. Thank you, and I'll try to keep your spirits up whenever you need a lift too."

Jenny smiled at Carol. "Just having you up here is all I need. Another mother going through the same journey as me. Who else could understand this better?"

Carol smiled and jumped a little as Steve and Fred carried in the dessert and a tray of tea cups and a teapot.

Steve boasted. "Now ladies, how good can this get? Tea, dessert, good company. Katie's getting ready for bed without a fuss. All is well."

Carol and Jenny just looked at each other and smiled.

Carol looked at the group. "All is well, Steve. Very well."

CHAPTER THIRTY-ONE

Jimmy was munching on his corn muffin when Will sat down beside him. Jimmy looked at him. "Well, what did you find out?"

Will shook his head. "Apparently, their relatives have special gifts too, but Miria doesn't think anyone else has Beya's gift. However, Beya's father was killed on a trade mission a long time ago. I've got a sneaky suspicion that he wasn't killed and these ugly tribesmen enslaved him for his gift."

Jimmy stopped chewing. "Whoa, that's some theory. But if these guys just disappeared like Timtuk was told, how else could they do it?"

Will nodded. "Exactly, and how do you think Beya will feel if he finds out his father is still alive?"

Jimmy looked at Will. "All good questions, Sherlock, but for now I think we should keep this to ourselves; okay?"

Will nodded in agreement. "Jimmy, why would they kidnap a baby elf? What's the point? They don't have any special powers except flying. What would make them do that?"

Jimmy sat up and whispered to Will, "I was thinking the exact same thing when you were speaking with Miria. I wasn't getting far with any really good theory, and then I began to watch Buddy. He was laying his head by Timtuk, licking his hand, snuggling close to him. It was at that moment that I came to a real sick theory, for a pet. They took the baby so they could raise and teach her their ways. No memories, so therefore no real problems. She won't even remember her family or where she came from. Think of it Will, a pet."

Will let out a slow gust of air. "Jimmy, that's an excellent theory, and it makes the most sense. This rogue tribe is really something to worry about. Miria says she prays every night that we don't cross paths with them. I wonder if in three years we can be so lucky."

Jimmy snuggled down into his bedroll. "You, dear cousin, have said a mouthful. Goodnight."

Will grabbed his bedroll. "Yeah, goodnight, Jim."

***

In the morning all was packed up early for the next step of their journey. Will greeted Miria as she was getting breakfast for everyone. She gave Will a plate with an mushroom omelette on it.

"Miria, this looks fantastic. But where did you get the eggs?"

She smiled. "The king sent them to us with a wonderful basket of mushrooms. We will be eating them for days, I think."

Will smiled as he took a big bite of the omelette. "Oh man! Miria, this is delicious. I could eat mushrooms for a month and never tire of them."

She smiled at him as Jimmy approached with Timtuk.

"Hey Mom, what's for breakfast?"

Miria chuckled at the mom reference and handed Jimmy and Timtuk their plates.

Jimmy looked at it. "Wow, a mushroom omelette. Where did you get the eggs?"

Will started to laugh. "Miria, you should make a sign. It would save you so much time."

Miria laughed and looked at Jimmy. "The king sent them to us. And the mushrooms. We have enough mushrooms for our journey to Quintoke. We will get more supplies there."

Jimmy and William looked at Miria before William asked. "How far is Quintoke, and what makes it special?"

Miria answered as she began to clean their plates and forks. "Lian believes it is about a three-day journey. As to what makes it special, we just don't know. None of us have ever journeyed so far, so each village is as much a surprise for us as it is for you."

Jimmy and Will began to fill the last boxes with the bedrolls and the breakfast dishes. Lian walked over and began to speak to Miria, she nodded and continued on with her work. Will looked at Lian and gave him a courteous nod and a small smile. Lian said nothing but just walked over to Beya and Donat.

Will picked up Timtuk and began to walk him away from Miria. Without speaking, he asked Timtuk in his thoughts, what did Lian just think when he looked at me?

Timtuk whispered in his ear, "Stay away from Miria, you snake."

Will chuckled a little. *Now, isn't that so special,* he thought. Timtuk laughed at his Dana Carvey impression. Will hugged Timtuk as he placed him on his box.

"Timtuk, this game we're playing is going to be so much fun. But you must keep it a secret; okay?"

Timtuk nodded. "Okay."

Buddy bounded over to Will and jumped up on his chest. "Whoa, Buddy, you're too big for that kind of play. Now stay by Timtuk; okay?"

Buddy gave him an understanding woof and Will smiled and patted his chest.

Everything was ready and Miria did her magic again and the boxes floated. Lian pulled on the lines and the gang was off again.

But before they entered the cave, the elves fluttered to them waving and blowing kisses. It was a beautiful send off, and the gang waved and said their goodbyes as they entered the cave.

* * *

They had travelled for several hours and the caverns were filled with colourful crystals and what appeared to be green jade-like stones. The odd thing that Jimmy noticed was that they were continuously going downhill.

Jimmy looked at Will. "I swear, if we hit lava, I'm going back to the elves."

Will smiled at him. "Me too. How deep down do you think we are?"

Jimmy looked at his cousin. "The way my ears keep cracking, I'd say five or six thousand. Can we get the bends down here?"

Will laughed. "Don't think so, but I sure have to wonder about the air quality down here."

As if on cue Donat starting blowing inside the cave. It was cool and refreshing as if an air conditioner had just been turned on. Jimmy turned to Donat and gave him a thumbs up. Donat smiled and nodded his head in understanding.

They finally came out of the cave and entered a cavern that had arches of stone. They resembled bridges, and yet they just went from one side of the cave to the other. Jimmy counted twenty-two of them and everyone was astonished by the beauty and the vastness of the cave. Lian shouted an order and everyone knew it was time for a rest.

Jimmy came up to Will. "Look at this place. It's like the Grand Canyon meets the Himalayan Mountains. It's incredible!"

Will nodded. "Jimmy, can you believe the colours down here.

There's the orange and purple over there, and the green arches are breathtaking. I hope we can stay here for a while. I'd like to explore, wouldn't you?"

Jimmy looked at his cousin. "Absolutely. Do you think Chuckles will let this happen, or will we have to drug his food?"

Will laughed. "Let's hope it will be a long pit stop."

As everyone was getting settled for their lunchtime break, Jimmy asked Miria how long they would be staying here? Miria looked over at Lian and asked the question.

When he answered back Miria looked back at Jimmy. "For a few hours. He hopes to make a plateau before dinner."

Jimmy jumped up. "That's great. Will and I would like to explore this cave for a while. We won't be long."

Miria watched as the two boys scurried off in the direction of the arches. She wondered if they would climb one or two of them then came to the conclusion that they most likely would, throwing caution to the wind. *Please keep safe,* she thought.

Timtuk turned his head and looked at her. He just smiled his toothy grin. But for one moment Miria felt like he knew what she was thinking.

Will and Jimmy climbed over rocks and crawled along small arches as they were heading for the larger ones up ahead.

"Look at this, Will. This rock is called Chinos Flerix, and it is like a bunch of agates all stuck together making it appear like it's made of glass. When you cut and polish it, it has depth like glass caves throughout the rock. It's really unique and special, though not valuable like a gem stone. But it is rare."

Will looked at his cousin. "We're down about six thousand feet. I hardly think this rock is in abundance on the surface. It even looks like it has flecks of gold in it."

Jimmy looked closely at the rock. "No, it's just mica, but it sure is pretty."

They continued to climb the side of the cavern. It was like rock climbing only more edges to grip. They reached the tallest arch and began to cross it. Half way they searched the cave for their group. When they saw Miria and Timtuk way off in the distance, they howled and waved to them. Miria looked in their direction and saw two specs on the arch.

She thought, *Oh my God! They are going to get killed.*

Timtuk started to cry. Miria turned around. "Timtuk, what is wrong?"

Timtuk realized his mistake and the secret he had to keep. "I have a tummy ache. Can you make it better?" he tried to sound convincing to his sister.

Miria scooped him up in her arms. "Of course, my little one. Let's get you to lay down."

Timtuk lay on his box, and Miria spread her hands over his stomach. After she crossed over his stomach two times, he smiled at her.

"Thank you, Miria. I feel better."

Miria looked at Timtuk suspiciously. "So soon? Are you sure you had a stomach ache?"

Timtuk couldn't look her in the eyes, but he did read her thoughts, and she was sure he was faking.

"Maybe I have to go and poop," he said with all innocence.

Miria smiled. "That could be the reason for your tummy ache. Go over to the hole Beya dug. And please be careful."

Timtuk ran towards their makeshift outhouse, glad to be away from Miria and her suspicions.

Jimmy and Will sat down on the arch bridge and looked at the vista around them. Jimmy was the first to speak. "How high do you think we are?"

Will looked over the side. "I don't know. Two maybe three hundred feet."

Jimmy gave out a slow whistle. "Wow, and there is at least a hundred feet on top of us. This cave is incredible, and no one up above knows of it. Now I know what the early explorers felt like. What a great feeling!"

Will laughed. "Yeah, if we had a flag we could claim it and name it."

"Oh good point, what do you think we should name it?"

"I don't know, the Golden Arches has already been used."

Jimmy looked at Will with enthusiasm.

"But the Wright Arch Cavern hasn't been used."

Will smiled. "That does have a nice ring to it. Okay, let's do it."

He started to pick up some loose stones and began to pile them in a small mound. He smiled as Jimmy added a few to the top as well.

Will cleared his throat. "I claim this cave as the Wright Arch Cavern, and forever it shall be protected as a National Park for those that wish to visit."

Jimmy snickered. "Yeah, we have high season traffic right now. Please call ahead for reservations."

They both laughed and stood again to survey their new claimed land. Will whispered, "I wish Dad could see this place. He would love it."

Jimmy nodded. "Yeah, and we can't even take pictures since everything was quarantined after our boat ride. Wouldn't matter, though. No power."

Will nodded. "Besides, our oath to them, remember? We can't jeopardize their world. Not for anything or anyone."

Jimmy smiled. "I'm with you on that, cuz. We' better get back. Lian will be chomping at the bit to get under way."

Will mumbled, "Yes, let's not disappoint Lian!"

Jimmy just laughed quietly to himself as they descended the

huge arch.

***

As the boys reached Miria and the others, she smiled and was secretly relieved to see them safe and sound. Beya and Donat smiled and waved their greeting, but Lian just leered at them and started to assemble the lines on the boxes.

Jimmy whispered to Timtuk, "Is Lian mad at us?"

Timtuk whispered back, "He was thinking you two should be tied up, so you don't go off like that again."

Jimmy laughed. "Really! Well, isn't he just so funny."

Timtuk looked at him and started to laugh.

"Yeah, funny Lian."

Jimmy rubbed his hair and returned to Will.

"Seems our dear leader thinks we should be tied up to avoid us exploring."

Will looked at Jimmy. "What a jerk. But as long as he keeps those thoughts to himself, we can't complain. Besides, Miria would never stand for it. This I know!"

Jimmy smiled and walked to Miria.

"Can I help you with anything, Miria?"

She smiled at him. "Oh thank you, Jimmy. Could you put the plates in the box for me and the forks as well?"

Jimmy picked up the pile of dishes. "No problem." He placed them in the box. When he moved some small boxes to make more room, a small box flipped open and a watch fell out. Jimmy picked it up and recognized the name brand immediately. He quickly put it back in the small box and neatly returned it to the original spot. *Must be her father's*, he thought and chose to forget about it. If Miria wants to talk about it, he would listen, but only when she was ready.

Will was settling Timtuk on his box and giving Buddy extra hugs and pats for taking care of Timtuk.

"You're such a good dog, Buddy. Now stay with Timtuk. You watch my dog too; okay, Timtuk?"

Timtuk gave the thumbs up sign.

"Okay, Will." Will just laughed as he took his place in line.

Lian screamed his command and everyone started to walk down the path to another cave and another adventure.

✶ ✶ ✶

Another four hours of walking and everyone was starting to show their exhaustion. Lian wasn't happy with the area for overnight camping, but he relented when he saw how tired Miria and Timtuk looked. Fortunately, they found a small stream of water behind some large boulders, so Lian seemed a little relieved. Everyone took out their bedrolls and chose their sleeping arrangements. Miria always looked for a small cavern where Timtuk could sleep in, and she could block his way if he tried to get out.

Then Miria started to take out the food she had planned for dinner, the dishes, the cutlery and her heating rocks.

Will came up to her. "Hi, need any help?"

She smiled at Will. "I like your culture, Will. It is not beneath you to help with a job that my culture considers woman's work only."

Will laughed. "In my culture it's help with all chores or be killed."

She looked at him with shock and Will burst out laughing. "I'm kidding, Miria! But my mother makes sure we help with all chores. If you eat, you help with dishes, and when you get older, you help with the cooking. I must admit, I make really good pancakes."

Miria looked at him. "Pancakes? What are pancakes?"

Will smiled. "I wish we had all the ingredients. I know you have corn flour, but I also need baking powder, sugar, eggs and milk. Though I think water would do in a pinch."

Miria began to think. "We have eggs, corn flour, but what is baking powder?"

Will put his hands together and slowly started to separate them. "It makes the pancakes rise up and get fluffy inside."

Miria scratched her head. "I think I have something like this. What else do we need?"

"Sugar, do you have something sweet we can use?"

She went into the large box with the food supply and came back with a stone canister. She lifted the lid and a golden sand was inside. "Do you mean this?"

Will poured a tiny bit on his hand and wet a finger and touched the sandy substance and licked it. It was sweet. "Perfect," said Will loudly. "You're in for a treat tonight, Miria!" And he went about looking for a large bowl to make the batter. He whistled as he broke three eggs into the flour, sugar, and Aztec baking powder mixture and started whipping the batter together adding water when needed. He dropped a small scoop on the fire rock and Miria enjoyed watching them bubbling and Will flipping them over. When three were ready, he gave one to Timtuk, one to Miria and one to Beya (because he was standing and watching Will cook.) When Miria took a small bite she was surprised as to how good it was. Timtuk gobbled his down in four bites. Miria looked amazed at Will.

"These are delicious. What are they called again?"

"Pancakes," said Will proudly.

Beya held up his thumb in satisfaction. Donat and Lian came over to see what all the fuss was about. Miria quickly explained Will's talent for cooking the pancakes and how they must try them. Donat nodded his willingness, but Lian spoke to Miria in a very firm voice, and she quickly nodded and went to get food for him.

Will knew just by the way Miria looked that he was chastising her for not doing her woman's work.

Will walked over to Lian and handed him a plate with a pancake on it. Lian put his hand up and walked away.

Will yelled at Timtuk. "Timtuk, tell Lian to try the pancake, or I will be insulted."

Timtuk relayed the message and Lian stopped in his tracks and turned around. He had a strange sneering smile on his face. He slowly came back to Will and took the pancake from the plate. He then walked over to Buddy and gave it to him. Buddy of course ate it with gusto. Lian then turned and walked away. Will mumbled under his breath,

"You son of a …"

Jimmy cut in. "There's always a food critic when you least expect it. Come on Will, everyone else enjoyed them. Cook some more."

Will turned and faced his cousin. "Okay. More for everyone else, even you, Buddy."

And he continued to cook until the batter was done.

Miria took out some dried fruit, a muffin and some jerky and went to Lian. She placed it on a rock near him and just walked away. She made her feelings known just by the look on her face. Anger and a whole lot of disgust.

* * *

Dinner was over, Timtuk was getting ready for bed and Will was still grumbling about Lian.

Jimmy looked at his cousin. "Don't let him get to you. I swear that is his game with you. Walk away, even though you would really like to give him a black eye. Be a better man than that. The only one who would really get hurt in all of this is Miria. She has to stay with him when we go home. Do you want her life to be miserable after we leave?"

Will looked at Jimmy. "No, of course not. I guess I wasn't thinking clearly. You're right Jim, I have to rise above that creep, no matter what. Thank heaven I still have you to help me do it."

Jimmy smiled his cheeky grin. "Yeah, I'm a regular Dalai Lama."

Will looked over at Timtuk.

"Our little secret agent is about to go to bed. Why don't you go and talk to him about his discovery of minds today? I'm afraid he'll tell me what Lian was thinking, and your speech to me will go right out the door."

Jimmy chuckled under his breath. "Good point. Where are the berries?"

Will took out ten berries from his stash and gave them to Jimmy. Jimmy stood and walked to Timtuk's bed. He sat down beside him but only used his thoughts to communicate to Timtuk.

Hey guy, what did you hear today?

Timtuk whispered, "Lian thinks Will is a girl. Why would he think that?"

Jimmy touched Timtuk hand and thought, *Because Will cooked for us tonight. In our culture, we all help with all chores. It doesn't make you less of a person when you help someone, does it?*

Timtuk shook his head. Jimmy continued. *And did you think less of Will because he cooked for us?*

Timtuk whispered, "No, I would like to do that too."

Jimmy smiled. *We can arrange that, Timtuk. What else did you hear today?*

Timtuk whispered into Jimmy's ear, "Miria, thinks Lian is dung for not trying a pancake."

Jimmy laughed. *So did I. But it was his loss, wasn't it?*

Timtuk nodded his head very quickly.

"They were so good, Jimmy. Do you think he will teach me how to cook?"

Jimmy smiled. *I'm sure he will. Now how about Donat and Beya? What did you hear today?*

Timtuk whispered closer to Jimmy, "They liked the pancakes, and they think Lian is mean to Will on purpose. They both said they will protect Will if Lian gets mean again."

Jimmy swallowed hard and hoped the group would get back on track and not take sides to any issue. *You've done well, Timtuk. Here's your payment.* and he slowly emptied the berries into his hand. Timtuk popped two into his mouth and grinned. *Don't choke on those. Eat them slowly before you fall asleep,*

Jimmy thought. Timtuk held up his thumb and Jimmy laughed. Timtuk loved to use this way of communicating, AOK.

He tussled his hair and said, "Good night, you little bandit." And Timtuk smiled and rolled over and snuggled in for the night. Before Jimmy could rise, Buddy came over and lay down by Timtuk. Jimmy patted his head, "Good boy, Buddy." And Buddy wagged his tail.

Jimmy went to sit by Will. Will looked at his cousin, "Well, do I want to know?"

Jimmy smiled. "Miria thinks Lian is dung. Timtuk wants you to teach him how to cook. And Beya and Donat are swearing to protect you from Lian."

Will started to chuckle. "Really, they said that?"

Jimmy nodded. "Yeah, but we have to be careful here, Will. The team has to work together as a unit. We can't divide ourselves up like this. Everyone has a purpose, and together as a team we work well. What would happen if Lian decides not to help us if we meet any scary bugs or lizards again? I'll tell you, someone may get killed. It might be Miria, Timtuk or me. Can you live with that?"

Will shook his head slowly. "Absolutely not."

Jimmy continued, "And I can't live with the thought that it might be you. So come on, Will. It's time for a pow-wow with the rest of the team. Let's get this settled tonight; okay?"

Will nodded his head and stood up. "Okay, cuz. You're right. Let's go talk to the troop."

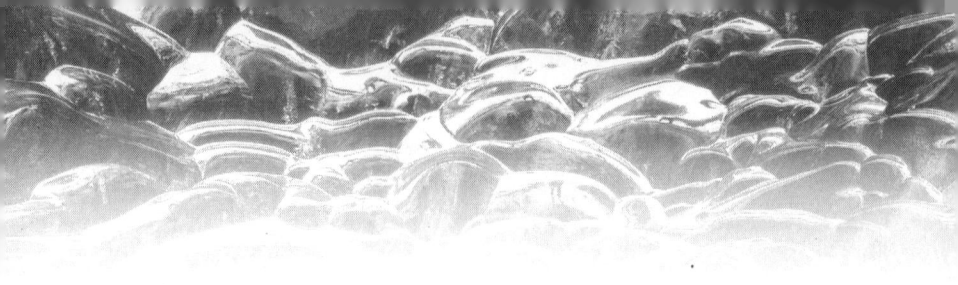

CHAPTER THIRTY-TWO

After their wonderful dinner with Steve and Jenny, Carol was surprised at how tired she was as Fred drove her home. She could hardly keep her eyes open. When Fred turned into the driveway and shut off the truck, she woke with a start.

"Oh Fred, are we home already? I must have zonked out."

Fred came around to her door and opened it.

"If you're not too tired, I'd like to show you something."

Carol slipped out of the truck holding his hand.

"No, I'm okay. I had a power nap."

Fred smiled as he led her down a path using a penlight that he always carried in his jacket.

He smiled at Carol. "Come and sit on a lawn chair. If you're cold, I'll get you a blanket from the house."

Carol settled into the lawn chair. "No, Fred, I'm fine. And oh my God! Look at these stars!"

Fred snickered. "That's what I wanted to show you. I know you never get this in the big city."

Carol looked up at the sky in awe of the vastness and beauty.

"Fred, I honestly don't think I have ever seen so many stars, and so bright too. I've missed this my whole life? That's a travesty."

Fred held her hand. "You don't know how happy it makes me

feel to introduce you to our heavenly galaxy."

Carol looked at him. "Fred, you've introduced me to so much up here."

He snickered. "Not that, you jerk! No, it's here. Mother Nature at her finest. The mountains, the rivers and lakes, the beautiful trees which I can't wait to see in the fall. It's everything."

"This way of life, it's slower yet comforting. I feel like I belong. Do you know what I mean?"

Fred rose from his chair and straddled over Carol. He gave her a sweet, long kiss. As he pulled away he looked into her eyes.

"You do belong here. I know exactly what you mean. This part of our world gets under your skin, into your lungs and then your heart. I'm so glad you found out so soon."

She pulled him down to her and gave him a long endearing kiss.

"I'm a quick study, and you're a great teacher!"

He smiled and settled back in his chair. He held her hand, and they just sat in the dark, saying nothing as the starry night played its own symphony.

***

As Jenny and Steve were settling down into their bed he said, "Carol looks happy, doesn't she?"

Jenny laughed. "Carol is over the moon in love. So that goofy smile she wears is upside down happiness. I could kiss Fred for doing this to her. I haven't seen her glow like this since..."

Steve looked at her. "Since Mike. Go ahead. You can say it."

She smiled at her husband. "Yeah, since Mike. Do you think he would be happy with her choice?"

Steve looked up at the ceiling. "I do. You know, Jenny, I always felt Mike when there was a problem with Jimmy. Not just feel him, but knew he was beside me, egging me into action to protect him. I have not felt him since the boys disappeared. He showed me the marking on the rock. He was the reason I looked. I didn't know what I was looking for, but when I found it I knew that is what he wanted me to find. But honestly, since Carol and Fred started connecting, I swear he is at peace with her choice."

Jenny looked at Steve. "Where do you think he is right now?"

Steve shook his head. "Quite honestly, I think he is with the boys. And I don't think I will feel his presence again until the boys return home."

Jenny snuggled into Steve's arms and lay her head on his chest. "You know something, Steve? That makes me feel good. I hope you don't feel him until then. If you do, that could mean the boys are in trouble and there is sweet nothing we can do about it. So Mike if you can hear me, stay with the boys. We'll take care of everything here."

Steve smiled and kissed Jenny's head.

She looked up at him. "I want a better kiss than that, big boy."

Smiling he took her and pulled her up for a long romantic kiss. They made their own symphony that night.

✱ ✱ ✱

Reed entered Steve's office quietly shutting the door so as to not disturb him from his paperwork. When Steve looked up, he smiled and jumped up to shake his hand.

"Nice surprise, Reed. What do I owe this honour?"

Reed sat down on the chair next to Steve's desk.

"I was wondering, Steve, how do you know the boys will be back in three years? Who is this old man you spoke about?"

Steve put his hands over his face for a second and then took a deep breath.

"Okay, Reed, I'll tell you what we know, but you have to keep it a secret. Someone might want to throw a net over you and haul you away. Know what I mean?"

Reed laughed. "I thought that was going to happen to me twenty-one years ago. So please, the story will stay with me only. My word to you."

Steve smiled. "Okay, buddy, get comfortable. This is going to take a while."

***

Reed said nothing, he just looked at the floor deep in thought. When he finally spoke, his voice was barely above a whisper. "You see, Steve, it was what you told me about the girl and the child. If the girl lost the necklace, then it only makes sense that Dean gave it to her. Therefore I have to reason with the thought that she may be his wife and the child might be his child."

Steve nodded his head. "That's a fair conclusion."

Reed went on. "So I was wondering, if you know when the boys will return and where they are coming from. I was wondering if I might join you when you go to meet them?"

Steve sat up straighter in his chair. "For what purpose, Reed?"

"I was hoping that I might get the answers to all my questions. Maybe your boys will know something or maybe their companions will know. I would really like to be there when they come out."

Steve sat quietly for a moment. "Can I get back to you on this, Reed. I'm sure it will be okay, but I really want to discuss it with Carol and Jenny first. Do you mind?"

Reed stood up. "No, Steve. I totally understand. This is a group decision, and I will respect your answer. Will you call me soon?"

Steve put out his hand. "Just give me a day or two. Have to get the group together again, but I'll promise you an answer as soon as possible."

Reed took his hand and shook it. "Thanks, Steve. I appreciate your understanding in this matter. I would desperately like to get closure here."

Steve walked him out. "I'll be in touch. Take care," he said as he watched Reed walk slowly to his truck.

As Steve watched his truck drive away he said to himself, *You've lost the most of all in this tragedy, Reed. I'll speak on your behalf and hope the mothers will understand.*

✱ ✱ ✱

Katie came running out with her arms wide open to greet Steve. "Daddy, pick me up."

Steve grabbed her as she shot into his arms.

"Oh man! Katie Bug, you are getting too heavy for this game. You're going to throw your old man's back out."

She gave him a big hug and kissed his cheek. "You're not an old man, Daddy. You're Superman."

Steve laughed as he carried her to the front porch. "Superman? How can I be Superman? I can't even fly."

Katie giggled. "You are so strong. Strong like a dinosaur."

Steve whispered, "Yeah Katie, but they're extinct. Do you know why?"

Katie looked at him in wonder. "Why Daddy?"

Steve put her on the porch. "Because the little girl dinosaurs broke all the daddy dinosaurs' backs when they came running for a pick up."

Katie laughed. "No! That's not true."

Steve started to growl. "It is so true, and the daddy dinosaurs sounded like this." Steve started to roar and growl and chase Katie. She screamed and screeched so loud that Jenny came flying out the door to see what was the matter.

"Oh, you two! You scared me half to death."

Steve laughed and grabbed Katie. "And that's what happened to mommy dinosaurs. They got scared to death by their kids."

Katie laughed. "Is that true, Mommy?"

Jenny shook her head. "No, honey, but Daddy sure tells a great story, doesn't he?"

Katie giggled. "Yeah, but I like it best when he chases me."

Steve grabbed Katie and threw her over his shoulder,

"Come on, Katie Bug. Wash up for dinner. I'll bet Mom made us a great dinner for two hungry dinosaurs."

Katie screeched as Steve carried her into the house upside down. He put her down gently on her feet and held her shoulders until she got her balance. "Okay, Doodlebug, let's get washed up."

Katie ran for the bathroom and Steve washed his hands in the kitchen sink.

Jenny came over to him and gave him a kiss on the cheek. "How was your day? Full of fun and adventure? Wrestle a grizzly bear? Outrun a cougar? Come on, big storyteller, tell me a story."

Steve laughed and hugged his wife. "Dull as ever, but still better than a city job. I did have a visitor today. Reed George."

Jenny looked at him as she began mashing the potatoes.

"Oh, what did he want?"

Steve looked at Jenny.

"Do you think you can get Stacey to babysit tonight for a few hours. I'd like to go and see Carol and Fred and tell you all about my meeting."

Jenny started dishing up the plates. "Well, that sounds suspicious. Are you going to share?"

At that moment Katie skipped into the kitchen. "Share what, Daddy?"

Steve smiled at Jenny then at Katie.

"My extra scoop of ice cream. Who wants it?"

Katie jumped up and down. "I do, I do!"

Steve picked her up and placed her at the kitchen table.

"Okay, but Mom really wants you to eat a good dinner. Okay? Vegetables too."

Katie laughed. "For an extra scoop of ice cream I'll eat Brussel sprouts."

Steve laughed. "Man, I don't think I'd do that, not even for ice cream or chocolate fudge cake."

Jenny tapped the back of his head.

"Stop that! At least our daughter is more adventurous than you."

Steve mumbled, "I have my standards, and Brussel sprouts is not on my list."

Jenny chuckled and said, "You're impossible."

Steve took a bite of the roast chicken Jenny had placed on his plate. "Do you think we can get Stacey for a few hours tonight?"

Jenny looked at him. "Did you call Carol or Fred to see if they are available tonight?"

Steve stopped chewing. "No, but Fred's always home."

Jenny chuckled. "Yes, but now he has a girlfriend, and he just might have a social life."

Steve looked at her and scrunched up his nose. "I just knew that things were going to change. Freddy could always come out to play whenever I called him. Now he has a girlfriend. Boy, that just sucks."

Jenny sat back in her chair, crossed her arms and started to laugh. "Are you done?"

Steve looked like a contrite child. "I think so, but it really does suck."

Katie started to giggle and Jenny looked at her. "Don't use the word 'sucks' Katie. It's not a nice word."

Katie looked at her mom. "Is it a swear?"

Jenny looked at Steve with the look of 'you started this'. "No, honey, it's not a swear, but it's not a nice word. Like the word 'stink.' It's better to say smells."

Katie curled up her nose. "What's a better word than sucks?"

Jenny thought for a moment and then looked at Steve for help. He smiled at her and offered, "stinks."

Jenny looked at Katie. "Can I get back to you on that?"

Katie giggled. "Okay, Mommy. I finished my dinner, may I please have my ice cream?"

Jenny rose from her chair happy to change the subject. "You bet, Katie. And an extra scoop for our girl, just as promised."

Katie's eyes popped out as she was handed the bowl with three scoops. "Wow, thanks, Mom. And Daddy too, for sharing."

He tussled her hair. "You're welcome, Doodlebug."

Katie finished her three scoops in record time. *If only they did the same with their dinners,* Steve thought. She smiled at her dad.

"Can I go play with my dolls now?"

Jenny smiled at he., "Sure honey, but wash your face and hands first. I think you're sticky."

Katie jumped from her chair and skipped into the bathroom. Jenny went and picked up the phone, dialing Fred's number. She waited several rings before she got the answering machine. She left a message and the hung up.

"Just as I suspected, they're out. I left a message, but I can't get a babysitter on speculation. Why don't we make it for tomorrow night? Maybe meet for dinner at The Bistro Café and have a nice night out."

Steve chuckled. "Boy, what a sneaky way to get a date out of me."

Jenny laughed. "Anyway I can get it, buster, I'll take it."

He nodded his head. "This is all Freddie's fault. And his girlfriend too."

Jenny just laughed and sat on his lap. "I'll be so appreciative for a night out."

Steve whispered, "Really? How appreciative?"

Jenny smiled and whispered in his ear.

"Oh, man," Steve chuckled. "How about I take you out for breakfast too?"

Jenny just laughed, kissed his cheek and started clearing the table.

Steve got up. "Let me help you, honey. Maybe you'll be appreciative tonight too."

Jenny just gave him a giggle and a wink.

All was well in the Wright home.

***

Carol stood on the dock at the side of the huge lake, holding a fishing rod. She slowly wound the reel to bring the fly back to her.

"That's it, honey. Nice and slow then cast it back in," Fred encouraged.

"I've never done this before. Didn't think I had the aptitude for it."

"You don't need aptitude for fishing, just patience."

Carol was just about to reel in again when she felt a tug on her line. "Oh Fred, I feel something. What do I do?"

Fred put his line down and walked to her, putting his arms around her and holding the rod with her. "Just let him play for a minute, tire him out. When you feel him stop pulling, you reel in until he starts to play again. That's it. You got it?"

Carol looked up at him, enjoying the closeness. "Is this how you teach everyone to fish? It's kind of hot."

Fred muffled his laughter in her hoodie. "Only you would think fishing is hot. Now come on, concentrate. Bring it in, slowly. There he is just under the water. Do you see him?"

Carol started laughing and screaming, "Oh my God, I caught a fish. I caught a fish!"

Fred helped her reel it to the dock then he went for the net, scooped it up and presented it to her. "It's a keeper."

Carol looked at him. "What does that mean?"

Fred laughed. "Well, sweetie, if it was too little we would have to throw it back."

Carol looked at Fred with shock.

"We're going to throw him back anyways; right? I won't be party to a killing."

Fred snorted. "What about fresh trout for dinner?"

Carol shook her head. "Nope, he goes back, right now."

Fred started to laugh and took the fish from the line. He handed it to Carol. "Here, you let it go. This goes against the fisherman's manual."

Carol held her breath and took the slimy fish in her hands. Kneeling down she let it slip from her hands and back into the water.

"There now, Fred. Isn't that better than killing it. The thrill of the hunt but as big a thrill to release it back."

Fred snorted. "Okay, if you catch any fish, you can release them. But I catch a fish, I get to keep it."

Carol looked at Fred and then moved her hands up and down in front of him and his fishing rod. "Whoogy, whoogy, whoogy!"

Fred looked at her. "What the hell are you doing?"

Carol laughed. "Putting a hex on you and your rod. You won't catch any fish tonight."

Fred dropped his rod and began to chase her.

"I'll catch me a fish, a big land sucker."

Carol screamed and tried to run, but he was on to her in seconds. He threw her over his shoulder and jumped off the dock with her screaming and laughing. As they came up for air she splashed him with all her might.

"You idiot. We're soaked."

Fred laughed. "Well, I thought you liked being with the fish. Since you won't let me fish for them, let's scare them."

And he splashed her and jumped at her and took her down again. When she started to fight him off, he grabbed her hands and held them behind her back. Then he kissed her and all the struggling just seemed to disappear in the water. He let her hands go, and she slowly put them around his neck. The kiss lingered, and he smiled at her as he slowly let her go.

"Remind me to never take you hunting; okay? I got a feeling you'd scream every time I spotted a deer or a moose."

Carol laughed. "I wouldn't scream. I just blow off an air horn and all would be fine."

Fred kissed her again. "Some wilderness woman you're going to make."

***

Jenny smiled as Steve took her coat from her and handed it to the waitress.

"I just love this restaurant. A little bit of Paris way up here in the wilderness."

Carol smiled. "Yes, French cuisine. My first meal up here was goat stew."

Fred looked at her with a shock on his face. "Hey, I thought you liked it."

Carol started to laugh. "I did, but, gee honey, I think this restaurant is more to a city girl's standards. Especially on her first night up here."

Fred chuckled. "You're just being a snob. I take you to the best wilderness joint and now she tells me, it wasn't up to her standards."

Carol laughed. "Oh honey, I loved the restaurant you took me to our first night. Every city girl should try goat stew. It's how you turn our heads and make us swoon with ecstasy."

Fred laughed. "See, mission accomplished!"

Steve laughed. "Don't let me take any woman's advice from you pal. I think Katie could do better."

Fred laughed. "I got my girl, didn't I? I schmoozed her right off her feet."

Carol smiled. "And tossed me right into a lake."

Jenny laughed. "What the heck are you two talking about?"

Carol looked at Fred. "He threw me in the lake because I kinda put a hex on him and his fishing rod."

Fred looked all innocent. "In all fairness, she wouldn't let me keep her fish. And it was a keeper."

Steve looked at Fred incredulously. "So you threw her in the lake?"

Fred started to feel a little ball of sweat under his collar. "I guess when you say it like that, it doesn't sound too good."

Carol started to laugh,. "He didn't just throw me in. He came too. All because I didn't want to keep the fish I caught. I wanted to catch and release and Fred thought I was crazy. But hey, the kissing part was real nice, honey."

Fred smiled. "Thanks, sweetie, but I'm never taking you hunting. You stay home and defend people, and I'll go hunt and fish and be caveman for my woman."

He put his arms up to flex his muscles to look like a body builder.

Jenny started to laugh out loud. "You two are not dull. I'll give you that. But Fred, don't forget to take Barney when you go play caveman. He'll be unbearable to live with if you don't." And she gave Steve a wink and a smile.

Steve winked back. "Yeah Fred, don't forget your old pal, Barney. I want to play caveman too!"

Carol looked at Jenny. "Are they like this all the time?"

Jenny laughed. "Only on days that end in "y"."

Carol burst out laughing. "Oh my God, what have I signed up for?"

Fred chimed in, "A lifetime of fun and laughter. I guarantee it!"

Carol smiled at Fred through glistening eyes. "I could handle that." Opening her menu. " Yes sir, I could handle that just fine."

Everyone smiled and opened their menus. Fred took Carol's hand and gave it a loving squeeze. She smiled at him and gave him a wink. Fred opened up the menu.

"Now let's see if we can order Carol some yak testicles in a nice French wine sauce. I'm sure she'll love it."

And the fun and laughter continued.

As they sat quietly sipping their wine after a delicious meal Jenny sat up straight. "Hey, aren't we supposed to be talking about something, Steve? Didn't you have something important to discuss with us?"

Steve smiled at Jenny. "You know, I was having such a good time I almost forgot why I called this meeting. Reed came to see me yesterday, and he wanted to know everything. So I told him with the promise that it doesn't get discussed with anyone but us. But then he made a strange request. He wants to be with us when we meet the boys in Peru."

Jenny looked a Steve. "Why?"

Steve put his hand on his chin. "Says he wants to find out what happened to his brother. Maybe our boys will know or their companions. He is desperate to put closure to this."

Carol sat up and sounded like a lawyer rather than a mother. "Is there an ulterior motive, Steve? He doesn't want to go underground and leave this world or anything?"

Steve shook his head. "No way. He has a beautiful wife and family that I know he adores. No, he just wants answers as soon as possible, and personally I can't blame him."

Fred cut in, "From what I've seen from Reed, he is a totally devoted family man to his own family and the band. I can understand his reasons for wanting closure."

Then Steve tapped the table.

"Then let's take a vote. All in favour of inviting Reed on our Peru expedition, say aye." A unanimous "aye" was heard.

Steve smiled and said, "Good. I'll call him in the morning. Thanks, guys."

Carol looked at Fred and Steve. "What do you two believe happened to Reed's brother? I have my lawyer Spidey sense going off. You're not telling us everything, are you?"

Steve and Fred looked at each other and tried to keep emotionless faces. Fred shrugged his shoulders.

"We found Dean George's necklace. And we believe the woman dropped it when she run back into the cave. The necklace was important to Dean, so we are presuming this was his wife and child who came out."

Jenny sat up straighter. "Why didn't Dean make contact with his family? They must all be wondering what happened to him?"

Fred and Steve said nothing but just looked at each other.

Carol made a startling sound. "Because you believe he's dead. The professor told us these were peaceful people. How did Dean George die?"

Fred grabbed her hands. "Honey, we're speculating. If Dean George died, it could have been an accident. He might be alive, though, and didn't want to leave his new life."

Jenny whispered in terror. "So you're saying our boys might not want to come back?"

Steve looked up at the ceiling in frustration. "No, Jenny. We're saying we only have hypothetic scenarios to go on. That's why Reed wants to be with us. He needs to know. Did his brother marry someone and have a child? Can he meet them? Why didn't he take the three-year portal like our boys will? These are questions he would like answered."

Tears started to well up in Jenny's eyes. "What makes us so sure our boys will travel to the portal in Peru? Dean didn't, why are we so sure our boys will?"

Steve was quiet for a moment. "Well I'll tell you, Jenny. If they don't come out, we're going in."

CHAPTER THIRTY-THREE

Will and Jimmy walked up to Lian, Beya and Donat. They looked over at Miria and Will called out. "Miria, we need you to interpret for us. Would you come and join us?"

Miria walked over to the boys and sat on a large flat rock.

"What do you wish to discuss?" she asked quietly.

Will took a deep breath. "Jimmy and I would like to discuss us, this group and how we have to work together. If we don't, someone may get killed."

Miria translated to the others. Lian only smirked in disgust.

Jimmy piped in, "That's what we're talking about, Lian. You have to stop hating us and see us as part of this team. We want to get this cleared up."

Lian looked at Miria and spoke. She looked down at her feet. Will looked at her.

"What did he say?"

Miria spoke softly. "He said you're not part of the team. You're just the problem."

Will was about to blow up when Jimmy held his arm and looked directly at Lian.

"We're not the problem, Lian. You volunteered for this journey, not because you wanted to help us get home, but because you wanted to keep Miria safe. We get that. But you have to understand that Will and Miria are just good friends. They both know that falling in love with each other would be irresponsible and fruitless. She must stay in her world, and Will must return to his. Where's the happy ending? But you have to put your pitiful jealous feelings aside and accept that they are not a threat to you. However, you will never win Miria's heart if you don't start treating her as an equal human being too. Be nice to her, talk to her with respect, compliment her. We know she is wonderful, why don't you? If you want to win a girl's heart, Lian, quit being an ass."

Miria translated and stumbled on a few areas, especially about herself and then calling him an ass. But she did it and Lian stayed quiet the whole time. At first everyone thought he was going to start yelling and screaming, but to everyone's surprise he got up slowly and walked over to Jimmy and Will. He put out his hand and Jimmy and Will slowly rose, each taking a turn to shake his hand. When he spoke, his tone was calmer, not commanding like it usually was. He looked at Miria and began to speak.

Miria looked at the boys. "He says he is sorry for being an ass. He knows that he has been jealous of Will and his judgement of you two has been unfair. He agrees with Will that we must work as a unit, and teamwork is essential. He will be a better leader in the future. As for me, he will take what Jimmy said and try to be a better man to me as well. He apologized to me for not treating me as the lady I am."

Donat and Beya stood up and approached the boys. There was a whole lot of handshaking and smiles. Donat looked at Miria and spoke, and she translated.

"Will and Jimmy are our friends. We trust them and like them very much. You have our solemn oath that we will protect you as we know you will protect us. And Miria, we will always treat you with love and respect. You are as valuable to our team as any man here."

Miria's eyes welled up with tears as she wrapped her arms around Donat's neck.

Will could see he was taken aback with this show of affection, but everyone laughed and all was well. Even Lian was laughing. It was a miracle of miracles.

***

The next morning everyone seemed in better spirits. Lian and Donat were laughing as they packed up the boxes. Beya and Jimmy were practising language skills with each other. Will looked around at the group, and he marvelled at the difference. He walked over to Miria who was putting the breakfast dishes away. Will smiled at her.

"Miria, is it just me or is everything different with the group this morning?"

She giggled at him. "Will, I have been complimented by everyone this morning.

They have thanked me for the delicious breakfast, and Lian even mentioned that my hair was especially lovely today. I can't thank you and Jimmy enough for this.

For the first time since we started this journey, I feel relaxed."

Timtuk came running up to Will with Buddy at his heels. "Up, Will!" he held his arms out to him and Will picked him up instantly.

Will laughed and kissed his cheek.

"So little brother, what kind of adventure are we going to have today?"

"A fun one! With a ride from Donat."

"Oh, you think it's that kind of day, do you? Well, we're going to have to ask Lian if that will be possible. After all, he is our leader."

Timtuk looked at Will with a puzzled look. "You like Lian

now, Will?"

Will smiled. "Yes, Timtuk, I like Lian now."

Timtuk smiled at him and hugged him. "Not a jerk anymore?"

Miria piped in, "Where did you hear that word?"

She then looked at Will with an accusatory face. Will turned and walked away with Timtuk.

"Come on you, little monster, before you get me into more trouble."

Miria started to snicker under her breath and continued with her chores.

"Children, I'm surrounded with children."

✳ ✳ ✳

All was ready for the journey. Miria placed Timtuk on his box, did her levitation magic and Lian called out to everyone. Places were taken and they were off.

Through a cavern that seemed to go up rather than down. Jimmy looked at Will. "This is different. We've never gone up before."

Will nodded. "Yeah, I wonder how far we have to climb. This could be tricky with the boxes."

No sooner had he said it than Timtuk started to cry.

Miria lifted him from the box. "He's afraid he is going to fall. I'll carry him for a while."

Jimmy came to her side. "No, Miria, let me. Come on, Timtuk. Piggyback ride!"

Timtuk let out a howl of glee and jumped on Jimmy's back. The smile on his face was from ear to ear as he bounced on Jimmy's back.

"Let me know when you get tired, and I'll take over," said Will as he patted Timtuk on his back.

Jimmy smiled. "Thanks, maybe sooner than you think. Come on, Timtuk. You have to hold on and stop bouncing; okay?"

Timtuk laughed. "Okay, Jimmy. Come on, Buddy!"

Buddy was at Jimmy's heels, and Will shook his head at how he stayed so close to Timtuk. *What a great dog he is*, he thought.

"Yeah, he's the best," piped in Timtuk.

Miria looked at Timtuk. "Who's the best, Timtuk? What are you talking about?"

Timtuk looked at Will shocked at his forgetfulness about their secret.

Will covered for him. "I whispered that Buddy is a great dog and Timtuk just agreed."

Miria looked at Will. "I never heard you. My goodness, Timtuk, your hearing is very good."

Timtuk just smiled and buried his face into Jimmy's back. Will sent him a quiet thought. *Come on, Timtuk, don't blow our secret.* Timtuk just started to giggle. Miria couldn't help but feel there was something fishy going on with these two. But she shook the thought from her mind as they continued to climb.

※ ※ ※

They climbed for over an hour. Will and Jimmy took turns with Timtuk on their backs. Finally they came through the cavern to a large plateau. Lian called out to everyone to stop for a rest. Miria got out the water jug and tumblers for everyone.

When she went to Lian and handed him his cup, he took the water jug from her and poured her a cup. He smiled at her, and took the jug to Beya and Donat and poured their water too. He quietly came to Will, Jimmy and Timtuk and gave them each a cup. When he finished pouring their water, he filled his cup and drank deeply. He smiled at them and walked away and sat by Miria. Will thought to Timtuk. "What was he thinking, Timtuk?"

Timtuk whispered back, "If this is how to win Miria, I'll do it."
Jimmy looked at Will. "It's what we want; right?"
Will just nodded his head but said nothing. He hoped Timtuk didn't pick up on the agony he was going through at this very minute.
Will squatted down by Buddy. "Come on, boy Let's get you a drink too."

***

As they continued on the climb, they entered a cavern that was totally pink. The rocks were pink and speckled with some black. It felt warm and peaceful. Everyone seemed to feel it as they all became quiet. Lian called out that this was where they would camp for the night.

Will looked at Jimmy. "What kind of stone is this, Jim?"

Jimmy picked up a small piece from the ground.

"My guess is Rhodonite. It's one of the healing crystals I've read about. You'll love this. It is supposed to promote forgiveness. Guess it wouldn't hurt to stay here for a night, eh?"

Will snorted. "Yeah, if you believe it. I'll keep an open mind."

Miria began to set up the dishes preparing for an early dinner. Jimmy walked over to her. "Can I help with anything, Miria?"

"Would you mind taking out the fire stones for me? I don't know why, but I feel so tired right now."

Jimmy looked at her with concern. "Miria, are you feeling okay? You do look a little pale."

Miria looked at Jimmy and then everything went black. Jimmy grabbed her before she hit the ground.

"Hey guys, Miria's in trouble," screamed Jimmy.

All the men ran towards Jimmy who was holding Miria. Lian started to talk to Jimmy, and Jimmy looked at Timtuk. "Timtuk, what did Lian say?"

Timtuk translated. "He wants to know what happened."

Jimmy placed Miria on the blankets Will had laid out for her. "Timtuk, tell Lian she said she felt very tired and then she just fainted."

Lian, Donat and Beya all started to speak at once. Timtuk started to get upset and began to cry. Will quickly picked him up.

"It's okay, Timtuk. We'll make Miria better. Do those guys know what to do, or are they just as confused as you?"

"Lian says we need a medicine that might be in one of the boxes, but they are not sure what medicine it is."

Jimmy looked at Timtuk. "Ask Lian what he thinks might have caused this."

Timtuk quickly translated and waited for Lian's reply.

Timtuk looked at Jimmy. "He said it has to do with how high we are right now. Some people are affected by this."

Jimmy snapped his fingers. "Altitude sickness. Timtuk tell everyone she just needs rest and to drink liquids. As soon as she wakes up, we must give her water and sweet tea."

Lian came to Jimmy's side and asked a question. Timtuk translated, "He wants to know how do you know this?"

Jimmy smiled. "Back home I climbed many mountains. Sometimes if you forget to keep the liquids in you, you get dehydrated. You get dizzy and might even pass out like Miria did. She'll be okay with rest and liquids."

Miria started to moan and everyone went and sat by her. She slowly opened her eyes. "What happened? How did I get here?"

She tried to sit up but everyone shouted, "No" and eased her back onto the blanket.

Will was the first to speak. "Miria, you are dehydrated. With all the climbing we did today, it has affected your body. You need rest, water and sweet tea. Doctor Jimmy's orders."

She began to protest. "No, I must make dinner for everyone."

Timtuk translated this to Lian, Donat and Beya. Lian was the first to speak, and Timtuk could hardly believe his ears. He looked at Jimmy and Will.

"Lian says she is to stay in bed. He said we can make the dinner for a change. Will can teach all of us."

Will smiled and nodded at Lian. "First, sweet tea for Miria."

He took out the fire rock and poured water into the stone pot. When it boiled he added the tea leaves that Miria kept in a small container. Then he looked for the container with the sandy sugar he used for his pancakes. He added a heaped spoon into her cup and poured the hot tea in. He stirred it slowly and then sat down by Miria.

"Careful, Miria. This is really hot," he warned.

Miria sat up slightly and sipped the tea. It felt like silk going down she thought.

"Thank you, Will."

"My pleasure, Miria. Now do as the doctor and all his interns say. Stay in bed and drink lots of liquids; okay?"

She smiled. "Okay, I will," she said, and she continued to sip her tea.

Will looked up at everyone. "Right, now let's get dinner started. Let's see what we have got to eat."

Inspecting the box of food supplies Will was surprised at his findings. He looked at Timtuk.

"Timtuk ask Lian when he believes we'll be at Quintoke."

Timtuk translated and Lian responded. "He believes we should be there tomorrow, in the early afternoon."

Will smiled. "Great, then we can splurge a little on our rations since we'll be restocking tomorrow. Everyone, real men eat quiche.

Wait until you try mine."

Timtuk translated but didn't know how to translate quiche. Will just thought to him. "Don't worry, it's just an omelette on steroids," he said and he winked at Timtuk.

The men watched Jimmy and Will cut veggies into small pieces and whip up the eggs into a fluffy froth. Will used a corn muffin base for his quiche and placed it on the fire rock to cook up a bit. Then he poured the egg mixture and veggie mix on top. He put a lid on the pot and placed it on the fire rock. The aroma was intoxicating for everyone. Jimmy cut up some sweet potatoes and planned to fry them up on the other fire rock. But he could not find any oil. He looked at Will.

"Any ideas how to fry these up without oil?"

Timtuk began to translate to the others. Beya jumped up and went into the food box and came out with a container with a gray cream. Jimmy looked at it with apprehension, but Beya kept nodding and pointing to the pan. Jimmy shrugged his shoulders. "Okay, bro. If you say so." And he took a big spoonful and placed it into the frying pan. It melted in seconds and Jimmy picked up the sliced sweet potatoes. "Well, here goes." He dropped them into the strange grease.

Within ten minutes everything looked and smelled fantastic. Will and Jimmy dished everyone some quiche and fried sweet potatoes. Will and Jimmy waited until they all tried the dishes.

Their smiles and nods was all the boys had to see to exhale in relief. Lian was the first to compliment them and asked if they would show him how to cook this meal someday soon. Will and Jimmy laughed and nodded. Miria looked at Will and Jimmy.

"Are you two trying to steal my job. You cook better than me."

Jimmy just laughed. "Not better, just different. Your steamed fish dinner we had the first night with you was fabulous. And your corn muffins are worth going to war for."

She smiled weakly. "You're just being kind. I don't cook that well, but maybe you two can teach us all on this journey. We'll have many months to learn."

Timtuk was busy translating and to Will's surprise the men all nodded in agreement.

Slowly, one culture was courting another, and it was good.

Lian, Donat and Beya jumped up and began to gather the dishes. When Will and Jimmy got up to help Lian looked at Timtuk and started talking very fast.

Timtuk said, "He said you did the cooking; they will do the dishes. It's only fair!"

Will and Jimmy laughed their approval and showed them a thumbs up sign.

Everyone showed their thumbs up and laughed.

Miria quietly watched this performance in front of her eyes and silently prayed her thanks to the gods for answering her prayers. They were all at peace with one another. And she slept soundly that night, the best sleep she had had in weeks.

CHAPTER THIRTY-FOUR

Fred drove into Steve's office parking lot and wasn't surprised to find him in at such an early time. He quietly stepped into the outer office and got a cup of coffee from the kitchen area. Then he rapped on Steve's door to announce his presence.

Steve looked up. "Hi, you're up early too. How was your night?"

Fred started to chuckle. "I got raked over the coals by my lady lawyer. Man, she is good. I was almost ready to confess to crimes I have never done just to get her to calm down."

Steve laughed. "Jenny was not to thrilled with me either. She believes we've been holding back too much information to protect them. In hindsight, I guess we should have known this was going to blow up in our faces. She made me tell her everything, and she still thinks I was holding back."

Fred smiled. "Got the same treatment too. Do you think they take lessons on this?"

Steve laughed. "Yeah, Ball-busting 101. Jenny got an A, I'm sure."

Fred laughed. "Let's face it, bro, we can't fool them or protect them. They're just too good at seeing through us."

Steve chuckled. "And that my friend is our lesson for the day. Never underestimate your wife. She knows you too well."

Fred laughed. "I'll take that to my grave, bro. I promise. Now tell me, how did Jenny react to us going into the cave if they don't come out."

Steve shook his head. "Oh boy, that was fun. You should have heard the pros and cons on that little diddy. Where do we go to find them? What about Katie? How long before we find another portal? What if we never find them? Man! Fred, we didn't sleep much last night. I was trying to put out that fire for hours."

Fred laughed. "I got a different angle thrown at me. We'll have to take the professor with us. He's the only one who can help us in there. He might know the language. How much food and water should we prepare for? What if we meet another culture of people before we meet the boys? Why didn't Dean George come out? When did you first suspect he was dead? Why didn't you tell us? And so on. You get the picture."

Steve nodded. "Yup, sounds a lot like the same movie at my house. Suffice to say

I've been here since five a.m. Did you have breakfast?"

Fred smiled. "I'm holding it in this cup. You want to go to Belle's Diner?"

Steve smiled. "Yeah, I'm sure I'll feel better with some ham and eggs in me. Right now I feel as empty as a donut hole."

Fred smiled. "Come on. I'll drive. You look weak."

Steve laughed. "If I fall asleep in my plate, just turn my head, so I don't snort any eggs or hash browns."

Fred chuckled. "I got your back, bro."

And they drove to Belle's Diner in a much better mood.

✱ ✱ ✱

Carol tapped quietly on Jenny's back door. She was hoping Jenny was up, but she didn't want to wake Katie in the process. Jenny came to the door in her robe and gave Carol a huge smile when she saw her standing on the porch. "Good morning, Carol. Did you have a lousy night too?"

Carol smiled. "I'm sure Fred is having second thoughts about marrying a lawyer."

Jenny got two mugs from the shelf and poured coffee. "Oh, I'm sure he's not thinking that. Maybe being a little more careful withholding information. That I could believe."

Carol snickered. "Yup, he'll think twice about doing that again. How about you?"

Jenny smiled. "I think I was more upset about the going in after the boys' routine.

Carol, I'm not good as the explorer. I like my life normal and calm. That scares me half to death just thinking about it."

Carol took a sip of the coffee. "I'm just the opposite. If we go, I want to be prepared. Take the proper supplies, take the professor as a guide, you know. Maps, compass, weapons."

Jenny looked shocked. "Weapons! What kind of weapons?"

Carol smiled at her. "Rifles, crossbows and lots of chocolate. Ever seen me needing a chocolate fix. I could take on the army and navy for a chocolate bar.

It's not a pretty sight, let me tell you!"

Jenny laughed. "Yup, know exactly how you feel."

Carol whispered quietly, "But I think what bothered me more than anything else, is that they have a suspicion that Dean George is dead, and they refused to tell us. I'm not a hysterical woman. I want all the facts and theories. And I'm a little ticked off that Fred doesn't know that about me."

Jenny whispered back, "I'll bet my last dollar that it was Steve's idea to keep it quiet. I went to pieces over the boys, and I'm sure he thought I would lose it again. And to tell you the truth Carol, I don't know how I would have reacted to this news. I didn't overreact last night because there was so much to take in. But when we got home and I had time to digest all the information, I was a pit bull with lipstick."

Carol laughed. "I would have loved to be a fly on the wall for that one. You always seem so calm to me. I can't imagine my sweet sister-in-law as a pit bull."

Jenny smiled. "Got you fooled, haven't I?"

Carol laughed. "No, you're just a mother who cares. I'm sure Katie's well-being was brought up last night."

Jenny nodded. "You bet. I certainly won't leave her behind, but I can't imagine her going underground with us either."

Carol smiled. "Your two options are take her with you or leave her for at least three years with your mother."

Jenny looked shocked for a moment. "Counsellor, you have a nasty habit of coming to the point." Jenny took a deep breath. "There is no choice. She comes with us."

✳ ✳ ✳

As Fred and Steve were enjoying their breakfast together they were surprised to be greeted by Reed George as he entered the restaurant. He smiled at them and Steve motioned for him to join them. He came over and took a seat.

"Good morning. Didn't think I'd see you two so early in the morning. It's barely daybreak."

Steve smiled. "Yeah, that's us. Dedicated workers right from the start."

Fred laughed. "What are you doing here, Reed? This is pretty early for you too."

Reed smiled. "Got two loads of wood I'm delivering to my aunts in Smithers. Thought I'd get an early start, so I'll be home by late noon for my boys' soccer practice tonight."

Fred smiled. "You're a good dad, Reed. It's so nice to see."

Reed smiled. "Thanks, Fred. Appreciate you saying so. By the way, have you had a chance to talk to your wives about my request?"

Fred smiled and then coughed. "Yes, we had the discussion last night. It was a unanimous decision that you join us when we go to Peru."

Reed smiled from ear to ear and his dimples popped out on his face.

"Thank you so much. This means a lot to me. Really!"

Steve smiled. "Our pleasure, Reed. The girls agreed you have so many questions that need to be answered, and if it was them, they would want to go too."

Reed smiled. "Thank you so much. And there is one more thing. My father, he would like to meet with you as soon as it is convenient for you both."

Fred looked a bit confused. "What does he want to see us about?"

Reed took a deep sigh. "The necklace. He found it on my kitchen table, and I had to tell him where I got it. He would like to talk to you both if that's okay."

Steve looked at Fred. "Why do I get the feeling that we're being sent to the principal's office?"

Reed laughed. "No, it's nothing like that. He would like to hear your theories on Dean and your boys. For the first time, I think he finally believes me and my story.

I think he just wants to talk to you about it."

Fred and Steve both nodded their heads and Steve replied, "Okay, Reed. How's your afternoon tomorrow, Fred?"

Fred looked at his cell phone.

"I'm open after three o'clock. Does that work for you, Steve?"

Steve adjusted his phone. "Yeah, I can rearrange my schedule a bit. Tell your father we'll come after three tomorrow. Will that be okay?"

Reed stood up. "That will be great." He held out his hand to shake each man's hand. "Thanks so much, guys. I really appreciate all this."

Fred smiled. "Our pleasure, Reed."

And Reed left the diner with a coffee and some muffins for his long drive ahead.

***

When Steve arrived home that late afternoon, he didn't know how the mood would be in his home. But when he opened the door, he could smell Jenny's cooking and all the bad feelings just melted away. He came into the kitchen and held out a huge bouquet of flowers to her. Jenny looked at them and then at Steve.

"Thank you, honey. You didn't have to do this." She gave him a sweet kiss on the lips. "But I'm so glad that you did."

Steve smiled. "What are you cooking? It smells delicious."

"Roast chicken with your favourite dressing. I kinda feel guilty for last night, Steve. I wanted to make it up to you somehow."

Steve hugged her close. "Why are you feeling guilty?"

She put her head on his chest. "Because I know now that you were only protecting me. You didn't want me to worry for three years. And if I knew about your theories about Dean George, I guess I might have overreacted. I've been known to do that lately."

Steve gave her a kiss on the top of her head. "Oh honey, as long as we stick together, pray for the best for our boys and don't lose faith, I think everything will turn out okay."

Jenny looked up at him. "It will. I just don't see it any other way."

He kissed her again as Katie ran into the kitchen and latched onto her dad's leg.

"Hi Daddy. Wanna see the pictures I made at school?"

"Absolutely. Go get them for me; okay?" She ran out of the kitchen and skipped back within seconds holding three large pieces of construction paper. She put them on the table.

"This one is Buddy holding onto a fish he just caught."

Steve laughed. "What kind of bait did he use? That's some fish he caught."

Katie laughed. "No bait, Daddy. He dove for it."

Steve smiled. "Didn't know he was that talented."

Katie flipped to the next picture. "This is Will and Jimmy on their expedition."

Steve looked at Katie surprised. "Wow, big word and you used it in the proper context. Good job. Now what are the boys doing?"

"They are searching for a way home to us. They're having fun, but they miss us."

Steve looked at Jenny who just smiled and stayed quiet. Katie flipped to the last page. "And this is all of us greeting them when they get home."

Steve looked at the picture. He noticed the mountains in the background, a nearby lake and that there were many people in her picture.

"Katie, who are all these people?"

Katie smiled and pointed. "That's you and mommy, Auntie Carol and Uncle Fred, the professor, that's me, Will and Jimmy. That's a man, but I don't know his name."

Steve looked at Jenny. She could read his expression, and she slowly shook her head.

"Honey, these are fantastic pictures. Where did you get the idea of the mountains and the lake?"

Katie giggled. "In my dream. It all came to me in my dream. Will and Jimmy are fine, you know. They are learning so much about the new people too. Can I go play in my room now?"

Jenny spoke up, "Sure, honey. Dinner should be ready in about twenty minutes; okay?"

"Okay, Mommy," she said and she skipped back to her room flapping the pictures up and down as she went.

Steve looked at Jenny. "How could she know? Did she overhear us talking last night?"

Jenny shook her head. "Steve, you and I both know a train could run through her room at night, and she wouldn't even rustle a toe. She dreamed this, Steve. And then had the fortitude to put it on paper for us. I think somehow she's channelling them. And I for one feel so much better knowing what she just told us."

Steve shook his head. "How did she know about Reed? We didn't discuss this at home. We discussed it at the restaurant. How did she know that he was coming?"

Jenny shook her head. "I don't know, Steve, but right now I'm calling her my little miracle girl, and I'm accepting what she told us."

Steve sat back on the chair and crossed his arms. "And a child shall lead the way."

Pretty humbling when you begin to think of it."

Jenny put her arms around his neck and kissed his cheek. "I always thought she was an amazing child. Now you know too."

Steve smiled. "She's just like her mother! I have two amazing women in my life, and I promise you I'll never take either one of you for granted."

Jenny smiled. "That's sweet, honey, but Katie is not like me. She just like her grandmother, and I think we should give her a call."

✱ ✱ ✱

Jenny waved to her mother as she came through the arrival gate at the airport.

"Hi, honey," she said as she gave Jenny a big hug. "Oh, I thought you would have brought Katie. I'm dying to see her."

Jenny smiled as she took her mother's suitcase. "She's having a playdate. We'll pick her up before we go home. I kind of wanted to talk to you alone, Mom, without little ears around."

Jenny's mom looked suspiciously at her. "Is something wrong? I've been picking up some odd feelings about you guys lately. I hoped it was just me being overcautious, but I'm beginning to think I was on the right path."

Jenny smiled. "Come on, Mom. We've got a long ride ahead, and I've got so much to tell you."

***

Jenny had just finished the whole story as she pulled up to Katie's friend's house.

Jenny smiled at her mom. "I'm sorry to just drop this whole bombshell on you, Mom, but when Katie showed signs of your gift, I knew I couldn't keep quiet anymore."

Her mom smiled at Jenny and took her hand. "I'm a little disappointed you didn't call me right at the beginning. Don't you understand that I can channel Will? Thank heavens Katie is starting to show signs of the gift. I think you need to hear positive feedback where the boys are concerned. Now go get my little Katie Bug, and I'll wait in the car. Does she know I'm coming?"

Jenny smiled. "Nope, thought I'd surprise her. That and she would have never agreed to a playdate if she knew I was going to pick you up."

Jenny's mom laughed. "Just the perfect words a grandmother

likes to hear."

Jenny jumped out of the car. "I'll be right back."

A few minutes later Katie was walking towards the car when she spotted her grandmother stepping out of it.

Katie ran to her with her arms outstretched. "Nana! Oh, I've missed you."

Jenny's mom laughed. "Oh, I've missed you too!" She gave Katie a hug and a kiss on her cheek.

Katie jumped up and down. "How long are you going to stay? A month?"

Katie's Nana looked into those beautiful blue eyes. "Oh, I wish I could Katie Bug, but ten days is all I can leave your grandpa for. After that he might be out of dishes."

Katie looked at her in a confused way. "Huh?"

Nana laughed. "He has a tendency to forget to wash dishes. So ten days is all the dishes I think we have in stock before we have to declare my kitchen a disaster zone."

Katie laughed. "But Nana, you have a dishwasher."

Nana laughed. "True darling, but the kitchen fairy is on vacation, and Grandpa just doesn't know how to open the dishwasher. Maybe you can teach him the next time you come and visit."

Katie giggled. "Okay, Nana."

She jumped into the backseat and buckled up. Jenny and her mother did the same, and they drove back to their homestead.

✲ ✲ ✲

Katie pulled her grandmother's hand as she walked towards the front door.

"Katie, honey. I'm an old woman. Slow down a bit."

"I want to show you the pictures I made at school. And the ones

I made this morning before I went to play at Hannah's."

Jenny looked at her mother and shrugged her shoulders.

Nana smiled at Katie. "Wonderful, why don't you go and get them while I put my suitcase in my room."

Katie ran off like a jumping rabbit. Jenny's mom looked at Jenny. "Just an ounce of that energy. I'd pay a fortune for it."

Jenny laughed and took her mother's suitcase to the bedroom. "Why don't you go into the kitchen and get settled, and I'll make us some lunch," Jenny called out.

Jenny's mom nodded. "That would be lovely, dear."

As she went into the kitchen Katie came into the room with a handful of construction paper. Nana smiled at her little granddaughter.

"There now. I'm all comfortable and waiting for the Katie Wright Art Show."

Katie snickered and showed her grandmother the first three pictures she showed Jenny and Steve two days ago. Then she showed her the new ones she did this morning.

"See Nana, Will and Jimmy are making dinner for everyone. There's Will and Jimmy, a little boy, I think his name is Timmy, a pretty lady and three other men that Will and Jimmy are cooking for."

Nana looked at the picture. "Do you believe they are with this many people?"

Katie looked up with a serious face. "Yes, Nana. Don't you see them too?"

Nana smiled. "To tell you the truth, Katie, I didn't know until today that Will and Jimmy were on an adventure. I will concentrate on them tonight and see what my dreams tell me."

Katie smiled and nodded her approval. "This one is Buddy playing with Timmy. He plays catch with him all the time."

Nana took the final picture and laid it on the table. "Tell me about this one, Katie."

Katie laughed. "That's the ride they all took. It's like a sailboat train. They all laughed and had a good time. Timmy hopes they can do it again real soon."

Jenny quietly came in and sat down at the table. She looked at the new pictures and then at her mother.

Jenny spoke quietly to Katie. "Honey, why don't you go and play with your dolls, and I'll make us some lunch; okay?"

Katie jump off her chair. "Okay, Mommy. Nana do you want to keep the pictures?"

Nana smiled. "Really Katie? You'd give all these lovely pictures to me?"

Katie nodded and smiled. Nana smiled too. "I'd love to keep them. Thank you so much," she said and she hugged and kissed her granddaughter before she scooted off to her bedroom.

Jenny got up and started to pull bread and salmon from the refrigerator.

"Well, Mom, what do you think?"

Jenny's mom looked at her. "I'm so proud of that little girl I could just cry.

Jenny, her gift is real and strong. She can channel the boys, I'm sure of it. She even knows how many are in their party. Jenny, this is huge!"

Jenny started putting together the sandwiches. "Do you think you can channel them too? See if you get similar visions."

Her mother nodded her head. "Probably. I could have been doing this a long time ago if someone had let me in the loop."

Jenny stopped making the sandwiches and looked down at the floor. "I know, and I'm so sorry for this delay, but really, Mom, I was afraid you would think we were crazy parents being hysterical and all."

Jenny's mom got up from the chair, walked to the counter and put her arms around her daughter. "I would never in a million years think you and Steve were crazy hysterical parents. You two are the best parents I've ever seen. Both so dedicated to their well-being, educating them about nature and our world. Raising two wonderful respectful kids. As a grandmother, I could not be prouder of them and you and Steve. So sweetie, never be afraid to share anything with me. I'm on your team, remember?"

Jenny whispered into her mother's ear. Her mother held her back, so she could see her face. "I know. I picked up on that a week ago."

CHAPTER THIRTY-FIVE

As the team edged out of a tight cavern, below them was Quintoke, a beautiful village of white stone beside a sparkling blue lake.

Will blew out a huge breath. "Wow, that's beautiful. Jimmy what do you think this village is built from?"

Jimmy looked down on the village as if it was in a small valley. "Not sure, bro. I have to get closer to make an analysis."

Miria smiled at her companions. "It's so pretty. I hope the people are good too."

Will laughed. "Once they meet you, Miria, they'll be in love."

She blushed at such a compliment. Lian called out for the group to take formation as they descended down the path. It was tricky as the path narrowed in a few places, but Miria lifted the boxes higher, so they glided over the path with ease.

As they slowly entered the village a large man came out of an official looking building with many windows and steps leading up to the huge front door. He walked over to them, took a small bow and began to speak. The language was a different dialect than Miria and the team spoke, so Timtuk was called to translate.

"The man says we are welcome and wonders if we have anything to trade?"

Miria whispered to Timtuk. "Tell him we have some light stones that we would like to trade for food and supplies."

Timtuk relayed the message. "He says they are very interested in trading. Does anyone have any special skills that would be useful to this village?"

Miria felt a twinge in her stomach. "Timtuk, tell them we are on a journey, and we only have the light stones to trade. None of us are gifted. We are just weary travellers."

Timtuk relayed the message. The man seemed sceptical but motioned for them to come with him. "He says he is going to show us where we can set up our camp."

Miria was a little disappointed. She had hoped for a lodging with beds for everyone.

The man led them to a beautiful spot by the lake. He told Timtuk they were welcome to stay for as long as they liked. Lian did not like the spot. He felt it was too dangerous. There was only one way in, leading him to believe they were trapped. Will picked up on his apprehension and asked Timtuk to translate for him.

"Ask Lian what's wrong?"

Timtuk relayed the question and Lian told him his feelings of entrapment. When Timtuk relayed that back to Will, he looked around and agreed with Lian.

"Jimmy, Lian feels we are being trapped here. I can't help but feel he's right.

Any suggestions?"

Jimmy looked around and agreed with Lian's feelings. "We are going to have to use our secret agent in town and see what these people are about. In the meantime, we take turns and keep watch. At least we can be prepared if anything should go wrong. I hope these are just jittery feelings, but let's be on the safe side of caution."

Timtuk translated back to Lian and he nodded his agreement to the plan. They began to set up their camp while Buddy and Timtuk ran about chasing a rolled up rag, Buddy's favourite toy. When all was settled Miria suggested they walk into town and explore the village. Lian and Donat chose to stay and guard the camp, so Beya joined them on the excursion.

At first everyone in the village seemed happy and welcoming to the newcomers, but Timtuk became uneasy, and Will picked him up and asked him what was wrong.

Timtuk whispered, "These people want something from us. Not the light stones. They want gifts."

Will thought back to him. "Do you mean your special gift or everyone's special gift?"

Timtuk whispered in his ear. "Everyone's. They especially want a healer. Someone is sick, and no one can help him. Should we tell Miria?"

Will thought back. "Not yet, Timtuk. We want to see if we can trust these people."

Timtuk whispered, "They already know I have a gift of language. So now they are going to watch us to see if we have any more gifts."

Will shook his head. "That was real stupid of us to introduce you to them. We should have used charades to communicate. I'll go talk to Miria."

Miria and Beya were looking into the shops that lined the main street. She was especially attracted to the material hanging in the front of one shop. It looked like it was spun with gold and green silk threads. It was stunning, and she was mesmerized by the softness.

The merchant wanted to trade with her, but Miria put her hand up saying 'no' as a purchase like this would be too frivolous. Jimmy walked into the shop and admired the material as well.

He smiled at her. "This would be beautiful on you. Why not trade for it?"

"Oh Jimmy, we have too far to go for me to be so frivolous with our stones. Another time maybe," Miria said and she stepped out of the shop.

Jimmy turned to the merchant and gave him a big smile.

❋ ❋ ❋

Will and Timtuk found a shop where food was in abundance. He called for Miria and Beya to come and see what kind of trading they could do. The merchants were willing to haggle, and it seemed like a good day of trade. They got enough food for a week, and it cost only three light stones. Miria said it was good trading, but how would they get it back to the camp. She did not want to show her levitation gift. Will smiled and walked over to an older man pulling a wagon.

Will spoke his thoughts to Timtuk.

Ask him if we can borrow his wagon and as a trade cook him a nice dinner at our camp tonight.

Timtuk translated to the older man, and he happily relinquished his wagon to them. Will bowed to him and said, "Mena, Mena."

Will pulled the wagon to the shop and started putting the supplies into it. Beya immediately helped, and Miria wondered how he acquired it.

Will smiled. "Simple horse trading. A wagon for a meal. We will have a guest for dinner tonight."

Miria started to laugh. "You are really starting to understand trading, my friend."

When the wagon was full, Beya and Will started to pull and push as a team effort.

Jimmy came running up to them, put a package in the wagon and started pushing the wagon as well. Will noticed the package and looked at Jimmy.

"What's that?"

Jimmy smiled. "I'll tell you later. You know, how to score points with a girl. I've got it covered."

Will shook his head in confusion but continued to push the wagon as Beya pulled it along to the campsite.

As they approached the camp Lian and Donat rushed out to meet them and assisted with the wagon. When Miria explained their day of trading, Lian was whooping with laughter and slapped Will on the back in appreciation. For the first time Will felt closer to Lian than ever before. It was a good feeling.

As they all took the food and supplies out of the wagon, Beya and Donat gave directions as to what box should contain what food or supply. When all was done Miria went about setting up for dinner. Since they were expecting company she planned a fish and vegetable dish and sweetened dried berries for dessert. She placed the fish dish on the fire rock and let it simmer slowly. The aroma drove Buddy crazy.

Jimmy laughed at Buddy. "Sorry, my friend. You'll have to go and catch your own fish."

And Jimmy threw a rock into the lake. Buddy chased after it and plunged his head into the water. After a bit of splashing Buddy came up with a fish in his mouth and walked over to Jimmy to show him. He dropped it at his feet as if to say,

"There! Now will you cook it for me."

Jimmy laughed hysterically. "Man alive, Buddy. You are one special dog, and I'll be happy to cook this for you."

Buddy gave him a little woof and a huge wag of his tail. Jimmy walked over to Miria.

"Could I use the other fire stone to cook Sir Buddy's royal meal?"

Miria looked at the fish and then at Buddy. "He caught this?"

Jimmy laughed and nodded his head. "All by himself. Now I

have to cook it for him. Do you mind?"

"No, he absolutely earned it. Good boy, Buddy."

Buddy woofed again and wagged his tail. And when it was cooked, it was the best meal for a champion fisherman, a.k.a. fishing dog.

✱ ✱ ✱

The older man who lent them the wagon came slowly up to the campsite. He carried a small bouquet of flowers and handed them to Miria. She smiled at him, curtsied and replied, "Mena." She ushered him to a seat by a small table that Lian had set up. She placed the flowers in a small bowl and put them on the table. The older man seemed pleased. Lian came over and started to introduce everyone, ending with Timtuk. Timtuk took the man's hand and shook it gently. He then turned to Will and gave a strange look to him. Will sat down beside him and thought.

What's wrong, Timtuk? What does the old man think?

Timtuk whispered slowly in Will's ear. *He thinks it's a shame that people as nice as us will have to be chained to our poles.*

Will's stomach dropped like a rock. He tried to stay positive for Timtuk.

"Why don't you get Buddy's ball and go play fetch; okay?"

Timtuk never needed to be asked twice to play with Buddy. He ran off like a rabbit.

Will went to Miria. "I have to talk to you as soon as possible. I think we are in danger, and we have to get out of here as soon as possible."

Miria looked at Will with a confused face. "How can you say this? No one has threatened us or made us feel uncomfortable. Not since this morning."

Will whispered to her, "Miria, let's get dinner finished and get our guest on his way. I have to talk to you and the group. It's important."

She nodded slowly but still did not understand the importance. So she started dishing up dinner for everyone as Will requested. Dinner was completed in less than an hour, and Will and Jimmy helped the older man with his wagon as he pulled it over the gravel walkway. They waved to him as he entered the village, and he waved back to them too. "Mena" he cried back. Jimmy and Will waved and nodded to him.

Jimmy then looked at Will. "What was that all about? You practically stuffed the food in his face to get him to eat faster. What's wrong?"

Will whispered to him. "Timtuk picked up on his thoughts. He thought it was a shame that people as nice as us need to be chained to the poles. Want to spend the night here?"

Jimmy ran back to the group. "We're in danger. Miria tell the others. we have to go and quickly. The villagers want to imprison us."

Miria looked at them. "How do you know this?"

Will and Jimmy both looked at each other knowing it was time to let the cat out of the bag.

Will took a deep breath. "It's Timtuk. He has another special gift. He can read minds. He read the old man's mind, and he thought it was a shame people as nice as us had to be chained to their poles."

Miria shook her head. "Timtuk can read minds. How long have you known this?"

Jimmy looked at Miria. "Not for long. Miria, we don't have time. Tell Lian and the others we have to go. And tell Beya we're going to need his gift right about now."

Jimmy could see people starting to gather on the outskirts of the town.

"Miria, now!" Jimmy shouted.

Miria went to the others and quickly relayed he message. Lian,

The Seven Sacred Caves

Beya and Donat took no time asking questions. They threw the boxes together in a flash and had Miria levitate them. Beya put them in the mist and they quietly walked back towards the town. Their only exit to freedom. Lian whispered for everyone to be quiet until we were back in the cavern. Even Buddy seemed to understand the danger. Miria carried Timtuk and held him close to her chest.

They slowly walked past the group gathering by the official building they were first greeted from. The men whispered and Miria could see some of them carried chains. She looked away and shivered. Timtuk looked at her and read her thoughts, but she gave him a warning look to be quiet. He did.

Slowly the group headed up to the cavern that brought them to this village. Will wondered how they would continue since this village was in their direct path. But for now, getting as far away from this place seemed the only option for them.

They could hear screams coming from the villagers. They must have discovered their escape. They began to run in every direction looking for them. Jimmy and Will smiled at Beya and gave him the thumbs up for his gift. He smiled at them and kept concentrating. Some of the villagers came running up the same path the group was on. Lian led the group off the path and gave the hand signal to sit and be quiet. Everyone did as they were asked and the villagers ran past them and up into the cavern.

After about thirty minutes later they came back walking slowly and grumbling. They walked into the village with defeat in their walk.

Lian slowly gave the signal to stand and quietly climb the path. Everyone did as requested, and they were inside the cave and safe for the moment.

Beya released his mist and everyone smiled and gave a huge sigh of relief. Lian gave another order and Miria translated to Jimmy and Will.

"We're going back to the outer cave, there is another path to take. It's way off our route, but he believes it's definitely safer for all of us."

Jimmy and Will nodded their approval to Lian.

Miria whispered to them, "And when we get settled there, you two have some explaining to do."

Jimmy whispered to Will, "I think Mom's really ticked off at us."

Will whispered back, "We've only known about it for a few days. If they find out the truth, they might put us in chains. Two days, Jim. That's all."

Jimmy groaned inwardly. "I hope this doesn't come back and bite us in the butt."

Will looked at Jimmy and shrugged his shoulders. It was a very quiet walk back to the outer cave.

***

They arrived back at the outer cave two hours later. Everyone was exhausted, but no one was complaining. Timtuk was asleep on his box all cuddled up in his blanket. Jimmy was feeling envious of the little guy. He could hardly wait to climb into his bedroll.

Camp was set up quickly and everyone was getting settled into their bedrolls.

Miria walked over to the boys.

"Not so fast you two. I want answers. How long have you known about Timtuk's other gift?"

Will sat up and looked at her. "Two days."

She squinted her eyes as she didn't seem to believe him.

"Why didn't you tell me?"

Jimmy coughed a little before answering. "You're not going to like this answer, but we thought we could have some fun with it. Find out what everyone was thinking. No harm, really."

Miria repeated back to him, "No harm? You used my little brother like a toy to be played with. You have no right to listen to other's thoughts. That's personal and private. I am so ashamed of you both, and I swear if Timtuk's story doesn't match your story tomorrow morning, there will be a penalty to pay. Now goodnight, gentlemen."

Miria stormed back to her bedroll and Timtuk. Will and Jimmy gave each other a look of dread.

Jimmy whispered first. "Any suggestions?"

Will whispered back. "I have to get to Timtuk before she does. How many berries do we have left?"

Jimmy looked into his bag. "About twenty."

Will nodded his head. "That should do it. I'll pay off the little guy."

Jimmy looked at Will with a look of shock. Will looked back.

"What? Do you want Miria stripping our hides if she finds out the truth? Cover our bases, cuz, it's all we can do. Unless you can think of something better."

Jimmy looked at Will. "Let me think about it. I hate involving Timtuk in this charade. She'll never forgive us. You know that, don't you?"

Will looked at his cousin. "Okay. Try to think of a better plan. I'll back you up."

Jimmy smiled and rolled over in his blanket. Saying a small prayer to himself, "Please God, let me think of something that won't make Miria mad at us."

***

The next morning came too quick as far as Jimmy was concerned. He tried to think what to say to Miria, but he kept coming up blank. Then it came to him, and he smiled his approval at the thought.

He gave Will a pat on the shoulder. "Wake up, cuz. I've got a better idea."

Will rustled in his bed and turned to his cousin.

"A better plan? Let's hear it."

"Nope, just follow me and remember, you got my back!"

Will slipped on his shoes and tied them up and followed Jimmy as he stopped at one of the boxes and took out a package. He looked at Will and gave him the follow me look, Will did.

They approached Miria. She looked up at them.

"Good morning. You two look like you have something on your mind. Do I have to call Timtuk to find out what it is?"

Jimmy sat down beside Miria. "No Miria, you don't have to do that. We're here to tell you the truth. We've known about Timtuk's gift since the cave of arches. About two weeks. We didn't mean any harm. We just wanted to find out what Lian thought of us, and Beya and Donat. When we did, we realized that our team needed help. That's when we gave the speech to everyone about how to treat each other and especially you. Timtuk's gift is incredible, and yesterday it just might have saved our lives. So Will and I were planning to give this to you later but now seems like as good a time as any."

He handed her the package. She looked at them suspiciously and slowly opened it. Inside was the beautiful material she admired in Quintoke.

"Oh my heavens! How did you get this? What did you use to trade?"

Jimmy smiled. "I think it's rude to ask what one paid for a gift, Miria. Please take this gift from us as an apology for using Timtuk's gift. We meant no harm, truly we didn't."

Miria looked at the boys and then at the material. "You certainly make it hard for a girl to stay mad at you. I forgive you and thank you from the bottom of my heart for this gift. It is beautiful."

She hugged each of them, and Will and Jimmy walked away to

wash up.

Will looked at Jimmy. "If you ever decide to run for office, you got my vote, cuz. You are a real diplomat, do you know that? I am so impressed!"

Jimmy walked to the river to wash, feeling a foot taller and grateful for answered prayer.

CHAPTER THIRTY-SIX

Steve and Fred drove up to Chief George's house. He was sitting on an old chair in his garden watching the children play around him.

Fred waved. "Afternoon, Chief. How are you today?"

With a smile and a wave, the chief tried to get up without letting his old bones show his age.

"Good, my friend. I'm old, but I'm good."

Steve put his hand out to shake the man's hand, but secretly he just wanted to steady him.

"Hello, Chief. Nice to see you again."

The chief smiled. "Come into the house. My wife has coffee and a special cake made just for you two."

"Oh, she didn't have to go through all the trouble," said Fred.

The chief smiled. "No trouble for good friends." And he led them into his house.

The chief's wife had the table set in the kitchen and welcomed them with a warm smile and handshakes.

Fred smiled. "Thank you for going through all this trouble, Mrs. George. You really didn't have to."

"My pleasure Mr. Fred and Mr. Steve. But we are friends, call me Clara. Please sit down as I get the coffee." She went to the stove for the coffee pot.

Steve smiled as he hadn't seen a coffee pot like this in years. Everyone has electric ones, and he was curious to know if the coffee tasted different. While Clara poured the coffee, the chief brought out the necklace.

He spoke slowly. "We gave this to Dean on his sixteenth birthday. The carving is of a whale. He loved to study about them. I wanted to get him a bear, but his mother insisted on the whale. A man should wear the animal of his choice, she told me. And she was right."

He smiled at his wife. He took a deep breath before he started again.

"I did not believe my son and his friend about Dean's disappearance. Though I did not say this to Reed, it was just such a tall tale it was hard for an old man to believe. But Reed never changed the story. He always insisted the cave swallowed him up. Then when I spoke to the eldest of our band; he read to me from the book about the cave people. It was then that I came to believe my son.

Sadly, it was many years later, and Reed didn't want to talk about it anymore.

Then one night, I was sleeping by the fireplace and dreaming. Dean came to me riding on a white stallion. He waved to me and looked so happy. I knew when I woke up that Dean had crossed over to our ancestors. That was many years ago.

Then you found this." And he held up the necklace. "This made no sense to me. I need you both to explain what you feel is the answer to this question. How did it get here?"

Fred gave Steve an 'I've got this look.'

Fred began. "The search and rescue team found it a week ago. They brought it to us to see if it belonged to either of the missing boys. It didn't, so Steve made a phone call to Reed and asked if Dean owned such a piece. The initials on the back gave us a clue as to the ownership. When Reed confirmed that Dean did own this necklace, we had a few theories to share with him. One is he gave it to someone special in his life, maybe a wife. Or two, he passed away and his loved one wore it in his memory. The third theory --and this one has already been shot down, he left it for you to find it and know he is alive and well."

The chief spoke slowly, "He would never leave the necklace. Anyone could have found it. He would have made a Hocuta. That would make more sense to us."

Steve nodded. "That's what Reed told us too. So we believe that the woman and child that came out of the cave might be related to Dean."

The chief and his wife said nothing for a very long time. Finally Clara spoke, "My son has left this life. We both know this, but if we have grandchildren from another world, we would like to ask a favour from you."

Steve nodded. "What can we do for you?"

"We know that Reed has asked to join you on your quest in three years. We would like to make a book of memories that we would wish you to put in the cave when it opens. We would hope our grandchildren would recognize their father as he grew up and photos of his earth family. We want them to know that we are one with them, though we shall never meet. Can you do this for us?"

Fred smiled and touched the chief's arm. "We would be honoured to do just that."

The chief and his wife both breathed a sigh of relief and smiled. "Thank you so much," they both said in unison.

Steve stood and shook their hands. "You're very welcome. And thank you Mrs. George for this lovely cake and delicious coffee. I think I'm going to insist to my wife that we start making our coffee this way again. I like it so much more."

She patted Steve on his back as he walked to the door.

"You are so welcome, Mr. Steve. Please come back and visit us soon."

Steve and Fred both laughed. "If you make us cake, we'll come!" said Fred.

And the men walked to their truck waving back at the wonderful couple they called "friends."

✱ ✱ ✱

Carol drove into Jenny's driveway and noticed her mother walking around the yard with a mug in her hand. Carol got out of the car and waved to her.

"Pat, it's so nice to see you. It's been too long." Pat walked over to Carol and gave her a big hug.

"Oh Carol, it's so nice to see you too. And congratulations on your engagement. I'm so happy for you, dear."

"Thank you. I can't wait for you to meet him. You will let me know how you see our future together."

Pat laughed. "Already did. And you know the answer in your heart now, don't you?"

Carol smiled. "Yeah, I do, and I'm so happy, Pat. In all this craziness with the boys, out of the blue I find love. Go figure."

Pat put her arm around Carol and they started walking towards the house.

"Now when do I get to meet this hunk of burning love?"

Carol almost choked with laughter. "Soon, Pat. In fact he's coming in the driveway right now behind Steve."

Fred smiled when he saw Carol with Jenny's mom. As he hopped out of the truck he called over, "Hi honey, nice surprise to find you here. I get an early hug."

Carol laughed as she hugged Fred and gave him a quick kiss.

"Pat, this is my fiancé, Fred. Fred, do you know Jenny's mom?"

Fred smiled. "Only by the photographs in the house. So nice to finally meet you, Pat."

Pat smiled as she took his hand. "And I you, Fred." She held his hand a little longer than normal and Fred wondered why.

"Fred, be careful when you lift things this week. I feel a really bad back spasm in your future if you don't."

Fred looked at her with a shocked look an then looked at Carol with a "huh" look.

Carol started to giggle. "Jenny never told you her mother is psychic. You better listen to her. She's really good."

Fred looked at Pat. "Are you here about the boys?"

Pat smiled. "That's not the whole reason. I came because of Katie."

Carol and Fred both looked at Jenny before Fred spoke.

"Is Katie okay?"

Steve smiled. "Why don't you go and ask Katie to show you her drawings, and then we can talk."

Pat smiled. "They're on the counter in the kitchen. Take them into Katie's room and enjoy her stories."

Fred and Carol looked at each other with confusion written all over their faces, but they went inside. They took the drawings and went into Katie's room. About twenty minutes later they returned to the kitchen both with stunned looks on their faces. Pat, Jenny and Steve were at the table waiting.

Carol spoke first. "How can she know all this? Did you tell her about Reed coming with us?"

Jenny and Steve shook their heads.

Fred spoke. "Then how?"

Pat stood up and held onto the back of her chair. "My granddaughter is channelling her brother and cousin. She does it in her dreams and then draws the pictures she remembers in the morning.

She has a gift, and I am so proud of her. Don' be afraid of it. She has a firm grasp on the boy's well-being. She is your link to the boys right now. And as far as she is concerned, they are having a marvellous adventure with some new friends."

Fred shook his head slowly. "I always knew she was special, but this one came out of left field. Steve why didn't you tell me?"

Steve laughed. "Would you have believed me? Jenny and I wanted you and Carol to see this first hand and draw your own conclusions."

Carol looked at Jenny still with a shocked face. "I'm speechless. Overjoyed but speechless."

Jenny came and hugged Carol. "I feel better, though, don't you? The boys are safe. We really know this now."

Carol nodded. "Yes, I feel good about that too. Who would have guessed our little Katie would be the one to put our minds at ease?"

Jenny and Steve smiled at each other and held each other's hand.

Pat spoke up, "Now is there a nice little restaurant in town, where I could take you all for dinner?"

Everyone spoke in unison, "No, Pat. You don't have to do that."

Pat laughed. "But I insist. Now where shall we go?"

Carol spoke first. "Fred took me to a very nice log cabin restaurant just this side of town. The food was excellent."

Fred laughed. "Yeah, Pat. How would you like to try goat stew. It's their specialty."

Pat laughed, "I'm always up for an adventure. Now let's get Katie and be on our way."

✱ ✱ ✱

Fred and Carol were quietly watching the stars, having a glass of wine and each deep into their own thoughts.

Carol smiled at Fred. "So what did you think of tonight? A little hair-raising, wasn't it?"

Fred laughed. "To say the least. How long have you known about Jenny's mom?"

Carol smiled. "Jenny confessed it to me about five years ago. She told me her mom picks up on things she doesn't totally understand all the time. Pieces of clues for a better definition. But Pat was always sorry she didn't pick up on Mike. She said on that day she felt upset but didn't know why. When Jenny called her that night to tell her what happened, she realized what the apprehension and anxiety was all about. She always felt bad that she couldn't have done something for him. But just like you, she warned you about your back. Are you going to be careful?"

Fred laughed. "Yes ma'am, after tonight with Katie I'll believe anything."

Carol gave a big sigh. "I can hardly believe what Katie picked up. It's amazing. Especially about the mountains, the lake and Reed. You must admit, it's darn spooky."

Fred smiled. "Not spooky. Fascinating."

Carol smiled at Fred. "But she put my mind at ease. I'll give her that. I bet I sleep better tonight since this nightmare began."

Fred smiled at her. "How about a dip in the hot tub. The warm water will help you relax even more? I'll get more wine."

Carol laughed. "Oh Mr. Avery, I do believe you are trying to seduce me?"

Fred snickered. "Moi? No way. I'm a gentleman."

Carol laughed. "I'll go get my bathing suit."

Fred laughed out loud. "Sweetheart, we're miles from anyone. We don't need suits."

Carol said with innocence in her voice, "But what if someone comes to visit?"

Fred chuckled. "It's eleven o'clock at night. Believe me, we won't have guests arriving for cocktails at this hour."

Carol smiled. "Last one in is a rotten banana." She jumped up and started to run tearing her jacket off as she did.

Fred lunged after her. "You know what they say. Rotten banana, great banana bread." As he stripped down to his underwear in a full run.

The last sound you could hear was a splash, a lot of laughter and then silence.

***

Katie had fallen asleep on the ride back from the restaurant. Steve carried her into the bedroom while Jenny carefully undressed her and put her into her favourite nightie. Each parent kissed her softly on the forehead and Jenny whispered to her,

"Good night, Doodlebug. Sweet dreams."

Pat was sitting in the living room looking at a magazine from the coffee table.

She smiled at them as they joined her.

"Aren't William and Kate's children simply adorable?"

Jenny smiled. "Absolutely, and you can sure see the resemblance too."

"Aren't all babies cute and adorable?" asked Steve.

Pat smiled. "All babies are adorable but not all babies are cute."

"You did it right Jenny, both our babies were cute and adorable."

Jenny laughed. "Thank you, sir, I pride myself on my work."

Pat looked at her daughter and smiled, "Can I make you two a cup of herbal tea?"

Jenny jumped up. "That would be wonderful, Mom, but I'll do it."

Steve looked at Pat. "You've had a busy day, Pat. How come you're not asleep on your feet?"

Pat smiled. "I don't know what it is about being here, Steve. I always get energized, just like that little bunny."

Jenny walked back in holding a tray with a tea pot, cups and a small sugar bowl.

She smiled at her mother. "Okay, everyone, a nice cup of tea and then bedtime. I'm exhausted."

Pat took her cup and smiled at her daughter. Jenny winked at her mom and sat down with her cup. Steve was oblivious to the code of women.

CHAPTER THIRTY-SEVEN

After breakfast Will asked Miria if she would translate to Lian for him.

Will looked at Lian.

"Could we see the route you have chosen for us to take to avoid Quintoke?"

Lian nodded and spread the map on a large rock. Will and Jimmy both looked at the route before Jimmy spoke.

"It looks like we're backtracking for a while then we're heading for Barthilimbo?"

Lian nodded as Miria translated. Then Lian spoke to Miria.

Miria looked at the boys. "He says we will backtrack for one day and then get on the proper route for Barthilimbo. This village is the birth place of his grandfather. Lian has relatives in this village, so he feels we will be very safe."

Jimmy smiled. "Good. Have you met these relatives, Lian?"

Lian shook his head as Miria asked the question but assured them they would be welcome.

Miria looked at the boys. "It will take us about eight days to get to this village. It's a good thing we got lots of supplies at Quintoke."

Jimmy smiled. "I'm sure they didn't plan for us to leave with all those supplies. I think they had it in their heads they would get them all back after they captured us."

Will nodded in agreement. "Thank heaven for Timtuk. Come to think of it, where is the little mugwomp anyway?"

Miria looked around and realized he wasn't where she left him.

"Timtuk!" she yelled. But there was no answer.

"Timtuk, please! Let me see you."

There was still no sign of him. Will looked around for Buddy. He gave a shout, "Buddy! Here boy." But Buddy didn't appear.

The whole group realized Timtuk was AWOL and everyone started shouting his name. Miria was getting a little panic in her voice.

Will held her arm. "It's okay, Miria. Buddy is with him. He'll protect him no matter what."

Miria looked at Will and nodded, but he could read the fear in her eyes.

Jimmy shouted, "Okay, everyone spread out. He couldn't go far, so let's look in all the possible crevices he could be hiding."

Everyone started to search, calling his name and Buddy's. After twenty minutes' no one was any closer to solving the mystery. Will started down another path and noticed a small cave nestled between two large rocks. He called down and he swore he could hear Buddy way off in the distance.

Will shouted, "Everyone, bring some lights. I think I know where he is."

Lian, Beya and Donat brought lights and some rope if necessary. Will pointed to the small cave.

"I think I could hear Buddy."

Jimmy stuck his head in. "Timtuk, Buddy are you in here?"

From way down deep they could hear a small voice. Lian nodded and headed into the cave first. Everyone followed behind. Lian lit the path and it was covered with a lemon coloured crystal. Jimmy didn't have to wait for Will to ask.

"It's called Apatite. It really rare, and it is supposed to have a healing power that, wait for it, stimulates your appetite."

Will chuckled. "You made that up!"

Jimmy laughed. "No, really. It also helps invigorate you. Just what Timtuk doesn't need."

Lian started shouting Timtuk's name again. From a distance, you could just make out a small voice and then a dog bark. The walk was all downhill, but it was dry and didn't seem cold like other caves had been when they descended. Finally they turned into a large cavern with stylolites in the most beautiful lemon crystal. It almost appeared like chandeliers everywhere. Then they spotted Timtuk. He and Buddy were way up a wall and sitting in another small cave entrance.

Miria called out. "Timtuk, don't move. Lian and Beya will get you down."

Lian threw the rope as far as he could, hoping to catch on a jagged edge.

He tugged and it held. He spoke to Beya and Donat and they attached a line to him and held their positions. Lian started to climb the rock wall as Beya and Donat guided his ropes. It took a while but he finally reached Timtuk. He tied a line around him and put him on his back. Timtuk was told to hold on. Slowly Lian made the descent with Timtuk holding on for dear life. It was a slow job, but finally they were safe on the ground. Miria picked up Timtuk and gave him a big hug, and then put him down and started scolding him for putting everyone in such fear.

Timtuk lip started to quiver but everyone was leaving him alone. Finally Jimmy spoke, "Timtuk, as part of a team, one team member never goes off without another team member."

Timtuk sniffed through his tears, "But I had Buddy. He's part of the team; right?"

Jimmy tried to hide his smile. "Yeah, but you are still to discuss it with everyone before you go exploring, especially Miria."

Timtuk looked down at the ground and mumbled, "Sorry, Miria."

Miria spoke back crossly, "As part of your punishment, you will be tied to me for three days. Do you understand?"

Timtuk nodded and then pointed up to Buddy. But Buddy was missing.

Will started to shout, "Buddy! Buddy where are you?"

A far off bark could be heard from the cave trail they had just travelled.

Buddy came bounding out, a little dirtier and dustier than normal, but happy.

Will and Jimmy hugged him and he wagged his tail as he licked their faces.

Beya started to call Lian over to a trail he just found. Lian joined him, and they listened. They could hear running water. They told Miria and the rest of the team to wait while they investigated the cave. Everyone sat down and admired the beauty of the yellow cavern.

After about an hour Lian and Beya came back with smiles on their faces.

Miria translated. "Apparently this cavern has an underground river which meanders for miles. Lian believes this cave is a tube created by melted rock millions of year ago. He believes it may be a shorter path to Barthilimbo. He wants to go back and get our supplies and try this new route. He believes we will only take a few days as we can ride the river."

Will looked confused. "Ride the river. With what? We don't have a boat, do we?"

Miria smiled. "We can make one. It's not difficult."

Jimmy and Will jumped up. Jimmy laughed. "Let's go get our

stuff and then play Tom Sawyer and Huckleberry Finn."

Miria scrunched up her nose. "I don't understand."

Will laughed, "You will, Miria. You will."

And everyone scrambled back up the trail for the supplies and on to their new route.

✳ ✳ ✳

Hours passed before they finally reached the deep interior of the cave and the river. Lian, Beya and Donat started tying the boxes tightly together. Jimmy looked at Miria.

"Miria, no matter how hard you try, those boxes won't float. They're made of rock."

Miria laughed. "Yes, this is true, but you know what one of my gifts can do. Do you not think that I cannot make these rock boxes float on water with a little help from Donat?"

Jimmy looked at her, digested her words then smiled. "I guess it is possible when you put it that way."

She laughed. "It will be a long boat with a sail in the middle. Donat will control it's coarse."

Jimmy whispered, "What are you doing to prevent Timtuk from sliding overboard?"

Miria smiled. "Lian will clear the smallest box and place Timtuk inside. He'll be able to sit in it and enjoy the ride."

"No lid; right?"

"No lid. But it would be a good threat to keep him from any mischief."

Jimmy shook his head. "Aw, come on, Miria. He's only three. You have to understand you were that age once."

Miria started to smile. She remembered her father always saying she was a handful. She looked at Jimmy. "You may be right. I'll try to forgive him, but I swear if he ever scares me like that again, I will lock up the little monster."

Jimmy laughed. "I'll help you."

* * *

Lian called out to everyone. The boat and the supplies were all in place. Miria came over to the makeshift boat and did her levitating magic. She slowly floated the boat into the river and to Jimmy's and Will's amazement, it floated. The sail used on the wind-train was now set up for their boat trip. Will looked at it in amazement.

"I can hardly believe what I'm seeing. You need a train, it becomes a train. You need a boat, you make a boat. You guys are incredible."

When Miria translated what Will had said about them, Beya, Donat and Lian all laughed and nodded their appreciation.

Lian picked up Timtuk and securely tucked him into the small box. Timtuk grinned from ear to ear as Buddy was placed beside him. He felt like he had the best view on the boat with his best friend at his side. Miria sat behind him to ensure his safety. Donat sat in the middle just behind the sail. Beya was in the bow of the boat, with Will and Jimmy just behind him. Lian took to the stern and used a long rod to control their rudder. All was ready as Lian gave the order to Donat.

With one giant breath, the boat moved with ease. Beya hit the light stone to guide their way, and Lian controlled the direction while everyone else enjoyed the ride.

The cavern they were in sparkled like starlight. Will looked at Jimmy.

"You're going to tell me; right?"

Jimmy smiled. "It's Dolomite with Pyrite. The Pyrite makes it sparkle. It is cool though, isn't it? Since we can't be with our stars, this has to be the next best thing."

Will smiled. "I agree. I must admit I do miss the sky and clouds too, but the light stones are so bright it's like bringing our own sun with us wherever we go."

Just as Will and Jimmy were quietly talking a huge splash was made from the river. Everyone looked to the port side to see what it was. Buddy started to growl and everyone went into alert mode. All was quiet and the boat floated along with the current and small wind.

Then a crashing wave came up on their port side. It was a serpent like the one they encountered on the boat so long ago, but this one was three times the size.

It lashed at Lian while he threw his first fire ball at it. Miria lay over Timtuk and Buddy to protect them. Will and Jimmy picked up rods used for handles on the boat. They poked at the serpent as it lunged at them. Its fangs were the size of walrus tusks but twice as deadly.

He lunged again at the boys but Lian and Donat worked together and made a blow torch to scare off the beast. He dove underwater and all was calm. Everyone looked at each other and then back at the water, unsure if it was wounded or coming back for another strike.

Buddy started to growl again, so everyone was on their guard. It rose again. This time at the bow and straight at Beya. Beya used the light stone to blind the beast but not before he struck him in the arm. Beya screamed and Lian and Donat threw another fire wall at it while Jimmy and Will went to get Beya out of danger. The beast was ready to strike again, but Lian's aim was as deadly as this animal. He struck it right in his chest, and it fell backwards into the river. It caused a huge wave which rocked the boat from one side to the other, but everyone held on.

Lian and Donat returned to their places and drove the boat into a shallow shore. They pulled the boat up on the bank and ran to their friend's side.

Miria was already doing her healing on Beya's arm, but his colour was too pale for her to feel comfortable with her powers. She looked at Lian and started to cry out for supplies in one of the boxes. He quickly came back with a chest full of herbs and salves. Miria poured some clear liquid directly into the fang hole, it bubbled and smoked and Beya tried to hold back his scream. She looked at her friend and spoke to him in a soothing voice. He responded by taking deep relaxing breaths.

Miria looked at Will and Jimmy. "Do you think you can boil me some water. I need to make a special herbal tea for him to kill the poison in his body."

Will jumped up. "No problem. We'll have it for you in three minutes."

Miria looked at Will and said, "Make it two."

It was right then that Will realized the severity of this situation.

Jimmy had the fire stone in his hand while he handed Will the water rock and the stone pot. In seconds the fire stone had the water bubbling, and Will brought it to Miria in record time. Miria placed three different herbs into the boiling water and stirred slowly with her measuring stick. She asked Jimmy and Will to sit Beya up, which they did slowly, as he was swelling and in great pain.

Miria held the cup under his lips and encouraged him to drink. Beya did as asked but quickly started to scream as the anti-toxins began to do their job. Miria held her hands over his body and slowly move them up and down over his whole body. Beya began to feel sleepy, but Miria called out to him, which woke him immediately. She continued to move her hands over his body, and he seemed to breathe easier. The colour in his face was coming back, and Miria asked Will to give him more tea.

Jimmy held him up as Will poured a little more tea into his

mouth. Lian and Donat had finishing securing the boat and came to help out. This time Beya did not cry out in pain when the tea entered his body.

Miria stopped moving her hands and concentrated on one particular area of his upper body. Will and Jimmy were both amazed to see the swelling go down right before their eyes. Miria rubbed her hands together and placed them directly on top of the bite mark. She slowly raised her hands and from the fang marks oozed an ugly brown and red slime. Jimmy started to gag at the smell as Lian took a clean cloth from the box and wiped the ooze away from his skin.

Will looked at Miria. "Is that the poison?"

She did not speak but nodded to him and continued to raise her hands over his wound. The wound oozed for a few more moments, and then nothing came out.

Lian cleaned the wound as Miria placed her hands over Beya's head. He quickly fell asleep, and she smiled at him. Miria took a powder from the box, sprinkled it on his wound and placed a clean cloth over that. She wrapped the wound gently and placed his arm over his body as he slept.

She smiled at everyone. "He'll sleep for a few hours, but his strength will not be back for a few days."

She looked at Lian and spoke softly to him. He nodded and he and Donat went off to untie the boxes. She looked at Will and Jimmy. "We are going to camp here for a night and maybe two. His strength will come back slowly, but if we encounter any more of these serpents, Beya would not survive another strike."

Will and Jimmy jumped up to help Lian and Donat. Miria looked over to Timtuk who was still in his box with Buddy sitting right at his side.

Miria smiled. "It's okay to come out now, Timtuk. Beya is going to be fine."

Timtuk got out of his box and slowly walked towards Miria. Just as he was about to come into her arms, the serpent shot out of the water and struck down at him. Miria screamed as the serpent tried to strike again, but this time Buddy bit just behind his eye and he held on. The serpent flinched backwards and fell into the water. Timtuk began to scream for Buddy. Will and Jimmy both had crossbows in their hands as they ran to the edge of the water. Timtuk kept screaming for Buddy, but all was quiet. Will and Jimmy just kept looking with shock and disbelief on their faces.

Jimmy yelled, "Buddy! Where are you, boy?"

Will could hardly get the words out. "Oh, Buddy. This can't be happening."

Miria held Timtuk as he cried uncontrollably. Will and Jimmy felt the same.

Will kept walking up the shore hoping to see his dog make a miraculous appearance. But there was nothing but the sounds of the moving water.

Jimmy came up to Will and put a hand on his shoulder. Will looked at him. Both boys had tears welling in their eyes. Donat and Lian came to stand with them, each man saying nothing but speaking volumes.

CHAPTER THIRTY-EIGHT

Jenny woke up to the sound of Katie crying. She quickly got up and went into her room. Katie was sitting at her table with her felt pens and paper strewn everywhere.

Jenny went to Katie and put her in her arms. "Sweetheart, what's wrong?"

Katie stumbled through her tears. "It's Buddy. He's gone. The big snake took him."

Jenny's stomach felt like it dropped two feet. "What snake, Katie?"

Katie picked up her drawings. "The snake from the river. He tried to bite everyone, but he tried to bite Timmy and Buddy bit the snake. The snake took Buddy into the river. Buddy's dead." Katie began to cry uncontrollably.

"Oh Mommy, he can't be dead. He just can't be."

On hearing the crying and the word "dead" Steve came into the room with a shocked look on his face. He looked at Jenny. "What's happened?"

Jenny picked up Katie's pictures and handed them to Steve.

"It looks like our boys may be in some danger. And Buddy is missing."

Steve examined Katie's pictures and sat down slowly on the floor by Katie's bed.

Pat walked in to the bedroom. "What's wrong?"

Steve handed Pat the pictures. "Is this a snake, Katie?"

Katie nodded. "A huge monster snake. And he took Buddy into the water with him. Nana, Buddy's dead!" And she began to cry in her mother's arms.

Pat held the pictures. "Katie did anyone else get hurt?"

Katie sat up slowly. "Another man got bit, but the lady fixed him. Why can't she fix Buddy?"

And she slammed back into Jenny's arms crying loudly.

Pat got up slowly from the chair and went into the kitchen. Steve followed her.

"Pat, are you okay?"

Pat turned around. "Steve, do you have one of Buddy's toys? One of his favourite toys."

Steve went out to the porch and brought back a blue rubber ball.

He handed it to Pat. "This was his favourite. Your arm would fall off before that dog would ever tire of playing fetch."

Pat took the ball. "Thank you, dear. I'll just take this in my room for a minute."

And she returned to her bedroom.

Steve scratched his head in confusion and returned to Katie's room. Jenny was rocking her in her arms, and Katie had fallen back to sleep. She slowly slipped Katie back into her bed and tiptoed out of her room.

Jenny looked at Steve. "She must have been up for hours to complete all these pictures."

Steve looked at the drawings. "Do we believe these pictures? They look like they are on a boat in this one. Jenny it looks like seven people and Buddy are on this expedition."

Jenny took a huge sigh. "I have to talk to my mom. Where did she go?"

Steve looked at her with a confused face. "She took Buddy's favourite toy and then went into her room. What's she going to do with his ball?"

Jenny smiled. "Meditate on it. She wants to feel if Buddy is really gone. To do this, she needs something of Buddy's to hold as she meditates. I won't disturb her. Do you want coffee?"

Steve looked at his wife as if she was a complete stranger to him. "Jenny, you say this like it's a normal thing to do."

Jenny smiled at him. "Getting coffee is perfectly normal, Steve."

Steve shook his head. "Not the coffee. The ball, your mother, the meditation. What's that all about?"

Jenny laughed a bit. "Steve, you know my mom has a special gift. She feels things, and she goes off into that world, so to speak. I remember when I was about ten years old the police came to our house and asked Mom to assist in a missing child case they were working on. They gave her the child's favourite Teddy to hold. After about an hour of meditation, Mom knew the child was still alive and near a field with an old barn with green doors. There was writing on the roof of the barn, but it was so old that she couldn't make out the words. It had an large "R" and a large "B" on it. Within two hours the police found the boy sleeping in a field near an old green barn. The worn off letters were advertising Rainbow Nurseries."

Steve looked at Jenny incredulously. "How come you never told me this before?"

Jenny laughed. "I was afraid you would think my family is crazy and refuse to marry me."

Steve laughed. "Point taken. But, honey, I don't care if your family thinks they live in Care Bear Country or Munchkin land. I'd have married you anyway. You were my girl, and no one or nothing could have swayed my decision to love you forever."

Jenny smiled at her husband and embraced his hug. "You know, honey, you say the nicest things to me, just when I need them the most."

Pat walked onto this scene and smiled as she felt the happiness swarming in this kitchen. Jenny looked up and saw her mother. "Hi Mom. Did you feel anything?"

Pat smiled. "Buddy is hurt, but not dead. I fear if they don't find him soon, Katie's nightmare will be real."

Steve just shook his head. "And we have no way to text them with your findings.

God, it's like looking into a window, seeing things, but you can do absolutely nothing about it."

Pat looked at Steve. "There might be a way, but it's going to take some real hard meditation to reach him."

Steve looked confused. "Reach who?"

Pat smiled. "Why William of course."

Steve looked at Jenny with a 'you gotta be kidding look.'

Pat laughed. "I can't do it alone, Steve. I'll have to make some calls to a few friends, so they can help me."

Steve shook his head. "Help you do what, Pat? Make a telepathic phone call?"

Pat smiled. "Exactly. Jenny he understands more than I thought he did."

Steve whispered, "Pat, I was kidding!"

Pat laughed. "Steve, I'm not."

Steve looked at Jenny with a defeated look. She smiled at him, "You see, if you knew all this, would you really have married me?"

Steve rubbed his face and started to chuckle. "I plead the fifth, your honour. I plead the fifth."

Pat rubbed his back as she walked from the kitchen. "Hang in there, son-in-law. You'll come over to our side. I guarantee it."

As Pat walked out of the room Steve whispered to Jenny in a

Darth Vader voice, "Steve, come to the dark side. You know I'm your father."

Pat shouted back, "I heard that!"

Steve and Jenny both started to snicker.

❋ ❋ ❋

Carol knocked on Jenny's door before she entered. "Hi Jenny, are you here?"

Jenny walked out of the bedroom. "Yeah Carol, come on in."

Carol hugged her sister-in-law and looked at her with a serious look.

"What's the matter? You seem tense."

Jenny shook her head. "Oh Carol, it's been quite a morning. Come into the kitchen. There's fresh coffee and another round of Katie's pictures."

Carol stopped instantly. "Something is wrong, isn't it?"

Jenny put her arm around her. "Yes and no. Come on. Let's go get some coffee."

When Jenny handed Carol the pictures, she studied each one slowly and carefully.

She looked at Jenny. "They're on a boat and some big snake attacks them? I thought the professor said they would be safe!"

Jenny nodded. "I doubt he knew about the wildlife."

Carol sat up and studied the last picture. "The snake got Buddy! Buddy died?"

Jenny sat down beside her. "No, but he's hurt. But from Jenny's dream they don't know that he is still alive. And from Mom's meditation on Buddy, she's picked up that he's hurt and dying. And he's alone."

Carol sat back in her chair. "Oh Jenny, what can we do?"

Jenny smiled. "Mom's put out the Bat Signal to all her special friends. They are going to meditate at the same time and try to contact Will and tell him about Buddy."

Carol looked at Jenny with an expressionless face. Then she replied, "I've had to face that my son disappeared into a cave that just melted it's opening shut. I had to listen to the professor tell me about a culture that has lived below us for a thousand years. I had to accept that a young man disappeared twenty-one years ago and now may have relatives travelling with our sons. So Jenny, if your mom can send a telepathic message to William, who am I to argue with you? Go for it, Pat!"

Jenny laughed. "You take this so much better than Steve did."

Carol laughed. "Women understand more of this than men do. I don't know why. We just accept it to be true. Like I accept the sun to shine tomorrow and the day after that and so on. We don't put up walls. We open our minds to the potential."

Jenny smiled. "Well said, sister. Well said!"

They tapped their coffee mugs in a toast and took a sip. Pat wandered in.

"Oh hello, Carol. Did Jenny bring you up to speed on our little problem?"

"She sure did, Pat, and I'm awful glad you are here to help us. When does the inter-galactic phone call happen?"

Pat smiled. "In about one hour. I have nine of my friends helping. We're going to send William a short simple message. 'Find Buddy. He's alive'. All of us will be thinking only those four words while we meditate on William. I hope it works. If it does, Katie I'm sure will let us know."

Carol looked at Jenny "Katie, how is she? She must have been so upset when she drew these pictures."

Jenny nodded. "She woke me up this morning with her crying.

When she thought Buddy was dead, she was uncontrollable with the tears. But after talking to Mom, she feels so much better."

Carol shook her head slowly. "She is sure going through a lot for an eight-year-old girl. Do you think Auntie Carol could take her for the afternoon? I'd like to do some girl stuff with her and then take her out to lunch. Do you think she would like that?"

Jenny laughed. "If she doesn't, pick me, pick me!"

Pat laughed. "I think that is a great idea, Carol. Let me go and get her ready for you."

As Pat left the room Carol looked at Jenny. "You okay? You really look a little pale."

Jenny smiled. "I'm okay, just a little tired. Maybe I'll take a nap this afternoon while Mom's doing the meditation and you have Katie. Wow, what a luxury you just gave me."

Carol laughed. "Glad I could help, sis. Why not sweeten the pot and add a bubble bath to the scenario."

Jenny looked at her sister-in-law. "That's why I need you, Carol. You always have the best ideas!"

* * *

Jenny woke from her nap feeling like a million dollars. She didn't remember ever having such a sound sleep. She attributed it to the thirty-minute bubble bath she had just before the nap.

Her mother was sitting in the living room reading a book. When she saw Jenny, she put her book down and smiled. "Oh sweetie, you look so much better. You have wonderful colour in your cheeks again."

Jenny chuckled. "Mom, I slept like a log. It sure felt good. Is Katie home yet?"

Pat shook her head. "Nope, I guess Auntie Carol is really enjoying the time with our little girl. Let's face it, she only had Jimmy. Can't take a little boy for a manicure and a pedicure."

Jenny laughed. "Well, you could, but I doubt they would appreciate it."

Pat laughed. Jenny looked at her mother. "Oh Mom, I almost forgot. How did the meditation go?"

Pat smiled. "I think very well. We did our part, honey. I hope William heard it."

Jenny sat on the couch holding her knees up to her chest. She put her head down on her knees and whispered, "Please, Will, find Buddy."

CHAPTER THIRTY-NINE

Will was sitting by the river alone. He had cried quietly by himself and hoped no one would bother him until he was ready to join the group. He thought about Buddy and what he did to save Timtuk. He was an incredible dog, and he just couldn't get his head wrapped around the feeling that he was gone forever.

He put his knees up to his chest and then put his head on his knees. He closed his eyes and just let his mind wander. He felt like someone was calling him. He kept looking for the source but couldn't see anybody.

"Buddy's alive – Find him! Buddy's alive – Find him! Buddy's alive- Find him!"

Will jumped up as if woken from a deep sleep. He screamed for Jimmy.

"Jimmy! Jimmy, come quick!"

Jimmy ran over to him as fast as he could. "What's wrong, Will?"

Will tried to catch his breath. "He's alive. We have to find him."

Jimmy looked at Will and grabbed his shoulders. "Who's alive? Buddy? How do you know?"

"Jimmy, I know you're going to think I'm losing it, but I swore I heard my Nana's voice telling me Buddy is alive, and we have to find him."

Jimmy looked at Will with little expression at all on his face. "Will, we've seen melting rock block us from going home, water and fire from stones, a beautiful girl levitate stone boxes, a child understand our thoughts and our language. Lian can throw fire balls, Beya can make us disappear and Donat can blow a hurricane if he had to. You think I wouldn't believe you that somehow your grandmother is trying to reach you? Will, let's go find Buddy!"

Both boys ran to Miria and as quick as possible tried to explain that Buddy is still alive and needs to be found. Miria took no time in talking to the group and everyone was ready to search. Will was so happy that they believed him.

Lian and Donat went up the right side of the bank, Miria, Jimmy, and Will went up to the left. Timtuk was told to stay with Beya and be his protector. He seemed to enjoy that position as he sat beside him with a steel rod resting on his shoulder.

Will, Jimmy and Miria searched the bank of the river for any signs of Buddy. Will kept hearing the words, "*Find him*" in his head. Just when they were about to turn back Jimmy saw some strange pattern on the sand.

"Will, Miria, I think I found something."

He followed the mark until it came up against a large boulder. When Jimmy looked around the back of it, there was Buddy laying against another rock.

"Will! I found him!"

Jimmy quickly patted Buddy's head looking for any signs of life.

"Buddy! Buddy, can you hear me?"

Buddy lay quiet and still and Jimmy's heart skipped a beat with fear. Will and Miria came running towards him, but one look at Jimmy's face and Will feared they were too late.

Miria held her hand to Buddy's chest then rubbed her hands together very fast and placed them above Buddy's body. She slowly moved her hands up and down his body and suddenly they heard Buddy whimper.

"Help me to move him. I can't help him here. I can't see if he's been bit,"

Miria said with calm authority.

Will and Jimmy carefully started to pick up Buddy. Miria stopped them.

"No, just hold his head, Will. I'll do the rest."

She passed her hands over his body, and he slowly levitated from the rock. She floated him to a flat rock with Will cradling his head in his arms. She placed him gently down for a better examination.

Miria ran her hands along his back, his legs, and then his chest and head. She searched everywhere for a puncture hole or any blood. She found nothing.

She ran her hand along his spinal column and Buddy yelped.

She looked at the boys. "I think he has some broken bones. Especially here. The serpent must have hit him on some rocks to get him to let go. I can help him, though. It will just take some time."

She rubbed her hands together again and placed them above Buddy's spine. This time there was a green glow coming from her hands that covered Buddy's body. Buddy just lay there and whimpered softly. Will put his head close to Buddy's head.

"I'm so proud of you, boy. Let Miria help you. Please don't leave me," he whispered in his dog's ear. Buddy responded by wagging his tail a bit.

Jimmy watched Miria in stunned amazement. The glow coming from her hands was obviously healing Buddy. He was hypnotized into watching her every move. He felt an absolute awe for her and this gift she possessed.

After about ten minutes they were joined by Lian and Donat who seemed just as happy as Will, Jimmy and Miria to find Buddy alive. Miria placed her hands on Buddy's torso and rested them on a particular sore spot. After another twenty minutes of therapy, Buddy sat up. Miria smiled.

"I think he will walk now. Let's go tell Timtuk his best buddy is safe."

The scream of joy could be heard for miles! Timtuk danced up and down and hugged Buddy (carefully) as they walked back to the campsite.

Timtuk even started to cry which just about had the whole team joining him. Will and Jimmy both hugged Miria and thanked her repeatedly.

Will looked into her eyes. "Miria, there are no words that could express to you my appreciation for all your help. You, my lady, are a miracle worker!"

With tears in her eyes Miria said, "No, Will. I only repaid Buddy back for saving Timtuk's life. It is I who am grateful for Buddy. He is my hero forever. I am forever in your debt for bringing such a wonderful friend for Timtuk."

And she hugged Will. And he hugged her back.

When everyone was tucked into their beds, Jimmy and Will finally had time to talk quietly with each other.

Jimmy looked at Will. "Okay, cuz, now tell me about this message from your grandmother."

Will looked at Jimmy with a confused face. "Jim, I really don't know what to tell you. I was sitting on the bank away from everyone when I felt a real sense of sleepiness. I rested my head on my knees, and I just drifted away. Like I was floating with clouds. Then I thought I could hear my Nana's voice. She said, "Buddy's alive. Find him!" I heard it again and again. That's when I woke up and called to you."

Jimmy looked up at the cave ceiling. "Your Nana. Does she have any special gift?"

Will didn't say anything for a few minutes. "I'm not sure. There have been many weird moments with her now that I think about it. She called Mom about an hour after I broke my arm playing baseball. She said she picked up on my pain. And Mom said she knew that she was pregnant with Katie before Mom did. Stuff like that."

Jimmy raised himself on his elbows. "Your grandmother is psychic! But how did she know about Buddy? And how did she channel you to get the message he was still alive? Will, we might be able to use you to channel your grandmother. You might have some of her ability. You certainly picked up on her message quick enough."

Will just lay on his back and looked up at the ceiling of rocks. He looked at Jimmy.

"I honestly don't think I have any special gift, Jim. But I have to be honest with you about something."

Jimmy sat up slowly. "What is it?"

Will looked him in the eyes. "Katie. I've been dreaming about Katie for weeks now. I feel like she comes to visit me in my dreams, and I show her around and tell her about our adventures. Do you think there could be any connection?"

Jimmy lay his head down. "Cousin, I'm starting to believe everything is connected in one way or another. If Katie comes to you tonight, give her a kiss for me and be sure to tell her about Buddy and that the message was received."

Will smiled at him. "Will do, cousin. Goodnight."

Jimmy just mumbled as he quickly fell asleep. Will turned over and patted Buddy on his head. "Nice to have you by my side, Buddy. It's been a long time."

Buddy wagged his tail and gave a big sigh and fell to sleep. Will snuggled in and was asleep in moments, waiting for another visit from his sister.

* * *

Will was the first to wake the next morning. Buddy was snoring quietly by his side. Jimmy was still rolled up like a sausage roll and facing the other direction. He looked over to Miria and Timtuk, and they were still bundled up and asleep. Will looked at Donat and Lian, and they too were still snoring logs.

Will got up slowly and moved to Beya's side. His colour seemed so much better today, and his breathing wasn't as laboured as it had been yesterday. Beya opened his eyes and slowly focused on Will. Will put his hand up and waved. Beya smiled and tried to sit up. Will came in beside him and assisted.

Beya looked at him and said, "Sala. Sala, Will?"

Will thought for a second. "Water! Yes, Beya, I'll get water."

And Will took a cup and tapped the water rock and filled it for Beya. He brought it back and slowly helped him to take it to his lips. Beya smiled at Will and said weakly, "Mena, Will."

Will smiled back, "Pasha, Beya."

Miria came up quietly behind Will. "Good morning, Will. How is Beya today?"

Will smiled at her. "Weak, but on the mend. How long will it take him to feel strong again?"

Miria touched Beya's forehead. "A few days. The poison is

out, but it still did some damage. I will do two healings on him today and then one tomorrow. That should be enough to make him strong again."

Will looked at her. "So we should stay here another day? He should not be moved; right?"

Miria nodded. "Yes. He is as weak as a cup of water. I will make Lian understand the importance of another day of rest. How is Buddy?"

Will smiled. "Snoring happily by Jimmy. I think you did an amazing job on him too, Miria. I think he and Timtuk will be playing together in no time."

Miria smiled as she mixed some herbs for Beya.

"Would you like me to boil some water for you? For the herb tea?"

Miria shook her head. "You are always so helpful, Will. Yes, thank you. That's very nice of you."

Will got up. "No problem. Always nice to feel useful!"

He went to the water stone and filled the stone pot with water. Then he put the pot on the fire stone. Within minute it was boiling and steaming. He carried the pot to Miria and put it down on a flat rock beside her. She placed the herbs into the boiling water and stirred it slowly. When she felt it was strong enough, she poured some into the cup by Beya. She assisted Beya to sit totally upright and helped him to drink the tea. By the face he was making, Will could tell Beya was not impressed with the flavour. Miria gave him a gentle talking to, and he nodded and drank more of the tea.

Miria smiled at Will. "It is a little bitter, but it will help him with his strength and to rid him of any poison that might still be in his body."

Will laughed. "Remind me to sing the song, "A Spoonful of Sugar" to you later. It might help you with the medicine."

Everyone started to rustle and wake slowly. Lian and Donat came to Beya to check on his recovery. The concern in their eyes made Miria smile. They were such good friends who truly cared about one another. Lian asked Miria what she thought of his progress, and she persuaded Lian to stay another day, so Beya could regain his strength.

Timtuk came running over to Miria with Buddy right on his heels.

"Good morning, Timtuk. And to you, Buddy. It is so nice to see you so happy and healthy," she said to them.

Buddy gave her a woof and a little jump up to show her all was well. She shook her head.

"You are one amazing dog, Buddy."

And she gave him a hearty rub on his chest. He totally loved that.

Jimmy walked quietly to Will. "Good morning, cousin. How did you sleep?"

Will looked at Jimmy and smiled coyly. "Like a baby."

"Any midnight walks with Katie?" Jimmy asked quietly.

Will looked at Jimmy. "Been waiting for you to wake up, so we could talk. Come over to the bank of the river, where we can talk privately."

Jimmy started to chuckle. "Will, remember! The guys don't understand us."

Will whispered back, "But Timtuk and Miria do and right now I'd like to run all this by you first."

Jimmy nodded. "Okay, cuz. Let's meander over to the riverbank."

They slowly walked away from the group as if they were going to wash up or something. Will and Jimmy sat down behind some huge boulders and Will began.

"Jimmy, Katie came again. She asked about Buddy. Did we

find him? Is he okay?

Then she told me about Nana visiting her, and Nana told her Buddy wasn't dead.

How would my Nana know this Jimmy? I told Katie I thought Nana sent me a message, and she said Nana and some of her friends sent it. She overheard my mom and Aunt Carol talking about it."

Jimmy straightened up. "My mom! My mom is with your mom?"

Will looked down at the ground. "According to Katie, your mom lives up there now and is marrying Uncle Fred."

Jimmy jumped up. "Who the hell is Uncle Fred?"

Will looked at his cousin. "Calm down, Jim! The only Uncle Fred I can think of is Fred Avery. He's a good friend of my dad. They hunt together, and he works for the forestry as well. He's a real nice guy, though I thought he was a confirmed old bachelor."

"Will, my mom is engaged to a man I've never met and living up north with everyone. What happened to our home in Vancouver? What about her job?

Man, Will. We go away for a few months and everything changes!"

Will whispered back to him, "Jimmy, I'm not sure all of this is true. Katie comes to me, but is it just my mind playing games? But this I do know, my Nana sent me a message. And that message saved Buddy's life. So I have to wonder if these visits with Katie are real, and does Katie possess any special gift as well?"

Jimmy was quiet for a moment. "Will, we've seen too much down here we can't explain. Who are we to question Katie and your grandmother's gift? Did Katie deliver you any earth-shattering news? She's certainly shaken me up!"

Will was quiet for a moment. "Katie told me Mom is going to have a baby, but Mom hasn't told anyone yet, so she is only telling me."

Jimmy started to chuckle. "Again, how does she know this?"

Will only shook his head and shrugged his shoulders. "I don't know, Jimmy, but I sure do like walking with her each night. She brings a feeling of home with her, and it sure feels good."

Jimmy smiled. "Maybe you possess a special gift as well, Will. Ever thought of that?"

Will smiled. "I think it only hits the female side of the family."

Jimmy smiled. "You wish!"

Will just chuckled and gazed into the river.

CHAPTER FORTY

Katie ran into her parent's bedroom and jumped on their bed.

"He's alive!" she shouted. "He's alive!"

Steve sat up like a cannon ball being shot. "Who's alive, Katie?"

Katie started jumping up and down on their bed. "Buddy! They got the message from Nana. The lady saved him and Buddy is alive!"

Jenny sat up slowly and grabbed Katie. Pulling her down in her arms. She spoke quietly to her, "Sweetie, how did you know about Nana's message?"

Katie looked at her. "Will told me. He told me to tell Nana he got her message and that Buddy is alive because of her."

Steve sat back on his pillow. "Whoa, this is really spooking me!"

Jenny got up and grabbed her robe. "Come on, Katie. We have to talk to Nana."

Hand in hand they walked to Nana's bedroom and knocked softly. A very sleepy voice called out. "Yes. Come in."

Jenny and Katie peeked in. "Mom, we have to talk to you right now. Can we come in?"

Pat sat up in her bed. "Of course. Come in."

She held out her hands for Katie, who responded by hopping into her bed and into her arms for a hug.

"Now, tell me, you two, what's so important?" She said with a big smile on her face.

Jenny looked at Katie. "Go ahead, honey. Tell Nana what you told Daddy and I."

Katie looked up to her Nana. "Buddy is alive, Nana. You saved him! Will told me to tell you he got your message. The lady fixed him, and everything is good again."

Pat looked at Jenny. "This is not a coincidence. Katie didn't know about the message being sent, did you, Katie?"

Katie looked down at the bedspread. "I don't know. Maybe, but Will told me if it hadn't been for you Nana, they would have never looked for Buddy. He wasn't bit by the snake, but he had broken bones 'cause the snake smashed him into some rocks. But the nice lady down there fixed him, and Buddy is okay. Will said to say thank you!"

Pat hugged Katie and kissed her on her head. "I'm so proud of you, Katie. What you are doing is called channelling. You are visiting Will through your mind, and bless your heart you are remembering it all. This is a very special gift and over time you will get better and better at it."

Katie looked at her grandmother. "I will?"

Pat hugged her. "Yes, sweetheart, and your mom and Nana will be right here guiding you. Never be afraid of this gift. It's powerful but wonderful too."

Jenny leaned over and gave Katie a kiss. "Why don't you go and get some cereal, and I'll be out to make toast for you. I'd like to talk to Nana for a minute."

Katie jumped down from the bed. "Okay, Mommy. Can I have banana slices on my cereal?"

Jenny smiled. "Sure. Just be careful with the knife; okay?"

Katie smiled. "Okay, Mommy. I know how to use a knife now, Nana. Daddy and Mommy showed me how."

Pat smiled. "Atta girl. You're growing up so fast. Slow down a bit, so this old lady doesn't get dizzy watching you."

Katie laughed. "You're funny, Nana!" And she skipped out of the room.

Jenny looked into her mother's eyes.

"Wow! This is really amazing, and she seems to be getting stronger at this by the day."

Pat sat up and held Jenny's hand. "Darling, she's your link to Will. It's like having a direct line to him. This is fantastic!"

Jenny started to tear up. "I know, Mom, but it's also a shock too. I had no idea Katie was showing signs of a gift. You have it. I never had it, but now she has it. Does it skip a generation?"

Pat looked at her. "No, because my mother had a gift with animals."

Jenny shook her head. "Come again? What are you taking about?"

Pat giggled. "You seem to think the gift we possess is all psychic. It's not. My mother could understand animals. She knew when our animals were sick, and she told the Veterinarian exactly what was wrong. And my mom was never wrong. Doc Bellows, our Vet, hired her as an assistant. He said she was worth her weight in gold."

Jenny looked at her mom. "I knew Grandma worked at the Animal Hospital, but you never told me about her special ability."

"Yes I did. When the movie Dr. Doolittle came out, I told you Grandma could do that."

Jenny sat quietly. "I never understood what you meant. And I was so young, I didn't think to question it."

Pat smiled. "So Jenny, you may not have a psychic gift, but it's not to say you don't have a gift. You're probably doing something so naturally for you that you don't realize it's a gift that no one else has."

Jenny looked at her mom and started to tear up. "I talk to the baby. I talked to all of my babies. I knew what their sex was, if they were sleeping or if they needed me to sing to them to calm them down. Do you know babies get scared of loud noises? They love it when you rub your stomach. It makes the uterus move in waves. It kind of rocks them to sleep. This baby is a girl, and she can't wait to meet Katie. She says Katie knows about her. I just thought all mothers go through this, but I guess they don't, do they?"

Pat smiled and took Jenny in her arms. "Why didn't you ever tell me? This is so incredible. Jenny I always knew you were an incredible mother. I just never knew you were spiritually attached to them. I'm so proud of you."

Jenny sat up. "Katie knows about the baby. I haven't even told Steve yet."

Pat chuckled. "So when are you planning on doing that dear?"

"I guess today would be a good time. I have it all ready, I just needed the right moment."

Pat looked at her with a confused expression. "What do you have ready?"

Jenny jumped up. "You'll see. I have to fix Katie some toast."

And she left Pat still with a confused expression.

Jenny entered the kitchen finding Katie munching her cereal and sliced bananas.

"Good job with the bananas, Katie!" Jenny laughed.

Katie grinned with her mouthful.

Jenny took out the bread. "How about some toast and orange juice?"

Katie smiled. "Yes, please, and could I have peanut butter on my toast?"

Jenny smiled. "Absolutely, Doodlebug!" And she popped the bread into the toaster as Steve entered the kitchen.

He smiled at his girls. "Hey, did you eat all the cereal? Did you save any for your starving old dad?"

Katie laughed. "There's lots left." As she pushed the box

towards him.

Jenny smiled. "Would you like eggs and bacon instead?"

Steve smiled. "Oh baby, you know what I like!"

Jenny laughed and began making breakfast for him. Pat entered the kitchen,

"Oh my favourite family having breakfast together. I just love this Norman Rockwell essence."

Jenny just laughed and handed Steve a gift box. Steve looked at it.

"It's not my birthday. And our Anniversary is not until next month. What's this for?"

Jenny smiled. "Open it and find out."

Steve slowly opened the beautifully wrapped gift. As he lifted the coloured tissue from inside he began taking out each item, one at a time. A jar of baby food, a disposable diaper, a bib that says, "Daddy's Girl", a onesie, and a burp cloth. He looked at Jenny.

"Katie got her wish?"

Jenny nodded and started to well up in her eyes. Steve jumped up and hugged her and then kissed her on her mouth.

"Oh honey, this is great news. Are you happy about it?"

Jenny nodded and burst out laughing. Katie and Pat started clapping and cheering.

Steve laughed. "This calls for a celebration. Can I take my three favourite ladies to dinner tonight?"

Jenny smiled. "That would be wonderful. The Bistro, please. I feel like French cuisine tonight."

"Done! I'll make the reservations."

Katie gave a hearty yippee and Pat just smiled at the two proud parents.

Steve smiled. "Of course my girl can't have any alcohol, but I'll get some non-alcoholic sparkly for you; okay?"

"Okay, even Katie can share a glass with me."

Katie laughed and skipped off to her bedroom. "I'm going to pick out my dress, right now!"

Steve laughed. "Always my little girl."

Then he stopped and looked at the bib from the box. He looked at Jenny. "Daddy's Little Girl? Are you telling me we're having another little girl?"

Jenny nodded. "You okay with that, Daddy?"

Steve smiled. "I'd have ten Katie Bugs if we could, but I'll happily settle for two."

Jenny smiled and hugged Steve. Steve held her tightly, wanting her to feel how happy he was inside too.

Pat tiptoed out of the kitchen, not wanting to spoil this private moment these two young people were having.

✷ ✷ ✷

"A BABY!" Carol cried out with glee. "Oh Jenny, I'm so happy for you," she said as she hugged her sister-in-law. "How did Steve handle the news?"

Jenny laughed. "Like a really wonderful proud father. He's excited too, Carol."

Carol laughed. "I'll bet he's telling Fred right now, and they're patting each other on their backs like they just ran a full marathon or something."

"I also can tell you, it's a girl."

Carol clapped her hands in excitement. "Oh Jenny, that's so great. I get to see her grow up from the get-go. You know Katie and I had such a good time the other day going shopping, trying on clothes and shoes, pedicure, manicure and then lunch. I loved shopping with Jimmy, but it's so different with a girl. You know, nail polish looks interesting, but to a guy it just looks like really good model paint. Just not the same. You know what I mean?"

Jenny laughed. "Will always made any excuse he could think of to avoid shopping with me. I have a stomach ache was his favourite, but he used the 'Sorry. Mom, I'm going fishing with Dad' then go and talk to his dad and beg him to save him from a fate worse than death."

Carol laughed. "And did he?"

"Absolutely. He always told Will, we men have to stick together. Why do you think I was so thrilled to have Katie? Someone on my side for a change."

Carol was quiet for a moment and looked away from Jenny. Jenny touched her arm. "Carol, are you okay?"

Carol looked back at Jenny with tears in her eyes. "I really thought this chapter of my life was closed. I have a fifteen-year-old son, case closed. But here you are starting another new chapter in your life, and I just didn't think it was going to be possible for me. But for the first time in a long time, I feel I could do it too. I know Fred would love it, but it comes back to the marriage thing. I'd like to wait for Jimmy, but I would also like to have another baby too. Jenny, what do I do?"

Jenny hugged Carol and whispered in her ear, "You talk to Fred. Work together. You'll come up with an answer."

"He'll choke on his dinner if I bring it up at the table."

Jenny laughed. "Then might I suggest a glass of wine before dinner to avoid the choking bit."

"He'll spit the wine on the carpet. I just know he will!"

"Come on, sis. Live on the wild side. Take a chance."

Carol laughed. "Okay, I will."

***

Fred got home just before six o'clock, and he could smell the dinner cooking from the driveway. He walked into the house and smiled at the warm feeling and aroma he was encountering.

He yelled out, "Is there a gorgeous woman living here?"

She smiled as she came towards him with her arms spread out. "Don't know about the gorgeous part, but there is a woman living here."

Fred took her in his arms. "Don't kid yourself, lady, you're drop dead gorgeous!"

And he kissed her softly on her lips.

She smiled at him. "How about a glass of wine before dinner?"

He took off his coat and boots.

"Sounds great. I'll put on some music."

He went to the stereo and placed a few CD's in the slots and turned to Carol as she entered the room with two wine glasses and a bottle. He smiled at her and took the bottle from her, opened it and poured wine into each glass.

He looked at Carol suspiciously. "Are you okay? Did I forget your birthday?"

Carol laughed. "No! Besides, I would never let you. No, I was wondering if you and Steve saw each other today?"

Fred shook his head. "No, I had to go to Smithers District today, and he was in the Kitimat region. Why do you ask?"

Carol tapped his glass and took a sip.

"I saw Jenny today. She had some wonderful news."

Fred looked at her as she took another sip of wine. "Are you going to tell me, or do I have to guess?"

Carol chuckled. "Apparently, they are going to have a baby."

Fred just sat there stunned. Carol tried to read his thoughts but was coming up blank. "Fred, are you okay?"

Fred shook his head. "Oh yeah, I'm great. This is great news! I wish I had seen Steve today. He must be on cloud nine."

Carol nodded. "Jenny says he is. I'm so happy for them, aren't you?"

"Absolutely. Gosh Katie must be dancing like a butterfly over there."

He then got quiet again, and he took a slow sip of his wine. "Carol, have you ever thought of having another child? Like with me?"

Carol was surprised and yet a little thrilled that he brought this up first.

"Yeah Fred, after today I've thought of nothing else. But I have a small problem that maybe you could help me solve."

He took her into his arms. "I'll try. What's troubling you?"

Carol smiled and cuddled into his arms.

"Fred, until today I really thought having babies was off the table for options. But when Jenny told me about her baby today, it was like a floodgate inside me just opened. I really want another child, Fred. I want to have your child."

Fred hugged her and began to rock her. "Well, that's fantastic. So what's the problem?"

Carol whispered to him, "I want to be married first. I'm old fashioned, I know! But I want to be married first. And I also want Jimmy to be there, so what I'm having a problem with is I don't want to wait three years."

Fred smiled and chuckled a bit. "That is a problem. Somehow honey, you are going to have to make a compromise. Wait for Jimmy and the baby or marry me now and have the baby next year. The one thing about weddings is that you can have re-vows taken at any time. We could have a big family ceremony in the mountains of Peru. Look on the positive side, the baby could join us too. And right now, we could have a small private civil ceremony with just two witnesses. What do you think?"

Carol looked into his eyes. "You've been thinking about this, haven't you?"

He whispered into her ear. "I have sweetheart. I've wanted to marry you the day I asked you to be my wife, but I can respect your wishes about Jimmy. But do you want to wait three more years until you get pregnant? You are getting old, you know?"

She gasped at that comment and tried to hit him on the leg before he caught her arms. They wrestled all the way to the floor before he pinned her and kissed her passionately. When he finally released his hold on her she touched his face softly and kissed him on the lips.

She whispered to him, "Let's do it your way. I'm sure Jimmy will understand, as long as I get a big family wedding in the Andes. Not many girls can say that statement and make it come true."

Fred smiled and whispered back. "You've made me the happiest man on earth Carol. Can we do it tomorrow?"

CHAPTER FORTY-ONE

Miria finished her first healing on Beya and was just getting ready to make lunch when Will came and sat near her.

Will looked at her. "Will Beya feel stronger soon?"

She smiled. "Yes, in fact he should start to feel stronger within a few hours. I will do another healing before he goes to sleep and one again tomorrow morning. By mid-day tomorrow we should have our old Beya back."

Will smiled. "That's great, Miria. We are so lucky to have you with us. I can't imagine what this trip would have been like without you. Disastrous comes to mind."

Miria looked closely at Will. "I'm glad I'm here, and I could not be in better company. I feel very safe with all of you. I can't imagine losing any of you, and I refuse to believe that will happen. As a team, we are... oh what is the word?"

Will chuckled. "Super heroes!"

She laughed, "If that means really special, then yes, we're super heroes."

Will laughed. "Can I help Wonder Woman make lunch?"

Miria laughed out loud, "Wonder Woman? I like the sound of that. And yes, I would appreciate your help, Will. I have to make a hearty soup for all of us and corn bread too. How about cutting up some vegetables for me?"

Will smiled. "My lady, I'd be honoured." And he began setting out the vegetables Miria was planning to use for the soup.

* * *

Jimmy was quietly walking along the riverbank examining rocks. He could hardly believe the variety of minerals that were so readily available at his fingertips.

As a rockhound, he wished he could stay here for a week and analyze the variety he was encountering. Onyx marble, oolite and oncolite, all so readily available and yet in his world, rare. He was in his happy place as he examined each stone until he encountered something rarer than mineral rocks.

Jimmy called for Will and Miria to come take a look. When they finally joined him, Jimmy was so excited he could hardly keep still.

"Look, it's a stone statue carved into this rock. I'm positive the statue is made from black opal. It's so rare but here it is just sitting there. Who could have carved it and is this whole rock a huge black opal? Will, this would be priceless at home!"

Will patted his cousin on the back. "Jimmy, calm down. We can't take it with us.

Maybe you can chip off a small stone, but that's about all you can bring.

But this statue, Miria, do you have any idea who could have carved it into this stone?"

Miria said nothing but turned and called to Lian and Donat. They came running immediately. Miria showed them the statue. Both men showed a sign of shock and fear. They spoke quietly to each other before Miria turned to the boys.

"We believe this was carved by the Tepanex tribe. They are

marking their territory, and it stands as a warning for anyone passing through. We are in danger, and we must leave immediately."

Will and Jimmy both paled and Will spoke, "Miria, what about Beya?"

Miria spoke quickly as she began to walk back to the camp.

"We have no choice, Will. He will be bundled up safely. We must leave now!"

Everyone felt the seriousness of the situation. Lian and Donat started tying the boxes together to form the boat. Will, Jimmy and Miria packed the food and the bed rolls up. Timtuk and Buddy were placed inside their special box, Beya was put directly in front of them, so he could lay down. All was ready within twenty minutes, Miria levitated the boxes and they shoved off from the riverbank.

Donat provided a good wind as the sail filled and thrust the boat into the centre of the river. Everyone was on high alert, first, for the snake, and second, for the Tepanex tribe.

Jimmy sat behind Miria and quietly spoke to her. "Tell me about this tribe, Miria. Are they the tribe you warned us about at your village?"

She looked at him sadly and nodded.

Jimmy continued, "They want you all for your gifts; correct?"

Again, she didn't speak, just nodded her head.

Jimmy whispered into her ear, "And Beya won't be able to use his gift for a while, right?"

She nodded again but this time whispered back. "Jimmy, we cannot stop until we get to Barthilimbo. We will have to sail for at least a day if we are to remain safe. That is, if we don't encounter anyone on the river."

Jimmy got a cold chill down his back.

"When will Beya be strong again to use his gift?"

Miria shrugged her shoulders. "Maybe tomorrow or maybe in

a few more days. I truly don't know. All I do know is that we can't count on him at this time. This is scary Jimmy. The danger is real, and we must try our best to avoid it."

Jimmy took a deep breath before he asked the next question.

"Will and I do not have any special gifts. What will they do to us?"

Miria looked away. "Let's not think about that now. Let's think of getting safely to Barthilimbo. We'll be safe there."

Jimmy looked to the bow of the boat for any danger on the water. His gut was telling him there was trouble ahead, but his head refused to believe it.

***

After two hours of sailing without incidence everyone was breathing a little easier. Lian was still watching closely as they turned in the bends of the river. And Donat stood guard with a strange-looking weapon as he blew the boat on its path.

Lian spoke to Miria, and she nodded in agreement. Miria went to Jimmy and Will.

"Lian thinks you should have your weapons by your side, just in case."

Will nodded and went to the box containing the weapons. He took out the crossbows and arrows and then began to investigate the other weapons packed in the box. He asked Miria to explain the uses.

She laughed at him. "Will, the women do not get trained in weaponry. I have absolutely no idea what each weapon does. You would have to ask the men on our team. In your world, do woman fight?"

Will nodded. "Yes and very well too. If you would like, someday I'll teach you to use the cross-bow. I believe everyone should know how to protect themselves if danger arrives."

She smiled sweetly. "I would like that, Will. I look forward to my first lesson."

Jimmy came up beside them and looked into the box. "Wow, what do all these things do?" he asked looking at Miria. She smiled at him, looked at Will, winked and moved back to sit near Timtuk and Beya.

Will looked at Jimmy. "Take the cross-bow, just in case. Apparently women do not get any training in weaponry, so Miria has no idea what this stuff is. Did you see that crazy thing Donat is holding? It looks like a rocket launcher mated with a bubble gum machine. What do you think all those balls inside that case are?"

Jimmy shook his head. "I don't know, and personally I don't want to find out. To find out means we're under attack. And I for one would like to skip that course. Thank you."

Will chuckled, "You and me both, cousin. Never was thrilled with confrontation.

Some people thrive on it, not me. I'll take calm and peaceful every time."

Just as Jimmy was about to respond Lian screamed a warning. A small boat was spotted coming up from the back. Lian quickly ran to the box and took out a weapon that looked like a violin in shape, but it definitely had a trigger on it.

Donat picked up the wind and the boat went a little faster. The boat coming up the rear was being paddled by at least six men. But there was a man standing in the bow, he seemed to be shouting orders. And a man in the back was standing. Will could see he held something in his hands. A weapon, possibly.

Beya sat up and looked at Lian. He shouted some words, but Lian shook his head, and Beya lay down again. Miria looked at Will and Jimmy.

"We don't know who they are, and they don't know who we are.

Do not show your weapons unless they fire first. We're hoping this is just some fishermen from Barthilimbo, but we must be on our guard if they are not."

Will and Jimmy both nodded in understanding. Lian kept watching from the stern, and it was so hard to read his face. To look at him all you would see was a cold and forbidding look. Jimmy thought he could be in movies with that stare. He'd scare the poop out of him.

Though their boat was going at a good clip, the other boat was sleek and faster and was slowly closing the distance. Will could make out their faces but could not really see if they were friendly or if they were trouble. Lian called out to them and they stopped paddling. The man standing in the bow called back. Lian held his hand up, the man in the bow did the same. Miria whispered to Will and Jimmy.

"This is a sign of peace."

Lian continued to talk to the man, and he responded. Lian nodded and gave the hand motion to pass by them. The boat did just that as Lian and Donat watched carefully as they floated slowly by. The leader of the boat called out again and held up his hand. Lian nodded and held up his hand.

Miria whispered to Jimmy and Will, "They say they are fishermen from Barthilimbo, and that we may follow them safely."

Will stood up and tried to look into their boat. "Miria, if they were fishing what do they use to catch the fish? I see no net, no fishing rods, nothing to indicate they are fishermen."

Miria looked quickly at Will then called Lian to come over. She repeated what Will had noticed, and Lian nodded in agreement. He spoke to Miria quietly hoping Timtuk would not hear them. Miria looked at Jimmy and Will.

"Be prepared, we may still need to fight."

This sent chills up both boys' back. Will and Jimmy quietly

loaded their bows for a quick attack, if necessary. Just as Donat and Lian were quietly getting their weapons ready, Beya sat up and spread his arms.

In a flash they were in a mist and Jimmy and Will smiled as the boat full of men stopped rowing and wondered where we just disappeared to. Miria called to Beya sternly, but he just smiled at her and continued the cloaking mist. Donat blew the boat to the opposite side of the river, staying as far away from those men as he could get us.

Lian went to Beya and tapped his shoulder. Beya smiled at him and they spoke briefly. Lian returned to his post with a much happier face than he had just a few minutes ago.

Will looked at Miria. "Is he strong enough for this?"

"He tells me he is, so I must believe him. I don't know how long he can keep it up, but at least it will get us out of danger for now."

Jimmy looked at Beya, smiled and gave him the thumbs up. Beya smiled back, but would not drop his arms, keeping everyone shrouded in the cloaking mist.

Timtuk gave Will a come here look, so Will crawled over to his box.

Will smiled at him. "What's up, soldier?"

Timtuk whispered into Will's ear, "Those men. They want Miria. I heard them. They want Miria."

Will touched his back and said nothing but talked to Timtuk through his thoughts.

Timtuk, don't worry. There are five men on board here that will protect her with our lives. No one is going to take Miria; okay?

Timtuk nodded. "Okay. They are bad men, Will. They are not fishermen." Will nodded and spoke again in his mind.

I know, Timtuk, but right now thanks to Beya we are safe. Let's hope Barthilimbo is not too far away, and we won't have to worry about these men anymore.

Timtuk smiled and snuggled down by Buddy. Will smiled at them.

"You two protect each other, ya hear?"

Timtuk smiled and began to suck his thumb and cozy into Buddy. Will took it as a good sign.

Will resumed his post. "What did our little mind reader tell you?" Jimmy asked quietly.

Will whispered, "Those men want Miria. Now Jimmy, they don't know who she is and her special gifts, so I have to assume they just want her for their lousy desires."

Jimmy gave a huge sigh. "Well, now, they would have to get through our army of five before we would let that happen. I hope Beya can keep this up for a few more hours, the farther we get ahead of these creeps, the better it will be for all of us."

Will looked at Jimmy. "I gotta take Timtuk to Lian. He has to know what Timtuk just told me. I want everyone on red alert to protect Miria."

Jimmy nodded in agreement.

"I'll keep Miria occupied with our very late lunch or very early dinner. You get Timtuk."

Will nodded and waited for Jimmy to occupy Miria's time. He slowly crawled over to Timtuk and lifted him out of his crate and carried him to Lian. He asked Timtuk to repeat what he told him. Lian stood there frozen, his jaw clenching at every word. He spoke to Timtuk and Timtuk happily nodded his head and looked at Will.

"He said everything you did. No one on this boat is going to let anything happen to Miria. He promised me."

Will smiled at Timtuk and nodded at Lian. Both men understood the situation now.

Will quietly took Timtuk back to his crate and placed him

carefully inside. Timtuk smiled and cuddled back into Buddy's side. Jimmy continued to help Miria fill the bowls with food. He began to distribute them to Donat, Lian and Beya. He smiled at Beya and popped a small piece of dried fish into his mouth, so he could continue with his cloaking. He delivered to Will while Miria gave Timtuk and Buddy some as well. Jimmy took his bowl and went to sit by Beya. He offered Beya a piece of corn bread. Beya nodded and popped it into his mouth. They continued this until both men's bowls were empty.

Beya smiled at Jimmy. "Mena, Jimmy."

Jimmy smiled back. "Pasha, Beya. Sala?"

Beya nodded happily and Jimmy went to get him a cup of water.

✳ ✳ ✳

A few hours had passed and Lian went to Beya. They spoke and Beya put his arms down and the mist disappeared. Lian finally felt safe enough, so Beya could take a rest. Beya curled up under the mast and fell asleep immediately. Miria went to him and gave him a well needed healing. He slept through the whole process. He slept for three hours.

As the boat rounded a large turn, Lian called out. At first Will and Jimmy thought they might be in danger again, but Lian pointed in the direction straight ahead. Far off in the distance was Barthilimbo. Jimmy and Will were taken aback by the architecture. Jimmy looked at Will.

"Are we in Moscow? This place looks like Saint Basil's Cathedral on steroids."

Jimmy was right. The city was alive with the swirling onion dome architecture of Russia. As far away as they were, they could see the colours and the beauty of this large city.

Miria sat down beside the boys. "It's incredible, isn't it? I've never seen anything like it."

Jimmy smiled. "We have. In photos only, but this architecture is well known in Eastern Europe. How your architects got these plans is really a mystery I'd love to solve."

Miria looked at Jimmy. "What is a photo?"

Jimmy smiled. "I'm sorry, I keep forgetting where I am sometimes. A photo is a picture taken from a small machine one would carry. It's how we record our memories of vacations we take, special holidays, birthdays and so on. Believe me, Miria, I wish I had a camera with me. I'd love to take all these memories with me in my hand."

Miria smiled. "But you still haven't forgotten your oath?"

Will piped in, "Never, Miria. We'll keep this place a secret until the day we die."

And Jimmy laughed. "Maybe two days after, to be on the safe side!"

Miria laughed and just enjoyed the rest of the ride as they slowly floated into the small harbour of Barthilimbo.

Lian and Donat left the boat to find a private place to stay for a few days. They didn't want anyone seeing the floating boxes as it would draw attention to them. Lian hoped they could find a small place outside of the city for privacy.

They were gone for only a short time before they jumped back on the boat and said they had a place to stay. It was just a short ride downstream and close to the city gates but private in its surroundings. Miria could hardly wait to see where they would be staying. She hoped there would be beds to sleep in, instead of the hard ground.

When they came up to the little house they were renting for the next few days, Jimmy first sight of it reminded him of Frodo's house from Lord of the Rings. It was partially buried into the ground. The door was rounded as were the two windows. The roof was covered in moss.

Will looked at Jimmy. "It's Frodo's house."

Jimmy snickered and patted his cousin on the back. "Glad to see we think alike."

Miria was ecstatic knowing they were going to sleep on beds rather than a rock floor with bedrolls. On entering the house she was taken aback by the old stone fireplace with wood piled next to it for burning. The living area was cozy and warm. The kitchen had a small stone oven and a sink made from a large hollowed out stone. She smiled as she saw the bucket they would need to get water, but knew her water rocks and fire stone was all she needed for this area. There was an upstairs loft that could easily sleep three to four people. And the bedrooms off the kitchen and living area were small but cozy and inviting. Miria felt like she was in a palace after all the weeks they had been travelling.

Lian came in pushing the first of the boxes. Miria guided the food box into the kitchen area. The weapons box remained near the front door, and the other boxes were placed where there was room along the walls. Lian looked at Miria and spoke to her. Her happy face showed everyone she was pleased with the housing situation.

The furniture was polished stone, but the couches had large colourful pillows on them for comfort. The kitchen table was so shiny Miria could see herself in it.

Though the house looked small from the outside, it went on for quite a way into the ground, making it spacious for all seven of them. Miria asked if she and Timtuk could take the first bedroom and everyone agreed that would be fine. Beya and Donat wanted the loft, Lian took the bedroom beside Miria and Jimmy and Will took the third bedroom. Each room had two beds in it, with large pillow mattresses and again Miria jumped for joy. She wanted to stay for a week, but Liam reminded her that they were only here for a few days to trade for supplies and check on the next portion of their route for safety and speed.

Beya settled on the couch watching Timtuk and Buddy play tug of war with an old rag. Buddy was winning hands down, but Timtuk was relentless in defeat. Miria took out her knapsack and asked Jimmy and Will if they would like to accompany her into the town to look for some fresh food for their dinner. Both boys jumped at the chance to explore.

When they entered the city gates the smell of baked goods almost knocked them over. Jimmy took a deep breath.

"Oh, I haven't smelled fresh baking in ions. Can we get some for dinner?"

Miria smiled. "Absolutely. Let's go into this shop."

Upon entering a little old lady approached them and began to speak. Miria quickly struck up the conversation as Will and Jimmy enjoyed looking into the baskets of cookies, tarts and small cakes.

Jimmy's stomach began to growl loudly. "Down boy, it won't be much longer."

Will whispered to him, "Keep your voice down. We don't want to draw attention to ourselves."

Jimmy nodded. "Right. Sorry."

Miria pointed to the tarts and even to three small cakes. Jimmy and Will felt like little kids in a candy store. Miria paid with a small lantern stone and the older lady seemed genuinely pleased with the trade.

Miria smiled.

"Now off to find fresh vegetables and maybe some fresh fish."

Jimmy and Will were mesmerized by the colours, the entertainment on the streets and the people who all seemed happy and pleased to be a part of this community.

They did not notice the two men lurking in the back of the crowd, slowly following Miria and the boys wherever they went. When the boys stopped to watch two jugglers, Miria said she would go into the vegetable shop herself and meet them back here. Jimmy and Will were grateful and began to enjoy the entertainment. They did not see the two men slowly make their way to the same shop Miria entered.

Miria was admiring the variety of vegetables to choose from when suddenly a hand was placed over her mouth and a cloth over her face. In seconds all went black.

✳ ✳ ✳

Jimmy and Will enjoyed the show but realized it had been quite some time since Miria left them. Will stepped into the shop. He looked around but could not see her anywhere. *That's odd*, he thought. *Where else would she go?* He stepped out of the shop and looked at Jimmy,

"She's not in here. Where else would she go?"

Jimmy thought for a moment. "The fish store. She must have seen how we were enjoying the show, so she went there alone."

They walked along the street of vendors looking for anything that resembled a fish store. When finally they came to a small shop that definitely had fish, Miria was nowhere in sight.

Jimmy looked at Will. "Did we pass each other? That could easily happen in this crowd. Let's go back to the entertainment area. Maybe she's there."

Will nodded in agreement, and they headed back. They looked everywhere as they went, trying to find her face in the crowds. When they returned to the entertainment area she was not to be found.

Will looked at Jimmy. "I'm getting a really bad feeling here, Jim."

Jimmy looked around slowly, looking at each person with scrutiny. Then he saw someone that made his stomach drop to his feet.

"Will, that's one of the men from the boat that chased us this morning. They're here and now Miria has disappeared. Coincidence?"

Will shook his head. "I don't believe in coincidence. Come on, we have to get to Lian."

The boys rushed back to the house as fast as they could possibly go with such a large crowd of people to meander around. Jimmy kept looking back to see if they were being followed, but with the large crowds it was impossible to notice anyone suspicious.

When they reached the house, Will quickly scooped up Timtuk and yelled for Lian.

Lian, Beya and Donat all came out at the sound of Will's voice. Will looked at Timtuk.

"You have to be very brave for me Timtuk and translate everything to Lian; okay?" Timtuk nodded bravely.

Will described the events in the town, the man from the boat, and Miria's disappearance. Lian and Donat grabbed some small weapons from the box.

He spoke to Timtuk and Timtuk translated to Will and Jimmy.

"One of you must come with us and show where you lost Miria and where you saw the man from the boat. One of you must stay here to guard Timtuk with Beya's help."

Jimmy looked at Will. "Let me go with Lian and Donat. I'm understanding the language more and more, and I think I'd do better with them."

Will nodded in agreement but held Jimmy's arm for just a second. "Be careful; okay. And please find her."

Jimmy nodded and smiled a reassuring grin. "Failure is not

an option."

Will smiled and nodded. "Absolutely."

***

Jimmy led them to the last place they had seen her. When Lian entered the vegetable shop he noticed Miria's bag under a table. He picked it up and took it out to Jimmy. Jimmy looked at it and nodded.

"It's Miria's."

Lian started to search the crowd for a face that resembled any one of the men from the boat that chased them. Donat and Jimmy did the same. Donat spotted one of them first and motioned to Lian to follow him. They slowly came up on the man and touched him with a rod that Lian had in his pocket. The man collapsed but Donat caught him before he hit the ground. Jimmy wondered what he used on the man, but he bet it was like a Taser gun. They held the man between the two of them and dragged him back towards the privacy of their house.

It took what seemed like forever, but they finally lay the man down at the back of the house. Will came out when he heard the man moan. He looked at Jimmy.

"Where did you find him?"

"Near the entertainment area. Lian found this in the vegetable shop."

He held up Miria's bag. Will's stomach just dropped.

"What did they do to him?" pointing to their prisoner.

"Not quite sure. It was so quick, but I'm betting on something like a Taser gun.

He passed out as soon as Lian touched him with a rod."

Will turned to go inside. "I have to get Timtuk. I want to know what this creep is going to say when he wakes up. I hate involving the little guy, but we have no choice."

Jimmy agreed. His knowledge of their language was still weak. Timtuk's translations would definitely be needed. Will returned with Timtuk in his arms. Beya followed him out as well. The man on the ground started to moan louder. Lian gave him a kick on his butt and told him to wake up. The man slowly opened his eyes and noticed the men standing around him. He lunged at Will and Timtuk but not before Lian landed his fist to his face. He went down hard. Lian started yelling at him.

Timtuk whispered to Will, "He's telling him to get up and tell us where Miria is being kept."

The man did not get up but just looked at Lian and laughed through his broken teeth. Lian repeated the command but the man refused to move. Donat grabbed him by the shirt and tossed him in a chair like a rag doll. Both Jimmy and Will were amazed by his strength.

Lian pushed his thumb into the man's neck and he flinched with the pain. He tried to hit Lian but Donat pinned his arms behind him as Lian continued with the pressure. The man began to scream, but Lian just kept asking where Miria was being kept. Finally he said a word, and Lian took his hand away.

Timtuk whispered to Will, "Boathouse."

Beya brought out some rope and Donat tied the man to the chair. Lian spoke to Donat and Beya. They both nodded and headed into the house. They returned with weapons. Lian looked at Timtuk and relayed a message to Jimmy and Will.

Timtuk translated.

"Lian knows you two want to come, but he says he needs you to stay here and protect me. They can move faster in the crowds and understand the languages better than you and Jimmy. Do you understand?"

Will and Jimmy both looked at Lian and nodded. Jimmy looked at Timtuk.

"Translate this Timtuk. Please find her and all of you come back safe."

Lian, Donat and Beya nodded and left the man in their charge. Lian left Jimmy the rod, he touched it on a rock to show him the electric shock it provided. Jimmy knew it was for their guest should he become a nuisance. Jimmy nodded his understanding. Lian smiled and tapped his arm. And the three men were off to find Miria and the boathouse.

They moved swiftly and quietly. Lian found out from an old fisherman where the boathouse was situated. It was at the far end of the harbour. As they slowly made their way to the harbour Lian understood why they used this place. It was situated on a small island of rocks. Making a quick ambush impossible without being seen first. But they hadn't counted on Beya's gift and Lian was so glad he had his strength back.

Beya put them in the invisible mist and they walked up the small path that led to the island without any incidence. They found a small boat and slowly got in and paddled to the island.

There were two men standing guard by the front door. As the three invisible men approached them, Lian and Donat touched them with the stun rods and they collapsed to the ground. Lian quietly opened the door and the three went inside.

Miria was tied to a table and she looked unconscientious. Two men were sitting on large bench playing a dice game and shouting out their frustrations with each toss. Lian slowly led the group to Miria. He slowly began to untie her and touch her face to see if she was breathing properly. She moaned and the men stopped playing their game.

"Our little fish is waking up, I think," said one of the men.

The other man just ignored him. "She'll sleep for a while yet, then Rosen can do what he wants with her. Let's play."

Lian looked at Donat and Beya. Gave the motion to follow him to the men at the bench. One touch of each of the rods and the dice tumbled to the floor as well as the men.

Lian rushed over to Miria and quickly started to untie the rope. Donat took out his knife and sliced them like a hot knife through butter. Donat picked up Miria and Beya put the mist around them all as they quietly headed for the door. They could hear voices and men screaming.

The door flew open as Lian and the group hugged the wall. The three men came in and screamed at the men laying on the floor. They did not move a muscle. The leader, now known as Rosen smashed his hands on the table.

"Patta will never pay me if we don't get her back. Find her and kill all her companions if you have to. I want her back."

The two men rushed out of the boathouse. Rosen just leaned against the table and muttered to himself. Lian nodded to the group and they moved slowly to the table, Rosen never knew what hit him. He just collapsed on the table.

Lian and the group slowly made their way back to the boat. They laid Miria down in the bow and they slowly rowed back to their house, trying not to make a wake on the water for anyone to notice.

When they finally reached the house, Beya removed the cloaking mist and Timtuk screamed in delight as they materialized on the riverbed. When Timtuk saw Miria asleep in the boat, he looked at Lian for reassurance that she was okay. He patted him on the back and told him she was just fine, sleepy but fine.

Will and Jimmy came down to the boat as well. Will looked at Lian, Donat and Beya and smiled at them all.

"Mena, mena, mena."

They just laughed as Donat picked up Miria and carried her to her bed.

Lian returned to their prisoner tied to the chair. He just looked at him and sneered. Lian looked cold and emotionless as he spoke quietly to the man.

"You can sneer all you like my friend, but I want answers. Now, we can do this with or without pain. Which do you choose?"

The man just looked away from him. Lian smiled.

"Oh, you choose pain. I am only too pleased to accommodate your wishes." He pressed his thumb into his neck, and the man started to flinch.

"Who is Patta? And what does he want with the girl?"

The man squirmed and started to yell but said nothing. Lian put more pressure on his thumb and the man began to turn blue. Lian repeated the questions.

"Who is Patta and what does he want with the girl?"

The man started to scream, "A friend of her father."

Lian let go of his neck and let the man catch his breath. Lian repeated the last question again. "What does he want with the girl?"

The man looked angrily at Lian. "To sell her to the highest bidder. She has gifts. She will bring much wealth to him."

Lian leaned in again but did not touch the man, just the threat made him flinch.

"How did you know where to find us?"

The man started to chuckle, "By a mistake and good luck. We made a wrong turn long after Napo. We lost your trail, so we headed for Quintoke. When we heard about the travellers who swindled their villagers we knew you could not be far. We looked for any trace of you and found the cave you entered to use the river. We went back to Quintoke and borrowed a boat then followed your path. We were about five days behind you. We were surprised to see you as soon as we did."

Lian did not explain about the serpent attack to the man but chuckled how he said borrowed a boat from Quintoke. Stole it would have been more truthful.

Lian looked at the man again.

"How long have you been trailing us?"

The man shrugged. "Attaberra."

Lian looked as cold as a snake with this next question.

"So you said Patta wanted the girl. And her father got a message to him as to her whereabouts. What were you to do with the rest of the party she travelled with?"

The man looked down before answering, "We were told you were all too dangerous to capture. You were all to be killed."

Lian's face was stone cold. "And just how were you going to do this deed?"

The man shrugged. "Ambush. We're very good at it."

***

Miria woke slowly trying to adjust her eyes to the room she was in. She realized she was in a bed, and it looked like the bedroom in the house they had rented.

She sat up slowly and called out. Jimmy walked into the bedroom with a smile on his face.

"Well, hello. It's so nice to see you finally awake. Are you okay? Did those men hurt you in any way?"

Miria looked at Jimmy with a confused look. "What men, Jimmy? And how did I get here? The last thing I remember is looking at vegetables."

Jimmy filled her in on the day's activities. She lay on her pillow in total shock.

"Jimmy, I was kidnapped! Why? By who?"

Jimmy held her hand. "All good questions, my dear, and Lian is working on one of the culprits right now to get the answers. Hopefully he will be able to shine some light on this mystery. But right now, I'm going to get you some wonderful soup that you started yesterday, and Will and I completed today. So just relax and let me wait on you; okay?"

Miria smiled but objected to staying in bed. "I'm not sick, Jimmy. Let me come into the kitchen and eat at the table."

Jimmy nodded. "Okay, but be careful. We think they drugged you, so you might be a little wobbly on your feet."

As Miria slid off the bed she understood immediately what Jimmy was talking about.

"Oh my, I do feel a little shaky. Would you please hold me, so I don't fall, Jimmy?"

"Are you so sure this is a good idea, Miria? Wouldn't staying in bed for a while be better for you?"

She laughed a bit. "Please, Jimmy, I just need to walk about. I'm sure the shaky part will go away."

He helped her into the living area where everyone greeted her warmly. She looked around at all the wonderful faces and counted her blessings for such good men in her life to protect her.

She smiled. "Jimmy told me about this day. Thank you all for the rescue and thank you all for being my friends and protectors."

Everyone smiled and hugged her. Will settled her down at the table and served her some hot soup and corn bread. Until she smelled the soup, she never realized how hungry she was.

"Oh, this tastes wonderful. Did we get anything from this morning's shopping trip.?"

Will laughed. "Only what was squished in your bag. You dropped it when you were taken, but it's still edible if it doesn't look that great."

"My apologies to everyone. I will try again tomorrow," she said with a chuckle.

Lian entered the room just as she said this, and he spoke to her in a tone that Will and Jimmy could not recognize. Miria said nothing and then looked at the boys.

"Lian says we have to talk, everyone must know what has happened and what we must do to protect ourselves."

Everyone sat down in the great room waiting for Lian to share what he extracted from the man. He started slow, so Miria could translate to Will and Jimmy.

"Apparently, we have been tracked since Attaberra. My father sent word to a friend of his and gave him permission to kidnap me and sell me into slavery. The rest of the group was to be …" she stumbled over the next words, "ambushed and killed."

She looked at Jimmy and Will. "I think I've heard this story before. I think I lived it before."

She looked at Lian, Donat and Beya and relayed the story of her father's death.

Jimmy looked at Miria.

"Will and I always suspected he had something to do with Dean George's death, Miria. He wanted your mother, and Dean was in his way, so he used his friendly goons in Napo to get him. Now he wants you gone too though I'm not sure why. You are certainly no threat to him."

Lian and Miria talked, and she explained what Will and Jimmy suspected. Lian said something to her, and her eyes welled up with tears.

Miria looked at the boys. "Apparently he doesn't want the mongrel bloodline to continue. He wanted it to stop with me."

She burst out crying and Jimmy went to her side and held her.

Will looked at Lian and then at Miria. "What does Lian want us to do?"

She translated back to Lian and he pulled out the map and placed it on the table.

He pointed to three villages and began to tell them their options.

Miria translated. "We have three villages to choose from. Lian believes they can't hunt us in all three places, so we must make a wise choice as to our next move.

Dolo is the closest village. We could be there in two days. So supplies don't have to be too heavy to carry. Tesip is three days away. Again, our need for supplies will be low, but Fargana is at least a week away, so many supplies will be needed. Lian believes they will follow us to Tesip or Dolo, but he believes our best course would be to head for Fargana. It would be difficult for them to carry all the supplies needed for the journey. We however, have little difficulty, but it will slow us down a day or two. He would like to know what you think."

Will and Jimmy looked at Miria. "Tell Lian we vote for Fargana."

Miria relayed the message. Donat and Beya agreed with them as did Miria. Lian folded the map and began to give instructions as to what needed to be done before they embarked on the next expedition. Beya and Donat began to make a list of the supplies they would need, but Miria silently went out the door and headed for the riverbank.

Will followed her. She sat down on the ground and leaned up against a large rock. Will came in and sat down beside her.

He looked at her. "Miria, I know this is a nightmare for you, but I have to ask a few questions. Is it okay?"

She nodded as she wiped away the tears trickling down her face.

"Your mother didn't marry the chief for four years after your dad was killed." Miria nodded.

"Did she seem happy about the union?"

Miria looked at the river and then after a few moments looked at Will.

"Now that I think about it, no. She never seemed happy about it. I believe she still mourned my father."

Will shook his head. "I don't believe she really wanted to marry him, Miria. Somehow, I think he wore her down or maybe threatened to harm you unless she accepted."

Miria looked at Will in shock. "How do you know this?"

Will looked at her seriously. "Miria, he threatened you with a letter. He gave permission for one of his goons to sell you and he ordered the death of the rest of us. It kind of adds up that he blackmailed your mother for his own personal means. He's just not what you call a really nice guy, more like borderline psychotic!"

Miria looked at Will. "I don't know what that means, but it probably describes him perfectly."

"Did your mother ever let you go off with him alone?"

Mira shook her head. "No, never."

"Did she ever give you any advice about him?"

Miria thought for a moment.

"Just be a good girl and don't make him angry. Oh Will, my mother was terrified of him. I just never thought about it."

Will held her hand. "You were twelve years old, she would protect you from that part of her life. But seriously, Miria, he had your father killed, wants you to be sold as a slave, wants the rest of us dead. You can't go back to your village anymore. It's not safe for you."

Miria started to cry. "But Kitalla is where I grew up. It's the only home I know."

Will put his arms around her.

"It's not safe. We'll have to find you a new home. You could go to Attaberra and live with your aunt, but I honestly think it's too close to Napo and Kitalla. I think he would still try to harm you. And let's not forget Timtuk. He is going to need guarding as well."

Miria put her head on her knees. "Oh Will, what am I going to do?"

"We'll think of something. Maybe on our journey we'll find a nice village for you to go back and live. I'm sure every village would love a healer. Let's face it, you'd never be out of work." She smiled through her tears.

"How do I keep all of this away from Timtuk? How are we to keep our thoughts about his father out of our minds? How do I keep my hatred for this man a secret?"

Will smiled at her. "If anyone can do it, it's you. I have faith in you because I know how much you love Timtuk. And I know you will protect him the same way your mother protected you."

Miria leaned into his arms and hid her face.

"I pray Will that I can do just that. I cannot believe this is happening."

Will hugged her and rocked her a bit.

"No one can, Miria. But it's the hand we've been dealt, so we just have to learn how to play it."

Miria looked up at him with a confused look. Will snickered, "Someday, I'll teach you card games, then you'll understand that statement better. It means, this problem is what life just handed you. Now how are you going to fix it?"

Miria smiled. "With the help of my friends, we'll fix it."

Will smiled. "There you go. Your first step on your new life journey."